At the tempestuous annual convention two doctors fight for the highest prize in their profession!

H. Edward Danton—wealthy heart surgeon and clinic director, who desperately wanted the association presidency, and didn't care whom he ruined to get it.

Paul Rice—a young researcher, fired years ago by Danton, now back to challenge his leadership on the convention floor.

Aletha Danton—Danton's aristocratic wife, whose refined manners didn't keep her from laying her body on the line to help her husband.

Cary Posten—a medical professor who soon found himself involved in a far deadlier game than convention politics.

Marion Crowder—beautiful young author of the best-selling exposé, *Sexual Slavery*, whose cool efficiency in the cause of women's liberation hid a heart burning with need.

CONVENTION, M.D.
was originally published by
Doubleday & Company, Inc.

Books by Frank G. Slaughter

<table>
<tr><td>Air Surgeon</td><td>The Golden Isle</td></tr>
<tr><td>Battle Surgeon</td><td>The Golden Ones</td></tr>
<tr><td>Buccaneer Surgeon</td><td>The Healer</td></tr>
<tr><td>Code Five</td><td>In a Dark Garden</td></tr>
<tr><td>Constantine</td><td>The Land and the Promise</td></tr>
<tr><td>Convention, M.D.</td><td>Lorena</td></tr>
<tr><td>Countdown</td><td>Pilgrims in Paradise</td></tr>
<tr><td>The Curse of Jezebel</td><td>The Purple Quest</td></tr>
<tr><td>Darien Venture</td><td>A Savage Place</td></tr>
<tr><td>David: Warrior and King</td><td>The Scarlet Cord</td></tr>
<tr><td>Daybreak</td><td>Shadow of Evil</td></tr>
<tr><td>The Deadly Lady of Madagascar</td><td>Spencer Brade, M.D.</td></tr>
<tr><td>Devil's Harvest</td><td>The Stonewall Brigade</td></tr>
<tr><td>Divine Mistress</td><td>Storm Haven</td></tr>
<tr><td>Doctor's Wives</td><td>Surgeon, U.S.A.</td></tr>
<tr><td>East Side General</td><td>Sword and Scalpel</td></tr>
<tr><td>Epidemic!</td><td>That None Should Die</td></tr>
<tr><td>Flight from Natchez</td><td>Tomorrow's Miracle</td></tr>
<tr><td>Fort Everglades</td><td>A Touch of Glory</td></tr>
<tr><td>God's Warrior</td><td>Women in White</td></tr>
</table>

Published by POCKET BOOKS

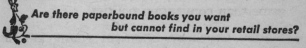

Frank G. Slaughter

Convention, M.D.

A Novel of Medical Infighting

PUBLISHED BY POCKET BOOKS NEW YORK

CONVENTION, M.D.

Doubleday edition published 1972

POCKET BOOK edition published October, 1973

6th printing..........................June, 1976

All characters in this book are fictitious, and any resemblance to actual persons, living or dead, is purely coincidental.

POCKET BOOK editions are published by
POCKET BOOKS,
a division of Simon & Schuster, Inc.,
A GULF+WESTERN COMPANY
630 Fifth Avenue,
New York, N.Y. 10020.
Trademarks registered in the United States
and other countries.

ISBN: 0-671-80387-5.
Library of Congress Catalog Card Number: 73-186043.

Printed in the U.S.A.

Convention, M.D.

CHAPTER I

Jerry Warren flicked the switch of the sixteen-millimeter projector and the two men in the audio-visual preview room of the Central City Municipal Auditorium settled back, while the credits of the motion picture they were viewing appeared on the monitor screen.

"Resection of Acute Myocardial Infract, with Coronary Bypass," the title read. Beneath it, in letters equally large, was the name of the surgeon "H. Edward Danton, M.D.," and slightly below that, the words "From the Danton Vascular Surgery Clinic."

The credits faded to a Hollywood-like shot of the Danton Clinic itself, with the buildings of the university medical school of which it was a part forming the backdrop. As a rasping voice, quite familiar to both viewers, took up the narration, X rays of the coronary blood vessels of a human heart, outlined sharply in white against the darker background of the lungs and other soft tissues in the chest by the contrast medium injected into them, filled the screen.

"Trust the bastard to use a single credit line, when most of that technique was worked out in the research lab." Jerry Warren's voice was bitter.

"*His* research lab," Paul Rice's tone was somewhat milder than Jerry's.

At thirty-two, Paul looked at least five years younger. With his dark hair brushed back from a lean intelligent face, warm brown eyes and a body honed by a half hour of jogging every morning, he was the image of the successful young surgeon and already a name to conjure with in the highly sophisticated field of heart and blood-vessel surgery.

"How could I ever forget?" Jerry's voice changed to a growl amazingly like that of H. Edward Danton. "*My* clinic, *my* laboratory, *my* patient, *my* operation, *my* stooges."

And my wife, Paul Rice added silently.

In the two years since he had joined the Central University Medical School Faculty as head of the Cardiovascular Research Center and chief surgeon of that section of the giant university hospital, Paul had almost managed to put Aletha Danton out of his mind. The challenge of building the center into a worthy competitor with the Danton Clinic for top place in the rapidly expanding field of heart and blood-vessel surgery had been enough to push old memories—however painful—into the background. But the rasping voice from the film he and Jerry were viewing, plus the picture of the new clinic—built only last year for H. Edward Danton by a grateful Texas billionaire, whose son had been saved from cardiac invalidism by a daring open-heart operation—brought memories of Aletha surging into his mind once more, sweeping away defenses erected carefully during these past two years and leaving him momentarily without a bulwark against erupting emotions.

When the final blowup had come two years ago, resulting in his leaving the Danton Clinic, it wasn't because of Paul's attentions to Aletha, but over Jerry Warren and the artificial heart, on which the two younger surgeons had been working together.

"Look at that!" Jerry's voice focused Paul's attention once more upon the small ground-glass screen of the monitor.

The gloved hands pictured there were now engaged in the delicate task of connecting a section of the saphenous vein, taken from the patient's leg, to form a shunt between the aorta, with its adequate supply of blood, and a narrowed coronary artery supplying part of the heart muscle. The stricture in the latter vessel caused by deposits of cholesterol and other material slowly building up inside it had lessened the amount of nutrients, particularly oxygen, going to a section of the heart wall. And this in turn had resulted in the sudden death of that section—in medical terms an infarct—when the artery had finally been completely closed by a clot called a thrombus, creating the most serious emergency to which humans are liable.

"What are you talking about?" Paul asked.

"Just now, when Danton was putting in the first suture, didn't you notice the difference?"

"I wasn't looking. What was it?"

"Wait a sec. I'll reverse the film and you can see it again."

The procession of frames flashed backward upon the monitor screen in a continuous stream of images, the sound of Danton's voice in reverse rising to a Woody Woodpecker screech.

When Jerry turned the switch again and the regular showing was resumed, Paul studied the screen closely, concentrating upon the hand using the instrument, whose jaws clasped a needle to which was attached a fine strand of nylon suture.

The surgeon's movements were noticeably slower, as Jerry had said. But what caught Paul's attention immediately was a subtle difference, perceptible only to someone familiar with this type of surgery, between the hands which had started the operation and those now performing the delicate task of connecting the vein to the artery, neither larger than the average size of a pencil.

The hands of H. Edward Danton, so large that he regularly wore a size eight surgical glove when operating, were particularly startling in a surgeon famous world over for the intricacy of the operative procedures he performed. But though obviously skilled, those now connecting the vein to the coronary artery could not have been much larger than a size seven glove.

"What do you think?" Jerry Warren asked.

"Whoever made the incision—"

"That was Danton. I'd recognize those big mitts of his anywhere."

"Another pair is suturing the vein to the artery. That much is certain."

"Only Danton's name appears on the film," said Jerry.

"If he's claiming credit for an operation he didn't do, you could file a protest as chairman of the Film Projection Committee."

"And have Danton claim I did it to get back at him? I'm not about to cut my own throat and yours just to embarrass him, Jerry. Let's start at the beginning of the film and see where the change came."

"I'd still give a lot to get back at our chief for stealing the credit for my pump," said Jerry.

"Your time will come. Besides, the artificial heart you've developed since we came to Central is twice as good as the one you made for Danton."

"He's welcome to it," said Jerry. "If you hadn't yanked me out of the Danton Clinic when you did, I'd probably have wound up murdering the guy."

"Don't forget what I saved you from then." When Paul Rice smiled, his normally somewhat serious expression took on a sudden warmth, like the sun emerging from the cloud. "You don't make artificial hearts in jail, so get off the soapbox and hurry with the film. We've still got a lot of stuff to go through before we knock off work."

"Did you ever stop to wonder why all these films are made of surgical technique, when less than ten per cent of the doctors attending this convention will have any real interest in just how a thin-walled vein can be sewed to a thick-walled artery without a leak?"

"What's bugging you about that?"

"These are advertisements. Paul, and doctors aren't supposed to advertise, at least not nowadays. If the people who go to so much trouble and expense to make these films were entirely honest about it, they'd run a commercial at the end. Something like: 'Come to the Danton Clinic for your blood-vessel surgery. Results guaranteed. Low discount prices every day!' "

"Not Danton. He wouldn't give a discount to his own mother."

"The money this film cost could still have been spent a lot more wisely by showing a man eating a lot of solid fats and taking no exercise. Then an animated sequence of cholesterol building up in his coronary arteries until one of them is blocked. And finally a shot of him in an Intensive Care Unit after his heart attack with a tracheotomy tube in his windpipe and a Mark Seven respirator pumping oxygen into him to keep his brain cells from dying."

"There's a flaw in that argument," said Paul. "Mostly only doctors see these films."

"So what? They're some of the worst offenders when it comes to courting heart trouble. If we shook doctors up a little, maybe they'd be more positive with potential coronary patients."

"If medical films are simply advertising like you claim, aren't you and I as guilty as the rest?"

"Sure. That's why I sometimes think I could accomplish more working somewhere in the ghetto, maybe in a Health Maintenance Organization like the Mile Square project in the Chicago slums."

"Come off it, Jerry," said Paul. "You're the best research man studying vascular conditions in the country. What the hell good would it do to hide your light under a bushel just because your skin happens to be as dark as mine would be if I ever got a chance to acquire a real sun tan?"

"That's the trouble with you whiteys." Jerry shook his head in mock despair. "No social consciousness."

"Why do you think I teach in medical school at twenty-five thousand a year, when I could make a hundred in private practice?" Paul demanded indignantly.

"Maybe because you're smart enough to realize that in a few more years there won't be any private practices, only something like HMOs delivering medical care in assigned areas paid for by a combination of government subsidy and prepaid health insurance."

"That may be a long time coming. All new ideas are."

"What's so new about that?" said Jerry. "I read a novel the other night that describes the whole setup, just like more and more people are coming to realize it has to be. Guess when it was published?"

"I don't have any idea."

5

"Nineteen forty-one. Over thirty years ago. Talk about prophets."

Jerry flicked the switch of the projector and, as it began to hum again, the familiar stubby fingers of H. Edward Danton—in full color—appeared on the monitor screen holding a scalpel. Like a sword thrust, the blade made a long, arrow-straight cut down the breastbone of the patient, slicing through skin, fat and even the periosteal outer lining of the bone.

While the hands of assistants worked swiftly on either side of the incision, clamping bleeding vessels and tying them off with fine ligatures, the whine of a oscillating saw sounded briefly on the sound track. Swiftly the rapidly vibrating half circle of metal cut through the soft bone of the sternum for its entire length. Then the soft thudding of a mallet against the blunt edge of a Lebsche knife followed, as the heavy blade was driven through the deeper layers of the breastbone. Rib spreaders next separated the halves of the sternum to reveal the heart itself, throbbing steadily inside its membranous sac, the pericardium.

"I'll say one thing for H. Edward." Jerry's voice was tinged with reluctant admiration. "Not even you could get into a chest that fast."

As the pericardial sac was sliced open, an X-ray film of the coronary vessels supplying blood to the heart muscle itself appeared upon the screen and the raspy voice of H. Edward Danton took up the narrative once again:

"This patient had suffered from angina pectoris for some time, indicating a definite lack of adequate blood flow through the coronary vessels to the heart. He was in the hospital, being evaluated for surgery to increase the flow of blood to the heart muscle by means of a conventional coronary bypass operation, when he sustained an acute coronary thrombosis, causing a large infarct in the section of heart wall supplied by the blocked artery.

"In view of the urgency of the patient's condition, with a heart rate which could not be stabilized, we had no alternative except to remove the damaged portion of cardiac muscle and bring a fresh supply of blood to the area by means of a saphenous vein graft between the aorta and the distal segment of the coronary artery which had previously been determined to be open and functioning.

"The patient was first placed on complete cardio-pulmonary bypass with the heart-lung pump." The rather stubby fingers of the surgeon appeared again as the view switched to a color shot of the operative procedure itself. "We are placing a purse-string circular suture in the right atrium, the upper thin-walled chamber that receives blood by way of the great veins called the venae cavae from the major portion of the body, except the lungs, which have their own circulation. This procedure will allow us to divert all the blood normally reaching the right side of the heart from the entire body except the lungs to the pump oxygenator, or heart-lung pump."

"Those are Danton's hands," said Paul.

"Keep looking. He hasn't come to the delicate part yet."

On the screen, plastic tubes with balloon-shaped segments at the end were being inserted into the two great veins through an incision in the wall of the atrium in the circular area formed by the purse string.

"At the same time," Danton continued, "we are lowering the patient's temperature and will shortly replace his own circulation with the heart-lung pump which is capable of taking over mechanically the entire task of maintaining life."

The lens of the camera swung to show the stainless steel and plastic central chamber of the vital pump. The metal disks that formed its heart were spinning, half submerged in a bath of blood within a long plastic tube, allowing the oxygen that filled the rest of the tube to be absorbed by the red film covering the exposed surfaces of the disks.

"The patient is now on the pump oxygenator." Danton's voice sounded overscene once more. "As you can see, the heart has almost stopped beating due to the decrease in temperature and the take-over of function for both heart and lungs by the pump. We can now proceed to the simple task of excising the section of heart muscle from which life has been practically shut off by the thrombus—a clot to the uninitiated—causing the acute coronary attack."

A hand wielding a scalpel appeared on the screen and Paul Rice gave a muffled exclamation of surprise. Leaning forward, he studied the scene carefully as the blade was plunged through the wall of the now almost still heart at the edge of the dark patch marking the junction between healthy muscle and that which was dying from lack of blood.

"See what I mean?" said Jerry.

"Stop the film, please. And back up a little—slowly."

The procession of images moved backward, coming to a halt with the first frame showing the scalpel moving toward the damaged muscle.

"Now move it forward—as slowly as you can."

The sprockets of the projector clicked as Jerry Warren eased the picture from frame to frame, while each tiny photograph upon the film was enlarged many times upon the screen.

"Did you notice how awkwardly Danton was holding the knife just before the blade penetrated the heart muscle?" Paul asked.

Jerry nodded. "That's what attracted my attention in the first place."

"Danton started to excise the infarct, but somebody else took over," said Paul thoughtfully. "The question is: why? And who?"

"Not much doubt there," said Jerry. "With you out of the clinic, there's only one man left Danton could trust with that kind of surgery."

"Elton Brooks?"

"It has to be Elton. Remember how we used to kid him because he had hands like a girl?"

Paul nodded. "What do you suppose really happened there?"

"Search me," said Jerry with a shrug. "But you can bet on one thing: H. Edward Danton didn't let someone else take over, while an important operation was being filmed for his exhibit at the convention, unless he couldn't finish the job himself."

"And didn't expect to be able to repeat it for quite a while," Paul added.

"What a break this is—with you scheduled to be nominated from the floor for president-elect against Danton Thursday." Jerry's voice was tense with excitement.

"With no chance of winning."

"That isn't the point. With the organization behind him, Danton will win, of course. But if you corral enough votes to make it look like a rebellion is brewing among his own following, the hierarchy at the AMA will never let him be elected president."

"We still can't use this operation against him," said Paul. "He may have had a perfectly good reason for letting Elton do the delicate part. A thing like that could backfire on us."

"You may be right," Jerry admitted. "But I sure would like to clobber Danton."

"Let's do it in an open election, then."

"Open election! What do you suppose he's doing right now but lining up votes? And why do you think he's spending a couple of thousand dollars on that cocktail party this evening, if not to get more?" Jerry calmed down with an effort. "You're going, aren't you?"

"If you get busy and run the rest of these films. How about you and Katie?"

Jerry chuckled as he started the projector once again. "Right now she's busy making over one of the dresses she used to wear, when she was singing with Duke Ellington. We'll probably be the only black faces in a sea of white ones there tonight, but you can be sure Katie will knock their eyes out. And just to make sure nobody misses seeing us, I've rented a white tuxedo."

The telephone buzzed on the console desk of the audio-visual center where Paul and Jerry were working and Paul picked up the receiver.

"Dr. Rice," Paul recognized the voice of Pete Sanders,

9

executive secretary of the CMA, "could you come by the CMA office on the second floor?"

"Sure, Pete. But why the formality?"

"I'll explain later." The telephone clicked in Paul's ear.

"Pete Sanders wants to see me about something," Paul told Jerry, as he hung up.

"Don't let him talk you out of letting your name be put in nomination. Pete has to work with the Establishment, so he's got a vested interest in maintaining the *status quo.*"

Jerry looked at the clock on the console. "It's lunchtime anyway, so I might as well grab a sandwich while you're with Pete."

"I'll see you in the cafeteria, unless he keeps me," Paul promised.

"Right. Maybe I can pick up some scuttlebutt from the Danton crowd."

ii

In the first-class cabin of Delta Flight 882 at the Atlanta airport, Dr. Marian Crowder took the window seat assigned to her and settled herself comfortably, buckling the belt and tucking her handbag beneath the seat itself. Watching the other passengers come aboard, the men chomping cigars, joking with the stewardesses, giving the women passengers a quick once-over for future possibilities, Marian wondered how much of that smug conviction of masculine superiority they'd be able to retain if they knew she was carrying in her briefcase a word bomb that would shortly explode in Central City before the OB-GYN section of the CMA Convention—the final proof that the last citadel of male supremacy, the need of male sperm to fertilize the ovum of the female and so enable the species to be reproduced, had now been destroyed.

"Human Parthenogenesis" was the main title of her scientific paper. But lest some alert newspaperman realize what it implied, she had added a subtitle, "The effect of several agents upon early maturation of the ovum," to becloud somewhat its sensational nature.

Ten years of continual work since she finished medical school had gone into the paper, but they'd been worth it. Ten years of research in the Laboratory of Experimental Embryology she headed at Johns Hopkins proving what had been common knowledge to women since the dawn of time—that man was an accident of nature, a phallic symbol which must inevitably topple and collapse into abject impotence, once it was proved that males had no function which could not be supplied by women alone.

Marian could find no reason to regret a single one of those ten years. During them she had not only earned a high position in the field of experimental embryology through her meticulous and brilliant research, but she had also become a literary phenomenon with her best seller of last year, *Sexual Slavery*.

What man would have been clever enough to open the book with one of the Marquis de Sade's most pornographic passages, an exercise in sexual brutality designed to titillate habitual readers of non-fiction, seizing their interest at the start and holding it with a shrewd mixture of legitimate philosophy and purely sensual appeal? What a monstrous joke it was that by using lurid descriptions of sexual behavior—all duly credited to the original author and therefore casting no blame for their nature upon the quoter—she had gained readers by the hundreds of thousands. What was more, critics had been lured into praising the book as an important literary document, as well as for its social appeal.

With readers trapped and critics disarmed, Marian had then proceeded to an anatomically detailed description of copulation itself in all its lurid variations, piling shock upon shock vicariously until, hooked beyond escape, even the hostile reader could not fail to continue.

Knowing men—both as a physician and as a sexually healthy and beautiful woman who had more than held her own in a largely male-dominated profession—Marian had deliberately sought to stir up at the very start of the book the sort of lust she diligently excoriated in the rest of it, through depicting the various forms of slavery men had inflicted upon women since the time of Adam in the name of love.

"We will be serving cocktails as soon as we're aloft, Dr. Crowder. May I take your order now?"

The voice of the stewardess had startled Marian from her reverie, although she was no longer surprised at being recognized. *Sexual Slavery* had taken care of that, plucking her from the ivory tower of her laboratory and shoving her into the public eye.

"Bourbon," she said. "With ginger ale, please."

As the stewardess moved on to the next row of seats taking orders, Marian relaxed in the embrace of the seat belt and closed her eyes, ignoring the bustle of last-minute passengers moving through the first-class compartment, although she knew from experience that many of them recognized her.

She had no doubts about her own appearance. Slightly heavy before *Sexual Slavery* had exploded her horizons, she had nevertheless always drawn, and enjoyed, her share of male attention. Once book-club, paperback and other commitments before publication had guaranteed the financial success of her book, she'd taken the precaution of going to a famous Palm Springs spa for several weeks.

Exercised, dieted, massaged, pummeled and instructed thoroughly in the art of make-up, Marian had emerged glowing with health, a slim size fourteen with just enough tint added to her somewhat sandy hair to make it vividly golden—plus all the confidence she needed to invade the world of men—and best them.

A few inches taller than the average for women, she was, at thirty-five, a woman to whom men's eyes—and women's, too—were drawn automatically. Long ago, when they were students together at Hopkins, Cary Poston had compared her to Diana, the huntress, and she was sure the appellation was as fully deserved now as it had been then —perhaps even more, since maturity often heightened real beauty.

An experienced air traveler, Marian didn't even look out the window as the plane trundled its way to the take-off strip assigned to it. She dozed off when the sudden cessation of bumping beneath the plane indicated that it was airborne, to be awakened some fifteen minutes later by the stewardess reaching across to pull down the seat table before her.

"The 'Fasten Seat Belts' sign is off and here's your drink, Doctor," the girl said brightly. "Shall I mix it for you?"

"No, thank you."

"Flying time to Central City is ninety minutes," said the stewardess. "We'll serve lunch in about twenty."

Two small bottles of first-grade Bourbon were on the tray with a setup of ginger ale. Opening one, Marian poured it into the glass, then emptied the second in, too, following it with the ginger ale. Liquor always exterted a marked relaxing effect on her, she knew from experience, and with it another kind of stimulation. For that reason, she usually limited herself to a single light Bourbon when in the company of attractive men lest those instincts she had described so vividly in print as a threat to womankind trip her up, hoisting her as it were upon her own petard. But she was on vacation now so she relaxed with the drink, enjoying it, as well as the anticipation of the next four days at the Central Medical Association Convention.

CHAPTER II

Seeing Marian Crowder in the departure lounge at Atlanta had been something of a shock for Caleb Downs. If he hadn't seen her picture in the New York *Times* during the fanfare connected with the publication of *Sexual Slavery,* he wouldn't have recognized her today as the same slightly heavy "Hen Medic" with whom he'd started medical school in Baltimore under the name of Eric Sands, with which he was born.

Even though Marian Crowder had rated near the top of

the class that first year, Caleb remembered, she had been popular with her fellow students, particularly the masculine nine-tenths of the class. His own rather clumsy attempts to achieve any degree of intimacy with Marian had been firmly rebuffed, even though in Anatomy I, he had dissected a hulking black cadaver with her, Cary Poston and a fourth man, whose name Caleb couldn't remember.

Cary Poston had possessed all the social poise a rather awkward first-year student named Eric Sands had lacked and Caleb Downs recalled now that a rather torrid affair had been going on between Cary and Marian that year. As Eric Sands, Caleb hadn't particularly resented either one of them, though envying them both their assurance and ability—until they had turned him in for cheating on Microscopic Anatomy.

Eric Sands had been summarily kicked out of medical school during the last days of the first year, with none of the credits that would have allowed him to transfer to a less prestigious school. And with the stain of having cheated indelibly upon the record, his resentment against Marian Crowder and Cary Poston had been a burning fire within him through the some fourteen years since.

Remembering again the bitterness of that spring day when he'd left the office of the Dean of Students, his world in a shambles and his lifelong ambition to become a doctor thwarted, Caleb Downs now felt a surge of even deeper resentment against the beautiful woman waiting in the lounge to board the plane. With it, too, was an even stronger conviction than he'd felt a month ago, when he'd seen Marian's name on the program of the forthcoming CMA Convention, that fate had at last intervened on his side.

Cary, he knew, was a professor at Central University Medical School and the program had listed him as chairman of the Arrangements Committee, so he would be moving about widely during the coming session. And since Caleb's company always had one of the most popular exhibits there, the opportunity he needed for revenge upon both of his enemies must certainly happen.

That the years had treated Marian very well indeed,

Caleb could easily tell, even from the corridor outside the departure lounge where he had stayed until the gate was opened for boarding and she had disappeared into the airplane. That they had also been kind to him did nothing to alter his determination to gain at least the revenge of which he had dreamed so often through the years.

The mustache Caleb had cultivated following his abrupt departure from medical school had probably been enough of a disguise in itself to keep Marian or anyone else from Johns Hopkins who might be attending the CMA Convention from recognizing an old classmate of one year. In recent years, however, he'd added the precaution of a glossy full beard which, with dark glasses, would have prevented his own mother from recognizing him. Considering his plans for the next four days, however, he had still taken no chances and remained out of Marian's sight until she entered the airplane.

Pharmacology had been Eric Sand's real bent from the start. He had changed his name to Caleb Downs in an attempt to erase from his record, if not from his mind, the stain of failure. And the year in medical school, added to his college training, had given him the knowledge he needed to succeed in pharmacology. Now, with his own pharmaceutical house and the newest in the procession of wonder drugs from his production-line laboratory promising to cure the penicillin-resistant gonorrhea, which had become almost a national scourge, he was an assured success in business—and with women.

Normally, salesmen handled the Central Pharmaceutical exhibits at the large medical conventions, where they were very popular. This time, however, Caleb had decided to be there himself ready for the opportunity which must certainly develop sometime during the four main days of convention activity, with several thousand doctors, plus both Marian Crowder and Cary Poston, milling about on the exhibit floor where the Central Pharmaceutical exhibits always occupied a prominent spot.

Marian, Caleb observed as he finally entered the airplane after the last call for boarding, already occupied one of the first-class seats. His ticket called for similar space, but he hurried past her into the coach section, where he found an empty one. As he settled into the seat, a slight twinge over his heart told him the demand pacemaker implanted in his chest cavity a year ago—after a severe heart attack had left the natural control mechanism defective—had resumed its task of initiating the heartbeat by a rhythmic electrical stimulation sufficiently rapid to maintain the all-important brain circulation.

In the excitement of seeing Marian at such close range, he'd quite forgotten the pacemaker. But that same excitement, he realized now, had sent enough adrenalin pouring into his bloodstream to increase the heart rate by chemical action directly upon the sinus node of sensitive Purkinje fibers in the heart muscle itself and inactivate the pacemaker.

Now that he was resting in his seat and safely beyond any danger of being recognized by her, however, the heart had settled down again to the dangerously slow rate it tended to assume when not stimulated. And in this circumstance the pacemaker's action was once more required to remedy the deficiency which had almost turned him into a heart cripple, until the remarkably effective electronic device with its stimulating electrodes, through which a tiny current passed rhythmically to the heart muscle itself, had been implanted in his chest.

That same heart attack had completed Caleb Downs's disguise, too, when a surgeon had opened his windpipe—the operation called tracheotomy—allowing air to enter his lungs. The operation had saved his life but had left him with a husky voice quite different from the one he'd possessed prior to the onset of the attack.

All in all, Caleb Downs thought with a good deal of satisfaction, as he buckled the seat belt and made himself comfortable, the particular set of circumstances which had placed both him and Marian Crowder on the same plane at Atlanta bound for Central City and the CMA Convention was a good omen for the fruition of a plan of action he had gone to a great deal of trouble to devise.

ii

When Carlota Montez came out of the cathedral after Mass, she saw that it had rained during the service. Inside the church, the air had been somewhat musty, but outside after the brief spring shower everything was fresh and green with the promise of spring, the sun shining brightly and coaxing from the earth the aroma of growing things.

Carlota had nodded through much of the Mass, except when she joined the procession of worshipers to the altar, where Father O'Leary dropped a consecrated wafer on her tongue, smiling upon her with the admiration even a celibate could feel for an extraordinarily pretty girl. Outside, the freshness of the air brought her wide awake, however, and she pushed back the lace mantilla that had covered the dark waves of her hair inside the cathedral, letting the sun caress the faintly olive skin of her face.

"We're going to the lake for a swim, Carlota," a boy called from a group getting into a car at the curb. "Coming with us?"

For a moment she allowed herself to be tempted, then shook her head. "Got to work on a biochemistry paper in the library this afternoon, Rafael. Sorry."

"You can do that tonight."

"There's a reception at that big medical convention in the hotel. I have to work.

As the car hurtled away from the curb, Carlota started walking home. It was only a few blocks away, for the cathedral was in the midst of the older and most Spanish section of Central City where the greater part of its Mexican-American segment lived.

Somewhat wistfully she found herself wishing she could have gone with the others. A cooler of Cokes and beer, with a basket from a Kentucky Fried Chicken stand, was all the food they needed. It would have been heavenly to rest in the warm sand on the banks of the big power lake just outside of town, before a plunge in the clear water, still cool from the winter that brought perhaps a dozen frosts a year and, rarely, a brief snowfall to this central southern area. The reality of tomorrow's paper for her biochemistry class was too much in the foreground, however, and threatening to push even that aside, was her worry about Raul.

They were only four years apart. Carlota, at twenty-three, was a junior at Central University while Raul, at nineteen, was in the first year of art school but, because the school had no academic status, was not protected by it from the draft. Carlota had been more mother than sister to Raul even when they were small. Her own mother was too occupied with the rest of the brood after her father's death in a tractor accident to have any real understanding of the problems life could cast upon a sensitive artistic boy.

She was halfway home when Raul stepped from behind a large palm where he'd been waiting. He was sweating, although the air was cool from the rain.

"It's come, Lota." His voice was tense.

"What came, Raul?" Several generations removed from the family's old home in the rolling uplands between Mexico City and Vera Cruz, the young Mexican-Americans of their generation rarely spoke Spanish any more except to older people.

"The draft call. I have to report tomorrow for the physical."

"But today's Sunday. There's no mail."

"The postman was a substitute. He left the notice at Pedro Montez's house by mistake."

Carlota accepted the explanation without question. With so many Montez families in Central City, it happened all the time.

"I've got to get away before they take me," Raul added and Carlota didn't ask where. Ever since he'd received the draft classification in 1-A, he'd been talking about going to Canada. Nor in her heart had she been able to bring herself to dissuade him.

The thought of gentle Raul, so kind that he was always bringing home sick cats and dogs and nursing them back

18

to health, involved in a war nobody really wanted to fight, was more than she could bear. The first time he had to pull the trigger and send a bullet smashing into the body of another person, she knew he was bound to freeze, every sensitivity within him repugnant to the idea of killing. Which meant that inevitably he would be killed—or court-martialed for cowardice.

"What does it say—the notice?"

The official-looking paper he handed her was simply a draft-board notification instructing Raul Montez to report to the Central City Induction Center Monday morning at nine o'clock for a physical examination.

"This doesn't mean they'll take you," Carlota protested.

"If you pass the test, the FBI starts watching you—"

"Who told you that?"

"Henrico Valdez. He says they wait at the Induction Center, so you won't have a chance to get away."

"The draft wouldn't even take Henrico. Besides, everybody knows he's a chronic liar."

"You don't want to help me." Raul's voice rose in a childish treble and, realizing the strain he was under, Carlota reached out to touch and comfort him. But he moved away, obviously afraid she would persuade him against the course he was steeling himself to follow.

"You know I want to help you," she protested.

"Then you'll get me the money to go to Canada?"

"H-how much do you need?"

"A hundred and fifty dollars. Father O'Leary says I can get a job in Montreal or Quebec."

"Doing what?"

"There's a lot of construction in Canada. The padre says draftsmen—people that can draw well—don't have any trouble getting jobs."

"But you could never come back home."

"Father O'Leary says it's just a matter of time before the government will have to grant amnesty to people that leave the country because they can't fight in an unjust war. You could come to see me sometime, too, Sis—after you graduate and get that job in the hospital laboratory you're aiming for."

"I won't graduate, if I don't get to work on my biochemistry paper." Carlota suddenly remembered her plans for the afternoon. "Promise me you won't do anything before you have the physical and know for sure they'll take you."

"But the FBI—"

"Henrico's been telling you tales. If you pass, I'll see that you get to Canada somehow."

"How will you get the money, Sis?"

"I'll manage. I've never failed you before, have I?"

"No, but—"

"Just leave it to me, dear. Let's go home, Mama's got Cuban sandwiches for lunch."

"I don't feel like eating. I'll just walk around for a while."

"You promised not to do anything drastic," she reminded him.

"I won't. But don't forget that you—"

"I'll have the money for you."

But when she reached the small house set back from the street and surrounded by azaleas, camellias and gardenias, Carlota was no nearer an answer to the question of where she could possibly dig up a hundred and fifty dollars than when she'd assured Raul she would find it somehow. Fifty she could probably get by selling some books and arranging for a small loan from the hotel employees' credit union. But a hundred more seemed as far away as the moon.

iii

In a small dining room at the Hotel Centralia, political headquarters for the medical hierarchy that controlled the Central Medical Association, Dr. H. Edward Danton pushed his dessert aside and wiped his mouth with a napkin. In spite of a penchant for fine food, he was only slightly overweight and carried his forty-five years well.

The piercing gray eyes that could strike terror into a nurse, intern or resident who made a mistake in the operating room, the mane of graying hair, cut long in accordance with the fashion of the moment, the expensive Italian silk cloth of his carefully tailored suit, even the flush of success on his cheeks—all eminently fitted one who was above the common herd of doctors and well aware of it.

"Well, Jack." Danton addressed the slight man across the table who, as a member of the CMA Council, rode herd on doctors in four Midwestern states. 'What's the prospect?"

"Your election is in the bag." Dr. Jack Hanson's voice was decisive, like so many small men who achieve considerable success. "The only question is the size of the majority."

"It needs to be unanimous." Danton's voice had a slight edge. "I threw my full support behind you for the Council and for vice-president next year, Jack. It's your turn to go to bat for me."

"I can't do anything about the rebellion in your own camp, Edward." Hanson's voice was sharp.

"Never mind that."

"We've got to mind it." Dr. Tom Heath, a round-faced man in his forties who controlled the Eastern District for the Council, spoke with the authority of one representing a heavily populated area. "To most of the younger members, we represent the Old Guard, the Establishment if you will, and the fact that a brilliant young surgeon like Paul Rice will be nominated from the floor in opposition to you, particularly when he was trained in your own clinic, could be enough to make a lot of them vote for Paul."

'To say nothing of the smart trick Cary Poston pulled in getting Senator Spurgess lined up to address the First General Session tomorrow morning," said Dr. Hanson. "We could have stopped that invitation, Edward, if you'd gone to bat with the Program Committee."

"I didn't want to stop it."

21

"Mind telling us why?"

"Just a little horse-trade psychology," said Danton.

"I don't get it," said Heath.

"Who's the greatest enemy the medical profession has in Congress?"

"Spurgess, of course," said Hanson. "If this health plan he's proposing ever becomes law, we'll practically be working for the government—on salary and with federal inspectors looking over our shoulders all the time. Cary Poston and the people supporting Paul Rice didn't do the medical profession any favor by giving Spurgess another opportunity to make political hay by attacking us."

"If what the newspapers call the Young Turks hadn't invited Spurgess, I was thinking of doing it myself," said Danton.

"Now I know you've lost your marbles," said Hanson.

"I'll explain it to you then," said Danton patiently. "When Senator Spurgess gets up on the platform tomorrow morning and attacks us head-on, a lot of doctors who've been riding with the current and not bothering to set any sort of a course for the future will see the handwriting on the wall. That means they'll swing over to our camp, whether they agree with us or not, merely because we're working in conjunction with the AMA and other large groups in organized medicine, to maintain the *status quo.*"

"I don't know," said Dr. Heath doubtfully. "The Young Turk rebellion is *against* the *status quo*. The whole thing sounds pretty devious to me."

"Somebody had better be devious if we're to stop Spurgess and nip this rebellion in our own camp in the bud at the same time," said Danton. "You don't think for a moment that Spurgess is really concerned about medical care for all the people, do you?"

"He gives a pretty good imitation of it," said Heath. "And a lot of people have fallen for it."

"Of course they have," said Danton. "With all this publicity lately about doctors' incomes, the profession is becoming Whipping Boy Number One for politicians. Spur-

22

gess is hammering on us because we're a small segment of the population, but one people can't do without. If he loses the entire medical vote in a nominating convention—or in the country if he gets the nomination for President—he hasn't lost enough to worry about. But in the process he'll have gained the liberal section in labor, along with the starry-eyed do-gooders in welfare who want a guaranteed income."

"What you're saying makes sense," Heath conceded. "But how do we fight him."

"I'll give a blueprint of my own plan in my acceptance speech after the election Thursday morning," said Danton. "And I'll answer all the lies Spurgess will be spouting tomorrow at a news conference right after his speech. What we have to do first is pull together to influence the people we see in our offices. A sick man is scared. His first instinct is to do as the doctor tells him, so we'll give him a little propaganda with his medicine."

"That makes sense," Heath conceded. "And also costs money."

"We'll need a lot of money to fight the Spurgess crowd," Danton admitted, "but Spurgess is solving that problem for us, too."

"How?"

"By tackling the pharmaceutical manufacturers, he's brought a powerful ally into our camp. If the government gets control of medical practice, we're going to have to prescribe medicines by their generic names, at a fraction of the cost of named drugs. The pharmaceutical houses stand to lose a lot of money if Spurgess wins, which means they'll have to pull with us, whether they want to or not, and help pay the costs of fighting him."

"You're pretty convincing, Edward," said Dr. John Towers. "But the important thing right now is getting you elected."

Scheduled to take office as president on the last day of the convention, Towers would preside over the election on Thursday. Theoretically, then, he was neutral, but medical politics wasn't played that way.

"Like Tom says, Edward," Towers added, "Paul Rice's nomination could be enough to make it look bad for you."

"Then shut off any nominations from the floor."

"You know we can't do that."

"It's been done before."

"But not in times like these, when a substantial element of the membership is already muttering against our leadership." Tower's voice was firm. "Someone would be sure to raise a point of order and the parliamentarian would then have to rule against me. I'm not about to start my tenure of office by splitting the association."

"John's right, Edward," said Hanson. "Why don't you try to talk young Rice out of letting his name be placed in nomination?"

"Who's scheduled to nominate him?" Danton asked.

"Jerry Warren, I think. Alex Klein is masterminding that end of it with Cary Poston."

"Alex is smart and he isn't afraid of the devil himself or you, Edward," said Hanson rather pointedly.

"Your best bet is to talk to young Rice," Heath urged. "He's highly respected in my area. If his name is put up, I'm not even sure you could carry the Eastern District. Think how that will look a few years from now?"

Nobody had to be told what Heath meant. They all knew the presidency of the CMA was only a step, but a necessary one, toward the presidency of the AMA a few years hence. But if Danton's majority in the coming election was less than overwhelming his base upon which to build the campaign for the larger job would be seriously undermined at the start.

"The one thing I can't forgive anyone is disloyalty," said Danton stubbornly. "Rice and Warren stole credit for something that was mine. I'll not go crawling to them for votes."

"The way I heard it, they have as much right to claim credit for that cardiac bypass pump as you do, maybe more," said Dr. John Towers dryly.

"All right, fellows." Danton had regained his calm.

"We've all been friends and political confreres too long to quarrel now. What do you recommend?"

"Keep Paul Rice from being nominated from the floor Tuesday," said Hanson, "and I'll deliver the vote of my district for you unanimously."

"What about you, Tom?"

"The same," said the Atlanta doctor promptly.

"John?"

"I'll have to go along with the others, Edward. Paul Rice could pull a lot of votes from the central region, too."

"Thank you for meeting with me, gentlemen." Danton pushed his chair away from the table and got to his feet. "I appreciate your frankness."

All of them recognized that Danton hadn't committed himself, but knowing his temper when crossed, none of them pressed for a more definite answer.

"I hope you're right about the effect Senator Spurgess' speech will have on the convention, Edward," said Towers as they were leaving.

"I am," said Danton confidently. "The sentiment is already building. Aletha and I are counting on seeing you and your wives at the cocktail party this evening. I don't have to remind you of the need to maintain a common front. And not a word about this conference. We don't want to warn the opposition ahead of time."

"The last thing I want during my first official act as president of the Central Medical Association is a floor fight over the election," said Towers. "So long, Edward. Thanks for the lunch."

"Think he'll talk to Paul Rice?" Hanson asked Tom Heath as they were waiting for the elevator to take them to their suites.

"Doesn't have much choice, does he?"

"With H. Edward Danton, you can never tell," said Hanson. "Just when you expect him to pull a rabbit out of a hat it turns into a wolf. And I don't have to remind you what happened to Little Red Riding Hood's grandmother."

"I'm glad I'm not running against him," Heath admitted. "What do you think he's liable to do?"

"We just acquired one of Danton's former residents as a surgeon on our clinic staff. From what he says Danton may have a secret weapon he doesn't even know about."

iv

"We are about to take off for Central City. Flying time will be about seventy-five minutes." The voice of the stewardess came over the plane's intercom system. "Please see that your seat belts are securely fastened and observe the 'No Smoking' sign. Seats should be in the upright position until we are airborne and all tray tables closed."

In the coach section Jethro Forbes pulled the buckle of his seat belt a little tighter and pressed the button in the armrest allowing it to move forward. This would be his tenth visit to a CMA Convention—and almost certainly his last. When the meeting was over, he would board a plane to Guatemala and the upland clinic where he'd volunteered to work the rest of his days.

It had taken almost a year to prepare for the first real adventure in the life of Jethro Forbes, M.D., and it seemed fitting that his final curtain call as a general practitioner in the Kansas town of Revere should be the act of going to the CMA Convention. Touted for decades as the "General Practitioner's Medical Society," the CMA conventions had largely been taken over lately, as with the Southern, the AMA, and all the other large medical organizations, by specialty groups to whom a slogging small-town GP was a creature from a far lesser world. But Jethro still enjoyed meeting old friends who, like himself, came to the convention year after year to relieve the awful boredom of general practice and, if they were lucky, learn something new they could use in their own work. For him, as for most of the doctors pouring into Central City, medical conventions were a working vacation made even more attractive because the expense was deductible on the yearly income tax return.

Outwitting Sarah had been easy enough. She was so busy with her endless complaining and her nerve pills that

26

she never bothered any more with business affairs. The Merrill Lynch purchase and sales slips always came to the office, as did the monthly statements and those from the banks. So as long as Jethro gave Sarah enough money to run the house and kept in repair the color TV before which she spent the passing hours, absorbed by morning game shows, afternoon soap operas, and nighttime talk programs, nothing else mattered.

Since adding the "Late Show" movies to her TV schedule, Sarah had stopped bothering to get up in the morning and give Jethro breakfast—for which he was actually thankful. In wrapper and slippers, with a net over the hair whose titian hue had attracted him so much years ago, but had long since faded to a salt-and-pepper gray because she didn't bother to use a tint, she wasn't exactly an inspiring sight.

The extra weight Jethro had acquired from the two cans of beer he drank every night to put him to sleep, while Sarah lay in the other bedroom half buried in a nest of pillows watching the "Late Show," left him a morning choice only between coffee and toast or a diet cereal. Fortunately however, the Snack Shop on Main Street had better coffee than Sarah's, so he usually met Wiley Blackston, the mayor of Revere, there. Jethro's closest friend in Revere, Blackston was also the local mortician and a widower.

Twice-a-week sex had dwindled years ago to Saturday nights only and lately they hadn't even bothered. General practice in Revere, Kansas, was a twelve-to-sixteen-hour-day job with only a few hours off for golf on Sunday morning, if you were lucky. And a man as tired as Jethro was by nightfall could hardly get much pleasure out of panting over a woman whose only response was to ask, "Are you through?" and reach for the remote control unit that activated the TV set. It was no use asking himself what had happened to him and Sarah. The answer was nothing except the drudgery of general practice, the passing of the years—and Sarah's "nerves."

Maybe, Jethro thought, as the plane winged its way

southward, he and Sarah had always been as dull and uninteresting to others as they had now become to each other. Probably only the hormonal alchemy of youthful sex had brought them together in the first place, when he was still a medical student at Hopkins and Sarah a student nurse. Certainly it was sex that had finally trapped them into the squirrel cage where they had spent the years ever since.

Sarah had become pregnant the first time they slept together at his insistence, six months before his graduation and a year before hers would have occurred. And she had never let him forget it since.

Jethro had planned to take a residency in obstetrics after graduation, feeling that he had a real bent for that field. But with a baby coming and an intern's salary not much more than enough to make a living for himself and his then rapidly expanding family, as evidenced by the size of Sarah's abdomen, the residency had gone by the board—along with most of his dreams.

It had started the summer after graduation when Jethro took a *locum tenens*—a fancy name for substitute medical slave—in Revere to get enough money for them to live on during the residency. When the doctor he was substituting for died of cholera during a world cruise, it had seemed a smart idea to stay on there, with a practice already established and Sarah just about at term in a pregnancy that hadn't gone well from the start. And by the time it ended in disaster, when the convulsions of eclampsia had almost killed Sarah and caused a stillbirth, debt had been a millstone anchoring them to Revere.

Every New Year's for a while Jethro had resolved that this year he was going to break away, maybe to take a residency in OB even at his age, or at least a short course before moving to a larger city. He'd told himself again and again as he lay in bed and listened to the shouts and laughter of celebrants outside—when they could be heard over the caterwauling of the TV in Sarah's room, as she watched the revelers in Times Square—that he had to find a new life in the coming year or die.

The whole thing had seemed hopeless, however, until he'd signed up a year and a half ago for the medical seminar trip to Guatemala. Arranged by Central Pharmaceutical Company for their physician stockholders, it had included a token program of medical lectures and clinics that made the trip deductible for physicians.

In the lush tropical climate of Guatemala, Jethro had discovered a breathtakingly beautiful new world so far removed from Revere, Kansas, that it had seemed a million light-years away. Though only a five- or six-hour air trip, including the change of planes in Mexico City, separated Guatemala from his own humdrum world, it had taken the whole four months between New Year's Eve and the spring CMA Convention to finally complete his plans for the ultimate break.

First, Sarah's future had to be assured with a lifetime trust, but Jethro's insurance, plus most of what he'd gained from the securities he had bought over the years, had taken care of that. In addition, Sarah would have her house, the TV and enough money to live on, so she'd probably be even happier with him not around.

Most widows past fifty were, he noticed. Once a man had fulfilled his biological function of providing sperm for the children they wanted, and his economic responsibilities by building up enough of an estate to supply their needs after he was gone, the average wife appeared to thrive as a widow. In Guatemala Jethro wouldn't need or want much for himself, so his own future had been much less of a problem. Food, a chance to work really helping people in a warm climate, beautiful surroundings and a place to sleep had seemed a vision of paradise after the terrible winters of Revere and the sickness they brought.

He'd ensured that nobody back in Revere would know where he was or where he'd gone by telling Sarah he was attending a seminar in Chicago. Buying a ticket for O'Hare Airport, he'd purchased another for Central City there and with that simple act Dr. Jethro Forbes had dropped out of the small world of Revere, Kansas, early that very morning.

The only person who would really miss him, Jethro was sure, would be Wiley Blackston. Wiley, who was always ready to share a joke as they munched toast and drank coffee together in the morning before going their separate ways, Jethro to the business of saving life and Blackston to that of closing it out with the customary amenities. And Wiley, Jethro knew, would understand why he'd had to embark on this first—and last—real adventure, if he were not to die in harness like most country doctors.

v

For the duration of the convention, the administrative offices of the CMA, as well as those of its dynamic lay executive secretary, Pete Sanders, had been moved from its location in a downtown office building to the second floor of the Civic Center Auditorium, where the large theater was located.

"Glad you could make it," said Sanders, when Paul came into the office. "I had to be formal on the phone. Dr. Danton was here."

Paul smiled. "It's just like him to start giving orders even before he becomes president-elect."

"How's the film program shaping up?" Sanders asked.

"We'll be ready by the time the closed-circuit telecasts to the convention hotels start this evening. What did you want to see me about, Pete?"

Sanders looked embarrassed. "We've had a request to add another film to the program setup."

"I doubt if there's room. The whole thing has been carefully arranged with the sponsor's messages and clinical meeting announcements already scheduled on video tape. Who's the newcomer?"

"Dr. Danton brought another film with him. He says it's very timely and wants to put it into the program."

"That means somebody will have to be bumped."

"I know." There was an odd note in Pete Sanders' voice and Paul suddenly knew the reason—as well as why Sanders had wanted to see him on such short notice.

"Has the Arrangements Committee already approved this?" he asked.

"Yes."

"When?"

"This morning."

"Unanimously?"

"Dr. Poston raised holy hell but he was outvoted."

"All right, Pete," said Paul. "Jerry and I will pull out our own film on left ventricular bypass and put Danton's latest opus in place of it. But pass the word around that we know we've been given the shaft—and why."

Pete Sanders didn't even try to deny the truth of what Paul was saying; obviously, H. Edward Danton had skillfully maneuvered his young political opponent out of the public eye during the convention, doubling his own exposure at the same time. It was a smart maneuver and, had anyone else but himself been on the receiving end, Paul might almost have admired the smooth way in which it had been done. Yet he had no choice for, as chairman of the Film Projection Committee, he couldn't remove some other doctor's film while keeping his own and Jerry's as part of the closed-circuit TV program.

"Is that all you need me for?" he asked.

Sanders nodded. "I want you to know I'm not very happy about being the one to tell you."

"No offense, Pete; you've got a job to do. But from what Jerry and Alex Klein tell me about the way the campaign is beginning to shape up, it might be a good idea to cover some of your bets."

Pete Sanders grinned. "Dr. Towers told me Dr. Danton would like to keep nominations from being made Thursday morning from the floor, so I alerted the parliamentarian."

"I guess the only thing I have to worry about then is keeping Jerry Warren from gunning for our old boss."

At the door of the office, Paul turned back. "How's the registration going?"

"The advance figure is very good, just over a thousand.

31

The exhibit space is all sold, too, which will pay our bills, with the city's subsidy added to the kitty."

"Maybe all this we hear about young doctors not joining organized medicine isn't true," said Paul.

"Some of our good showing may be due to the fact that Senator Spurgess is going to speak at the opening session tomorrow morning. He's always good for some fireworks when he attacks doctors. And then there's the way the newspapers have been playing up the contest between you and Dr. Danton."

"That wasn't my doing, Pete."

"We both know where it came from. What I don't understand is why he would build you up, when you're opposing him."

"It hardly makes sense, unless Danton's planning to clobber me with something before the Thursday voting."

"Any idea how that might happen?"

Paul shook his head. "I'm afraid I'm not very smart when it comes to politics. Jerry's always after me to get with it, but I don't seem to have the knack."

"Being thoroughly honest *is* something of a handicap," Pete Sanders said with a smile. "Will you be able to make the College of Surgeons specialty group session this afternoon? They've got an excellent registration total."

"Not a chance—with a dozen or more films still to go," said Paul. "I'd better grab a hamburger and meet Jerry in the audio-visual center."

vi

As with most large meetings, the Sunday before Monday's official opening of the CMA was devoted to programs put on by organized specialty groups, theoretically leaving the main program during the week for papers of more general interest. Reluctantly turning away from the UP ramp leading to a meeting room on the third level, where the members of the CMA who were also Fellows of the American College of Surgeons were holding a preconvention specialty session, Paul Rice took the DOWN ramp leading to the ground floor of the auditorium building. Heart of the massive Civic Center, the Auditorium, with the adjacent hospital-medical school complex and the cluster of nearby hotels, made Central City particularly suitable for large medical conventions like the CMA, second only in size to the American Medical Association.

Broken up into more than a hundred assigned spaces, the exhibit floor had been carefully arranged to make it practically impossible to go from the main entrance at ground level and the battery of registration booths at the front of the building to the ramps leading to the upper levels, without passing the exhibits. The upper floors contained the theater, where Senator Frank Spurgess, current congressional scourge of the medical profession, would address several thousand doctors on Monday, and the many smaller meeting rooms, reserved during the next four days for the various sections devoted to scientific papers.

Less than half of the exhibit space was given over to strictly professional subjects. There, with films, photographs, charts and text—printed in block letters so bifocal wearers could read them from the aisles—medical accomplishments could be presented to the convention registrants by those responsible for them. Included among these scientific exhibits were Paul and Jerry's own presentation on coronary blood-vessel surgery and the usual elaborate battery of models and films from the Danton Clinic describing further research in the improvement of coronary circulation for which Dr. Danton and the clinic were most famous.

The major part of the exhibit space was given over to commercial subjects. By far the larger number of these, too, were the booths of pharmaceutical manufacturers eager to familiarize doctors, by means of samples and high-powered sales presentations, with their latest drug products, all ready to be prescribed by the trade names rather than the generic—or chemical—ones.

A close second in the number of exhibits were the booksellers and instrument manufacturers, followed by various miscellaneous exhibitors. Among the latter were commercial clinical laboratories which would process a single blood sample in the dozens of clinical tests required by modern medical practice and airmail the reports to busy doctors in all parts of the country. Space rentals for commercial exhibits paid much of the convention costs. They were high, however, and small-time exhibitors were therefore largely excluded, leaving room only for enterprises with a high profit margin, notably prescription drugs.

Many booths were still being set up, Paul saw as he moved through the exhibit floor, but two of the largest and most popular appeared to be ready for business. For several years Central Pharmaceutical Company had supplied free beer to thirsty doctors attending the country's major medical conventions. And for an even longer period, the Vibrassage booth had provided comfortable lounge chairs where "electric fingers" gently massaged weary muscles and induced relaxation, while a high-powered sales appeal was poured into the ears of those enjoying the gently rhythmic vibrations of the chairs.

In the Vibrassage booth, strategically located at the crossing of two major aisles on the exhibit floor, a remarkably well-built and handsome blonde looked up as Paul Rice approached.

"I've got one chair ready and going, Doctor Rice." Alice Perrault's smile was warm and friendly. "You look harried enough already to need it."

Paul stopped before the booth, tempted for a moment to accept the invitation.

"Didn't I see you at the Southern last fall, Miss Perrault?" he asked, reading the name plate pinned on the snug white sweater she wore above a yellow miniskirt.

"I was there," said Alice. "We make all the big conventions."

"You certainly had a popular booth."

"The only sure-fire one, except Central's beer." Alice picked up a small vibrator and, switching it on, handed it to Paul. The metal sausage was like a living thing in his hands, smoothing tense fingers with rhythmic massage.

"Mornings we get the hangover trade," Alice confided. "You'd be surprised what one of these little machines on the back of your neck can do for a morning-after headache. This year we've got a foot attachment called Pedassage, too, that works wonders for tired arches. And we've added a short-wave diathermy arm that can be swung across the big reclining chairs for that between-the-shoulders fatigue."

"You do seem to have all the answers," said Paul as he handed back the small vibrator.

"We strive to please and usually do, Doctor. Come in any time."

"I'll remember. Thank you."

Paul moved on toward the sandwich shop and Alice watched him, until he turned a corner into a side aisle and disappeared. Playing the medical convention circuits as she did, she knew enough about medical politics to recognize that the young heart surgeon was already marked for a high place in his rapidly growing specialty and in the profession at large. She could understand why, too, for there was a wholesome quality about him, an engaging friendliness that told you he was a real person, not just an aggressive doctor on the make for personal acclaim—and the wealth it brought.

Even before the official opening of the convention the next morning, the hotels and restaurants were already abuzz with news of the hitherto unheard-of challenge to CMA leadership represented by Paul Rice's announced candidacy for the office of president-elect against his former chief, Dr. H. Edward Danton. And however much that challenge might seem like David going against Goliath, Alice knew enough about the smoldering revolt of young doctors over the country against entrenched medical organizations and their usually narrow view of social progress to realize that this time Goliath was likely to have the fight of his life.

CHAPTER III

When the "Fasten Seat Belts" sign appeared on the bulk-head before her, Marian Crowder shuffled together the manuscript pages she'd been giving a full editing. Slipping them into a large manila envelope, she placed it in the attaché case she had brought on board and shoved the latter under the seat behind her feet.

The double Bourbon had been just the stimulation she needed and, rather than dampen the warm, exhilarating effect it had stirred within her, she'd eaten very lightly at lunch, topping the meal off with a crème de menthe.

Attaché case in hand and over her arm the light coat she had worn in deference to the considerable difference in climate between Baltimore and Central City, Marian joined the passengers leaving the plane at Central City Airport. Accustomed to taking care of herself, she didn't even glance at the faces of those waiting in the lounge to greet debarking passengers—until a male voice called her name.

The voice was only vaguely familiar, but she recognized its owner at once, a tall handsome man in an impeccable cashmere sports jacket and pale yellow slacks. A lean and obviously athletic body and a smiling face were crowned by a shock of dark hair cut moderately long.

"Cary Poston!" she cried. "Is it really you?"

Dr. Cary Poston took Marian's briefcase with one hand and put his other arm around her with the same movement. Before she realized what was happening, she was being kissed, not just perfunctorily on the cheek in a gesture of greeting, but thoroughly on the lips.

"Is this the way you greet all the women who come to Central City?" she managed to gasp.

"Only very beautiful ones, whom I haven't seen for ten years."

36

Cary took her arm and, holding her close to him, guided her into the main corridor leading to the terminal.

"How did you know I'd be on this plane?" Marian asked.

"You had a letter from the Arrangements Committee asking when you would arrive, didn't you?"

"Yes."

"I'm chairman of the committee so you and Senator Spurgess are my personal concern. I have to meet him between six and seven this evening."

"Isn't inviting him to address the CMA rather like nursing a viper to your bosom?"

"A lot of the membership thinks so," he admitted. "But a few of us who want to break the hold the Old Guard has on the CMA, hope Spurgess' speech will help gain a compromise and modernize the organization a little."

"How did you manage to get him?"

"I grew up in West Texas with Hal Stimson, Spurgess' chief administrative assistant. When I called Hal up in Washington, he fixed it for Spurgess to appear."

"I hope things turn out the way you want them to, Cary," said Marian. "As busy as you must be with the convention, you shouldn't have gone to the trouble to meet me."

"Surely you wouldn't deprive me of the pleasure of meeting the girl who dissected the same cadaver with me back at Hopkins. Remember?"

"How could I forget?"

Just out of the relatively cloistered protection of Radcliffe, Marian had recoiled from the messy task of dissection that first morning in Anatomy I. Noticing her reaction, Cary had protected her as much as he could from the rather boisterous humor of the anatomy laboratory. They had dated fairly regularly that year and had briefly been lovers. But treasuring her independence even then, Marian had avoided a more intimate relationship.

"You married after leaving Hopkins, didn't you?" Marian asked as he helped her on the moving belt that carried passengers from the departure lounges to the terminal.

"Two years out of medical school. Mary was a fine girl. She died two years ago of a uterine malignancy."

"I'm sorry, Cary."

"You get over the death of someone you love—eventually." His voice was warm with the memory of something Marian realized she had never known. "Fortunately, time has a way of healing things. And, besides, I stay busy with my own practice."

"Internal medicine and cardiology. I remember you were headed that way, even the first year."

"I enjoy my work, just as I remember your enjoying embryology even in medical school. I guess the patterns for our lives were really cut out for us from the start." His grip on her arm tightened momentarily in what was almost a caress. "Including our meeting again, all of ten years after graduation."

"Careful," she warned laughing. "You'll be revealing my age next."

"You're the youngest-looking and the loveliest thirty-five-year-old woman anybody's liable to see. I'm only a couple of years older but you make me look positively ancient."

In the terminal they moved toward the baggage claim area, but Marian's luggage had not yet arrived, so they were forced to wait.

"You were married once too, weren't you?" Cary Poston asked.

"Let's say I made a mistake. It lasted a year."

"No present attachments?"

"Just liaisons. I've been working very hard lately on a research project and don't have time for anything else." For an instant Marian was tempted to tell him the real subject of the paper she would deliver on Tuesday to the Obstetrics and Gynecology Section of the CMA, then thought better of it.

"I read your book," he told her.

"What did you think of it?"

"Mostly hogwash. But high class, and a beautiful job of selling."

Marian had stiffened a little at the words. "What do you mean?"

"That first chapter, largely written originally by the Marquis de Sade. Don't tell me starting off with a salvo of purple pornography was an accident."

"Well—no."

"You're much too smart not to know those descriptions of sex play would hook readers at the start."

"But the greater part of what I had to say wasn't contrived."

"I realized that, of course. After all, I knew you when you were an inexperienced, but very independent, hen medic."

"So why do you label the book hogwash?"

"Because most of this women's inferiority business is just that. You know as well as I do that nurses run the average hospital the way a top-kick sergeant rules his company. And without my secretary, I'd be a bumbling idiot most of the time."

"It's nice to know we're appreciated," Marian said a little crisply.

Cary laughed. "I discovered a long time ago that the only way to live in peace with the feminine half of the world is to make it a partnership. I do my part and I expect them to do theirs—the way it was with Mary and me."

"But you were still boss, weren't you?"

Cary smiled. "Let's say I did what I could to preserve that illusion for the protection of my fellow man."

"Which makes you a fraud," she said on a note of triumph.

"No more than you are, enticing people to read your book by describing the very thing you're inveighing against —sexual domination of women by men. And in such words that the reader is hooked."

"You're very assured, Cary. That's a sign of the masculine urge toward domination, too."

"And you do your best to cut us down to size, which is the same thing."

"Then we're adversaries?"

"I'd rather be friends—or friendly enemies. O.K.?"

"O.K.," she agreed.

An idea was already beginning to take form in her mind, however. Cary was too assured, too certain of himself, too handsome, and above all too much of a threat to her own independence to let the gauntlet be thrown down without picking it up. But it would be in her own way and on her own terms.

"Didn't I see your name on the program of the scientific session?" Marian asked as they were waiting for the baggage to be transferred from the plane to the terminal.

"Just a report on a so called 'Morning-after Pill' we've been prescribing on the Student Health Service. You and Senator Spurgess are the real star attractions of the convention. I hear that the Auxiliary is very much excited, too, about having the author of *Sexual Slavery* speak at their annual luncheon tomorrow."

Bags had started coming through on the moving belt, so Cary took her checks. "Back in a minute," he said.

When Cary returned, he was followed by a skycap with Marian's luggage, which was placed in the trunk of a waiting taxi.

"Parking is so much trouble at airports these days that I usually take cabs," he said as he helped her in and told the driver to take them to the Hotel Centralia.

"By the way," he said, as they settled themselves against the worn cushions, "word has come down that you'll explode some sort of a bombshell in your paper."

"When did you hear that?"

"The press was alerted yesterday, but not by the CMA. Some of the fat cats of the organization aren't happy about it either, particularly H. Edward Danton."

"How could anything I say in the paper possibly affect him?"

"He's running for president-elect. If you steal the limelight before his election, it could mean less press coverage for H. Edward."

"That's ridiculous."

40

"Danton sometimes is a bit ridiculous: It's one symptom of megalomania. He did Central University a favor nearly two years ago, though, by kicking a sharp young cardiac surgeon and his research assistant out of the Danton Clinic because they spoke of some work they were doing before H. Edward was ready to give it to a waiting world."

"This rumor you spoke of about me—is there anything more definite than that?"

"Two of the national TV networks have arranged for their local affiliates to have camera crews ready for the press conference after your paper. There'll be live coverage of Senator Spurgess' address tomorrow morning, of course; he wouldn't agree to come without it. But to avoid confusion, we decided not to allow any coverage of the professional papers presented inside the meeting rooms themselves, so I couldn't make an exception in your case. We'll be handing out short summaries of the papers to the press, while they're being delivered at the professional sessions, and scheduling a press conference immediately afterward so the author can answer questions. In your case somebody seems to have jumped the gun."

"Jake Hirsch probably did that," said Marian. "He's my publisher."

"It would still have to be something very newsworthy to get such coverage."

"It will be," she promised as the cab drew up before the entrance to the hotel and the doorman opened the door.

"I don't doubt that," said Cary. "You've certainly developed a flair for the spectacular where your writings and utterances are concerned."

Marian's eyes narrowed a little. "I'm not sure that's a compliment."

"It was meant to be," he assured her. "Got a patient to see so I won't go in. You're preregistered in the Tower, I picked out your suite myself. The Danton cocktail party starts at six-thirty. I'll pick you up at seven if that's okay, Spurgess ought to be safe in the hotel by then. We'll stay at the party awhile and then have a nice quiet dinner at a place I know you'll like."

41

"Sounds inviting," said Marian. "And thanks for the VIP treatment, Cary."

"Nobody could deserve it more. See you at seven."

ii

Caleb Downs had waited until the other passengers debarked before leaving the airplane, in order to keep from coming near Marian Crowder. He was pretty sure she wouldn't recognize him but there wasn't any point in taking chances, considering his plans for the next few days and her involvement in them.

He came into the lounge, where relatives were greeting debarking passengers, in time to see Cary Poston kiss Marian and take command of the situation with, now that he recalled what Cary had been like in medical school, characteristic efficiency. Come to think of it, there'd been something of an affair between them during that first year, all of which made his plans for the next four days more certain of being fully as rewarding as he'd expected them to be.

In the terminal, Caleb waited near the baggage claim area until he saw Cary and Marian leave in a taxi, then gave his own check to a skycap and was shortly ensconced with his luggage in a waiting taxi.

"Regency House," he told the driver.

Settling back in his seat, Caleb lit a slender cigar with a gold-plated lighter. He'd made a reservation at the older hotel where the members of his sales staff, who operated the Central Pharmaceutical exhibit and dispensed the free beer that was its greatest attraction, usually stayed during the CMA conventions. Now he was glad he'd avoided the much more opulent and newer Hotel Centralia adjoining the medical school and hospital complex of Central University and across the boulevard from the Municipal Auditorium and the rest of the Civic Center.

iii

Arriving a half hour later by Continental from Chicago, Jethro Forbes went immediately to the Braniff counter.

"I'd like a reservation for Guatemala City by coach," he told the clerk.

"Certainly, sir. We have two flights daily, morning and afternoon."

"How about Friday afternoon?"

"Round trip, sir?"

"One way."

Jethro had burned his bridges, when he took a plane for Chicago at Kansas City, then retraced much of the first leg of the trip by boarding another for Central City at O'Hare, making it almost impossible for anyone to discover where he'd really gone, so nothing was to be gained by leaving himself an out now, in the form of the return half of an airplane ticket.

"Both flights to Guatemala City are booked completely for Friday, sir," the clerk reported, after checking by phone.

"How about Saturday?"

"There's space on the morning flight."

"Put me down for it then and call me if you have a cancellation for Friday. I'll pick up the ticket about an hour before."

"Your name, sir?"

"Forbes. Dr. Jethro Forbes. I'll be staying at the Regency House."

"The ticket will be ready for you Saturday morning, Doctor."

As he turned away from the counter toward the baggage claim, Jethro saw a pile of newspapers on the newsstand and paused long enough to buy one. It carried a headline on the front page:

HEART SURGEONS TO VIE FOR CMA PRESIDENT-ELECT

The pictures of two men occupied columns just below the headline. One was Dr. H. Edward Danton, looking confident and successful as usual, the other a younger man whom Jethro didn't know, identified only as Dr. Paul Rice, aged thirty-two and associate professor of surgery and head of cardiovascular surgery at the Central University Medical School.

Jethro knew enough about the academic side of medicine to realize that thirty-two was a rather young age for a doctor to have achieved so important a position. But then cardiovascular surgery was so new that the field would still be limited largely to young men—and H. Edward Danton, who had trained most of the leaders. For one of them now to be opposing Danton was a bit like father striving with son to prove himself, Jethro thought. All of which promised to make this convention one of the most interesting he had ever attended, even though it would be his last.

CHAPTER IV

As chairman of the Film Projection Committee for the CMA Convention, Paul Rice was required to be within range of the electronic pager carried by all doctors of the hospital staff, until the closed-circuit showings on monitor screens throughout the Auditorium of the Central City Civic Center and over room television sets in the major hotels ended at eleven o'clock. Film breaks, equipment failures and projection difficulties were common in the complicated setup of the close-circuit system and someone had to be available to authorize sudden changes in the film schedule.

Since his apartment was in another part of the city, Paul had taken a room for the duration of the convention in the Hotel Centralia. Located across busy Auditorium Avenue from the Civic Center, and connected to it by an underground passage, the hotel adjoined the skyscraper University Hospital and Medical School, an arrangement particularly adapted for large medical conventions, with adequate hotel, auditorium, exhibit and clinical medical facilities all within easy reach.

When Paul found, after a quick sandwich and coffee at the Civic Center Cafeteria, that Jerry had not yet returned to the audio-visual control center where they had been previewing films, he crossed through the underground passage to the hotel. A letter was in his mailbox and, when he saw the familiar flowing feminine script and the perfume from it reached his nostrils, he knew the identity of the sender immediately.

Almost two years had passed since he'd last seen Aletha Danton, but his pulse still quickened as he moved away from the mail desk and tore open the envelope.

The message was brief:

Paul, dearest,
I'm going to be busy most of the afternoon getting ready for the cocktail party this evening, but I'd like to talk to you for a few minutes before it. Please be in your room around five and I'll try to come by. We need to talk as soon as possible.

Love,
Aletha

Moving to a wastepaper container at one side of the lobby of the Centralia, Paul tore the note and envelope into small bits and dropped them into it. But he couldn't erase the words or the perfume from his brain any more than he could the eagerness stirred within him by the thought of seeing Aletha again.

The last thing he would have thought of when, fresh from a surgical residency in Houston, he'd come to the Danton Clinic five years ago for postgraduate training in heart and blood-vessel surgery was to fall in love with the director's wife. During the whole first year of residency, he saw Aletha perhaps half a dozen times, mainly at clinic receptions for visiting medical potentates and the like. But things had changed rapidly during the third year when Paul had become H. Edward Danton's first assistant. And particularly during the fourth, when talk that his hands were even swifter and more dependable than those of the Great Man himself had begun to circulate inside the clinic and elsewhere in the world where the surgical elite, those who dared to tackle the heart itself, moved.

Aletha had gone out of her way that fourth year to be gracious, and in a dozen ways, had made it clear that she preferred Paul's company to that of the other men from the clinic staff, who always clustered about her whenever opportunity afforded itself, as young men will about a strikingly beautiful and desirable woman, particularly when she's the wife of their chief. In spite of the encouragement, however, Paul had been almost shocked when she had finally evinced a willingness to come to his apartment one evening, while H. Edward Danton was away on one of his frequent tours, speaking to medical societies on his work in heart and blood-vessel surgery.

The Danton Dacron aorta, the Danton plastic heart valve, the Danton coronary grafts—all were used by cardiac surgeons in many parts of the globe. And wherever the most famous heart and blood-vessel surgeon in the world spoke, other and less capable men came to listen and to watch, hoping to learn just how the stubby fingers of Dr. H. Edward Danton managed to perform the miracles of surgery that were regularly announced from the famous clinic.

What did it matter that in each case the research making the final brilliant results possible had been done by younger men, whose names were rarely mentioned in the lectures given by Danton to admiring groups of doctors? Or, for that matter, in articles describing the final results which appeared in the most important medical journals in the world?

One field alone had refused to be conquered by Danton and his brilliant staff—the left ventricular bypass device known to newsmen and the public at large as the "artificial heart." Jerry Warren, then head of research at the Danton Clinic and the most promising young man to be developed there besides Paul himself, had come closer to it than anyone else. Working as a team, Paul and Jerry had devised a promising apparatus and appeared to be on the verge of a real breakthrough. Until Jerry made the mistake of mentioning their work during a forum discussion at a medical meeting when an alert medically oriented science writer happened to be present.

That had been the end for Jerry Warren at the Danton Clinic—and for Paul Rice when he stood up for his friend. Half the upper echelon staff of the clinic had walked out as an aftermath of that volcano when, in a towering rage, Danton had made it clear that only one voice spoke for the clinic and only one person received the credit. Snapped up by medical school faculties all over the country, the fallout, so to speak, of the Danton mushroom cloud had benefited medical science immeasurably by making heart surgery no longer the private preserve of H. Edward Danton.

A month before the explosion, Aletha had dashed all of Paul's hopes for a more intimate relationship. The break had come when a seriously ill child was admitted on the evening of the very night Aletha had promised to spend in Paul's apartment. The cyanotic lips and straining lungs of the child with the strange congenital heart malady called the Tetralogy of Fallot—because the development of the heart had gone awry in four places—had banished from Paul's mind all thought of the bliss he'd waited so long to attain—until it was too late and a gravely affronted Aletha had gone home angry. She had refused even to speak to him afterward and, before he'd been able to explain, the final explosion had seemed to remove all possibility of a reconciliation—until today.

ii

When Paul Rice returned to the audio-visual control room a little after two, he found Jerry already at work.

"What did Pete Sanders want?" Jerry asked. "Or is it none of my business?"

"It's very much your business. Danton wants to put another film into the closed-circuit schedule."

"In place of the two-hands one?"

"In addition to it."

"Whose film comes out—as if I didn't know?"

Paul shrugged. "What else could I do but jerk ours?"

"Nothing, of course," said Jerry bitterly. "But I still hate to see that bastard—"

"You're repeating yourself."

"That *white* bastard then—get away with it."

"Me, too," said Paul. "But this time it looks like checkmate."

"Did you see the film?"

"No."

"This must be it; somebody left one here while we were at lunch." Jerry picked up a reel lying on the console desk before the control panel. "Give me a minute to thread it into the projector and we'll see what Danton has produced this time."

The film was in color and the hands were skilled—but not Danton's.

"Elton Brooks again," said Jerry. "He's improved a lot since we left the clinic."

The operative procedure was intricate, even daring. Performed much of the time beneath a large magnifying glass, it consisted of a careful dissection of one of the larger superficial arteries from the temple and its connection with an artery at the base of the brain by means of an extremely delicate anastomosis.

The narration, as with the other film, was Danton's and nothing in the presentation indicated that he had not performed the operation himself, except the size of the surgeon's hands, which those not intimately familiar with Danton's operative technique would hardly have noticed.

"Looks like he's got himself a new procedure," said Jerry when the film was finished.

"I don't think it's original with Danton," said Paul. "A

very similar one was described a few months ago in a foreign medical journal, Swiss, I believe."

"This wouldn't be the first time Danton appropriated an operation for himself, without giving credit to the originator. Are you going after him on this one?"

Paul shook his head. "He's headed us off at the pass again. As I remember it, the original procedure used a different artery for the outside source of blood."

"Either way it appears to channel an extra supply of blood to each half of a brain that's being crippled by arteriosclerosis."

"It's a brilliant idea," Paul conceded. "Which should teach us not to underrate our old chief."

"So what are we going to do?"

"Nothing, unless Danton happens to mention this during the panel discussion on coronary circulation that's on the convention program. If he does, one of us will rise to discuss and casually mention this procedure, in a way that lets everybody know it isn't really Danton's."

"Then I'd better run some pressure tests on the vessels involved to see whether connecting an artery like the superficial temporal to the circulation at the base of the brain really delivers more blood to one side of the cerebrum. Which means Otto and I will be working late."

"I'll help you, if I don't get tied up," Paul promised.

Jerry frowned. "I wonder——"

"What's wrong?"

"It just occurred to me that this double-barreled blood supply for the brain could put a pretty heavy strain on the lenticulostriate artery that usually ruptures in the classic type of apoplexy. And that could also mean stepping up the number and maybe the severity of strokes."

"You've got a good argument."

"What surprises me is that Danton would go to the trouble of developing this procedure, when the scuttlebutt is that he's got everybody at the clinic working on the artificial heart."

"Maybe he's heard we've already got one," said Paul. "Is everything O.K. for the exhibit?"

"Working like a charm," said Jerry. "I'll try to catch Elton Brooks at the old man's cocktail party tonight—or before, if I can. Maybe I can pry some information out of him."

"Good luck."

"By the way, I saw Mrs. Danton at lunch." Jerry's tone was studiedly casual. "The Auxiliary was having some sort of party at the Sheraton. She even spoke to me."

"How did she look?"

"More beautiful than ever. Why can't men look better as they grow older the way women seem to be able to do?"

"I guess that's because men have to work like hell to pay for the upkeep. You're married, so you ought to know the answer to that better than I do."

"Katie's still in the warranty period, thank God. I saw Alex Klein at lunch, too. He says support for the Young Turk movement is snowballing. That headline in the *Dispatch* pitting you against Danton was a stroke of genius on Alex's part."

"The king can still do no wrong."

"But he can have it done to *him*. We just might give Danton the shock of his life Thursday at the election."

CHAPTER V

The doorman at the Hotel Centralia whistled softly when Carlota Montez stepped down from the bus in front of the hotel.

"Hi, Countess." A warm smile crinkled Jack Reeves's weatherbeaten face. "Boy, do you look good! If I were only twenty years younger—"

Carlota took Reeves by the lapels of his blue uniform and kissed him on the cheek. "That's for cheering me up when I'm low, Jack."

"Nobody'd ever know it to look at you."

Carlota was indeed a picture of beauty in the uniform

worn by the Centralia's cocktail waitresses. H...
eggshell white, as were the patent leather boot...
to just below her knees. The pleated skirt was s...
ering barely a third of her thighs, and the faint ...
of her skin between its perky hemline and the bo...
blended perfectly with both, as did her dark hair. Shoulder
length, it was held back from her face by a ribbon of the
same color as the dress, but allowed to fall free in the
back with a natural curl that gave it the sort of wave
most girls achieved only through hours of roller curlers.

"You must be serving at Dr. Danton's cocktail party
tonight," said Reeves.

"I am," said Carlota. "One of the other girls couldn't
make it."

"If one of them young doctors here for the convention
gets a good look at you, he's liable to carry you off like
that fellow Lochinvar I used to read about when I was a
boy."

Carlota laughed. "I'd better get upstairs then, Jack.
They say everybody at the convention will be at that
party."

"It's going to be a real bash," said the doorman. "Dr.
Danton's wife has already chewed out the head chef over
the *hors d'oeuvres*—as if anybody will be noticing what
they eat with all that free liquor."

ii

Aletha Danton stepped from the shower and rubbed her
body briskly with a large towel. Peeling off the cap that
had protected her blond hair, she inspected her face carefully in the bathroom mirror. No sagging yet, she noted
with approval. Of course, a woman of almost forty couldn't
expect to look like an eighteen-year-old. But when the
inevitable signs of age did begin to appear, she could always go to Los Angeles and the plastic surgeon who
specialized in keeping movie stars eternally young.

"What time is it, darling?" she called into the bedroom

...e suite, where H. Edward Danton was lying on one of ...e two beds.

"Four o'clock. Aren't you dressing early?"

"I want to check on the *hors d'oeuvres* again before the crowd starts coming. I don't entirely trust that chief pastry cook. How did things turn out at the luncheon?"

"Lousy. Paul Rice will still be nominated from the floor."

"I thought you already had more than enough votes to carry the election."

"I did—six months ago before a lot of people got agitated about changes in the way medical care is delivered. This isn't an old doctor's profession any more, Aletha. These days medical schools are full of long-haired radicals who think they can run things better than men who have devoted their lives to upgrading medical science." Danton's voice sank to a growl that was quite familiar to interns and residents who had worked in his clinic, presaging one of his famous rages. "Damn young punks!"

"Don't excite yourself, darling," said Aletha. "You know what Jim Merrill said—"

"Damn Jim Merrill! You'd be excited, too, if you were only two stages away from everything you'd always worked for and saw yourself crippled in the prime of life because a damned artery on one side of your brain sometimes shuts down."

Aletha had finished putting on her lingerie and wrapped a silk dressing gown about her body, before moving into the other room and the dressing table there.

"You shouldn't have let the strategy conference upset you this way," she said.

"It isn't just that," said Danton. "I'm pretty sure Paul and Jerry have a workable left ventricular bypass operation."

"Better than yours?" Aletha knew very well what perfecting an artificial heart could mean for its discoverer.

"If it works at all, it's better than mine. I managed to keep Paul and Jerry from showing a film describing theirs on the closed-circuit TV in the hotels—"

"How did you do that?"

Danton chuckled. "Put the screws on the Arrangements Committee to let me show two films instead of one. Cary Poston raised hell, but I had the rest of the committee in my pocket, so he couldn't stop me. And with Paul chairman of the Film Projection Committee, he couldn't very well jerk somebody else's film at the last moment and keep his own in the schedule."

"That was clever."

"But only a stopgap," Danton admitted. "Paul's giving a paper on the bypass Tuesday morning. He'll certainly show the film then, so I'll have to figure a way to clobber him again."

"Paul couldn't possibly beat you in the election, could he?"

"He doesn't have to beat me, just make a good showing. If he gets enough votes to even crimp my majority, I'll never be elected president of the AMA."

"Which film did you put into the closed-circuit program?" Aletha changed the subject.

"The one on direct anastomosis between the cerebral circulation and the superficial temporal artery."

Aletha frowned. "Isn't that taking a chance? I've heard you say you only looked into the operation because you—"

"Might need it sometime myself?"

"Yes."

"This was an emergency, Aletha. Besides, the only person here who could leak anything on my condition is Elton Brooks."

"Can you be sure he won't speak of it?"

"Elton wants that vascular surgery job in the new medical school in Arizona but knows he'll never get it without my recommendation." Danton settled himself comfortably on the bed. "Run along and give the hired help hell. I've got to do some tough politicking tonight at the reception and I want a nap before I dress."

"I'll be back in time to help you with your studs." Aletha leaned down to kiss him, but moved away quickly when he reached up to hold her.

"Careful, darling," she said lightly. "You've got your arteries to think of."

"Right now a couple of them are thinking for themselves. And they're not in the brain."

iii

It was four-thirty before Paul and Jerry finished checking films and Paul returned to his room. He was knotting his tie, after taking a shower and changing clothes, when a knock sounded on the door. He opened it to see Aletha Danton standing outside, smiling warmly.

"Aren't you going to ask me in?" she said.

"Of course." He stood back and closed the door behind her. "You're looking especially lovely, Aletha."

In a short cocktail dress of gold chiffon, setting off to the best possible advantage her blond hair and the long slender legs he remembered so well, she was enough to arouse desire in a monk, to say nothing of someone who had carried her image in his memory for the nearly two years since he'd seen her last.

"You've changed, Paul," she said. "Or maybe grown up is the better word."

"They say the quickest way for a young man to grow up is to be kicked out of the house by his father. Or in my case by a father image."

"Even so, the change has been good for you." She crossed over to the bed and, sitting on it, reached for an ashtray on the bedside table.

"I've been following your career," she added. "You're really making a name for yourself, not only here but in the country as well."

"I was taught by a master."

"Not married yet?" She took a cigarette from a jeweled case and lit it with a matching lighter. Like many surgeons, Paul had long since given up smoking.

"That's another fallout from being so close to feminine perfection those last two years at the clinic," he said. "It

54

sort of sours you on any really permanent connection with another."

"What a nice compliment!" Her eyes sparkled. "It's easy to see you've had more experience with women, since you left the clinic."

He shrugged. "You're part of a medical complex, too, so you know they're available."

The wariness he'd shown when he opened the door and found her there hadn't left him yet, Aletha saw, and decided that it had been a wise move on her part to have this conference with him before things really got under way at the convention. Besides, his newfound assuredness excited her far more than his almost puppy-like eagerness had, when he'd become her husband's second-in-command some three years ago.

"I came to apologize, Paul," she said. "I didn't learn until much later how you saved that child's life the night we were to have met in your apartment. Edward said if you hadn't had the courage to bubble oxygen directly into the bloodstream, the little girl would have died."

"Probably."

"No woman likes to be stood up—especially by a man she's falling in love with."

She saw from the sudden softening of the stiffness in his posture, as he stood at the foot of the bed—almost as if to keep it between them—that the words had scored a hit on his defenses.

"That's why I reacted so violently," she added. "And why I didn't listen to your explanation."

"You don't need to apologize, Aletha. It was presumptuous of me even to imagine you might—"

"Imagine?" Her laugh was warm and intimate. "But I promised. And I did come to the apartment that night—waited an hour in fact."

"Will you accept my apology now?"

"It's I who owe you an apology, Paul. I want us to be friends."

"And Dr. Danton?"

Aletha laughed. "You know how Edward is. He worked

hard to get where he is, and he doesn't give up easily, particularly if you and Jerry Warren have really developed an artificial heart that works as some people claim."

Deep inside Paul Rice's brain a warning bell rang faintly, but still loud enough to alert him to a reason for Aletha's coming to the apartment that afternoon, other than the desire to renew what had almost been an intimate relationship just before he left the Danton Clinic so summarily.

"Jerry's making progress," he admitted. "Our paper to the Vascular Surgery Section Tuesday will give some details of what we've been able to do."

"You're smart not to announce it ahead of time. Edward always keeps a trick or so up his sleeve, one he doesn't show publicly until he's got the right sort of a setup."

"We're not hiding anything," said Paul. "There's plenty of room in the field for everybody who's working on ventricular bypass."

Aletha stubbed out her cigarette in the ashtray beside her. She'd learned what she had come there to learn—and what Edward wanted very badly to know—although she couldn't tell her husband about it just now. Still, she decided, there was no harm in tying Paul Rice more closely to herself once again, with the emotional bonds she had long ago discovered were a potent means of influencing men. And besides, Paul was the only man in the field who could possibly step in almost immediately and take over at the clinic, if the trouble which had already forced Edward to give up some of his more difficult surgical feats, to his considerable anger, continued to increase.

Equally important—and stimulating—was the stirring of excitement inside herself she saw reflected in Paul Rice's eyes as she got to her feet and smoothed down the chiffon skirt, quite conscious that the movement also called attention to the long fluid thighs, the slender roundness of her hips and the general desirability of her body.

"Tell Jerry I'm proud of both of you," she said. "So is Edward, though you'd never get him to admit it. He was particularly fond of you, Paul, almost like the son he never had. I'm sure that's why he reacted so violently when he thought you betrayed him.

"But I didn't."

"He knows that now, but he's a stubborn man. It's hard for him to back away from a position, once he's taken it. If you could—"

"I'm willing to meet him halfway, Aletha."

"I'm afraid it would have to be a little more than that."

"Shall I go to him during the convention?"

"Not yet, darling." She gave the usually casual endearment a throaty tone that made it considerably more than casual. "He's very much concerned about the election right now."

"It should be in the bag for him."

"Oh, he'll get elected but that isn't what counts. The presidency of the CMA is a giant step toward the AMA. If Edward wins Thursday morning by a landslide vote, the effect on the AMA election several years from now will be much stronger than if there's a substantial vote for other candidates."

"Are you asking my help—for Dr. Danton?"

"For *me,* darling. I'm quite human, as you would have discovered if you hadn't been stopped by that heart case. And I enjoy being in the limelight."

"There's no reason why you shouldn't. You're a very beautiful woman."

"And you're everything Edward Danton was fifteen years ago, with an even greater future in the right place and with the right connections. Our party will be starting soon, so I've got to go, but there'll be other times."

Aletha moved closer and looked up at him, obviously expecting to be kissed. His arms went around her and as he pressed the loveliness he remembered so well against his own body, his lips found hers parted and eager. For a single instant they might as well have been as naked, in the flesh, as they were in the surge of passion that gripped them both. But when he started moving her gently toward the bed, she broke from his embrace.

"Really, Paul!" She was breathing quickly, her cheeks flushed, her eyes bright with what could only be a passion almost equal to his. "You've come a long way in a few years. And so impetuous."

"Aletha, I—"

"Not now, darling."

"Later then? You can't deny what you felt just now. What you still feel."

"I won't deny it." She was repairing her mouth in the mirror over the dresser with a lipstick from her handbag. "Why else would I have come to your room alone?"

"But—"

"I'm Caesar's wife, Paul." She was at the door now, turning the latch. "With nearly a thousand people coming soon for cocktails, I have to preserve the illusion of untouchability—at least for a while."

"Tonight then?"

She shook her head—with just the right note of regret. "We're going out to dinner after the party—more politics. But Edward will be busy with strategy conferences as the election approaches. I'll let you know later."

She was gone, leaving her perfume and the fire in his body to remind him of her presence, plus the nagging suspicion that he was being used—as women have used their sexual desirability since the beginning of time—to advance the political career of H. Edward Danton.

iv

In Meeting Room C on the second level of the Civic Auditorium, reached by the ascending ramps from the exhibit floor, the preconvention session of the Academy of Family Medicine for the central region was winding down its annual meeting Sunday afternoon. The room was barely a third full, though Jethro Forbes could remember when, at the time an organization strictly for general practitioners had first come into being about ten years ago, the number of doctors attending this broadest of all

58

the specialty groups would have packed the room and spilled out into the corridor.

Created for the twin purposes of giving the general practitioner a feeling of status and encouraging him to improve his medical knowledge by discussing problems peculiar to his work, the Academy had flourished for a while as it sought to inject some life into the dying concept of the family doctor.

But the constant increase in the number of specialists, lured by large fees and less demands upon after-work time, had gradually whittled away the ranks of general practitioners and with them the membership.

Jethro had been one of the first to join the Academy and still made it a point to attend the annual preconvention meetings held, like the gatherings of specialty groups such as the American College of Surgeons and others, on the Sunday afternoon at the start of convention week. But through the years he had seen the programs become more and more concerned with shoring up the tottering prestige of general practice and less with the particular medical problems with which any family doctor must cope.

This afternoon's session had been no exception. A professor of family medicine at the University of Florida had described how, with a number of towns in the vicinity of the university unable to find and keep family doctors, the medical school had finally had no choice except to organize what might be called satellite clinics in surrounding areas. That the record of the clinics was excellent, as well as their acceptance by the community, had nothing to do with family practice, Jethro decided. In fact, it was but another evidence of what had been apparent to him for a long time, that he was a member of a bulldog breed whose death had long since been assured by the steadily increasing complexity of medical science.

The second speaker talked about the question of whether general practitioners should accept assignments of Medicare B payments for their services. The doctor bill section of Medicare, open to all over sixty-five who were willing to pay the monthly fee, was a source of constant conflict between patient and doctor. Patients were not very happy about being forced to go to the trouble of filling out insurance blanks and attaching receipted bills from their doctors, before sending them to Medicare payment offices, where more often that not, the fees were scaled down arbitrarily to considerably less than the bills already paid. Doctors, on the other hand, already busy with more bookwork than they liked in a day when practically everybody carried some form of health insurance insisted upon having financial dealings only with patients, avoiding the implication that they were already being paid by the government.

Only two papers in the program had proved to be worth Jethro's time. One discussed a cold-water test, designed to identify potential sufferers from high blood pressure, which an office nurse could easily carry out by immersing a patient's hands in ice water for a minute before taking the blood pressure and noting the rise over the level before the test. The other paper discussed a program to train nurses as midwives, not only reducing the cost of childbirth for women who had previously borne children and usually only had to give a good push away to deliver themselves, but taking a considerable burden off the few overworked practitioners remaining in rural areas.

It was five o'clock and the dreary program was almost at an end, when the chairman, a professor of family medicine—who had not been engaged in anything resembling its day-to-day routine for twenty years, Jethro suspected—called for comments from the door before adjourning. Usually Jethro just sat and listened during these sessions, but today, somewhat to his own surprise, he found himself rising to his feet.

"Dr. Jethro Forbes, Revere, Kansas," he said. "I'd like to say a few words."

"Certainly, Doctor Forbes," the chairman said hurriedly, heading off a plump doctor with rimless glasses who invariably delivered a diatribe against the government at every Academy session. "Please use the microphone in the aisle just ahead of you."

Jethro moved forward to the microphone stand in the aisle, placed there so it could be used by questioners or those commenting from the floor, as he was.

"Mr. Chairman and members," he said. "Some of you may know that I was a charter member of this Academy. Like most of you, I suspect, I intended to be a specialist —obstetrics was my field—when I graduated from medical school But I was sidetracked into general practice, where I promptly found myself a specialist in obstetrics without having to bother with going through a residency."

There was a round of laughter, and some applause.

"I don't feel exactly moribund," Jethro continued, "but this afternoon I haven't been able to escape the conviction that I've been attending a wake—with myself, as a general practitioner, the central character."

There was no laughter now. Looking around and seeing hardly anyone under forty, no doctor could escape the truth of what Jethro was saying.

"General practice, gentlemen, is for old men and all of our whitewashing by organizing courses in what we call family medicine, or setting up chairs in various medical schools isn't going to change it. We're a dying breed and maybe medicine will be the better for it; I don't pretend to know. This afternoon you've heard the doctor from Florida tell how small towns, which couldn't get a family doctor to settle there for love nor money, are receiving excellent medical care through what he called satellite clinics from the university. I happen to be one who thinks this is a good trend for several reasons.

"For one thing, it puts people on record as realizing the need for adequate medical care and requires that the community undertake at least part of the financial burden. For another, these satellite clinics also give young doctors an opportunity to tackle the diagnosis of disease by using their eyes, ears and fingers, instead of something like the machine that mechanics use to diagnose the trouble in your engine, before putting in a lot of new spark plugs and stuff that you don't need.

"All this is good, gentlemen, even if it means that you

and I who belong to the old breed of family doctors will soon vanish from American medicine. Look around the room and see how few of us are left, even at the convention of the largest medical association outside the AMA. Review the program of this meeting and you will see that half the papers today have been concerned, not with how we can function more efficiently in the care of our patients, but how to collect our full fees, although the patient who thinks himself adequately insured gets stuck, when Medicare B cuts down its allowance on our bills.

"We're a dying breed, gentlemen, and this meeting today might as well be our swan song. Tomorrow a United States senator is going to preach part of your funeral, of all our funerals, as independent physicians. And on Tuesday, the secretary of the government bureau, to which doctors are rapidly becoming slaves, will add the ashes to ashes and dust to death theme. As for me, I can ony give the salute of the gladiators: '*Ave Caesar! Morituri te salutant.*' "

Jethro sat down, to considerable applause. Now that he had said his piece, he felt a little embarrassed by his own eloquence. Essentially a taciturn man, however, he had spoken from the heart on a subject to which he had given considerable thought in the long hours of driving from farmhouse to farmhouse, when he wasn't listening to recorded medical lectures on the tape player that operated through the radio of his car. He'd felt the urge at other Academy of Family Medicine sessions to say just what he had said that afternoon but had never yielded to it before. But then he'd only broken his last tie with his practice in Revere that very morning, so in a way his speech had also been his swan song.

v

Ted Kraus had every reason to be weary. However slickly efficient they might be, surgical instruments were made of metal, which meant weight. He'd brought the entire collection for his booth up from Houston in the station wagon and the job of setting up the exhibit of

Surgical Instruments, Inc., had taken all day. Now he looked at his work, like the Lord at the end of the sixth day, and saw that it was good.

Pure inspiration had made him spend all his available spare time in the shop of the old surgical instrument maker in Stuttgart while he was stationed in Germany. With the further training the GI Bill of Rights had made possible after his discharge from service, he'd sharpened his skill in making the miniaturized surgical instruments used in many brain and blood-vessel operations.

The opportunity to exhibit his work to the doctors who flocked to the CMA Convention had been one he couldn't afford to turn down. And when he compared his own products with those exhibited by other instrument manufacturers at the convention, he was sure he could hold his own in competition with any of them.

Ted Kraus hadn't been too busy all day for an occasional glance at the well-stacked blonde working across the aisle in the Vibrassage exhibit. Now, as he stood back to survey the results of his labor, he wasn't at all surprised when she crossed the aisle to where he was standing.

Broad shouldered, narrow hipped, handsome in the roughhewn sort of way that seemed to appeal to most women. Kraus had taken their admiration for granted since he'd gone out for high school football as a freshman and discovered that he had a knack for broken field running. Gena was always warning him about other women, but the job of getting his own surgical supply house in operation had been so demanding that he'd hardly had time for Gena's own particular needs, although managing to father two fine boys and a girl in the process.

Now here he was at the second most prestigious medical convention in the country with his own exhibit of glossy instruments, many of which he had designed himself in the garage workshop, and a blonde with a gleam in her eye was crossing the aisle toward where he stood. It was a Solomon's dream come true and Ted Kraus, at thirty-five, was no man to turn down opportunity when it knocked.

"Looks good," said Alice Perrault. "The way you've been working, you must be bushed."

"I'm dead, Miss Perrault." Like most of the exhibitors, her name and that of her company were printed on the plastic-sheathed convention badge she wore pinned to a snug sweater. "Drove all night from Houston and I've been working all day setting it up. I'm Ted Kraus. Haven't even had time to pin on a badge."

"Better have it on tomorrow or the cop at the entrance won't let you in." Alice reached across the display table and lifted a small cylindrical object that was tapered almost to a point at one end. "What's this?"

"A magnet for removing metallic foreign bodies from the eye—you know, bits of steel and the like. This one is ten times more powerful than the average but doesn't weigh any more."

"Ten times?" Alice's quick glance at his shoulders, his lean body and narrow hips made it seem as if she were speaking of him instead of the magnet.

"It's a real gadget." Ted took the magnet from her hand and held it near one of the metallic buttons on her sweater, instantly drawing the button to the magnet.

"You could undress a girl with that thing, Mr. Kraus." Alice pushed the button back into place, not without some difficulty.

"Hardly, but it would do for openers." Ted put the magnet back on the table.

"What's this?" Alice reached over to pick up a curved shaft of plastic with a light bulb imbedded in one end and a white electric cord attached to the other.

"It's a sterilizable lamp used during operations where the surgeon needs a lot of light in a confined area."

He plugged in the cord and held the end containing the bulb behind his hand. Immediately the powerful lamp transilluminated the tissues, making it possible to detect the shadows of the bones.

"Put it behind the heart during surgery," he said, "and you can see what part is getting the blood supply it needs and what isn't."

"Ingenious. What won't they think of next?"

"Right now I can't think of anything except a hot bath and a massage," said Ted. "My back feels like the Seven Dwarfs have been pounding on it all afternoon with cudgels."

"Just step across the aisle with me," said Alice briskly. "Twenty minutes of Vibrassage will make you feel like a new man."

"Guaranteed?"

"Or your money back." She guided him to one of the reclining chairs, helped him take off his coat, had him stretch out and loosened his belt with practiced fingers. When she pressed the switch on a small console built into the arm of the chair, the whole surface beneath his body began to vibrate with a soothing motion.

"How's that?"

"Wonderful."

"Now I'll add Thermassage—"

"What's that?"

"Actually nothing but a fancy name for a diathermy unit. Vibrassage takes care of the surface but to really get down inside those muscles you've been punishing all day, you need Thermassage to put the heat right into the deeper tissues."

She adjusted a flat pad expertly beneath his back, then lay another one across just above his lower abdomen and switched it on.

"Lie there while I run over to the Central Pharmaceutical exhibit," she told him. "They started serving free beer about an hour ago. I'll bring some back."

Ted Kraus lay back and relaxed. He could already feel the pulsing warmth of the diathermy attachment deep inside his muscles, flushing away his fatigue while the gently kneading mechanical fingers of the Vibrassage chair stimulated the skin and superficial tissues.

By the time Alice Perrault came back carrying a large paper cup filled with foaming draft beer, he was drowsily content.

vi

Jerry Warren was putting the final touches to the exhibit of his and Paul's work which they had prepared for the convention, when Paul returned to the Auditorium about five-thirty for a final check. Their exhibit had been assigned to a somewhat out-of-the-way spot in the scientific exhibit area, where it was less likely to be noticed when the mainstream of visitors started passing through after the convention got under way at full speed the next morning.

The normal movement of traffic inside the ground floor exhibit hall was from the front of the building, where the registration booths were located, toward thc back. From there ramps led upward to the meeting rooms located on three floors of the Auditorium building above the exhibit area, as well as to the main theater. In all of these regions, papers would be delivered during the week to the various sections into which a convention of this size was customarily divided, as well as to the General Sessions.

It was no accident, Paul was sure, that their exhibit was relatively difficult to find. A word from Dr. H. Edward Danton to the Exhibits Committee had no doubt quickly settled the question of just how much prominence their particular efforts should receive, but the location didn't particularly trouble him. Neither he nor Jerry were quite satisfied yet with their latest model of a left ventricular assist device, popularly, and not quite correctly, known as the artificial heart.

The major difficulty with a pump of this type lay in the fact that the controls, tied in with the electrical impulses that initiated the several phases of filling and emptying which characterized the normal heartbeat, were not sensitive enough to cope with sudden changes in the function of the heart itself. If the electrical pulse actuating the normal heartbeat came a fraction of a second early, the valve in the left side of the pump letting blood into the ventricular chamber was not fully open. The supply available to be pumped out was thus partially nullified by lack of complete filling before contraction, making the pump much less efficient than it needed to be.

On the other hand, if the impulses activating the pump were a fraction of a second late, the left ventricle of the heart would overfill, the very thing the pump was designed to prevent, causing it to contract on its own account and dissipating much of the assistance the pump was designed to give. Thus on either count the device could fail to carry its real share of maintaining a normal pressure of blood in the great vessels of the arterial system connected to the left ventricle, the strongest pump of the heart itself when not damaged by disease. And until controls as sensitive as those governing the beating of the heart itself could be devised, the pumping device was considerably less than perfect.

"I had a drink in the Auditorium cocktail lounge with Elton Brooks this afternoon," Jerry said casually as they were giving the final check to the exhibit.

"Discover anything?"

"Elton's playing it cagey, but he obviously isn't very happy about his name not being on the credits for that infarct excision."

"It was brilliant surgery but he's been with Danton long enough to know the Great One doesn't share credits with anybody," said Paul.

"Something's happened at the Danton Clinic, but I gathered that everybody's afraid to talk about it for fear of getting the shaft."

"Is that all you learned?"

"Elton wouldn't admit it but the whole thing—whatever it is—has to be connected with medical politics."

"Are you saying there's a skeleton in Danton's closet?"

"Something like that—and I'd sure like to start rattling its bones."

CHAPTER VI

The waitresses for the Danton cocktail party were lined up outside the office of the restaurant manager, awaiting his approval before taking the service elevator to the rooftop lounge and the adjoining dining room which had been cleared of tables for the Danton cocktail party. The girls wore identical uniforms with short pleated skirts and boots, yet as she hurried to her place in the line, Carlota still stood out among them like a jewel among rubble.

The manager stood in the door of the office with the inevitable clipboard in his hand.

"Peters," he called and a thin-faced, perky blonde stepped forward for inspection, received the nod and moved to the other side of the door.

"Martin." Another girl, sultry, dark-haired, moved out of the line and was approved.

"Kelsey." A redhead, freckled, sparkling, stepped forward but the manager frowned when he saw the gold wedding band on her finger.

"Do you have to wear that?" he asked. "This is a convention and you girls want to give the illusion—the illusion, mind you, not the reality—that you're available."

"I'm sorry, Mr. Kimball." Kelsey expertly slipped off the ring and secreted it in her uniform pocket. "I forgot."

"Mind you, I'm not instructing you to accept any propositions." Kimball said wearily. "*That* concession already belongs to someone else."

There was a laugh as he turned back to the clipboard. Everybody knew the bellmen controlled the bodies-for-rent concession.

"Montez," he called.

"Here, Mr. Kimball."

"You're late again."

68

"I'm sorry, sir. I was working in the library on a bio-chemistry paper."

"One of the girls on the regular Polo Lounge shift called in sick just now," said the manager. "With free liquor flowing on the roof, the bar downstairs won't be needing help until after the party is over. Can you work in the Polo Lounge until midnight after the crowd from this reception starts drifting away?"

Carlota hesitated only a moment. Staying on until twelve would mean she would probably have to spend most of the night finishing the chemistry paper. But late-night drinkers in the main cocktail lounge were good tippers and she needed the money to help Raul—except that even with an emergency loan of fifty dollars she might be able to get from the hotel employees' credit union, it wouldn't be nearly enough.

"I'll stay, Mr. Kimball," she said.

As the manager turned back into his office the chattering girls took the service elevator to the roof, where a squad of barmen were already polishing glasses.

"This doctor must be rich to afford a reception for the whole convention," said Marian Kelsey. "What did Kimball say his name is?"

"Dr. H. Edward Danton," said Carlota. "He's the most famous heart surgeon in the country, maybe even in the world."

"That stuff gives me the willies." Marian Kelsey shivered. "I saw a movie the other night where the surgeon cut into a man's heart while it was beating—thought I'd shoot my dinner right there."

"The paper says Dr. Danton is going to have a tough fight for office in the medical association," said Carlota. "This cocktail party must be part of the campaign."

"Which means no tips," said Ilona Martin disgustedly. "I read somewhere that young doctors don't join these medical societies much any more so most of the ones you see at these conventions lately are older."

"The old ones tip better, though," said Ethel Peters. "I guess they've had a longer time to bring in the cash."

"All right, girls, let's get this show on the road," said Charlie, the head bartender. "And watch out for Mrs. Danton. The head pastry chef tells me she's hell on wheels."

ii

Marian Crowder was half dressed when a knock sounded on the door of the adjoining reception room to her suite. She cracked the door and, seeing Cary Poston outside, opened it to let him in.

"Remind me to tell you how lovely you are," he said as she moved into the bedroom, leaving him to take a chair in the sitting room with a magazine.

He made a handsome picture as she watched him in the mirror of her dressing table. He had changed into a dark blue double-breasted blazer and white slacks, with one of the light blue shirts that were so popular and a wide tie.

"Whose idea was it to give me a suite?" Marian called from the bedroom.

"Mine. You're the only bona fide celebrity of the convention as far as I'm concerned."

"Don't let Senator Spurgess hear you say that."

"By the way, I don't have to meet him this evening. Hal Stimson called a half hour ago to say Spurgess is hooking a ride here early in the morning on a military jet. He's going back tomorrow afternoon to get ready for the committee hearings on the pharmaceutical manufacturers next week."

Marian shrugged herself into a white cocktail dress and came into the other room, turning her back so he could zip her up.

Cary slid the zipper up expertly and clipped the hook at the top into place on the first try. Marian couldn't suppress a shiver of pleasure at his touch, nor did she object when his hands on her bare shoulders turned her gently to face him. She knew he was going to kiss her and made no resistance, meeting him halfway.

"Umm!" he said when he released her at last. "Don't tell me this is sexual slavery."

"Just the opposite," she said lightly. "Slavery is when a woman is married to a man and has to do his bidding because he supports her—even when it comes to going to bed. You kissed me because you wanted to and I let you because I enjoyed it."

Marian moved back into the bedroom to get her jewelry. "But don't go getting ideas. What we're dealing with here is a simple case of mutual pleasurable response."

"As long as it's mutual, I'm at least making progress," he said. "I hadn't really expected to kiss you, except for that welcoming peck at the airport, until at dinner tonight after the Danton party. I even had the hotel put a bottle of brandy in your suite so we can have a nightcap."

"The bottle's on the table in the other room." She came back into the sitting room with a small white beaded bag in her hand. "Aren't you a little sure of yourself?"

"I can't afford not to be. You got away from me once—"

"That was years ago."

"The years haven't hurt either of us—especially you. With less than a week to make you fall in love with me, I have to move fast."

"At least you're honest about your intentions," she said as he opened the door and dropped her key into the pocket of his jacket. "Which is more than I can say for most men where women are concerned."

iii

Jethro Forbes was enjoying himself at what he fully expected to be the last CMA cocktail party he would attend. Every year someone running for office in the Association could be counted on to spend a lot of money corraling votes with free liquor and glossy-haired women with bare shoulders. The fact that this one was on H. Edward Danton made it doubly pleasant, for he'd never liked the guy. Besides, there was no one here to tell him how many drinks he should have or when he should leave.

Danton had greeted Jethro warmly, something he'd

never done at other CMA conventions. And it was nice to be wanted. Jethro had to admit, if only because you were entitled to vote in the coming election.

He didn't even bother to feel guilty, as he gave his order for another scotch and soda to the beautiful brunette cocktail waitress in the short skirt, that there'd be no report from him on this year's convention to the medical society back home. By the next meeting he'd be far away in the mountains of Guatemala, helping care for the proud Indian race who inhabited the area.

Not that Trevor Hart's clinic in the Guatemalan uplands had much of a hospital, compared to the Danton Clinic. Jethro had visited the famous heart surgery center briefly, when the Revere Lions Club had raised enough money selling drinks and candy at local high school football games to pay the medical costs for Irina Kurz. Crippled from birth with an opening in the septum between the right and left sides of her heart, allowing blood to escape from the right ventricle without being pumped through the lungs, Irina had been a heart cripple until Jethro had diagnosed her condition and stirred the Lions into financing an operation.

It didn't matter that the Kurz's family still owed Jethro nearly a thousand dollars for looking after little Irina from birth through the spells of cyanosis that had so often turned her skin blue and threatened her with death before Danton had operated.

Jethro had cheerfully canceled his own bill and even paid his fare to the Danton Clinic. But Sarah had been looking after his books then, and when the bill came to him to be turned over to the treasurer of the Lions Club's "Irina Kurz Fund," she'd seen that it was four thousand dollars and raised hell, because Jethro canceled his own bill, while H. Edward Danton had not hesitated to stick the Lions with a full fee. But how explain to an indignant Sarah that during the long moments when he had held an oxygen mask over Irina Kurz's face and watched her skin lose some of its deadly hue he'd felt himself as much a medical god as even Danton was in his big clinic?

Irina Kurz was fourteen now and already budding into womanhood, but Jethro hardly ever saw her any more. Following the operation, Danton had referred her to a heart specialist in Kansas City and the family hadn't called on Jethro Forbes any more, or offered to pay their back bill. He still got that feeling of a god every now and then, however, when he pulled a mother and a baby through a tough delivery, whether he was saving a breech presentation with a glossy black hide, or even another slant-eyed baby for the Eurasian bride young Dick Calcott had brought back with him from Vietnam. What counted most was the fact that for a few moments, a human life—two in fact—was in the hands that were always callused from the wheel of the Chevvy he drove all over the countryside.

Next week all that would be changed. He'd be working in Trevor Hart's hospital like another Albert Schweitzer in his own private sanctuary at Lambaréné and might even take up the accordion again—Schweitzer, he remembered, had been an organist of fame. He'd have to order one from Sears Roebuck after he got to Guatemala, though, because Sarah would have been suspicious if he'd left Revere that morning with his old squeeze box in his baggage.

Looking again at Danton and his statuesque blond wife, as they received guests like the medical royalty they really were, Jethro tried to remember when he and Sarah had last gotten dressed up, but couldn't even recall the occasion, unless it had been a state medical convention at least ten years ago.

Usually the state meetings were held in Kansas City, where the Municipal Auditorium, like that in Central City, was large enough to house all convention activities. At first Sarah had gone with him to some of them, but she'd never had any real interest in his work, beyond the income that came from it, and had quickly tired of medical Auxiliary politics. The vicious infighting that characterized the afternoon TV serials had soon became a vicarious way of life for her and lately Jethro had given up trying to interest her in anything outside her twenty-one-inch world.

Briefly Jethro considered having the dark-haired waitress fill his glass again, if only for a chance to examine her youthful beauty at closer range, but decided against it and put the empty glass on a table. Maybe he'd go to a show, he thought. After all a man who was changing the whole course of his life was certainly entitled to some sort of a celebration bidding farewell to the old and anticipating the new.

CHAPTER VII

The Danton cocktail party was still in full swing shortly after eight o'clock when Paul Rice looked in through the door. Briefly he considered going in, but when he saw a radiant Aletha beside H. Edward Danton greeting a late-coming couple, he held back.

Could he trust her? He wondered for the tenth time at least since she'd left his room. Instinct told him not, but any man who had felt that vibrant body in his arms, even for a moment, with the promise of real intimacy later, would have to be made of stone not to go on. And Paul, as he very well knew, wasn't made of stone. Nor, he was sure now, was Aletha.

A beautiful girl in the uniform of a Centralia cocktail lounge waitress passed him carrying a tray of drinks. She was almost as tall as he was, with creamy skin and dark glossy hair, and the rather brief uniform set off to a considerable advantage her startling Latin beauty. To his surprise, she turned after serving the drinks and came back to where he was standing almost in the doorway leading to the lounge and the adjoining dining room.

"Can I get you something, Dr. Rice?" she asked, balancing the tray she carried with pacticed skill.

"No, thank you; I was just looking in. But how did you know me?"

74

"You operated on a relative of mine, Serafina Montez. We call her Sera."

"I remember Serafina well. How is she?"

"Fine. She's going back to college next semester."

"Please give her my regards, Miss—"

"Montez. Carlota Montez. Excuse me, please." Balancing the tray she carried expertly with one hand, she moved toward the other side of the room, where two bartenders were busy preparing drinks.

Looking at the famous head of the Danton Clinic from a slight distance, Paul couldn't see that the two years since he'd left the clinic had aged the older doctor at all. Tall, with a shock of gray hair and a ruddy complexion that made him look at least ten years younger than his actual age, which Paul knew was close to forty-five, H. Edward Danton was the epitome of the successful surgeon, handsome, competent, with an equally handsome wife, some eight years his junior, by his side. It was hard to believe anything could attack the skill and reputation Danton had built up over the fifteen years his famed clinic had been in existence. And yet the mystery of the change of surgeons in the midst of an important operation could hardly have any other meaning.

To soothe the clamor of his thoughts, Paul left the hotel and walked the block to where Central University Hospital, with its skyscraper tower, dominated the academic center in its shadow. He spent the next hour visiting his patients there and was just finishing rounds, when he noticed lights burning in the Experimental Surgical Laboratory behind the main building of the medical school adjoining the University Hospital.

Crossing a covered overhead ramp leading from the hospital to the laboratory, Paul found Jerry Warren and Otto Heinrich, the grizzled old surgical research technician they had lured away from the Danton Clinic, busy at work. A fourth-year medical student was giving the anesthetic to the large animal Jerry was operating upon, with Otto assisting.

Putting on cap, mask and gown in the adjoining dressing

room, Paul pulled cloth boots over his shoes, all designed to prevent the introduction of noxious bacteria from the outside into the operating room and eventually the surgical wound. Jerry looked up when he took a seat in the observation stand reserved for students, none of whom were here tonight because of the hour.

"You're supposed to be whooping it up at the Hotel Centralia," he said.

"So are you," said Paul. "What's going on?"

"After you left the Auditorium this afternoon, I ran that second film of Danton's again just out of curiosity," said Jerry. "Then, of course, I had to repeat the job to see if it works."

"Does it?"

"Otto and I have just finished proving that it's perfectly possible to make a shunt directly connecting the superficial temporal and the cerebral arterial circulation. Danton isn't original there, of course, but what bugged me was whether the pressure relationships would be changed by the shunt, so we're putting in catheters that will let us measure the pressure gradients between the two vessels."

"Have you learned anything?"

"I hate to admit it but Danton may have something," said Jerry. "Connecting the intrinsic brain circulation by way of the internal carotid and vertebral arteries to the external carotid flow through a vessel like the superficial temporal artery appears to increase the arterial pressure in the brain itself by roughly twenty per cent."

"That could really be something."

"I'm going to show Elton Brooks the results of this work tomorrow. Maybe he can shoot some holes in it, but if he can't, it looks like you and I may have overlooked something."

"We can't be up on everything."

"I still hate for Danton to show me up," said Jerry. "By the way, I didn't see you at the cocktail party. Katie and I made a token appearance there."

"I looked in about an hour ago."

"Don't tell me he welcomed you to his bosom."

"I didn't go through the receiving line, but to look at him, you'd never guess he isn't glowing with health."

"Alcohol is one of the best glow makers I know of, and our esteemed former chief can put away quite a lot of the sauce when he wants to."

"At least he's opened up a new area that needs to be explored," said Paul. "Could be we've been concentrating too much on heart pumps."

"I'd still like to solve the mystery of the shifting surgeons," said Jerry. "But I suppose we'll just have to wait and see."

Stepping back from the table, Jerry pulled off his gloves. "Can you run pressure checks on this shunt for a while, Otto?" he asked.

"Certainly. Doctor, I tink you got someting." The old technician had a thick Viennese accent.

"We should know by tomorrow at least," said Paul. "The intravenous anesthetic may have pushed the pressure inside the brain arteries up a bit, but the effect should wear off when the drug is detoxified in the liver. Then we ought to get some accurate readings."

In the adjoining dressing room, Paul leafed through a medical journal while Jerry was changing clothes.

"Why so glum?" the black surgeon asked as he was knotting his tie. "Day after tomorrow we'll be showing a waiting medical world the very latest thing in artificial hearts. And even though it's not perfect, it's still a lot further along than anybody else's work."

"Aletha came to see me this afternoon," said Paul.

"Talk about Mohammed coming to the mountain. Maybe you've really got as much sex appeal as Katie's always claimed you have."

"She wants to heal the breach between us."

"You and him? Or you and her?"

"Both, I imagine."

Jerry whistled softly. "Don't get the idea I'm knocking your qualities as the Great Lover, but that could mean Danton's in real trouble and needs your help."

"I'm thinking the same thing," Paul agreed.

"And wondering what it means for your own future?"

"Sort of."

"I'll never go back to the Danton Clinic," said Jerry firmly. "Working with the chief breathing down my neck always did give me the heebie-jeebies, but that's no reason why you can't go, Paul."

"I've got everything I need here."

"Technically, yes, but it will take years to build up the patient drawing power at Central that Danton already has. Aletha knows you're almost certainly the only surgeon in the country who could ever walk in Danton's footsteps and maybe go even further. So if he's in some sort of trouble physically, you could have the clinic—and Aletha, too."

"I'm not sure I want either."

"But still not certain you don't?"

"Almost."

"The way it looked to me, you wanted her once—and badly."

"I almost went off the deep end," Paul conceded. "After all, she's a very desirable woman."

"And six years older than you are," Jerry said pointedly.

"Aletha and the Danton Clinic wouldn't necessarily have to go together."

"She'd see that it did, you can depend on that. And much as I'd hate to break up our partnership, you'd be a fool to turn down the opportunity."

"Right now I feel more like getting drunk than anything else," said Paul. "Let's go over to the Polo Lounge at the Centralia and have a drink."

"Sorry, Katie's expecting me home. Besides, I can't wax very merry at the thought that our partnership might break up."

"Don't start the wake yet. I'm not even certain I'd take the job, if it were offered me."

"When you look at those fringe benefits, I still say you'd have to be a eunuch to turn them down."

ii

Jethro Forbes had drunk three Bourbons in rather rapid succession at the Danton reception. As a result, he was mildly exhilarated when he took the elevator down to the ground level, where the hotel coffee shop was located. So far, he'd met no one he knew very well at the convention. Which was just as well, considering his plan to drop out of sight when it was over.

The ribeye steak he ordered was tough and tasteless and the french fries soggy, as was the pie. Only the coffee was good and by the time he drank two strong cups of it, the stimulus of the Bourbon was gone, leaving him with a sense of melancholia.

Some of that came from the fact that the waitress, who took his order and slapped his plate on the counter when it was ready, could have been another Sarah. She was shorter and darker of skin, it was true. And once he heard her complaining querulously in Spanish about the tips to the short-order cook behind the serving window to the kitchen so she was obviously a Chicano. But even in Spanish her voice had the same querulous whine Sara's had most of the time. And the way her feet flapped on the floor behind the counter betrayed the fact that she was wearing carpet slippers, again just like Sarah did the greater portion of the day.

The night was warm and he stood outside the hotel entrance trying to decide whether he wanted to see a show or give up and look at TV in his room. A group of young people came by, laughing and jostling each other as they passed in the sort of horseplay youth indulges in the world over. Their son would have been close to eighteen, if he'd lived. Jethro remembered. But Sara had refused to follow the obstetrician's orders and lose weight during the latter part of her pregnancy and had wound up with a rapidly developing case of eclampsia. The baby had been born dead and, after that admittedly close call, Sara had refused to even consider becoming pregnant again.

Idly, Jethro considered the possibility of taking up with a young woman after he was established in the hospital in Guatemala. The work with the natives would be hard; he hadn't tried to delude himself into believing it wouldn't. But to come home at night to something other than complaints and a TV dinner which, as often as not, he had to prepare himself, would be like heaven compared to what he had known the past ten years.

He didn't kid himself that a somewhat stooped, spare man past forty would be able to find a girl one tenth as attractive as the dark-haired waitress who had brought him his Bourbon at the Danton cocktail party. Obviously something special, with her creamy skin and glossy dark hair against the shell-white uniform with its absurdly short pleated skirt, she was the answer to a young man's dream, not an old one's.

That glittering, statuesque wife of H. Edward Danton was something else, too; just the upkeep must cost Danton a fortune. But he already had the fortune and was well on the way to the sort of political honors successful doctors went in for, once they were firmly established professionally, so a wife like that was no doubt a considerable asset to Danton's political career.

A group in formal dress, obviously on the way to dinner, swirled gaily through the revolving doors of the hotel. The high-pitched voices of the smartly gowned women and the boisterous tones of the men indicated that they had prepared themselves well at the Danton cocktail party for the rest of the evening. If Sarah had been different, Jethro Forbes thought a little wistfully, they, too, might be part of just such another group tonight. But after the baby was stillborn, she had withdrawn into her own world and shut him out, largely, he sometimes suspected, because of the possible threat of another pregnancy.

Watching the group pile into a Cadillac parked in front of the hotel, Jethro Forbes found himself a little homesick. At least in Revere he could talk to Wiley Blackston and the stream of patients who poured through his office every day while here he might almost as well be in another galaxy, many worlds removed from where he was, moving endlessly through empty space.

At home, too, he'd long since learned to shut himself away from his loneliness by putting a cassette with a lecture on clinical medicine into the small tape recorder he carried with him even in his car, thereby keeping himself remarkably well posted on medical progress for a general practitioner. Or reading the *Wall Street Journal* where he'd found the financial information that had already made him a snug fortune——for a small-town general practitioner.

Better go up to his room, he decided, and watch TV. At least he could choose, for once, the program he wanted. Taking the elevator to his floor and his room, he switched on the television set to find that the last occupants had been looking at the local ETV station. And when that program turned out to be a panel discussion of problems related to malaria and other diseases indigenous to the tropics, Jethro shortly found himself absorbed.

iii

In the Falstaff Room of the Regency House, Ted Kraus had taken a stool beside Alice Perrault shortly after eight. She was wearing a magenta pants suit, with a scarf tied about her hair, and was nursing a tom collins in a tall frosted glass.

"Is that good?" he asked.

She shrugged. "As good a way as any to spend an evening."

"I could think of better."

"So?" She gave him an appraising look that left him with the absurd feeling of being stripped in public and Ted Kraus swallowed half of the gimlet the bartender put in front of him with one gulp, to hide his momentary confusion at her directness.

"There's a good way to find out," he said when he put down the glass.

"What did you have in mind?"

"Dinner—as a start."

"Let's go!" She slipped down from the stool and waited while he put a tip on the polished mahogany top of the bar.

"Where's the best place in town to eat?" he asked as they were leaving.

"The Cattleman's Grill, two blocks down and one over. It's expensive."

"I'll charge it off my income tax. Come on."

An hour and a half later Ted Kraus leaned back in his chair and sighed with deep satisfaction. "You weren't kidding about the food," he said.

"I never kid about anything," said Alice. "It isn't worth the trouble."

"Do you make many conventions?"

"That's *all* I do; Vibrassage has a local office in practically every large city. My beat includes conventions, fairs and other special events, direct selling to satisfied customers. I sell more Vibrassage units than anybody else with the company."

"Been with them long?"

"Ten years—ever since my ex beat me up and I landed in the hospital. They had a Vibrassage unit in the physiotherapy department and it put me back on my feet. So when I was able to leave, I went to the president of the company and asked for a job demonstrating the machines."

"What about the ex?"

"I shed him in Vegas. Since then I've been like George Washington—avoiding entangling alliances."

"You shouldn't give up just because you failed once."

"Once was enough!" Her tone was eloquent with disgust. "Let's go. I've got a hard day tomorrow."

"How was the food?" He tried to make his tone casual but didn't have too much luck.

"I picked the restaurant, didn't I? Better get a bottle of Bourbon at the package sales counter on the way out. I haven't gotten any yet."

The check, plus the Bourbon, made quite a dent in Ted Kraus's wallet. He couldn't put it on his American Express or Master Charge card either, because Gena worked in the office of Surgical Instruments, Inc., and would see the tickets when they came through. But he had an idea the results were going to be worth the expense.

Which they were, for Alice Perrault wasn't just an expert in Vibrassage. She knew a lot of other tricks, too—even some Ted himself didn't know.

The trouble was: How was he going to introduce Gena to them when he got back to Houston, without telling her where he'd learned them?

CHAPTER VIII

Closing the outer door of the laboratory behind him, Paul Rice crossed the hospital parking lot to the gate leading out to Auditorium Avenue, on which the hospital and hotel complex was located across from the massive pile of the Civic Center. His thoughts were tortured as he made his way through the warm spring night along the half block separating the University Hospital from the Hotel Centralia.

Paul had just entered the hotel lobby and was moving toward the bank of elevators at one side, when the sound of voices, two of them very familiar, reached him. Instinctively he moved behind a large potted palm where he could see and hear without being recognized.

Aletha was wearing the same cocktail dress she'd worn when she came to his room that afternoon. The group was obviously returning from dinner after the cocktail party, for Danton was still in a tuxedo with a brocade jacket of bright blue, as was his ruffled shirt. A half-dozen other doctors and their wives, most of them officers in the CMA, made up the party.

Danton's complexion was florid, as usual. But even at this relatively close range, Paul was almost certain now that Aletha's visit to his room had been for an entirely different purpose from the one she had given. That the Danton Clinic had not yet been successful in improving upon Jerry Warren's first version of the so-called artificial heart since Paul and Jerry had left, seemed certain. For if any real progress had been made Danton would already be trumpeting the news to a waiting world in motion pictures for showing at the convention and through the press.

All of which could mean that Aletha had actually been trying to discover just what he and Jerry had accomplished in the dramatic race to solve the age-old problem of building a substitute for man's ailing central circulation pump. It was a disturbing thought for one already disturbed, but what troubled Paul even more was the knowledge that, although she might well have come to him today for what she could learn that would help Danton, he still wanted her as badly as he ever had, with a craving that was like a fire within him.

When the Danton party disappeared into one of the elevators, Paul crossed the lobby to the entrance to the Polo Lounge. Moving through the crowd that filled it, he took a seat at a small table in the corner away from the crowd.

"Bourbon—double," he told the red-haired waitress who came to take his order.

When the drink was brought, he drank slowly while he watched the crowd of prosperous-looking doctors and their women thronging the lounge. Less than twelve hours ago he'd been excited at the prospect of presenting, at one of the most important medical conventions of the year, a paper describing the remarkable progress he and Jerry had made toward establishing the Vascular Surgery Clinic at Central University Medical School as a major center for the country. But since then, the seething torment of emotion within him had become a smoldering fire that not even the Bourbon he was drinking seemed able to quench.

ii

In his room at the Regency House, Caleb Downs switched the color television set to the ETV channel and stretched out on the couch. The station was showing a film on heart surgery prepared for laymen and, pouring himself a drink, Caleb sipped it slowly while he watched.

"The heart is the finest pump ever built," said the narrator, while a fluoroscopic picture of the chest in which the organ in question was contracting steadily was shown upon the screen. "Unlike most other pumps, it contains highly sensitive built-in controls, not only through its own intricate connecting system of specialized tissues that possess the quality of both nerve and muscle, but because the heart is affected directly by a number of chemical substances in the blood that reach it through an elaborate supply system called the coronary circulation. The heart also contains its own energy center, enabling it to function apart from the rest of the body, as long as oxygen is brought to it through the bloodstream and waste products like carbon dioxide are carried away to be excreted."

Caleb's knowledge of pharmacy had enabled him to stagger, half conscious, to the medicine cabinet that first time, when his own heart, severely damaged by the coronary attack that had put him in the hospital for six weeks, had slowed below the safe rate. Fumbling for a bottle of amphetamine tablets, he had managed to swallow enough of them to stimulate the heart rate until the rescue squad arrived and he'd been taken to a hospital, where a demand pacemaker had been implanted into his chest by a surgeon with its electric terminals in contact with the heart muscle.

"The ideal treatment following heart damage from an insufficient flow of blood through the coronary circulation would be to replace the failing pump, either by transplant of another organ or a mechanical substitute," the narrator of that film continued. "In December 1967, the world was electrified by news of the first transplant of a human heart from one person to another, performed by a Dr. Christiaan Barnard in Cape Town, South Africa. The dramatic and daring operation caught the attention of surgeons and potential patients alike to a degree never attained before by an operation. So popular did it become, in fact, that in November 1968, alone, twenty-eight heart transplants were performed in various parts of the world.

"It soon became apparent that however dramatic heart transplant was as an effective means of saving lives it had grave shortcomings. Most serious of these was the tendency of the patient's own body tissues to reject the transplanted organ by marshaling against it much the same sort of natural defense system with which our bodies fight noxious bacteria. By January 1, 1970, only twenty-two of the some hundred and fifty heart transplant cases throughout the world were still alive. The first patient, Dr. Philip Blaiberg, had already succumbed after nineteen months.

"In recent years, great progress has been made toward developing an entirely artificial heart, admittedly the ideal solution to the problem. So far, however, most of this progress has been limited to devices for assisting the left ventricle, which pumps blood to more than eighty per cent of the body, in performing its function following damage by disease or gradual deterioration from hardening of the coronary arteries. In order to understand how such artificial assistance to a heart might work, we must first understand some basic facts about the heart itself.

"To be ideally efficient, the substitute pump must drive the equivalent of four thousand gallons of blood through the body every twenty-four hours. Ideally, too, it should have its own source of energy, perhaps power from an atomic battery small enough to be implanted inside the body. The ideal mechanical heart should be able to function practically indefinitely and, above all, must not be subject to breakdowns in situations where the person whose life depends upon its action could not reach a center for heart surgery within minutes.

"This sounds like a large bill of particulars, doesn't it?" the narrator asked, then answered his own question:

"Well, it is—but heart surgery has come a long way in a decade and the next one has even greater promise. Today, tiny pacemakers inside hundreds of thousands of chests are stimulating flagging hearts into action, when they sense a demand, or remaining quiet when no demand exists. Now, new valves are being put into hearts to replace those damaged by rheumatic fever and other diseases. Perhaps most important of all, bypass channels now bring an adequate supply of blood to heart muscles starving for it because of artery hardening or a block by a fixed clot called a thrombus.

"In a few cases, the dead muscle produced by a severe heart attack has actually been removed before its weakness posed a threat of actual rupture. This last operation, a film of which, made at the famous Danton Clinic, will be shown during the CMA Convention, carries with it considerable promise if—and here is the main problem—some method can be devised to support the heart during the interim period while healing is taking place.

"Surgeons working experimentally to solve this problem think a usable artificial heart may be devised in three to five years, perhaps even less. Others, like Dr. Paul Rice and Dr. Jerry Warren of Central University Medical School, think they are already on the verge of a major breakthrough. In any event, doctors are now certain that no permanent frontiers which man cannot cross exist in the fight against death, for new hope is being given every day to hundreds for whom there was no hope the day before."

The picture flashed to the channel call letters and a different voice came on:

"During the coming week, more than two thousand doctors from various parts of the United States and many foreign countries will be meeting in convention here in Central City. Channel Seven will bring you news of outstanding developments as they are revealed during the progress of the convention, just as we have brought you this informational film on the subject of heart surgery because several important papers to be presented during the convention concern that field."

Caleb Downs reached over and flicked the switch to OFF. It would take more than a left ventricular bypass to save Marian Crowder from the death sentence he had vowed some fourteen years ago, as the train had taken him away from Baltimore and the end of his short-lived medical career. He had purposely left the method of her destruction flexible, although taking certain measures to insure that he would be ready to administer the *coup de grâce* when the proper occasion arose. But that the opportunities he needed to destroy both her and Cary Poston would come at some point during the next five days of the CMA Convention—and that he would be ready when they arose—he did not doubt even for a moment.

iii

It was nearly eleven when Marian and Cary came back to the hotel after a leisurely dinner at a Japanese Steak House he had selected. The table at which they had been seated by the smiling kimono-clad hostess was only about half normal height. It seated eight people but fortunately Marian and Cary had one end of it to themselves. In the middle was a metal hot plate about eighteen inches wide and some four feet long, whose use Marian didn't understand until preparation of the dinner actually began.

First they were served sake, the traditional Japanese rice wine, in delicate eggshell-like cups. Next came a fragrant, steaming broth, about whose ingredients Marian didn't inquire for fear they might turn out to be something as exotic—and as repulsive to American palates—as bird's-nest soup.

While they were enjoying their sake and broth, the waitress at their table was busy preparing the meal. First, she placed upon the hot plate several piles of chopped vegetables, string beans, bamboo shoots and other delicacies which she allowed to simmer along the outer edge, where the temperature appeared to be less intense. The steaks, cylindrical in shape and perhaps eight inches long, she placed in the center where they quickly began to cook, sending off, with the vegetables simmering on the outer edges, a pleasant fragrance that excited the appetite.

"This is a new restaurant in Central City," Cary explained as they watched. "I understand that it's a franchise operation out of Miami, but the authenticity of the Japanese decor has been strictly preserved."

"The aroma's authentic, too," said Marian as the waitress served them Japanese tea, again in delicate eggshell-thin cups. "I remember it from a visit last year."

"Nothing's too good when you're trying to rekindle an old flame," he assured her.

"I thought it might be part of your duty as chairman of the Arrangements Committee."

"Tonight we're two people who were once in love—"

"I don't think it was ever quite that, Cary. If it had been, I doubt that either of us would have let the other go."

"Almost in love, then," he conceded. "I guess in those days both of us were too much concerned about becoming the best doctors we possibly could to find much time for anything more than a casual romance. But as I recall it wasn't exactly casual."

Remembering how she'd felt that afternoon when he'd kissed her at the airport, Marian had changed the subject.

"Our dinner looks like it's about ready," she said. "How do we eat?"

"With these," Cary took a wooden instrument shaped like a pickle server and handed it to her. Gingerly she picked up one of the chunks of meat into which the steaks had been cut by the smiling waitress presiding over their table. Dipping the meat into a small bowl of sauce, she popped it into her mouth and exclaimed ecstatically at the flavor.

Everything else was delicious, too. The vegetables steaming, the steak exactly right with the juices sealed in by the first round of cooking at the center of the hot plate. Only when her pile of steak cubes were gone, and along with them the vegetables, did Marian sit back. Wiping her mouth with a napkin, she drew a long sigh of contentment.

"That was absolutely the most scrumptious meal I ever had, Cary," she said as she closed her compact after repairing the ravages to her lipstick. "I could kiss you for it."

"We're a little old to be carrying on in a public place," he'd told her. "But I intend to hold you to that promise later."

Marian remembered that promise now as Cary Poston opened the door of her hotel suite.

"The end of a perfect even—" she started to say but he cut her off firmly.

"You promised me a nightcap. I selected that bottle of brandy over there on the table myself and I refuse to go before I've had a drink."

"I have to make a speech tomorrow," she reminded him as he crossed the sitting room to where a bottle of brandy and several glasses were on a small table.

"One drink will relax you," he assured her.

"I'll need to be on my toes talking to a bunch of doctors' wives," she said. "They're always suspicious of women doctors, especially if their husbands work with them."

"Here's your chance to really give them reason to be suspicious," he said as he handed her a snifter of brandy. "We'll start by my claiming that kiss you promised me as a reward for the dinner."

iv

At eleven-thirty, business in the Polo Lounge was still going strong and Carlota Montez was beginning to feel as if little men with hammers were pounding fiendishly on her calves in the trim white boots. Ilsa Tonelli, a statuesque German war bride who was one of the regular waitresses in the Polo Lounge, stopped beside her as she waited at the end of the bar for an order to be filled, leaning against it to rest her tired muscles.

"I was just, as you say in America, propositioned," Ilsa said in her faint Teutonic accent.

"What's so novel about that? It's why they make us wear these miniskirts and boots."

"This one I would be tempted to accept, if it wasn't for my husband," said Ilsa.

"Who was it?"

"The dark-haired man, at the small table in the corner."

"That's Dr. Rice, the heart surgeon," said Carlota. "I wonder what's eating him?"

"Whatever it is," said Ilsa, "he offered to pay me well to help him forget it. And if my Tommy wasn't going to be waiting outside for me at midnight, I'd certainly take it."

Carlota's pulse had quickened at Ilsa's words, but she said nothing more to the other girl. She'd been racking her brain all evening for some way to get the money Raul needed. Now the answer could be within her grasp, though she wasn't quite prepared to accept the sacrifice it demanded. And yet, if it had to be, she couldn't think of anyone she would prefer to Paul Rice.

For the next few minutes, Carlota watched him as she passed back and forth across the room carrying orders to other patrons. He was nursing his Bourbon morosely, as he had been ever since he'd come into the Polo Lounge, apparently totally oblivious to the merriment around him, so deep was he in some private melancholy.

As the time for Carlota to go off duty approached, so did the necessity for her to decide. Oddly enough, however, it was Charlie the head bartender who settled the question for her.

"Dr. Rice's a little drunk," he said as he was filling an order for Carlota. "He's charging his drinks to a room number so he must be staying in the hotel, most of the doctors on the Arrangements Committee are. But he'll be lucky if somebody doesn't roll him before the night's over."

As Carlota delivered the order, she managed to pass near where Paul Rice was sitting. He wasn't really drunk, she saw, for his glass was still half filled. And he didn't even look up when she stopped beside him—until she spoke.

"Can I get you anything, Dr. Rice?" Carlota hoped her voice wasn't trembling the way her insides were, when he turned to stare at her. He had really beautiful dark eyes, she saw, in a face that was clean cut—if a little on the ascetic side.

"What?" His voice wasn't slurred, increasing her conviction that he wasn't just another drunk.

"I said is there anything I can do for you?"

She saw his eyes travel down along the uniform to the pleated skirt, the lovely legs, the leather boots and knew she was blushing.

"Where?" he asked when he looked up.

"Anywhere," she dared to say.

"When do you get off duty?"

"In half an hour."

"Room 1276," he said. "The door will be unlocked."

v

"Pour me a drink, Aletha." H. Edward Danton switched on the television in the living room of their tower suite at the Hotel Centralia and dropped into a chair before it.

"Don't you think you ought to go to bed, darling?" Aletha said as she moved to the dresser where the whiskey tray rested.

"I want to see the late news. What did you find out from Paul Rice this afternoon?"

Startled, Aletha turned with a glass in her hand. "What do you mean?"

"You went to see him before the cocktail party, didn't you?"

"Well, yes."

"Does he have a workable ventricular bypass pump yet?"

"The artificial heart?"

"It's not really that but the public likes to think it is."

"He and Jerry have something, I'm sure," she said. "But I didn't learn anything else."

"You will." Danton took the drink she handed him. "That's what ambitious wives are for."

"And it doesn't worry you?"

"On the contrary. After all the clinic is my monument and Paul is the only cardiac surgeon I know of who could take it over if anything should happen to me. You're a smart woman. Aletha, and I'd be the last person to resent your hedging your bets when it comes to the future."

"Nothing's going to happen to you, darling. This new operation—"

"Hasn't proved anything except that the circulation of the brain can be increased somewhat by using the shunt. The danger lies in what increased pressure might do to the arteries of an old—"

"You're not old."

"A man is as old as his *corporae cavernosae*. And in case you don't know where those are—"

"I get the message," she said with a smile. "But what makes you think Paul would have any interest in the clinic after the way you threw him out?"

"That was a mistake," Danton admitted. "I let my temper get the best of my judgment."

"I still don't understand why you tossed Paul out. Surely there's room at the clinic for two fine surgeons."

"He made the mistake of taking up for Jerry Warren, when I'd already decided to get rid of Jerry."

"Why? When he was doing so well?"

"That was the touble." Danton had shed his jacket and cummerbund, now he started taking off his bright blue evening shirt. "I pioncered in work on a lcft ventricular bypass long before Paul or Jerry came into the picture, but Jerry went far beyond anything I had even conceived of. By tossing him out, I expected to set his work back at least a couple of years, while he found a place in another clinic. In the meantime I could pick up where he left off, finish the job myself and take credit."

"Wasn't that rather cold-blooded?"

Danton shrugged. "I didn't get where I am by being squeamish about the way I use people, Aletha. You operate on the same principle that people who let themselves be used deserve to be used, so that shouldn't surprise you. Unfortunately, Paul stood up for Jerry and forced me to

fire him, too. And the two of them were too good a combination for some clinic not to snap them up together as
soon as they left me—like Cary Poston did here at Central."

"So what can we do?" Aletha asked.

"I saw Paul just now through the open doors of the
Polo Lounge while we were waiting for the elevator. He
looked like he might be drunk, so why don't you go down
for a nightcap in the lounge and see how much you can
get out of him? Get me a Nembutal out of my medicine
kit before you go. And don't forget that your chances of
becoming the wife of an AMA president may depend on
what you manage to worm out of Paul."

vi

It was nearly twelve-thirty when Carlota Montez left
the Polo Lounge and took the elevator to the second basement, where the locker room for employees was located.
Ilsa Tonelli and another of the waitresses came down with
her, but they were in a hurry and left after getting their
purses and repairing lipstick and hair.

Carlota found herself wishing she'd worn street clothes
to work, but the hotel management liked its decorative
cocktail waitresses to be seen outside in the brief-skirted
uniforms and boots that were their badge, so she had no
choice. The trouble was that any bellman seeing her above
the lobby floor now would know she was probably on her
way to an assignation with someone in the hotel and she'd
be fired as soon as the bell captain could report to the
restaurant manager in the morning.

When Carlota was certain the basement corridor was
empty, she hurried to the back and the bank of service
elevators located there. The door to one of them was open
and she stepped inside quickly, pressing the button for
the twelfth floor. Her luck held and the elevator went
straight to twelve and the door opened.

She had worked out an excuse for her presence in case
someone got in before the elevator reached twelve, that

she had left a compact in the rooftop cocktail lounge where the Danton reception had been held. But a quick glance down the hall told her it was empty and, leaving the elevator, she hurried to the door of 1276.

The door was unlocked as Paul Rice had promised and, her heart beating wildly, Carlota quickly slipped inside and pushed it shut. The TV was playing softly and the lights were on, enough for her to see that he was already in bed and apparently asleep. That he wasn't drunk was proved by the way he'd hung up his clothes when he undressed, emptying the contents of his pockets—a wallet, a ring of keys and some change—atop the dresser. Obviously he had been watching TV and had dropped off to sleep when she'd been late in getting away from the Polo Lounge.

Quickly Carlota switched off the overhead light and, going to the windows, closed the blinds so no one could see in, leaving the room illuminated only by the light burning in the bathroom. Her movements didn't disturb the sleeping man at all, and she approached the bed hesitantly, not knowing exactly what to do next.

Gingerly, she reached out and shook him by the shoulder, lightly at first, then a little harder. When he didn't respond. she turned to leave, filled with a tremendous sense of relief. Halfway to the door, however, she remembered that if she left without the money she needed, nothing would have been gained.

Turning back to the bed, she was looking down at Paul Rice and steeling herself to wake him, with what would certainly follow, when she heard the door open softly behind her. Realizing she must not have quite shut it since. like most hotels, the Centralia doors could not be opened from the outside when fully closed, except with a key, she whirled quickly.

Half expecting to see Mr. Beardsley, the night house detective, or one of the bellmen, warned by Charlie, the bartender in the Polo Lounge downstairs, who could have overheard the brief conversation she'd had with Paul Rice, she was startled to see, instead, a tall woman in a cocktail dress, very beautiful, very blond and obviouly as much surprised to see Carlota as she was to see her.

Carlota recognized the other woman immediately. And when she saw a sudden light of anger burn in Aletha Danton's eyes, as she glanced past her to where Paul Rice was lying upon the bed, she realized that Dr. Danton's glitteringly beautiful wife had come to Room 1276 for the same purpose as she, though no doubt without expectation of the same sort of recompense. Only momentarily did Aletha Danton betray her surprise and anger that another was there before her, however. Then turning quickly, she was gone through the door into the hall, slamming it shut behind her.

Carlota's first impulse was to run, until she remembered the trouble she'd gone to in getting here and the reason for it. Besides, she told herself, if Paul Rice was the sort of man who had midnight assignations with other men's wives, she needn't feel obligated to waken him at all.

Moving to the dresser, she took two fifty-dollar bills from his wallet and put them in the pocket of her uniform, before leaving the room.

Luck was with Carlota on the return journey to the locker room via the service elevator and, pausing only to get her handbag from the locker, she hurried from the building. Fortunately, too, a taxi was standing before the main door and, not at all sure her still trembling legs would support her much longer, she hailed it and was soon home.

vii

Exhausted from strenuous attempts to reach orgasm and failure, again as usual, Alice Perrault had dropped off to sleep as soon as Ted Kraus left. It was a routine she'd gone through so many times that she didn't even bother to be depressed any more by the pain across her lower abdomen that awakened her perhaps twenty minutes later.

Swallowing a Seconal, she plugged in the small Vibrassage unit she kept in her room and placed it across her lower abdomen. Usually the soothing vibrations relieved some of the ache of unfulfillment that sometimes lasted until morning, so she always kept one of the compact units in her room for that reason.

It had almost happened with Ted Kraus, she told herself, more as a reassurance that it could happen again some day than as an actual fact. She'd chosen him because he was big and strong, promising to be something of a bull in bed and he'd played his part well—but as usual to no avail. Now, she was left only with the bellyache that seemed to grow worse after each fruitless encounter, the certainty of a hangover in the morning, and the Vibrassage unit that, although helping the pain a little through its soothing action, couldn't remove the block that always kept her from complete fulfillment, no matter how hard or how often she tried.

Alice had taken only one of the ubiquitous red Seconal capsules tonight, in deference to the half bottle of Bourbon she and Ted Kraus had killed during the preliminary lovemaking. One night, though, she knew she'd take two, then three, maybe four, until some morning a hotel maid would find her with the Vibrassage unit still going but unable to stir warmth in a body that had been cold for hours.

viii

It was just after dawn when a chauffeured limousine deposited Senator Frank Spurgess and his administrative assistant Hal Stimson, at Andrews Air Force Base, just outside Washington. An Air Force colonel was waiting inside the door and shook hands with the two men as they came in.

"Your plane will be ready in ten minutes, Senator," he said. "You've time for a cup of coffee in the lounge, if you need one before we take off."

"Sounds like a good idea, Colonel Peters," said Spurgess. "Hal here isn't awake yet."

In the VIP lounge, a smartly uniformed WAAF served

them coffee and doughnuts. Spurgess took a silver flask from his pocket and poured a liberal shot of whiskey into the coffee, offering the flask to the others, but they declined.

"I'm glad you had a jet going to Central City this morning, Colonel," said Spurgess. "If I'd had to take a regular commercial flight, I would have had to leave yesterday evening."

"Our operations are pretty flexible, Senator," said Peters. "As soon as Hal called me I checked flight schedules and found this one open for additional passengers."

Spurgess didn't comment. All three of them knew the jet flight had been put on schedule for this morning, as soon as Hal Stimson telephoned the congressional liaison officer for the Air Force—and that Spurgess and Stimson would be the only passengers.

The Senator studied a sheaf of typewritten pages while he drank coffee and munched a doughnut. Warmed by the whiskey, the famous craggy face with its oddly boyish chin began to take on some of the animation that characterized it when he was fully in action, although in actual fact, the limousine with Hal Stimson had picked him up less than an hour before at the door of one of Washington's most decorative—and often divorced—hostesses.

"Going to give the doctors hell again, Frank?" Hal Stimson asked as they walked to the waiting plane.

"Wouldn't you?" Spurgess didn't slacken his pace. "It was your idea, remember?"

"Cary Poston and I grew up in the same town," said Stimson. "I hated to take advantage of Cary when he asked me to try and get you to speak to the CMA Convention. But with medical care costs going up all the time, doctors as a class make good whipping boys for ambitious politicians."

"Good political reason, yes. The last two years have seen more sentiment building up for a national health program than during the past century, maybe since the beginning of time."

"Did you get a roster of the drug manufacturers advertising at this convention?" Spurgess asked.

"It's in the file you have there. At least half of the main financial supporters of the CMA in the drug field are represented."

"Good work."

Hal Stimson grinned. "Might as well kill two birds with one stone, I always say—especially when we're going to lower the committee boom on pharmaceutical manufacturers next week."

As they settled themselves into the luxurious cabin of the jet, which served most often as a general's private conveyance, Hal Stimson took two typewritten sheets from his attaché case and handed them to Spurgess.

"Here's some background information on the Democratic Party organization in Central City and a few names you may want to remember," he said.

"Whisper them to me when they come in sight at the luncheon." Spurgess settled himself into the swivel seat and fastened the seat belt. "I'm going to get a little sleep."

An active night, no doubt, Hal Stimson thought, as he buckled himself in when the plane began to shudder with the increased throttle to the two powerful jet engines. He was willing to bet, too, that even out in the hinterlands, where she was campaigning, Spurgess' decorative wife, Paula, would soon have a full report on where and with whom her husband had spent the night. All in all, it was a very convenient arrangement, with each spying on the other so nobody got an advantage, while both were free to find entertainment where they chose.

Just the same, Stimson thought, he'd like to know why Cary Poston had asked him to persuade Senator Spurgess to address the CMA Convention. Cary was no fool and considering the way the Senator had attacked even the austere AMA, he must know what Spurgess' speech would be all about. Plus the fact that to most of Cary's profession simply the mention of Spurgess' name was like waving a red flag in front of a bull.

Sunday's Central City *Dispatch,* flown to Hal Stimson

yesterday by the Democratic committeeman in the city, had featured an article about a coming election battle between Dr. H. Edward Danton and a group calling themselves the Young Turks, who were putting up another cardiac surgeon, an unknown in medical politics as far as Hal knew, for president-elect. When he'd called, Cary had admitted that he was speaking for a rump group, which could hardly mean anyone except the so-called Young Turks. But why they would want one so violently liberal as Spurgess was another matter—unless they were deliberately seeking to polarize the membership of the convention, with the hope of electing a compromise slate.

Politically it made sense, Hal Stimson told himself. Which could mean that, instead of resting their case as before with simply being "against the government," doctors were starting to wise up politically rather than continue worshiping the *status quo* long after its demise, thereby setting themselves up as whipping boys for ambitious and clever politicians like Spurgess, who had the good sense to surround himself with a staff even more politically acute than he.

It was likely to be an interesting day, Hal Stimson decided, as the plane completed its bumpy journey down the runway and took to the air. Pulling down a seat table in front of him, he opened his briefcase and was soon deep in the mass of figures it contained, ammunition for Senator Spurgess' coming attack on the "ethical" drug industry, with its high markups on the prescription drugs doctors ordered for their patients.

CHAPTER IX

Carlota Montez had a ten o'clock class at the University but she was up long before that. Raul was due at the Central City Induction Center at eight and had planned to drive the family car, a battered old Chevvy Carlota had bought out of her own earnings. But by the time he finished breakfast, Raul was so nervous that she decided to drive him there herself, not only to make sure he got safely to the Induction Center without an accident, but that he went there in the first place.

Afterward, she planned to go to the hotel before class to negotiate the fifty-dollar loan through the employees' credit union. This, with the hundred she had taken from Paul Rice's wallet last night, would complete the amount she had promised to get for Raul, if he needed it—which she had devoutly prayed earlier to the Holy Mother that he would not.

When she parked in front of the Induction Center, Raul got out and started toward the entrance, but came back to the car.

"You're sure about the money, Sis?" he asked for the umpteenth time.

Carlota opened her purse and showed him the two fifty-dollar bills. "I'll have the other fifty from the credit union before you get back home," she promised.

"But if they say they're going to take me, I'll have to leave this afternoon."

"We'll talk about that when you get home. If I'm not there, call me at the Polo Lounge. I have to be at work around four."

"Maybe I ought not to go into the center at all," he said doubtfully. "I could get a bus out of here for Canada this afternoon."

"Go through with it anyway," Carlota urged gently, knowing that flaring up at him would only serve to cement his resolve to leave the country and avoid the draft. "I hear they sometimes don't call people up for months. Maybe by then the rules will be changed."

"Not with this draft board; they're tough. Only gave Rafael Gomez five days and less than six months later he was dead."

"Go through the physical anyway," she urged. "At least it can't hurt you."

After Raul entered the Induction Center, Carlota drove

around the block and past the entrance again, just to be sure he hadn't panicked and bolted. When she saw no sign of him, she drove on to the hotel.

The strain of getting Raul to the center had given her a headache and, after getting the check for the loan from the credit manager's office, she stopped in at the coffee shop before going on to her class. Beryl Reagan, a friend, was working behind the counter. She drew Carlota a fresh cup of coffee and half filled one for herself.

"You Polo Lounge waitresses have it made." Beryl leaned on one elbow wearily while she drank. "Serve a guy a few drinks and he's all loosened up when it comes to tipping. Down here we don't get nothing but a bunch of tightwads."

"This is a doctors' convention, Beryl. They all make a lot of money."

"Makin' it they may be, but givin' it out they ain't. The way most of 'em tip, they must be planning to take it with 'em. And the wives!" Beryl's snort of disgust was eloquent as only an Irish girl's could be. "Come in here dressed to the hilt and what do they leave the waitress? A measly dime."

"I read somewhere that the medical divorce rate is second only to actors. The wives have to put something away for later, when their husbands shed 'em for a younger woman."

"The way some of 'em act, I don't blame the men." Beryl moved away to draw glasses of water and set them before two men who had just taken stools at the counter.

Carlota finished her coffee and paid the cashier. At the door, she stepped back to let a woman enter. Too late to seek the protection of a potted rubber plant standing in the corner just inside the door to the coffee shop, she recognized the wife of the famous Dr. Danton—and the woman who had come to Paul Rice's room last night.

Aletha Danton recognized her, too, for Carlota saw a hot flash of anger burn in the older woman's eyes momentarily, before she moved into the coffee shop, forcing Carlota to step aside and make room for her to pass.

Carlota wasted no time resenting the older woman's haughtiness, however. As soon as the doorway was clear, she fled the coffee shop for the safety of the busy lobby outside.

ii

Marian Crowder's room telephone rang quite awhile and Cary Poston was about to hang up when she finally answered.

"I was in the shower," she said breathlessly. "Didn't even have time to grab a towel."

"In that case, I'll be right over."

"No you don't! I'm giving the luncheon address to the Women's Auxiliary at noon and it will take a lot of primping to get over looking like a debauchee."

"As I remember it, we debauched together, but I'm fit and glowing. And no woman is supposed to admit that a man can make her do anything she doesn't want to do."

"So I enjoyed myself, but I've still got to think pure thoughts this morning so I can tell the ladies of the Auxiliary how important they are to the medical profession."

"How about breakfast?"

"Don't you have to meet Senator Spurgess?"

"The local Democratic chairman called early this morning to say he'd meet the Senator and Hal Stimson at the airport and see that they get safely to the Auditorium. The opening General Session isn't until ten-thirty, but I've got to be in the building to see that nothing goes wrong at the last moment. There's a nice VIP coffee shop just outside the temporary CMA office. We can have a bite together there."

"Can you give me half an hour?"

"Sure. They're queuing up at the registration booths, but I'll pull some rank and get your envelope, so you won't have to bother."

"Thanks, Cary. You're a fine doctor and a perfect lover."

"That goes double for you."

"It's just my superb body you're enamored with. And of course my facile mind."

"What else is left?"

"You haven't seen the shrew in me yet. I'm going to show that to the Auxiliary at the afternoon luncheon."

"How about dinner?"

"I'm sorry, Cary. The local chapters of my college sorority are having a dinner tonight and asked me to speak as soon as it was announced that I would be at the CMA Convention. But if it will make you feel any better, I'd much rather be with you."

"A nightcap, then?"

"That would be nice. I'll call you when I get back to the hotel."

iii

Ted Kraus was hung over and looked it, when Alice Perrault arrived at the Vibrassage booth shortly after nine o'clock. In a white miniskirt, a snug sweater top and boots, she was fully conscious of the strong aura of sex she radiated—and needed—to attract the middle-aged doctors, who made up by far the greater part of those registering for the convention, to the Vibrassage booth.

On the way through the exhibit floors to her station, Alice had noted strong competition in another area. One aisle away, the most easily visible spot in the whole exhibit area, the CMA executive secretary had recruited a bevy of attractive young women in hot pants or miniskirts and boots to sell the new hospital expense and income protection insurance policies the association was underwriting for the membership. Doctors clustered around the booth signing applications for policies they would probably drop after the first year, when they discovered what the monthly premium costs would really be and that all their office personnel must also be included.

This early in the morning, the feet and backs of the conventioneers had no reason yet to become very tired, so

Alice wasn't doing much business. She wasn't disturbed, however; by half-past ten the comfortable battery of lounge chairs would seem like heaven-sent bliss to tired men. And the presence of a blonde in a short skirt pouring a soothing sales talk into their ears while they relaxed would somehow seem a part of the whole thing, too. Only when they received the chairs a month later from the factory, would they discover that the Vibrassage unit didn't seem half the boon it had appeared to be at the convention, without the presence of the blonde who had delivered the sales pitch.

After opening the exhibit and making sure all the appliances of the Vibrassage line were working perfectly in the hands of the local franchise dealer who was helping her, Alice crossed the aisle to where Ted Kraus was slumped behind one of the tables upon which the gleaming rows of instruments he sought to sell were arranged.

"You look like hell," she greeted him.

"I feel worse. How can you play around half the night, drink whiskey like it was water and look the picture of health the next morning?"

"It's all in your point of view," she assured him. "Before I go to bed I always leave an order with room service for a Continental breakfast at eight o'clock with an extra pot of coffee. A couple of shots in hot coffee does wonders to a hangover."

"I already had coffee, but it didn't help."

"What you need is some hair of the dog."

He brightened. "Don't tell me you've got some whiskey over there among the vibrators?"

"No. But there's free beer down the aisle a few steps at the Central Pharmaceutical booth. Right now a slug of lager will do you a world of good."

Caleb Downs was standing at the back of the exhibit while a salesman presided at the single tap dispensing beer this early in the morning. When he saw Alice and Ted Kraus, he moved to the front.

"I'm from Vibrassage, Mr. Downs," Alice introduced herself. "This is Ted Kraus from Surgical Instruments,

Inc. He needs some beer and anything else you've got for a hangover."

"Testamphet might do the trick, it's guaranteed to make the depressed male feel like a million bucks." Caleb picked up a packet of square yellowish tablets in the cellophane display packages pharmaceutical houses used in giving out samples at medical conventions. "Swallow a couple of these with some beer, Mr. Kraus. You'll feel better in no time."

"What's in 'em?" A Pennsylvania Dutchman who had defected to Texas, Ted still retained some of his native suspicion of things he knew nothing about.

"Confidentially, a shot of amphetamine to wake you up, a small dose of psychic energizer to knock out the depression that goes with a hangover, and some testosterone propionate to combat that all-gone feeling."

Alice's experienced eyes were assaying the cashmere sports jacket and pale gray slacks the solidly built man with the glossy black beard was wearing, along with a striped shirt and wide silk tie. They must have set him back at least five hundred dollars, she estimated, and could tell by the way Downs looked at her that he was interested.

"This your company, Mr. Downs?" she asked casually.

"Built it myself from a corner drugstore," he said proudly. "Can I draw you some beer, Miss Perrault?"

"I'll come by later when I'm real thirsty. Right now I'm full of coffee."

"I'd offer you some samples, too, but you obviously don't need any hormones," he told her. "In fact, I'd go so far as to say you're pretty much bursting with womanhood."

"I'd better get back to the exhibit," said Ted Kraus. "Thanks for the pick-me-up, Mr. Downs. I feel a lot better already."

"Any time," Downs told him and turned back to Alice. "Might I give you a ring for dinner some night, Miss Perrault?"

"Sure. I'm staying at the Regency House."

"So am I. It'll be simpler if you call me Caleb. All my friends do."

"I'm Alice, but if I don't get back to work my name will be mud," she said with a warm smile. "See you later, Caleb."

iv

In spite of its poor location, business started booming at the circulatory research exhibit of the Central University Medical School the moment the exhibit floor was opened. That much of it derived from the natural curiosity of the convention rank and file to see the work of the young surgeon, who was going to oppose H. Edward Danton in the election later in the week, and perhaps Paul himself, didn't bother Jerry, who had opened the exhibit that morning. The important thing was that their work was being seen and appreciated.

The central one of the three panels making up the exhibit showed techniques of improving the heart circulation. Jerry was explaining it to a group of doctors and students before the exhibit, when Jethro Forbes stopped to listen.

"In our experience," Jerry was saying, "a very useful procedure in treating coronary arteriosclerosis is gas endarterectomy. If you've been watching the TV films being shown over the closed-circuit network in the hotel rooms, you may already be familiar with this technique.

"First the heart is exposed surgically inside the pericardial sac. Then, with a twenty-five gauge needle, the portion of a coronary artery demonstrated in arteriograms to be blocked by arteriosclerosis is punctured several times and carbon dioxide injected under pressure directly into the core of the obstructed vessel."

"Why CO_2, Doctor?" an observer wearing the badge of a medical student asked.

"Any gas under pressure would do the same thing, I'm sure," Jerry conceded. "But since carbon dioxide is normally carried in the blood stream as a chemical solution and excreted in the lungs, it appears safe to use it. The gas acts as a dissecting agent and frees the obstructing core from the artery wall. Once this is done, a small incision can be made into the artery and the core itself extracted."

Opening a glass jar, Jerry held up a wormlike object. It was nearly six inches long and tapered gradually from one end to the other.

"This core was removed from a patient only three days ago," he explained. "He is now free from anginal pain for the first time in several years. If you will direct your attention to the fourth panel of the exhibit, you will see how a block in one of the heart arteries can be bypassed, using a section of saphenous vein from the leg to form a new blood channel.

"Here you see the operation actually being performed upon a patient by Dr. Paul Rice, who heads the Vascular Surgery Section here at Central. He and I have done more than two hundred of these operations with a mortality of less than four per cent, comparing favorably with the mortality from hysterectomy over the country in general."

One of the onlookers spoke from the back of the group. "I don't see an artificial heart in your exhibit, Dr. Warren. Might I ask why?"

"Our work on left ventricular bypass is still largely experimental," Jerry admitted.

"But you *are* working on it?"

"Oh yes—and with some promise of success."

"More than Dr. Danton has accomplished?"

Jerry recognized the questioner now as having been a medical student when he was at the Danton Clinic.

"I'm afraid I'm not familiar with just how far Dr. Danton has gone with his work," he countered.

"It's rumored that you have a bypass pump that really works," the questioner persisted.

Jerry smiled at the rather crude attempt to extract information from him. "We're not engaged in any secret research or in a race to come in first, Doctor. When we develop a workable bypass method, you can be sure it will be described in medical journals and at medical conventions for the benefit of others working in the field."

The crowd drifted away at the conclusion of Jerry Warren's lecture, but Jethro Forbes stayed on.

"You handled that rather well, Dr. Warren," he said. "Especially after being tossed out of the Danton Clinic because of your work on the artificial heart."

"The questioner was a Danton spy, Dr. Forbes." Jerry read Jethro's name on his badge. "Do you work in cardiology?"

"Me?" Jethro laughed. "I'm a general practitioner. Took a child with a Tetralogy of Fallot to the Danton Clinic some years ago and that got me interested in heart surgery."

"Did Dr. Danton operate?"

"He did a classic Blalock-Taussig procedure. The girl is doing fine." Jethro glanced at his watch. "It will be more than an hour before the Senator starts lambasting the doctors. Can I buy you a cup of coffee?"

"That would be nice," said Jerry. "Just let me switch on the audio and this exhibit will take care of itself—probably better than I could."

"I doubt that," said Jethro as the younger doctor flipped a switch on the panel beside the ground-glass viewing screen, turning on the sound which was synchronized with the film. "You have a knack of making complicated medical procedures seem simple even to a layman, which is what a GP is rapidly getting to be nowadays, with medicine getting more complicated every day."

In the coffee shop outside the temporary CMA headquarters at the second level, the two doctors chose coffee and Danish pastries at the serving counter and selected an empty table.

"I envy you, Dr. Warren." Jethro Forbes stirred saccharin into his coffee while Jerry doused his with sugar.

"Not many *white* men do, Dr. Forbes."

"Skin color has nothing to do with making a good doctor. When I was in med school almost twenty years ago, I spent part of each summer working on a farm in

North Carolina. Used to go with doctors in the area on house calls, but the only one I ever saw use sterile drapes and boil his instruments for home delivery was a Negro. He was a graduate of Howard and the best doctor in the whole county."

"You must have had an interesting life. Would it be impertinent of me to ask whether you have any regrets, Dr. Forbes?"

"Regrets?" Jethro Forbes put down his coffee cup and took out a small cigar, offering one to Jerry, who refused. "I'm not sure, Dr. Warren," he said. "Some days I feel pretty sorry for myself, but there are rewards too, so it all adds up. I make a fair amount of money and I've invested it wisely, so finances aren't a worry any more. I do some good as a doctor, plus as little harm as I know how to keep from doing, which seems to be about as sensible a philosophy for a doctor to have as any other."

"I never heard it expressed quite that way, but I think I agree," said Jerry.

"Aristotle once said the job of medicine as a profession is not to make a man quite healthy, but to put him as far as may be on the road to health," said Jethro. "His idea was that you can give excellent treatment even to those who can never enjoy sound health—I'm inclined to agree."

"I suppose that's what we're doing by putting some of the eighty thousand, who would die every year from coronary disease, on the road to health and whittling away at barriers that appeared to be insurmountable only a few years ago."

Jethro Forbes looked at his watch and pushed his empty coffee cup away almost reluctantly. "The one thing I miss most in a small-town general practice is the chance for bull sessions with coming young men like you, Dr. Warren, but I'd better be getting up to the General Practice Section. They've imported a hotshot to tell us for the thousandth time that we're the backbone of the medical profession even though everybody knows no one doctor can begin to keep up without the stimulus of the sort of continual professional needling working in a group gives you. I'm curious to know how this fellow is going to say the same thing the others have said and still make it seem like something new."

"Sounds like you're also interested in semantics."

Jethro chuckled. "Don't let it get around that I even know the meaning of the word. These specialists don't want the world to know any of us general practitioners are more than just dumb clucks who send in cases with wrong diagnoses."

CHAPTER X

By a quarter past ten Monday morning, fifteen minutes before the First General Session of the CMA Convention was scheduled to begin, the exhibit floor was practically empty, except for a skeleton staff in the larger booths. All who could attend, including many wives of CMA members and a large contingent of the press, were in the large Auditorium Theater and nearly all the seats were filled. Pharmaceutical manufacturers exhibiting their products at the convention were there in force, too, concerned by what the near control of medical practice by government could mean for them.

One thing the drug manufacturers could be sure of under the much-discussed health insurance bill already introduced into both Senate and House under the sponsorship of Senator Frank Spurgess was an emphasis on the use of generic names when prescribing drugs, a practice that would cut deeply into the profits of pharmaceutical houses. Still another reason for listening intently to the foremost enemy in Washington of both doctors and drug manufacturers was the possibility of gaining some hint of what course the announced investigation of the pharmaceutical industry by the Spurgess Committee would take, when it began in Washington next week.

When the current president of the CMA, a roly-poly

practitioner from Abilene, gaveled the opening session to order, the main floor of the theater was packed and only a few seats were available in the balcony. On the platform, flanked by some of the most famous names in American medicine, the famous Spurgess profile was as deceptively boyish as ever.

"The invocation for this opening session will be given by Bishop Paul Allen of the Episcopal Diocese for this area," the president announced. "Bishop Allen."

"We know upon the authority of St. Paul," said the Bishop, "that St. Luke, author of the Gospel that bears his name, as well as the Acts of the Apostles, was a physician and one of the leaders of the early Church. I can think of no way more fitting to invoke Divine blessing upon this assemblage, than by repeating the words of the Collect for St. Luke, the Evangelist's Day, from the Book of Common Prayer. I ask you now to bow your heads as I speak these hallowed words:

Almighty God, who callest Luke, the Physician, whose praise is in the Gospel, to be an Evangelist, and Physician of the soul; may it please Thee that, by the wholesome medicines of the doctrine delivered by him, all the diseases of our souls may be healed; through the merits of Thy Son, Jesus Christ our Lord. Amen."

During the brief pause while the president of the CMA waited for latecomers to be seated, Paul and Jerry moved into the theater and took seats at the back.

"Looks like Spurgess had a hard night," said Jerry. "If the bags under his eyes were any larger, they'd be dragging the ground."

"The paper this morning said his wife is out of Washington," said Paul. "According to the scandal sheets, he's quite a rounder."

"Welcome to the Seventy-fifth Annual Convention of the Central Medical Association," said the president. "You were all provided with programs, when you registered at

112

the booth near the Auditorium entrance or by mail, so you know what is happening onstage. The backstage activities you'll have to discover for yourselves."

A wave of laughter ran through the audience.

"Our Program Committee has gone to a great deal of trouble to provide discussions of professional subjects that will be interesting and instructive to everyone," the president continued. "We are very fortunate in being able to obtain a number of highly qualified speakers on special subjects, who will also participate in panel discussions on important phases of medical practice. All of these are listed in your program, but I want to remind you particularly of the one on coronary circulation to be presided over by Dr. H. Edward Danton on my right."

Dr. Danton rose and bowed, to considerable applause.

"Another panel discussion titled 'Problems in the Delivery of Medical Care' will take place during the Second General Session in this auditorium Tuesday morning at eleven. The panelists will be the Secretary for Health in HEW, who will come here from Washington for that purpose, Dr. Cary Poston, professor of medicine at Central University Medical School, and Dr. Herbert Pattishal from the administrative staff of the AMA. Following the panel discussion, the President's Luncheon will be held at Heritage House, where the Secretary for Health will deliver the main address."

There was another spattering of applause.

"The Final General Session will take place on Thursday at eleven, when the Nominating Committe will present its slate for the coming year and new officers will be elected. Let me remind all of you that if you have not already purchased your tickets for the President's Luncheon and also for the annual banquet and dinner dance to be held Wednesday night at the Hotel Centralia, please do so early. I know you are anxious to hear the featured speaker of this session, so I will turn the meeting over to Dr. Cary Poston who will introduce him."

From his seat beside Senator Frank Spurgess, Cary rose and moved to the podium, with its brace of microphones.

Directly before it was a platform from which three television cameras, bearing the call letters of three major networks, were beamed upon the speaker.

"Fellow members of the Central Medical Association and guests," said Cary, "I have been given the task today of introducing to you a man who can hardly be characterized as anything less than the most severe critic of the medical profession in this or any age. Whether you agree with him or not, however, Senator Frank Spurgess has done our profession a service by reminding us of deficiencies which we are sworn to correct. As a critic he therefore deserves our attention and as a distinguished member of the Congress, he deserves our respect. It is with these admonitions that I am honored to introduce to you the chairman of the Medical Subcommittee of the U.S. Senate, Senator Frank Spurgess."

Applause was perfunctory as Spurgess moved to the podium and arranged a manuscript there. For a moment, the famous smile warmed the craggy features.

"Thank you, Dr. Poston, for one of the neatest jobs of damning with faint praise I have ever heard," he said and a wave of laughter rocketed through the Auditorium, relaxing some of the tension in the audience.

When the laughter subsided, the famous voice, lowered now to the growl for which his committee sessions were famous, launched into his speech without the traditional humorous observations with which professional orators seek to soothe an audience into a false sense of well being before firing the opening shot.

"At the time of your graduation from medical school, many of you, I am sure, swore an oath as part of your commitment to your profession. For some it was the traditional Oath of Hippocrates, for others, the Oath and Prayer of Maimonides. Still others among you no doubt recited a more recent pledge, the Declaration of Geneva, now used by roughly a fourth of the country's medical schools. But since some of you may be unaware of its provisions, I will read them to you as a preface to what I have to say this morning."

Picking up a manuscript sheet from the lectern, Spurgess read:

"At the time of being admitted as a Member of the Medical Profession

I solemnly pledge myself to concentrate my life to the service of humanity.

I will give my teachers the respect and gratitude which is their due;

I will practice my profession with conscience and dignity;

The health of my patient will be my first consideration;

I will respect the secrets which are confided in me;

I will maintain by all means in my power, the honor and the noble traditions of the medical profession;

My colleagues will be my brothers;

I will not permit considerations of religion, nationality, race, party politics or social standing to intervene between my duty and my patient;

I will maintain the utmost respect for human life, from the time of conception; even under threat I will not use my medical knowledge contrary to the laws of humanity.

I make these promises solemnly, freely and upon my honor."

Putting down the manuscript sheet, Spurgess gripped the sides of the lectern and leaned forward until his lips were only inches from the battery of microphones attached to it. When his voice boomed from the loudspeakers, it was with all the force of a body blow.

"During the past two years, the cost of doctors' services has increased at a rate almost double the rise in the Consumer Price Index. On September 13, 1971, the New York *Times* reported that the median income of physicians under sixty-five years of age practicing in the United States was $40,550—after office expenses were deducted.

A little simple arithmetic reveals the startling truth that the some 443,000 doctors in the United States today earn over seventeen billion dollars a year, more than any other professional group, and in the top one per cent of the population.

"I can hear you saying now that my charge is not fair, because your share of the public's expense for medical care is only about twenty per cent. But how can you justify a rise, during just ten years, in the cost of a surgeon's services for the simplest abdominal operation you perform, an appendectomy, from $485 to $1,175 in New York and throughout the country as a whole from $265 to $785?

"I charge members of the Central Medical Association and doctors everywhere with failing to live up to the humanitarian principles of the Declaration of Geneva and the other oaths medical graduates traditionally swear in regard to their calling. I charge you with putting the accumulation of personal wealth above duty and of abdicating your responsibilities by doing nothing to control the spiraling costs of medical care except increase your share of it. I charge you with neglecting the poor, while you become rich, and with fighting every attempt by those really concerned with the health of the people to make the same quality of care available to all, regardless of their ability to pay."

When Spurgess paused to drink water from a glass beside the lectern, Paul Rice looked around him and saw only stern faces, many of them flushed and angry. Most, he knew, had spent—like himself—from twelve to fifteen years in preparing themselves for their profession, often at considerable financial sacrifice and thus could not be expected to approve a largely unjust charge.

"You will say I am being unfair," Spurgess returned to the attack, "but justify, if you can, two Cadillacs in almost every medical family garage. Explain why golf clubs have more doctors playing on Wednesday afternoons than the rest of the membership put together. Or why it is next to impossible to find a doctor over a weekend, except in overcrowded hospital emergency rooms. Even then, the patient is treated more often than not by an FMG—a Foreign Medical Graduate—who may not be able to speak enough English to understand them. And all because the doctors of the country did not have the foresight years ago to see that the new medical schools were begun and more interns provided to staff the country's hospitals.

"The cost of medicines in this country is also a national scandal. Just a simple example: Before the Federal Drug Administration was finally able to remove one antibiotic shotgun prescription from public sale recently the public was spending thirty million dollars a year on the product, although it had already been found to be useless by government scientists. This drug was prescribed only by doctors, not sold over the counter, so I ask you where the medical profession was while the public was spending thirty million dollars a year for a useless drug which you had prescribed?

"Many of you own stock in the pharmaceutical manufacturing companies whose products account for ten per cent of medical-care costs. Some of these make profits of over one thousand per cent on special items, but I have yet to hear that one doctor raised his voice at a stockholder's meeting to demand proof that the manufacturer's products delivered the curative power they were supposed to deliver. Your oath states that *The health of my patient will be my first consideration,* yet you betray that oath every day, when you prescribe a drug by the manufacturer's name for it—at a price often ten times what the patient would pay if you merely copied the generic name of the drug out of the United States Pharmacopoeia.

"But enough about manufacturers of pharmaceuticals." As Spurgess turned a page, an audible sigh of relief came from a group of exhibitors sitting near Paul and Jerry. "They will have their day before the TV cameras, when my committee starts hearings on the drug industry next week. I turn now to hospital costs.

"In the past decade, hospital bills have risen even faster than doctors' fees, in many cases a five-fold increase. A hospital bed cost nearly $100 a day and is still rising, while in one Eastern city, an intensive care bed costs $425.75 per day. I can see many of you looking smug as you prepare to deny any responsibility for this soaring cost, but how many of you have investigated the efficiency of the hospitals where you practice? How many of you have asked why facilities for open heart surgery must be available in every large hospital, when they may not be used more than once or twice a week? Why expensive radiation therapy units for treating cancer must be maintained by all, when millions could be saved by concentrating better facilities in one or two treatment centers in the average city of, say, a half million people.

"In one Southwestern city ten hospitals joined together recently to remove duplicating services and saved $90,000 the first year, simply by buying insurance for all in one unit. One health-care expert, himself a physician, says, 'The health delivery system is so full of glaring inefficiences and abuses that it is easy to give up in despair. For example, the providers of health care saddle the public with unnecessary, under-utilized and duplicated services which not only produce astronomical costs, but also often deliver low quality care.' "

Spurgess paused and drank again from a glass of water on the table beside the podium. He was sweating, his face was flushed and his voice was a little hoarse when he spoke again.

"Where, I ask you, were the doctors of this country when these inequities were developing? Twenty per cent of the cost goes directly to you, so you are among the 'providers of health care' to whom the quotation I have just read applies. You cannot therefore escape responsibility for a rise in expenditures for health services and supplies from $17.1 billion in 1955 to $37.3 billion in 1965, to $94 billion projected for 1975, unless drastic changes are made.

"A study by the federal government estimates that by 1980, eight per cent of the Gross National Product will go for health bills, five times the maximum cost of the Vietnam War in any single year. The United States was almost bankrupted by Vietnam. How can the economy survive a drain for health care five times as great?"

On the platform before the speaker, the unwinking red lights of the TV cameras burned steadily as the deceptively boyish-looking profile was recorded on video tape while the barrage of accusing words raked the audience.

"If the hospitals and other health delivery systems in the country are inefficient, wasteful and hopelessly antiquated in their business methods, *you* as doctors cannot escape your responsibility," said Spurgess. *"You* order patients to the hospitals. *You* order unnecessary laboratory work. *You* order needless and often useless drugs. *You* order expensive X rays and neglect to use the principles of physical diagnosis you learned in medical school. Many of you are on the governing boards of these hospitals and most of you take patients to them. If you used the pressure of refusing patronage, you could force the changes that need to be made. If you go on shirking your responsibility, gentlemen, how can you denounce those of us who are trying to save the medical care system of the country from bankruptcy?

"The refusal of doctors to see even their own patients over weekends or at night for minor illnesses has created a grave situation. Emergency rooms are cluttered with waiting patients who take up the time of the doctors and nurses trying to cope with the flood of accidents. As a result, accident mortality has become a national disgrace and emergency rooms little more than charnel houses over weekends and holidays, understaffed with doctors who are often not sufficiently well trained to cope with life or death situations.

"And why is this true?" Spurgess thundered. "Why else than because organized medicine has consistently fought against government subsidy of medical education to provide more doctors? Why else than because organized medicine consistently puts stumbling blocks in the way of young doctors, requiring membership in medical societies before they can obtain hospital privileges, plus the payment of exorbitant dues, much of which is spent lobbying against legislation to make medical care as fully available to the poor, as it is now to the rich.

"Why did the medical profession oppose health insurance through Blue Cross, Blue Shield and private companies, until the demands of an outraged populace forced them to capitulate? Why do doctors still oppose Medicare and Medicaid for the aged, the very young, and those unable to protect themselves against the costs of medical care? Yet when Medicare finally did come, who profits from exorbitant bills, often for visits not made, treatments not given, diseases not even treated?

"Who but doctors have fought against a system of peer review to set up a reasonable standard of fees? Who refuses to accept assignment of payment under Medicare B, forcing the elderly to pay exorbitant bills from pitifully meager savings, only to discover the charges were so outrageous that paying agencies have been forced to cut them —at the expense of the old and the poor?"

Spurgess paused and drank again from a glass on the table beside the podium. The hand that lifted the glass shook slightly, but there was no lessening of the anger in his voice when he resumed speaking.

"Look into your souls! Ask yourselves whether you are consecrating your lives to the service of humanity, as you swore to do. See if you can name yourselves guiltless for the death of the accident victim turned away from a hospital where you have staff privileges, because he didn't have insurance? See if you are guiltless for the agony experienced by a mother trying to find a doctor to care for a child choking with asthma. Or the desperation of an aging husband seeking help to allay the suffering of a wife dying of heart disease but unable to find a doctor to prescribe medicine to help her."

On and on the grating voice went, hurling charge after charge at the captive audience, relentlessly seeking out every possible chink in their armor for a probing thrust. Coughs, shuffling feet and other signs of displeasure from the listeners had no effect upon the steady flow of accusations, only the final sheer exhaustion of the speaker brought it to an end.

When Spurgess sat down, there was almost no applause. Even before the president hastily adjourned the meeting, a concerted rush for the doors had already begun.

ii

Outside the theater, Jerry Warren dropped a quarter into a Coke machine and handed Paul an open bottle, before getting one for himself.

"Now I know what it feels like to be burned at the stake," he said. "My hide is still smarting."

"Did that much of it hit home?"

"Enough. You naturally hate the guy's guts for calling you bad names, but nobody can deny that a lot of what he said is true."

"There were still enough distortions to give whoever answers him for the Association plenty of ammunition," Paul observed.

"Why not make that part of your acceptance speech on Thursday—when, as and if, of course."

"Mainly if," said Paul. "I saw Danton taking notes. When he sounds off Thursday, he'll get practically as much coverage from the media as Spurgess did this morning."

"Danton looked pretty good up there," said Jerry. "Any idea how much trouble he's really having?"

"No more than I had yesterday," Paul admitted. "I haven't had much time to think about it."

"So? What did you do last night after I left the lab?"

"Otto and I had a philosophic discussion, then I wound up getting tight, I suppose."

"Suppose?" Jerry's eyebrows shot up in an expression of disbelief. "Don't you know?"

"I have a vague recollection of having a few drinks."

"Maybe somebody gave you a Mickey."

"In the Polo Lounge?"

"Hardly," Jerry admitted. "Were you alone?"

"I don't know. That's the hell of it."

"You must have really tied one on."

"All I can remember is something about a girl with black hair wearing a miniskirt and white boots."

"You could be describing one of the Polo Lounge waitresses. They're all knockouts."

"I seem to remember two," said Paul.

"You made out with both of them? Wow!"

"I don't know that either. But when I woke up this morning, I was a hundred bucks short."

Jerry whistled softly. "For that you should have gotten something really special. But imagine not remembering whether you made out or fell—you'll notice that I use the word advisedly—by the wayside."

A plump man with wise eyes and an engaging, elfin smile stopped beside the vending machines and put in a coin.

"I'm counting on you to be at the Young Turks caucus in person tomorrow afternoon, Paul," he said as he peeled the wrapper off a candy bar. "A lot of our out-of-town support doesn't know you by sight yet."

"What time is is to be, Alex?" Dr. Alex Klein was masterminding the campaign to pit Paul against H. Edward Danton in the contest for president-elect of the CMA on Thursday.

"We stole a march on Danton by staging our caucus an hour after his," said Klein. "Being on the Council, I'm eligible to attend Danton's strategy conference, too, so I'll listen in and get the lowdown on what he's planning."

"Is that cricket?"

"Maybe not, but it's damn good politics. And don't think Danton doesn't have spies in our camp. Well, I'd better get back to my exhibit, somebody might stumble into the booth by mistake."

"I checked with Otto early this morning," said Jerry, as he and Paul started down the sloping ramp toward the exhibit floor. "The pressure gradient between the superficial temporal and the cerebral circulation by way of the shunt is still definite."

"So Danton really has something in that new operation?"

"Looks like it. Trust that SOB to get ahead of us."

"Trust him to think of something we didn't," said Paul. "If an extra channel by way of the superficial temporal artery can provide more blood to the brain, it's quite possible that the aging process in people with cerebral arteriosclerosis can be slowed considerably."

"Want me to stop working on the bypass and concentrate on this?"

"You've gone too far to turn back now," said Paul. "If you want something to do, try to figure a way to get my hundred bucks back."

"If you can't remember what happened, how do you know you didn't get your money's worth?"

iii

Cary Poston and Hal Stimson were waiting in the lobby outside the Auditorium Theater when Marian came out. Cary introduced Stimson to her.

"Wheres the Senator?" she asked.

"In there." Cary nodded toward the door to the Men's Room.

"Shouldn't you see about him?" she said. "Somebody might throttle him."

"Frank can take care of himself," Hal Stimson assured her. "He was an All-American halfback at Ohio State."

"Stick around a few minutes and I'll introduce you," said Cary, but Marian shook her head.

"I'd better get over to the hotel and put on some more make-up before tackling the ladies of the Auxiliary at luncheon," she said. "A lot of them were in the theater just now. It almost seems a shame to let them have the other barrel, like I'm going to do, after the shellacking Spurgess gave their husbands."

"Will you let that influence you?" Hal Stimson asked.

"Not a bit. I'm like your boss, Mr. Stimson. I hew away and let the chips fall where they may."

"That's quite a woman," Hal Stimson said as they

watched Marian move down the ramp toward the lower floor. "She could really make a splash in politics, if she wanted to."

"Speaking of politics," said Cary, "you realize that the Association will be making a full-dress answer to Spurgess' charges in a day or two, don't you? Some of the loopholes in that speech were big enough to drive a truck through."

"He made his point," said Stimson with a shrug. "The next shot's yours."

"Why would Spurgess lay himself open to attack by making such obvious distortions?"

"Who knows they're distortions?"

"Most of the doctors who heard the speech here or will hear it on TV."

"None of them would have voted for Frank anyway. Ted Kennedy proved that you M.D.s make fine political whipping boys and Frank Spurgess is only going him one better. Everybody who's had to pay a whopping medical bill lately or had his health insurance rate upped will listen to him on TV or read what he said in the papers and tell himself it's all true. That way we'll get his vote when the presidential primaries roll around."

Senator Spurgess came out of the Men's Room. He'd washed his face and combed his hair, but his eyes were still a little bloodshot.

"Can I offer you a cup of coffee or something, Senator?" Cary asked.

"Any chance of getting a drink around here?"

Cary looked at his watch. "The cocktail lounge doesn't open for a half hour, at noon."

"No time for that," said Hal Stimson firmly. "We're supposed to have lunch with the local Democratic Committee and the plane will be ready at three."

"There's free beer downstairs," Cary suggested. "Central Pharmaceutical operates a booth at all the large medical conventions in this part of the country."

"That's better than nothing," said Spurgess. "Let's go."

"Central's one of the companies we're looking into next

124

week," said Hal Stimson as they started down the ramp to the exhibit floor.

"Good." Spurgess grinned wolfishly. "We'll drink their beer and then tear them apart next week for bribing doctors with it."

iv

Caleb Downs had listened to Senator Spurgess' attack on the medical profession with mounting annoyance, as well as concern about what he would have to face next week, when he appeared before the Senate Medical Subcommittee with the other drug manufacturers, who had been subpoenaed. He left the theater as soon as Spurgess finished and was handing out sample drug packets to doctors as they approached the counter, where two of his salesmen were busy drawing beer in tall paper cups, when he saw Cary Poston in one of the lines.

Obeying a sudden impulse he stepped forward. "I'll take over for a while, Sam," he said to the salesman handling the tap serving the line in which Cary stood.

"Sure, Mr. Downs." The salesman moved back into the booth and started handing out the cellophane-wrapped packages of drug samples in Caleb's place.

Cary was now only two places away in the queue of doctors waiting for beer and Caleb Downs's heart had stepped up its beat to where the demand upon his pacemaker no longer existed and the electric stimulation was shut off. At any other time Caleb might have noticed the cessation of the faint prickly sensation that often accompanied pacemaker stimulation. But the tide of excitement surging through him, the sense of power that came with holding in his hands the life of one of the two people he hated most was so great that he could think of nothing except that this was one of the moments of revenge for which he'd waited and planned so many years.

As he filled the cups with the foaming draft beer and shoved them across the counter top to the waiting doctors, Caleb managed to drop his right hand unobtrusively into his jacket pocket and pick up one of the tiny effervescent tablets he carried loose there, so they could be ready when opportunity presented itself. Although free beer was traditionally featured in Central Pharmaceutical's exhibits, he hadn't thought of using it as a carrier for the lethal agent the tablets contained—until he saw Cary Poston waiting in the line.

Caleb didn't look directly at Cary as the internist moved forward in the line. And since Cary was talking to a doctor just in front of him, he had no chance to recognize in the glossy-bearded man drawing the beer his old classmate from medical school.

As the man in front was served and Cary took his place before the counter, Caleb Downs's right hand, in a movement he'd practiced dozens of times, passed across the top of the tall paper cup he had removed from the stack beside the tap with his left. The tablet had hardly reached the bottom of the cup, when Caleb's fingers on the faucet sent a stream of beer cascading into the cup and the foam from the beer effectively hid the slight effervescence, as the tablet was instantly dissolved.

With a continuation of the same smooth and practiced movement, Caleb slid the cup across and into Cary's waiting hand, while he reached for another cup from the stack.

"Another one, please." Cary looked at Caleb for the first time as his fingers closed about the cup but showed no sign of recognition. Startled by the unexpected request, Caleb Downs stared at him blankly for a moment. Then realizing that the worst thing he could do was to object, he quickly drew another cup, this time without the effervescent tablet since there was not time to get another from his jacket.

"Thanks," said Cary and carrying both cups moved out of the line while Caleb Downs stood watching him.

"Hey, mister!" the next doctor in line said impatiently. "If you aren't more efficient in dispensing your drugs than you are the beer, I'm going to start prescribing some other brand."

126

Caleb recovered control of himself during the burst of laughter that followed the sally and started drawing beer again. Thus he didn't see Cary Poston step into an exhibit booth several spaces away along the aisle, where Hal Stimson and Senator Spurgess were sitting.

v

"Here you are, Senator." Cary placed the first cup before Spurgess. "And one for you, too, Hal. I'll get mine later."

"No thanks," said Stimson. "Beer's bad for my ulcer."

Spurgess took a healthy swig from the cup, and made a wry face. "If that fellows drugs aren't any better than his beer, he ought to be put out of business," he said. "It tastes like somebody dumped red pepper in it."

Cary drank part of his while Spurgess removed the silver flask from his pocket.

"Mine seems to be all right," he said.

"Could be my throat." The Senator emptied the flask into the cup with the beer. "Air conditioning sometimes leaves my mucous membranes irritated."

Putting the flask back into his pocket, Spurgess picked up the cup again and got to his feet.

"Thanks for the pick-me-up, Dr. Poston; you saved my life. Let's go, Hal. Maybe I can get through lunch with the party bosses now."

The floor was crowded and hurrying people jostled the three men several times, as they moved along the aisle leading to the rear of the building. Progress was slow at best and Spurgess drank again but grimaced when he took the cup from his lips.

"If I didn't need the whiskey so bad, I'd throw this slop into a trash can," he said.

"You could hardly expect a 'boilermaker' to taste like nectar," Hal Stimson observed dryly.

"Mine tastes all right, Senator," said Cary. "What's wrong?"

"Feel's like my throat is tingling, but I need the shot to

get me through this luncheon." Spurgess emptied the cup and tossed it into a waste container. "Come on, Hal, we'd better be going."

"I'll walk with you to the loading ramp at the back," said Cary, as he dropped his own cup into the same container. "I told the limousine chauffeur to meet us there to avoid the crush outside."

It took them almost ten minutes to work their way through the crowd to the back door of the Auditorium. When he saw Spurgess and his party emerge from the building, the policeman on duty there blew his whistle and a limousine waiting nearby started to move into place before the ramp but was blocked momentarily by a panel truck. Cary turned to shake hands when the limousine finally reached the ramp but reached out instead to support Spurgess, who was leaning against the door through which they had just emerged, apparently gasping for breath.

"Anything wrong, Senator?" Cary asked quickly, but his trained physician's sense told him the answer before he even touched Spurgess. The other man seemed on the verge of collapse and, as Cary took his arm, he swayed and would have fallen, if Hal Stimson hadn't supported him on the other side.

"The combination of whiskey and beer must have been too much on an empty stomach," said Hal.

"The tingling in my throat." Spurgess' voice was hoarse. "It's getting worse." He was sweating, too, and his color was an ashen gray, warning Cary of an impending collapse.

"The convention aid station is close by," he said quickly. "You'd better lie down there awhile, Senator."

Spurgess made no protest. He was obviously quite ill and, by the time they reached the aid station, Cary and Hal Stimson were practically carrying him. Barely able to walk, Spurgess seemed to be in the grip of a strange sort of paralysis that affected his limbs and made breathing difficult.

The tall, dark-skinned resident physician on duty at the

aid station shut the door in the faces of the crowd that had followed the three men, then hurried to bring an oxygen tank and mask while Cary and Hal Stimson were lifting Spurgess to an examining table.

"Senator Spurgess collapsed outside the building, Dr. Singh," Cary explained as the breathing bag started emptying and filling with Spurgess' shallow breathing. Spurgess' eyes were bright with apprehension for whatever was wrong with him had obviously not affected his consciousness.

With the stethoscope Dr. Singh handed him, Cary listened over the patient's heart but could make out nothing to explain what could have happened—except that even while he listened, the pulse became perceptibly slower, as did the respirations.

Meanwhile, Dr. Singh had been taking the Senator's blood pressure in the left arm. When he looked up from watching the manometer dial, his face was grave.

"Ninety over sixty, Dr. Poston," he said softly. "This could be cardiac shock."

"Have the hospital send over a wheeled stretcher right away," Cary told Dr. Singh. "And a CPR team."

"What's that?" Hal Stimson asked.

"Cardiopulmonary resuscitation—just in case."

The startled look on Stimson's face told Cary he understood the gravity of the situation.

"I'll call the committee chairman and tell him we can't make the luncheon," he said.

"There's a pay phone outside," Singh told him. "We'll need to keep this one clear."

By now Spurgess' pulse beneath Cary's fingers had slowed to thirty-six beats per minute, while his breathing was roughly half the normal rate. His need for oxygen was becoming steadily more acute, too, as his circulation began to fail. And unless they could do something quickly to support both respiration and circulation, it was obvious that the supply reaching his vital centers through the lungs and the bloodstream would soon be unable to satisfy the demand.

"Do you have any digitoxin?" Cary asked Singh.

The tall resident nodded and moved quickly to prepare the injection. By the time he gave it intravenously at Cary's direction, however Spurgess' breathing was extremely labored, even with pure oxygen in the breathing bag. His pulse rate was now thirty, and the respirations had fallen to eight, but nothing they did seemed to have any effect upon his condition.

"Does anywhere hurt, Senator?" Cary asked.

The need for oxygen made the use of words a luxury Frank Spurgess could no longer afford and he was barely able to shake his head. The end came just before the wheeled stretcher and the resuscitation team arrived from the hospital, only a short hundred yards away across the street. The patient was conscious up to the very last, too, his eyes imploring Cary to do something. But the internist, for all his skill, was totally unable to control the gradual slowing of pulse and respiration, or the inexorable progress of death that accompanied it.

The skilled team of residents and interns went to work immediately in the routine of cardiopulmonary resuscitation. The emergency wheeled cart they'd brought with them, when the paging operator had sounded the alert call of "CODE FIVE, Convention Aid Station," contained everything needed to restart a stopped heart. While a husky resident physician pressed upon the now still chest of Senator Frank Spurgess, another pushed down his jaw and inserted a curved breathing tube, opening a clear airway to the lungs.

"This is odd," said the young doctor maintaining the airway, as air rushed from lungs compressed by the rhythmic squeezing of the patient's heart between the breastbone and spinal column. "His muscles are as limp as if he'd been given a relaxing agent."

"It's the same with the arm," said another young doctor who was injecting Isuprel and adrenalin intravenously.

While the skilled CPR team went expertly about its business, Cary Poston stood aside, stunned, and a little sick at the sudden death of a man who, though an avowed enemy of his profession, was still a human being deserving all that medical skill and knowledge could provide. That this was being given, no one could deny. But that it was accomplishing nothing was equally evident almost from the start.

When some fifteen minutes of continuous effort had brought not even a flicker of the pulse or a sign of spontaneous breathing, the Chief Medical Resident, who headed the resuscitation team, looked at Cary and shook his head.

"I'm afraid it's no use, Dr. Poston," he said.

"What happened?" Hal Stimson spoke from the doorway where he'd been standing, since he came in after telephoning watching with incredulous eyes the scene of furious, but obviously highly skilled, activity.

"He's dead, Hal," said Cary. "His heart ran down and his breathing stopped. We haven't been able to get even a flicker from either for the past fifteen minutes."

"But why?"

"We won't know until the post-mortem. Could be a coronary. Or even a brain hemorrhage into the vital centers, though it doesn't look like that. Either would cause cessation of the heart."

"And to think that a half hour ago he was giving the people who are trying to save him hell." Stimson took a deep breath. "What will we tell the reporters? They'll be swarming all over the place any minute."

"We don't tell them anything, until Dr. Pettigrew here says the Senator is dead," said Cary. "The CPR team has absolute jurisdiction as long as any chance of reviving a patient remains."

"Is there any now?" Hal Stimson asked.

"We don't think so." Dr. Pettigrew did not stop pressing on Spurgess' chest. "But we don't give up until we're sure."

After another quarter hour, even the CPR team chief admitted that it was useless to attempt resuscitation any longer.

"Thanks for getting here so quickly, Jack," Cary told him. "You boys did your usual expert job."

"What shall I give as the tentative diagnosis, Dr. Poston?" Pettigrew asked.

"Massive coronary thrombosis with cardiac shock, I suppose. It's not a textbook case but that diagnosis will have to do—until Dr. Huxtable gives the final one. Dr. Singh will call him."

Dr. Andrew Huxtable, professor of forensic pathology, was also County Medical Examiner. Until it was released to the family for burial, the body of Senator Frank Spurgess would be under his control.

"Will you help me prepare a statement for the reporters, Cary?" Hal Stimson asked. "This all happened so suddenly, I don't know whether I'm going or coming."

"I'm pretty much in the same fix," Cary admitted. "All we can tell the press at the moment is that Senator Spurgess died from massive coronary thrombosis."

CHAPTER XI

The press interview was short. The death of Senator Frank Spurgess, presumably from a heart attack, moments after he finished denouncing the doctors of the Central Medical Association to their faces as cold-blooded profiteers and betrayers of their professional oaths had all the elements of high drama. The reporters in the Press Room scrambled for the telephones even before Cary finished reading the statement he and Hal Stimson had prepared hastily in the elevator, while Spurgess' body was being taken to the hospital morgue by the CPR team from the hospital.

Pete Sanders, executive secretary of the Association, was kind enough to turn an office over to Hal Stimson, so he could notify Spurgess' wife and family and make arrangements for the body to be flown back to Washington, as soon as the post-mortem examination was completed.

When the press conference was finished, Cary Poston

stopped by the aid station to thank Dr. Singh for his help in what had obviously been from the start a hopeless cause. News of the dramatic turn of events was already being broadcast through the several floors of the Auditorium complex by that strange grapevine which allows both rumor and fact to spread through a large gathering such as the CMA—almost, it seemed, with the speed of light. Cary found Singh writing up the Emergency Room record on Spurgess, since there had not been time for him to be admitted to the hospital.

"I called Dr. Huxtable as you instructed, Dr. Poston," said the Indian resident.

"I hope you gave him a clinical history on the case," said Cary. "I haven't even had time to write anything down."

"I told him what transpired—also my belief that the Senator was poisoned."

"Poisoned! But that's fantastic!"

"Nevertheless, the symptoms are those produced by bikh."

"Bikh?" Cary looked at the Indian blankly. "What's that?"

"The alkaloid derived from the roots of *aconitum ferox*. It is a very popular poison in my own country of Nepal. Some forms are called bish or nabee, but the one most used is bikh. I have seen many cases."

"You mean where the drug was taken accidentally in fatal doses?"

"In Nepal and other parts of the Far East, bikh is frequently used as an agent of assassination."

"I find it hard to believe such a thing could happen here, Dr. Singh."

"Dr. Huxtable found it equally difficult." Singh's smile was wintry. "In fact, I'm sure he didn't believe me at all."

"What did you say the poison was again?"

"The real agent is pseudaconitine—one of the deadliest poisons known to man. It is practically impossible to identify in the body tissues and for that reason is much used in the Far East for assassination."

"Almost every doctor who heard Senator Spurgess speak this morning resented what he had to say, Dr. Singh. But that doesn't mean anyone would try to kill him."

"I have no idea how the drug was given to the Senator," Singh admitted soberly. "But I would stake my medical degree on the diagnosis."

Cary shook his head slowly. "Assassination of a United States Senator at a medical convention? It's still unbelievable."

"Not only is a murderer loose at the convention, Dr. Poston, he is armed with a weapon that is very difficult to identify in the bodies of his victims. Therefore, he cannot be proved to be a murderer, even if he is discovered."

ii

Although occupied drawing beer for the line of doctors waiting before the Central Pharmaceutical booth, Caleb Downs had managed to watch the aisle along which Cary Poston had moved after leaving the pharmaceutical exhibit. He saw Cary disappear into one of the exhibit areas between him and the Vibrassage booth but had no time to determine which one. When a few minutes later Cary, Senator Spurgess and Hal Stimson emerged from the booth, where they had been hidden briefly from Caleb's view, and started down the aisle toward the main entrance to the exhibit floor, he allowed himself to relax somewhat.

The agent he had dropped into the first cup he'd drawn for Cary had been selected because it was swift in its action and practically always lethal. Caleb still didn't want the effect to begin too near the Central Pharmaceutical booth, however, with the possibility of someone suspecting a connection. That once absorbed into the body, the dose he had administered would proceed inexorably to the death of the victim didn't trouble Caleb at all, since that was the very reason he had selected it from a host of other, and slower acting, poisons.

Even at a distance, Caleb could see that both Cary and Senator Spurgess were still carrying the tall cups in which the beer was dispensed. He would have given much to know which one contained the lethal drug, but the three men disappeared into a side aisle beyond his view.

Caleb's first clue to the success of his action, as well as to who the victim was, came when one of his salesmen returned from a visit to the Men's Room at the back of the exhibit floor.

"Senator Spurgess just suffered a heart attack, Mr. Downs." The salesman was so excited he could barely talk. "A salesman from the North Texas Laboratories booth saw them carrying him to the aid station."

"Couldn't have happened to a more deserving guy," said another salesman.

There was a sudden burst of activity at the entrance to the Civic Center, as a team of young men poured into the building. They were pushing a hospital cart loaded with special equipment and Caleb Downs remembered enough from his own near brush with death to recognize a CPR team. Two orderlies followed with a wheeled stretcher, all moving swiftly toward the aid station near the ramp leading to the upper levels.

For the next half hour, the exhibit floor was in a turmoil, as people crowded around the closed door of the aid station, hoping to gain some clue to what was happening. But the area was quickly cordoned off by security guards who would tell them nothing. Little knots of people gathered here and there around the exhibit floor, eagerly discussing the dramatic turn of events, some saying Spurgess had suffered a stroke, others a severe heart attack. The hospital resuscitation team was said by some to be giving him artificial respiration, while others were equally certain that daring surgery was being performed to restart a stopped heart.

Having been saved once by another CPR team Caleb Downs had more reason than almost anyone else to know just what was happening inside the aid station. But he couldn't be sure of the result for roughly half an hour, when the official report was finally made to the press that

Senator Frank Spurgess had suffered a fatal heart attack while leaving the Civic Center for another engagement.

Caleb accepted the news with a shrug. Obviously he had missed in his try to destroy Cary, no doubt because Cary had given the first of the two cups of beer to Senator Spurgess instead of drinking it himself. But in his attempt to destroy Cary, he had removed a real threat both to him and to his business. On balance, then, Caleb felt only satisfaction with the morning's work.

All of which, he decided, called for a small celebration. He could see that the Vibrassage booth, a hundred and fifty or so feet down the aisle, was busy and decided to wait until the clinical sessions on the upper levels were resumed and the number of people on the exhibit floor sharply curtailed, before seeing whether Alice Perrault was interested in a drink and perhaps lunch, as a preliminary to arranging what he was sure could be a very pleasant liaison that evening.

iii

The University Hospital and Clinics, where Cary Poston's office was located, were just across the street and down a half block from the Civic Center. He had just walked in when the paging operator at the hospital alerted him on the small device, roughly the size of a pack of Virginia Thins, carried by the hospital staff at all times.

Taking the pager from his pocket, he clicked on the switch.

"Dr. Poston," said the operator. "Please call Dr. Huxtable in Pathology."

Shutting off the pager, Cary rang Dr. Andrew Huxtable, the County Medical Examiner, who was also professor of forensic pathology in the medical school.

"I'm rushing the post-mortem on Senator Spurgess so the body can be flown to Washington this evening and thought you'd like to see it, Cary," said Huxtable. "Did Singh tell you about his crazy theory that somebody assassinated Spurgess with aconite?"

"Yes."

"What do you think of the idea?"

"On the face of it, the whole thing seems unbelievable. But Singh is a fine young doctor and he does come from that region so his diagnosis has to be considered, too."

"I don't agree with any diagnosis I can't make with an autopsy knife or a microscope," said the pathologist. "But I called Lieutenant Arthur Klinger of the Homicide Squad, just in case. We're ready to start when you are."

"I'll be right over. Don't wait on me."

The white tiled walls of the pathology amphitheater, with its rows of seats for students and staff to watch demonstrations of the ravages disease caused in the human body, had an oddly cheerful look for a place devoted to death. Dr. Huxtable, in surgical gown, rubber apron and gloves, was already opening the body when Cary arrived. Occupying front row seats were a small man with a fierce mustache and snapping dark eyes, Dr. Singh, Dr. Kendall Thomas, professor of pharmacology, Hal Stimson, and a gray-haired older man.

"You already know Dr. Singh and Kendall Thomas, Cary." Huxtable waved the bloody knife he held toward them. "Meet Lieutenant Arthur Klinger of Central City Police Department."

"Homicide Squad, Doctor." The officer with the mustache shook hands with Cary. "Glad to know you."

Klinger nodded toward the sixth man in the room besides the technician assisting the pathologist.

"Mr. Harvey Lawson, head of the local FBI office, Dr. Poston. We don't know that any federal jurisdiction is involved, but since a U. S. Senator died under rather tense circumstances, I asked Mr. Lawson to come along."

Cary shook hands with the FBI agent and took a seat beside Singh.

"I have—as you say here in America—gone out on a limb, Dr. Poston," said the Indian doctor. "Dr. Thomas and Dr. Huxtable will be very disappointed if I am not sawed off."

"I understand you were close to Senator Spurgess when

he collapsed, Dr. Poston," said Klinger. "Did you notice anything unusual?"

"No," said Cary. "I had stopped at the Central Pharmaceutical Company booth and got a cup of beer each for the Senator and myself. He poured some whiskey from his flask into the cup—"

"A boilermaker?"

"That's the popular term, I believe. Senator Spurgess and Mr. Stimson were in a hurry to get to a luncheon, so we took our cups with us and drank on the way through the exhibit floor to the loading ramp at the back of the building."

"Then all three of you had beer?"

"I don't drink, Lieutenant," said Hal Stimson. "Only the Senator and Dr. Poston had the beer."

Cary suddenly realized the import of Klinger's question. "Surely, you don't think—"

"If Senator Spurgess was poisoned, as Dr. Singh maintains, the drug must have been given him while you were with him, Doctor," said Klinger. "Possibly after you accepted the cup from the tap where you were served."

"*After?*"

"Didn't you say you drank yours, too.

"Yes."

"Obviously yours contained no poison," said Klinger.

Cary frowned. "I remember now that Senator Spurgess drank his more quickly than I did mine."

"But you drank all of yours?"

"Yes."

"And you felt no ill effect?"

"None." Cary looked at the body on the cold marble top of the table, where Dr. Huxtable was working busily and shivered. "None at all."

"That would seem to rule out your poison theory, Singh," said Dr. Kendall Thomas. "At least as far as beer is concerned."

"Why do you say that, Doctor?" the lieutenant asked.

"The various forms of the aconite alkaloids come from

the same genus of plants—ordinarily called monkshood or wolfbane," the pharmacologist explained. "Ironically enough, the plant belongs to the buttercup family but it's certainly the black sheep of that particular clan. The action is swift, so if the poison had been in the beer, Dr. Poston should be dead, too."

"Unless whoever administered the bikh deliberately put it into Senator Spurgess' cup," said Singh.

"Dr. Poston or myself would have to be the assassin," said Hal Stimson. "The three of us were together."

"I was the one who gave the cup of beer to Senator Spurgess," said Cary. "So I would have to be the prime suspect."

"We haven't reached the point of selecting suspects yet, Dr. Poston," said Klinger crisply. "At the moment we need to know more about the cause of death. How is the poison Dr. Singh suspects was used here prepared, Dr. Thomas?"

"Aconite is ordinarily extracted from the root as an alcoholic solution or tincture," said the pharmacologist. "In either form, it would have a distinctive flavor, so a lethal dose could hardly have been given in a paper cup of beer without the victim noticing a difference in taste."

A faint bell rang in Cary Poston's mind. There had been something peculiar about the cup of beer Spurgess had drunk, he recalled now, but couldn't remember exactly what it was.

"Is the drug hard to obtain?" Lieutenant Klinger asked.

"In a way—yes," said Thomas.

"What do you mean?"

"Nobody uses it any more in medicine but it's easier to grow than marijuana. Any gardener can do it."

"Any signs of poisoning, Andy?" Cary Poston asked the pathologist, who had almost completed the autopsy, except for the contents of the skull.

"None so far," said Huxtable. "But aconite is taken up so quickly by body tissues that I wouldn't expect to find any, except perhaps in the stomach contents."

"The poison acts directly upon brain tissues," the pharmacologist added. "It mainly affects the vital centers, slowing the pulse and decreasing the respiration until the heart is finally arrested."

"That's exactly what happened!" Cary exclaimed. Spurgess' pulse grew slower while my fingers were on his wrist, just like an engine running down. So did his respirations."

"So far you've given me only circumstantial evidence," said Dr. Huxtable. "We may know more after we examine the stomach contents and section the brain in the area of the vital centers, but as of now the cause of death can only be said to be unknown."

Dr. Singh shrugged. "As I said, I went out on a limb."

"Do you still think he was poisoned, Doctor?" Lieutenant Klinger asked the Indian physician.

"Without a doubt. Someone went to a great deal of trouble to prepare a pure form of pseudaconitine and administer it."

"But how could it have been put into Spurgess' drink?" said Cary. "I was right beside him all the time and so was Mr. Stimson."

"The floor was very crowded," said Hal. "I remember being jostled several times."

"So anyone who wished to do so could have dropped poison into either cup," said Lieutenant Klinger. "The question we need to answer is who hated the deceased enough to want to murder him?"

"Nearly two thousand doctors at this convention had every reason to resent Spurgess," said Cary. "But I still can't conceive of any one of them assassinating him."

The FBI man, Lawson, spoke for the first time. "If the poison was there, why didn't the Senator taste it?"

"Wait a minute!" The bell in Cary Poston's brain had suddenly rung again. "I think he did."

"What do you mean, Doctor?" Lieutenant Klinger was poised, like a ferret about to attack its prey.

"The first time he drank from the cup I gave him,

Senator Spurgess complained that the beer burned his throat."

"The initial symptom of acute bikh poisoning is a tingling in the throat followed by local anesthesia," said Dr. Singh quickly.

"Spurgess added whiskey to the beer after that," said Cary, "so the whiskey couldn't have caused the tingling."

"I remember Frank saying the drink still tasted bad," Hal Stimson added.

"He started to collapse right after he finished drinking," said Cary. "And after that I was busy getting him to the aid station."

"What about it, Kendall?" Dr. Huxtable asked the pharmacologist. "Do we have enough evidence to make a diagnosis of poisoning by aconite?"

"Not in my boo—" Dr. Thomas broke off in the middle of the word. "Do you have a textbook on legal medicine and toxicology in your office, Andy?"

"Sure. Why?"

"I seem to remember a simple test for aconite. If Spurgess got enough of it in a boilermaker to kill him, as Singh contends, we ought to find the drug in his stomach contents."

"The book's in my office," said Huxtable. "His stomach was practically empty but I'll wash off the lining while you're getting the book and we'll test the wash water."

"Just as I thought," said Thomas, when he came back to the autopsy room, "the standard test is to acidulate the stomach contents with acetic acid and add potassium permanganate. In the presence of an alkaloid of aconite, a reddish crystalline precipitate forms."

"We can do that easily enough." The Medical Examiner spoke from the side table, where he was washing the lining of Spurgess' stomach with water from a chemical laboratory wash bottle.

"Bring some acetic acid, potassium permanganate solution and several test tubes," Huxtable directed the technician who was assisting him. "We'll do the test right here."

When the technician returned with the necessary laboratory glassware, tubes and solutions, only a few minutes were required for Dr. Kendall Thomas to make the analysis. But though the two chemicals were added to several tubes of stomach washings and the pharmacologist even spread a film of both acid and permaganate over the mucuous membrane of the stomach lining, nothing resembling the reddish crystalline precipitate referred to in the toxicology manual developed.

"Looks like you're wrong, Singh," said Dr. Huxtable.

"The clinical signs are still indisputable to one familiar with the effects of bikh, Doctor. I have seen them often enough to be sure."

"I can think of at least one reason why you might not find aconite in Senator Spurgess' stomach now, Andy," said Cary Poston. "The alkaloid is highly soluble in alcohol; that's why it was almost always prescribed as the tincture, when it was used therapeutically. Since Spurgess was drinking alcohol in the form of the whiskey he added to the beer, the drug in the stomach could have been dissolved by the alcohol and absorbed into the bloodstream."

"I doubt that the drug would have been absorbed that quickly," Dr. Kendall Thomas objected. "From what you said, Cary, no more than ten minutes elapsed between the time Spurgess could have received the drug and the onset of symptoms."

"I have seen poisoning take place that quickly," said Dr. Singh.

"But wouldn't some have remained in his stomach, if the time was that short?" said the Medical Examiner.

"You're forgetting that the CPR team kept compressing the heart for a half hour," said Cary Poston. "During that time Spurgess was clinically dead but blood was kept flowing in his veins and arteries by the mechanical squeezing of his heart between the sternum and the spine. We were injecting cardiac stimulants into his circulation, too, so blood was flowing in his circulatory system all the time."

"Whether he was dead or not?" Lieutenant Klinger asked incredulously.

"Yes. And during that half hour all the aconite in his stomach could easily have been absorbed."

"I still think we need to wait for tissue studies," Dr. Kendall Thomas insisted.

"Unless we know Senator Spurgess was murdered, Mr. Lawson and I cannot initiate the sort of manhunt that might turn up his killer before he can get away or kill someone else," Lieutenant Klinger objected. "With thousands of doctors attending this convention, the murderer would almost have to be one of them."

"Possibly," Thomas admitted.

"Who else would know about this aconite and the way it acts?" Klinger insisted.

"At least a half-dozen exhibit booths are operated by pharmaceutical houses," said Cary. "It's true that most of those manning them are probably salesmen with very little actual knowledge of pharmacology, but all of those companies employ trained biochemical pharmacologists in their research."

"You forget one thing, Dr. Poston," said Singh. "Many of us from the Orient are in Central City, too, studying medicine or going through residencies. And most of us are familiar with the use of bikh in our own countries."

"In a form so refined that Senator Spurgess couldn't have tasted it when he drank the beer?" Cary asked.

"Apparently he did taste it," said Singh. "Tingling of the mucous membranes is one of the first effects from the local application of aconite. It is followed by the local anesthesia that is practically diagnostic of poisoning with bikh. In this case, the drug was in such a concentrated form and apparently acted so rapidly that the usual train of symptoms had no time to appear before complete collapse occurred."

"Where does that leave us then?" Lieutenant Klinger inquired.

"Just where we were before," said Dr. Thomas doggedly. "We haven't found the drug in Senator Spurgess' body, so we don't really know it was the cause of death. All we have to go on is what you might call an educated guess by Dr. Singh and, while I admit that on a clinical basis alone his knowledge is considerably greater than mine, I still don't consider the presumption of poisoning strong enough to shut down this convention and subject several thousand doctors to a police interrogation which in all probability would yield nothing. If there is a murderer, which I don't believe, and if he actually did use a highly concentrated form of aconite, it would have to be in a very small amount. Which means he could get rid of it quite easily and even a police search probably wouldn't unearth it."

"All that is true," the police officer admitted.

"You can all serve as the coroner's jury, although I'm not required to have one," said Huxtable. "How do you vote?"

"I agree with Kendall Thomas that we don't really have enough evidence to make a definitive diagnosis of death by poisoning," Cary admitted.

Lieutenant Klinger and the FBI man didn't vote.

"What about you, Singh?" Huxtable asked.

The tall Indian didn't hesitate. "I still say bikh. But I must admit that I cannot prove it."

A technician entered the room. "You're wanted at the convention first aid station right away, Dr. Singh," she said.

As Singh left the room, Dr. Huxtable moved to the wall and took a red telephone from a hook there. Above the telephone was the word "DICTATION."

"Cause of death not yet determined pending further investigation," he dictated to the recording machine in the central record room of the hospital, from which it would be typed by one of the secretaries in the stenographic pool. "Preliminary investigation suggests the remote possibility of poisoning, possibly with aconite or a related drug. Further tests are being carried out."

iv

"Hello, Mr. Downs," said Alice Perrault, when she saw Caleb standing at the entrance to the Vibrassage booth a little before noon.

"You're to call me Caleb, remember?"

"So much has happened this morning, I forgot—Caleb," she said. "The way you've been drawing beer you must be pooped. I've got an empty chair in case you need some relaxation."

Conscious that the tension he'd been laboring under since he'd seen Cary Poston in the line earlier had indeed left him more tired than he had realized, Caleb moved into the Vibrassage booth and stretched out in one of the large reclining chairs there.

"I could certainly use a massage," he told Alice. "My left shoulder aches like fury from handling that tap on the beer barrel."

"Just lie down and relax," she told him. "You're in experienced hands."

Her fingers were cool, efficient and quite impersonal, as she shifted his body about to fit better into the chair. At this range, Caleb could hardly escape the consciousness that Alice Perrault was an especially fine-looking woman with possibilities well worth investigating, he decided when the chair began a rhythmic vibrating motion that was as sensuous as the fingers of a woman massaging his body.

"Maybe I can help that shoulder for you, too," Alice told him. "You're the executive type and tending bar can be pretty tiring when you're not used to it."

Caleb closed his eyes and let the gentle fingers caress tired muscles. He didn't even notice what she was doing, when she swung the arm of an attachment across in front of his shoulder and moments later, he felt a deep warmth penetrate the tissues of his shoulder.

"Hear about Senator Spurgess having a heart attack,

145

Mr. Downs?" Jethro Forbes asked from the next Vibrassage chair.

"What happened?"

"I guess he let himself get too excited lambasting us doctors. They worked over him a half hour with a CPR team from the hospital but couldn't get his heart started again."

"Those resuscitation squads do a fine job," said Caleb. "I had a coronary several years ago in Jacksonville, Florida. If a Fire Department Rescue Squad hadn't gotten to me in four minutes, I'd have been dead."

"Didn't one of their rescue squads win first place in a national contest not so long ago?" Jethro asked.

"The year I had my attack. Still I guess you can't save 'em all."

"I've lost my share," Jethro agreed.

Caleb shifted position slightly. "This is quite a gadget you've got here, Alice. I may buy one for my office."

"I'll give you some more deep heat." Alice fiddled with the controls of the machine attached to the chair. "Got to keep you in shape; I might want a beer myself after a while."

"Any time. And something stronger, if you'd like it."

Caleb was feeling drowsy and satisfied. If Cary Poston had diagnosed the cause of Spurgess' death as coronary thrombosis, all danger of anyone's recognizing the real cause of death appeared to be past. And by the time they posted the body, the aconite would either be destroyed or so fixed in the tissues that it would be undetectable—which was what made it the perfect poison that it was.

Alice Perrault straightened up brushing the sweater against him, quite, he was sure, by design. Caleb wasn't so uninformed about conventions that he didn't recognize an invitation when he heard—and felt—one. He'd been pretty careful ever since his heart attack, but that was all of two years ago. And with the demand pacemaker in his chest ready to take over whenever it was needed, a little stimulation certainly couldn't hurt anything.

Absorbed in that pleasant prospect, Caleb didn't even realize when the pacemaker in his chest suddenly shut off. Or that the blackness which descended upon him was anything other than sleep.

CHAPTER XII

The first intimation Alice Perrault had that anything was wrong with Caleb Downs came when his head, no longer under normal muscular control with the circulation to his brain and the supply of vital oxygen to its cells reduced below functioning level by the slowing of his pulse, suddenly dropped to one side. His tongue, too, sagged back in his throat, partially obstructing his breathing and causing a harsh, snoring sound.

"Hey, mister!" Alice cried. "Wake up!"

When her frantic shaking brought no response, she turned in panic to Jethro Forbes, who was dozing in the adjoining chair, while the rippling waves of the vibrator massaged his body.

"Dr. Forbes!" she cried. "This guy passed out."

Jethro was out of the chair in a second, reaching across to lift Caleb's sagging chin and allow a clearer airway.

"Can you let the chair down flat?" he asked Alice.

She moved quickly to obey, manipulating the controls to let the back of the chair down and make it almost a couch. Pushing the diathermy attachment aside at the same time, she shut off the electricity both to it and the chair. By that time, Jethro's fingers on the unconscious man's wrist had discovered that Caleb's pulse rate was extremely slow, explaining the mechanism, though not the basic cause, of his sudden blackout.

"Call the aid station and have them bring oxygen." As he spoke, Jethro opened Caleb Downs's shirt and pulled up his undershirt part way, revealing the pale white scar of a surgical incision extending across his chest.

"He's had chest surgery—possibly cardiac."

Jethro's mind was working like a computer now, noting pertinent findings and discarding unlikely diagnoses while he appraised the likely possibilities. Loss of consciousness and a very slow pulse fitted the diagnosis of Stokes-Adams Syndrome, medical name for a block in the central communication channel within the heart itself. It didn't, however, explain the scar where the chest had been opened in a region that would allow access to the heart—until everything suddenly began to fall neatly into place.

Microwave ovens, diathermy machines, and many other commonly used electronic devices were able to shut off a demand pacemaker, he remembered, leaving it unresponsive to the needs of a patient whose pulse had slowed to a point below the critical level. That memory gave him the diagnosis and also the treatment, for one of the methods recommended to restore the function of a stopped pacemaker as quickly as possible was to apply a magnet to the chest wall over the heart.

"Were you using the diathermy attachment on him?" he asked Alice.

"Yes. But how could that—?"

"Look at the surgical scar on his chest. It probably means he's had a pacemaker put in to make his heart beat faster."

"Oh, my God!" Her eyes suddenly widened with horror. "The company warned us that diathermy could stop a pacemaker. But he didn't say anything about it, and you'd think a doctor would know—"

"Downs isn't a doctor." Jethro was searching for Ted Kraus's face in the crowd now jamming the aisle.

"Kraus!" he called when he saw the instrument maker standing at the entrance to his booth, trying to see what was happening across the aisle. "Bring me that ophthalmic magnet you were showing me earlier."

Seizing the magnet from his exhibit, Ted Kraus brought it to the Vibrassage booth and handed it to Jethro who immediately placed it over Caleb Downs's heart. Jethro had no time to notice—and it would have made no difference if he had—that a TV news reporter with a portable camera happened to be roving among the exhibits. Seeking something newsworthy to photograph, he had been attracted by the sudden massing of the crowd in the aisle before the Vibrassage booth and now climbed upon the chair Jethro had just vacated.

"Shut that damned thing off, will you?" Jethro snapped, when the sudden glare of the floodlight attached to the camera almost blinded him.

The reporter continued to let his camera run, however, while Jethro moved the magnet back and forth across Caleb's chest, seeking to localize its waves directly over the pacemaker—whose presence he could still only surmise.

"Oxygen's on the way," someone called from the crowd in the aisle, which had grown even more dense, since the TV reporter's floodlight indicated the presence of the newsgatherer there.

Jethro didn't bother to look up, knowing that even pure oxygen couldn't restore function to sensitive brain cells, unless the heart action could be increased to where it could keep an adequate supply of blood flowing to them. Each second that passed made the situation more critical for a few minutes of deprivation could turn what had been a man into a vegetable, since brain cells were the most easily damaged by oxygen lack of all those making up the body tissues.

"Is he dying?" Alice Perrault asked anxiously, visions of a suit for damages against herself and the Vibrassage Company foremost in her mind.

"His heart's beating too slowly, but he's still alive."

Jethro didn't stop scanning the unconscious man's chest with the magnet when the crowd parted to let a stretcher and two white-coated men pass through. One was Dr. Singh, panting a little after sprinting from the autopsy room across the street to the exhibit floor. The other was a medical student who was helping him man the aid station, after morning classes.

"What happened, Doctor?" Singh's appraising glance

told him Jethro was acting with competence and professional skill and the green-bordered convention badge he wore identified him as a doctor.

"Bradycardia. Stokes-Adams Syndrome," said Jethro as the Indian physician placed a small oxygen mask over Caleb Downs's nose and mouth and opened the valve, sending the vital gas into the small breathing bag attached to it. "My guess is he has a chronic heart block and his pacemaker was stopped by a diathermy attachment on this chair. I'm trying to start the pacemaker with an ophthalmic magnet."

"Most ingenious," said Singh.

"Check his pulse, please, Doctor. I haven't been able to take it since Mr. Kraus gave me the magnet."

Dr. Singh picked up Caleb Downs's wrist and felt the pulse for a moment.

"The pacemaker just started again," he said with a note of awe in his voice. "The pulse jumped markedly."

Jethro lifted the magnet away and waited, but the smile on the dark-skinned doctor's face before he'd counted more than fifteen seconds told him the pacemaker was functioning well.

"You saved his life by thinking about that magnet, Dr. Forbes," said Singh. "Congratulations!"

"Maybe not his life yet, but I hope, his brain," said Jethro.

A spattering of applause from the crowd now jamming the aisle for twenty or thirty feet in each direction from the booth startled Jethro, and he looked up to find himself staring directly into the lens of the reporter's camera.

Meanwhile Dr. Singh, helped by dozens of willing hands, was moving Caleb Downs from the chair to the stretcher. Even before the stretcher was ready to leave the Vibrassage booth, however, Caleb had already begun to move and show other signs of returning consciousness.

"Would you like to come with us to the aid station, Dr. Forbes?" Singh asked, but Jethro shook his head.

"He's your patient now, Doctor, but I advise you to take Mr. Kraus's magnet with you. If he hadn't shown it to me earlier, I wouldn't have known where to find one."

"And the patient would probably be a vegetable," said Singh crisply as the stretcher moved away. "Or dead."

The TV camera floodlight was shut off now and the reporter climbed down from the large chair he had used as a perch while photographing the dramatic scene from a distance of only a few feet.

"Could I have your full name and address, Dr. Forbes?" he asked.

"Why?" Jethro was getting his wind back.

"For one thing, so they'll get it right on the Carnegie Medal you're sure to receive for what you just did." The reporter was young and obviously still awed by what his camera had recorded.

Jethro gave him the information he needed and the reporter jotted it down.

"Can you tell me when this will be shown?" Jethro asked. "I've never been on TV before."

"You'll be on it now—and big," said the reporter. "I'm going straight to the dark room and develop this film. If it turns out okay, we'll put it on the cable to the network for the six-thirty news. The world will get it tomorrow."

Only then did Jethro remember that he was supposed to be in Chicago, but it was too late to change things now. He could only hope that, when she looked at the news tonight, as she always did, Sarah wouldn't realize where the film had been made.

ii

With five Vibrassage chairs, two Pedassage units and one portable vibrator sold that morning, Alice Perrault had been very busy until the advent of Caleb Downs. When the stretcher carrying him to the aid station was out of sight, she sank into one of the chairs, filled with relief that he hadn't died right there, but still torn by fear of what he might do to her and the company with a suit for damages, if he lived.

"You look like you need a drink, young lady," a male voice said from the entrance to the booth.

Alice looked up to see a plump man with thinning hair, horn-rimmed glasses and wise eyes standing there. The green border on his convention badge told her he was a doctor and she remembered seeing him in one of the exhibits farther down the aisle.

"You don't happen to have anything on you, do you, Doc?" she asked.

"Better than that, I know where we can have one in comfort. I'm Dr. Alex Klein, by the way."

"I certainly need a doctor—to examine my head." Alice swung her legs over the side of the chair and sat up. "The company warned us about diathermy machines turning off pacemakers. But I was so busy giving the sales pitch, I forgot all about it."

"I doubt that you'd do much business if you stopped to warn everybody who sits in one of those chairs that it may stop his heart," said Klein. "As Dr. Forbes said just now, being a layman, Downs wouldn't have known about it anyway. But neither would the average doctor, for that matter."

"What kind of a doctor did you say you were?" Alice asked.

"A psychiatrist."

"I went to one years ago." Alice was examining her lipstick in the mirror of her compact. "But he didn't help me."

"My exhibit is just down the aisle a few spaces, so I've been watching the way you sell these gadgets," said Klein. "I've got to admit that I've never seen a more concentrated exhibition of sex appeal than you've been putting on— outside of a brothel."

"I'm not sure I like that remark," said Alice doubtfully.

"It's meant to be a real compliment, Miss Perrault. The restaurant at the other end of the building ought to be open about now. Shall we go down and discuss the question further over a drink and lunch?"

Alice didn't waste time in debate. The pick-me-up she'd

had with breakfast had worn off already, so her vigor had begun to sag, even before the Downs episode. And if anything about her sagged very much, she knew from experience that her sales approach would soon begin to suffer.

"Take over, Asa, will you?" she said to the man from the local Vibrassage agency, who was helping her in the booth. "I'll be back in a little while."

"What'll you have?" Dr. Klein asked when they found a small booth in the restaurant, which was already beginning to fill up with prelunch drinkers.

"A bloody mary. Double the gin."

"Make mine Bourbon on the rocks, please, waiter."

"What are you selling anyway, Dr. Klein?" Alice asked while they were waiting for the drinks.

"Nothing—just saluting a stellar performance—"

"Are you implying that Vibrassage is a fake?" Alice demanded somewhat indignantly.

"On the contrary, a half hour on one of those can make even a tired and waning male raring to go."

Alice couldn't help laughing. "I'll have to use that in my sales pitch. Are you perhaps waning, Dr. Klein?"

"Only a little, about normal for a man of fifty who's naturally lethargic in temperament." Alex Klein grinned. "I have three children, Miss Perrault, and a wife ten years younger than I am and still sexually active. In other words, the best of all possible worlds."

"Then why did you—?"

"Pick you up?"

"Well, yes."

"I like watching an expert do his—or her, in this case— thing. How long did it take you to discover that the way to sell the Vibrassage unit is to make the sucker—the possible buyer—fancy that he's buying YOU. Or at least some further attention from you into the bargain?"

"You're all right, Doctor." Alice laughed. "I'll take back anything I said against you or the other shrinks."

"I'm still curious to know how you worked out that technique."

"Let me see, it must have been four, maybe five years ago—when miniskirts first came out."

"They do make a difference, especially when teamed with the superb equipment nature endowed you with."

Alice finished the bloody mary, considered ordering another but reluctantly decided against it and settled for a bacon-lettuce-and-tomato sandwich. On an empty stomach, two doubles might work too fast. Besides, the whole convention would be breaking for lunch in another hour with potential clients by the score surging through the aisle to examine the exhibits, and in her case the exhibitor, too, so it wouldn't do to get loaded.

"I guess my sales pitch *is* pretty stimulating," Alice admitted with some modesty.

"*Very* stimulating," Alex Klein assured her.

"Is your wife here with you?" Alice still wasn't sure the psychiatrist was as innocent in his intentions as he claimed to be.

"I live in Central City and spend my days listening to the troubled love lives of my patients, Miss Perrault. There's very little room for dalliance in my life."

"Tell me something," said Alice. "This equipment you were speaking of just now, if it's so superb, why doesn't it work?"

"But it does. I'm sure your sales record proves that."

"I'm not talking about the men. They all want the same thing."

"I'm afraid it's the nature of the beast."

"I don't blame them, Doc. After all if I enjoyed—" She stopped, leaving the sentence unfinished.

"What were you going to say?"

"Nothing."

"I take it you don't enjoy sex with men?"

"This isn't your office, Doctor. And if you're implying that I'm a dike—"

"Believe me, Miss Perrault, it would be a shame to waste such superb equipment on anything less than heterosexual activities. If I have offended you, I apologize."

"I guess it comes natural for you to ask a lot of questions," said Alice. "And I'd be a fool not to take free advice from an expert."

"I won't send you a bill," Alex Klein assured her. "And I'll be glad to help you with any problems—"

"The trouble is that no matter how hard I try to reach the top of the mountain, I never can."

"Do you mean you've never achieved orgasm?"

"Oh, I made it plenty of times when I was a teen-ager. I grew up in a West Virginia coal mining town and if a girl hadn't made it with a fellow by the time she was thirteen, she felt something was wrong with her. There certainly wasn't anything wrong with me then."

"And afterward?"

"Everything was fine until one day my daddy caught me naked in the bed with this fellow I was going with. He'd come home unexpectedly, there was an accident at the mine or something and Daddy's shift got off work early. Jimmy hightailed it out the back window—bare-assed—but there I was."

"What happened?"

"Daddy raped me, that's what. Gave it to me proper."

"And that was the last time you made the grade?"

She turned on him suddenly, her eyes wide with surprise. "How did you know?"

"A lot of women are locked up in mental institutions because of just what happened to you, Miss Perrault. Still more go through life always trying to make the grade, like you."

Alice looked as if she was going to be sick. "I—I need another drink."

Alex Klein signaled to a passing waitress. "Another bloody mary for the lady, please. Nothing for me."

"You're putting me on, aren't you, Doc?" Alice managed to ask after the drink had calmed her somewhat.

"I'm giving you free what most of my patients pay twenty-five dollars an hour to hear, Miss Perrault."

"Why?"

"Maybe I'm just feeling generous. Or again it could be that I enjoy seeing an artist at work sucking some stuffed shirts into buying something they don't really need, and feel an obligation to repay you."

"You're a weirdo, Doc," said Alice. "But a nice one. In a way I'm sorry you're so happily married."

Alex Klein chuckled. "You just paid my fee, Alice, so I'll tell you a few more things about yourself—if you're sure you want to hear them."

"Fire away, Doc."

"I imagine you went to church when you were a little girl—?"

"Pentecostal Holiness. Daddy said our immortal souls would burn in Hell if we didn't go every Sunday—twice. But what's that got to do with—?"

"When your father raped you, your subconscious mind rejected the truth that you enjoyed it because deep down inside you was the conviction that incest was a mortal sin. So ever since you can't reach the top of that mountain because your unconscious mind is afraid the man who's with you at the time may turn out to be your father again."

"But Daddy's dead."

"Not in your mind. He's just the way he was that day."

"If you know so much about me, tell me why I can't seem to stay away from men."

"That's typical, too. You're always hoping that next time you'll bingo."

"So what does that make me—a nympho?"

"No. What's happened in your case seems to be that you have channeled much of your libido drive into becoming a very successful saleswoman for Vibrassage."

"The *most* successful," she corrected him. "Not even the men can top my record."

"Congratulations!' said Alex Klein. "Not only do you make your employers at Vibrassage happy but a considerable portion of the male population, too."

"What about me?"

"In a way I'd say you're following the Golden Rule, Alice. You do unto others as you would have them do unto you."

iii

Caleb Downs had recovered consciousness by the time the stretcher reached the first aid station.

"Think you can make it without oxygen, now, Mr. Downs?" Dr. Singh asked as they were transferring him to an examining table.

"I'm sure I can."

"You had a close shave back there," said Singh as he was putting the tank back into a rack against the wall.

"The last thing I remember is lying on one of those vibrating couches. What happened after that?"

"You do have a pacemaker, don't you?"

"Yes. Did it stop?"

Singh nodded. "They have a new gadget on some of those chairs now, a diathermy attachment. When your pacemaker was put out of action by the microwaves of the diathermy, it failed to respond to demand and your pulse rate dropped to less than thirty. You went out, as you say here in America, like a light."

"How did you start it again?"

"I didn't," Singh admitted. "Fortunately for you, a Dr. Forbes happened to be in another chair. He knew the surgical instrument exhibit across the aisle contained a large magnet and used it to restart the pacemaker. If he hadn't moved fast, you might never be conscious again.

"I'll call the University Hospital and have you admitted for a routine check." Singh moved toward a wall telephone and reached for the receiver. "The battery in your pacemaker may be running down."

"My heart specialist put in a new one only a few months ago," said Caleb. "It wasn't really the pacemaker's fault, was it?"

"No. Even a new one could have been stopped by the diathermy machine."

"Then what's to be gained by admitting me to the hospital?"

"It's only for your own protection, Mr. Downs."

"Don't get the idea that I'm ungrateful, Doctor, but I've had enough of hospitals, with my coronary and then the operation to put in the pacemaker. I'll be all right."

Singh shrugged and hung up the phone. "It's your decision, Mr. Downs. But you'll have to sign a routine outpatient release."

"Gladly."

"And I must insist that you lie here for another half hour with the magnet nearby, just in case."

"I've been drawing beer at our exhibit for the last several hours," said Caleb. "I can certainly use the rest."

"I had one of your beers as I was coming on duty," said Singh. "An excellent brew."

"We serve only the best. Our medical convention exhibits have featured it for years."

"This is my first experience with one of the Central Medical Association conventions since I came here two years ago from India for my residency in medicine," said Singh. "I find it most interesting."

"Did you get any samples of our products—besides the beer, I mean? We don't produce that."

"I was in a hurry this morning so I didn't stop."

"Give me your name and address and I'll see that you're placed on our mailing list," Caleb told him. "It's the very least I can do to show my appreciation."

The Indian physician wrote briefly on a prescription blank, tore out the slip of paper and gave it to Caleb, who put it in his wallet. He was pleased to discover that the three small tablets of aconite he carried in his pocket— the main reason why he hadn't wanted to go to the hospital —had not been disturbed.

"What kind of pharmaceuticals do you manufacture, Mr. Downs?" Singh asked.

"The usual line, both ethical and proprietary. My factory is in Oklahoma."

"I have just come from the autopsy of an interesting case, a man poisoned by aconite."

"By what?" Caleb caught himself in time to control his voice.

"Aconite."

Caleb pretended ignorance, though his pulse had jumped at least ten points, he was sure, when Singh mentioned the drug.

"I can tell you one thing," he said. "We don't manufacture that."

Singh laughed. "Few people do any more—except in Nepal from whence I come. There it is the main ingredient of a poison called bikh."

"You must know a lot about pharmacology, to recognize something as obscure as that."

"Not really. It's just that in Nepal we still grow the most potent form of the plant that produces aconite. It has been used there for ages as an agent of assassination."

"It all sounds like an oriental whodunit," said Caleb. "Are you sure of your diagnosis?"

"I am but nobody else seems to believe it," Singh admitted. "That's why I must ask you to forget that I mentioned the possibility."

"Of course, Doctor. Did they do a post-mortem?"

"Dr. Huxtable just finished. I was called from the autopsy room to the aid station here, when you became unconscious."

"And they found the poison in the man's body?"

"Dr. Huxtable and Dr. Thomas, the professor of pharmacology, will be making further tests but all of them will probably be fruitless. You see aconite is not only one of the most sophisticated and powerful poisons in existence— except perhaps the toxin produced by the *bacillus botulinus*—it is also very difficult to discover in the body. The drug is fixed in the tissues very, very quickly and affects the centers of the brain controlling the heart and respiration."

"Incredible."

"I'm afraid the rest of those present found it so, too," Singh admitted wryly. "Particularly the police lieutenant who is investigating the case."

"You mean the police are in on it already?" Caleb was careful to keep his voice casual but his mind was far from it, as he evaluated what he had heard and what danger of detection and prosecution it might hold for him.

"Dr. Huxtable of our pathology faculty is also the Medical Examiner for the county," Singh explained. "When I made a clinical diagnosis of poisoning by aconite before the post-mortem was performed, Dr. Huxtable called the police. A Lieutenant Klinger was present at the autopsy. Also an agent from the FBI."

"Then the patient must have been Senator Spurgess."

Singh looked disturbed. "I have said too much—"

"You can trust me, Dr. Singh," said Caleb quickly. "I won't say a word to anybody."

It was a stroke of ill fortune, indeed, Caleb thought, that after he'd managed to create the perfect situation to get rid of Cary Poston, another man had been felled in his place. And an even worse piece of luck that someone as knowledgeable concerning the effects of aconite as Dr. Singh was had been around.

Momentarily Caleb considered the advisability of getting rid of the Indian doctor, but decided against it. The occurrence so close together of two failures of the heart in apparently healthy men could lead to a closer examination of the post-mortem findings than was likely to occur in what seemed to be a simple case of sudden cessation of the heartbeat, a by no means uncommon occurrence under natural circumstances. Besides, if neither the police nor the Medical Examiner accepted the startling diagnosis made by Dr. Singh, it seemed very unlikely indeed that any possible suspicion could fall on Caleb himself.

Singh's identification of the poison that had killed Spurgess meant that he would have to change his plans somewhat, of course. But then he had purposely kept them fluid against just such an eventuality. Any attempt to kill Marian Crowder would have to be postponed, too, at least until near the end of the convention—unless he were lucky enough to come upon her and Cary Poston under circumstances that allowed him to strike them both down at once.

iv

In the Civic Center Restaurant Caleb Downs ordered scotch and water and sat drinking it slowly, while his small steak and salad were being prepared. When they came, he ate slowly and with relish.

The more he thought about it, the more pleased he was with the events of the morning. Although he hadn't planned it that way, he could feel a distinct satisfaction in having removed Senator Spurgess from the national scene. Spurgess' staff, particularly Hal Stimson, were known to be very thorough in their investigation of people scheduled to testify before the Senate Medical Subcommittee. And if they had dug far into his own dossier, it might have been embarrassing to explain why he'd changed names after flunking out of Johns Hopkins, to say nothing of the relative uselessness of some of the drugs Central Pharmaceutical sold most widely, and a profit on new combinations that sometimes went as high as a thousand per cent.

Having finished lunch, Caleb was enjoying a cup of coffee when a small man with snapping dark eyes slipped into the seat across from him.

"Lieutenant Klinger of the Central City Police, Mr. Downs," said the visitor. "Mind if I talk to you a moment?"

"Not at all, Lieutenant. Can I offer you a drink—or something?"

"No thanks," said Klinger. "They took out half of my stomach with an ulcer here at University Hospital a couple of years ago. Since then it's no alcohol for me."

"What can I do for you?"

"I hear you had a close shave this morning, Mr. Downs," said the lieutenant.

"They tell me that if a Dr. Forbes hadn't recognized what happened to my pacemaker, I would probably have been stopped permanently," Caleb admitted.

"I saw a special broadcast about it on one of the TV

monitors as I came through the exhibit hall," said Klinger. "It was very impressive."

"I must find Dr. Forbes and thank him for restarting my pacemaker. They hustled me away from the Vibrassage booth to the aid station so fast I didn't have time to do it before."

"Dr. Cary Poston tells me he and Senator Spurgess enjoyed some beer from your exhibit shortly before the Senator suffered the heart attack."

"They could have. We were filling cups as fast as we could during the break after Spurgess' speech. I even had to pitch in and—" He stopped suddenly in pretended surprise. "Surely you don't think there could be any connection?"

"We're checking everything," said Klinger. "After all, Senator Spurgess was an important public figure."

"I thought the Senator died from a heart attack."

"The Medical Examiner hasn't given me a final diagnosis of the cause of death, Mr. Downs. I'm merely rounding up some loose ends before the case can be marked closed."

"You're welcome to inspect our booth if you like," said Caleb. "But if anything was wrong with that beer, half the doctors on the exhibit floor would have been laid out by now, plus a lot of the exhibitors."

"Your beer seems to be okay, Mr. Downs. I was just by the exhibit, and one of your salesmen remembered seeing Dr. Poston in the line. He said they were drawing from about the middle of a keg then, so a lot of people who were served from that same tap are still alive."

"That would seem to put us in the clear, wouldn't it?"

"Unless some other evidence turns up," said Klinger. "And I see no signs of that."

"I'll be here all week," Caleb assured him. "You can find me at our booth or at the Regency House, where I'm staying."

"We appreciate your cooperation, Mr. Downs." Lieutenant Klinger got to his feet. "Good day."

CHAPTER XIII

It was one-thirty when Marian Crowder moved to the podium to give the address at the annual luncheon of the Women's Auxiliary to the Central Medical Association. The tables were packed in all the way to the back of the long room and, as Marian looked down the triple rows of women now, she considered how to shatter their sleek assurance that they dwelt in the best of all possible worlds.

"Most of you, I am sure, are convinced that you already possess the new freedom for which so many other women are fighting," she began. "Just as you are quite certain that you need have no fear of ever having to worry about equal job opportunities, equal intellectual opportunities and, above all, financial security.

"Well, I've got news for you ladies. Of all social groups, medical marriages rank next in divorce rates below those of actors and actresses. I don't need to tell you what that means but what deserves even more concern from you: Among marriages which have lasted twenty to twenty-five years, as many of yours have, divorce rates are up to twenty-five per cent. Where marriages have lasted twenty-five to twenty-nine years, divorce rates are up thirty-six per cent. And when the census takers come around every ten years, the listing 'Spouse not living in the domicile' is higher for medical families than any others. Which simply means that as high as divorce rates are in the medical community, even more couples choose not to be divorced but to live apart for reasons of taxation and the effect upon their husbands' positions."

Here and there in the small sea of faces before her Marian saw a look of shock and surprise where her thrust had found a tender spot, a chink in the armor of wealth and assurance which so many of the audience put on to protect themselves from facing the truth.

"Today," she continued, "I want to ask you a pertinent question that will tell a lot about whether you are the fortunate group you fancy yourself to be—if you answer it honestly. Or whether you shouldn't be called sexual slaves in a very high white-collar neighborhood, just as much as the woman who obviously does slave in a blue-collar area, living in a walk-up flat and doing her best to make a husband's wages support eight children."

From a folder she took a reprint made up of several pages and held it up for all to see.

"We are attending a medical convention and your husbands are busy listening to scientific papers. So if you are as integral a part of this best of all worlds as you think you are, why shouldn't you listen to a scientific paper too? Here is a reprint of an article from the *American Journal of Psychiatry*. It is the text of a paper presented at a meeting of the prestigious American Psychiatric Association, to which, I am sure, some of your husbands belong. The report comes, furthermore, from one of the most famous and respected private institutions for the care of the mentally ill in the United States.

"The title is 'Psychiatric Conditions in the Physician's Wife,' and the report covers fifty cases. But it could just as well have been five hundred, since it represents a cross section of the medical population of any large American community. I will hold it up so those at the front can read the title."

When she held up the reprint, several women at the front row of tables just before the platform stood up to read it better, while a murmur of displeasure swept over the room.

"I am not surprised that you are startled and shocked," said Marian. "As you sit here, I am sure you can think of many women you have known at other CMA conventions who are no longer here—although their husbands are. Who no longer can be members of your Auxiliary, because they are no longer the legal wives of doctor-husbands.

"Let me read you a list of the reasons the women described in this report wound up in a psychiatric clinic: Only nine out of the fifty, less than one in five, stated that they experienced frequent and mutually satisfactory sex relations. Which means that only one in five, who sought psychiatric help, were sexually emancipated to the point where they enjoyed sex with their husbands—or lovers—unreservedly, as it should be enjoyed by the happily married woman. The other four were sexual slaves, except those who had been released from bondage when their husbands found willing—all too willing, in fact, as many of you can testify—nurses, technicians and other women on the make with which the average hospital population virtually teems."

Marian paused again so the full impact of her words could be felt by the audience. Many more faces were shocked and fearful than before and, certain now that she had really shaken them up, she moved on to twist the probing scalpel.

"Make no mistake about it: Plenty of other women envy you your social position, your Cadillacs, your luxuries, your lovely homes in the finest part of town. They stand ready to move into the favored places from which, before the year is out, some of you will be uprooted by divorce or by separation.

"Since this is a medical report, we must identify the cause of the 'Doctors' Wives Disease' that brought these fifty unhappy women, and will bring hundreds of others every year, to the point where they needed help so badly that they had to be hospitalized, often to save their lives. Here are the major symptoms:

"Anxiety and muscle spasms. Sound familiar?" Marian asked. "Psychiatrists in several large university hospitals have found that a large part of the young women who come to them for emotional disorders are the wives of interns, residents—or faculty. Anatomically a direct line called the vagus nerve extends from the emotional levels of the brain to the gut. So let's hope some of you do have a spasm of the digestive tract already. It may save you from a so-called nervous breakdown and from losing your husband.

"Depression and excessive drinking. Familiar again? How many of your friends are lushes? Seven out of these fifty were really alcoholics. Even worse, twenty-two were using drugs as crutches to compensate for their unhappiness and half of those were real addicts. You need not look for drug addiction only among the young. Just run down a list of the medical marriages you know that are still functioning, at least on the surface, and you can easily spot a few."

Pausing to turn a page of the article from which she was reading, Marian looked down at the women occupying the front table and saw both fear and stubborn resentment mirrored in a dozen pair of eyes. She would make no friends here today, she realized, but was untroubled. Like a painful injection of a drug, it was a necessary treatment, if many of her listeners were to be saved even greater pain.

"I look at you and I see a group, many of whom are busily engaged in the usual activities with which bored and lonely women of the upper income and social levels try to fend off confessing their own unhappiness. You are pillars of your communities, leaders in women's activities, in promoting good schools, in your churches, in the cultural activities without which any community gradually dies. Believe me, I didn't come here to censure you, rather as a woman and a doctor I would like to help those among you in whom the symptoms of the 'Doctors' Wives Disease' are already beginning to appear, help you to see those symptoms for the deadly illness they are so you may build your own defenses before it is too late.

"I can hear you saying in your minds: 'Those fifty were the weak ones, the kind who couldn't stand up to the difficulties of being a doctor's wife.' But listen to what the author of this article says: 'Prior to illness, they had been quite successful. They were well educated and pursued a variety of intellectual and cultural activities in their leisure moments. They were able to marry men with high sociocultural standing.'

"Sound familiar? It should, for you may be looking in a mirror. Listen to this: 'As a group, they had successfully weathered the difficult years of their husbands' medical and specialty training and the early years of practice.'"

Putting down the reprint, she leaned forward and gripped the sides of the lectern.

"I won't even ask how many of you worked in those early years, how many of you were nurses, secretaries or technicians while your husbands were completing their training. You, I am sure, can take no comfort from the fact that the symptoms of incompatibility noted in three quarters of these women, particularly alcoholism and drug addiction, didn't usually develop until *after* they had raised families averaging three children. These women had already reached the peak of wifely success, measured by the common standards of social relationships. Yet, they succumbed to an amazingly common weakness, the fact that they no longer participated in their husbands' professional activities, the intimate sharing in his professional life that drew the two of them close together in the early years. No longer considering themselves necessary—except as what might be considered routine bed partners and not always that—their defenses were too fragile to protect them against the conviction of their own uselessness in a marriage gone sour.

"I don't have to tell you that success in medicine does things to a man, things that often make him difficult to live with. In the hospital and in the office, people follow a doctor's orders unquestioningly! He has but to speak and the willing slave, usually female, is quick to leap and answer his bidding How can he be treated like a god in the professional sphere and not take that expectation over into his personal life?

"How long can you continue to carry the idealized image of the enthusiastic lover, the happy partner you married, when he begins to be—in your eyes—a harried man who as often as not misses the dinner party you have worked so hard to arrange? When he has no knowledge or understanding of the cultural satisfactions that come to mean so much in your lives as you grow older? When all too often he is but a vague father figure in the eyes of your children, leaving to you the difficult tasks of discipline and guidance, sometimes even putting you in the untenable position of incurring the resentment of your own children, and alienating you from them?

"Isn't this a high price to pay for your Cadillacs, your country club memberships, your charge accounts and particularly your frustrations, when your own sexual needs are either ignored or only perfunctorily attended to? Being married to a god, you may find it difficult not to become slaves to the feeling of omnipotence so carefully encouraged in your husbands throughout that better part of their lives which exists away from you.

"It is easy then to understand why three symptoms recurred again and again in the fifty unhappy women who made up this case study. Why those same themes of depression, addiction—to drugs, alcohol or both—and somatization, a lovely medical term for vague complaints which have no discernible cause, keep popping up when doctors' wives consult physicians other than their husbands.

"Mind you, husbands are the poorest doctors for their wives to consult, according to this article. Again and again, where addiction was present, the husband's medical bag, like some malignant Pandora's box, was the source of the drugs to which they became unhappy victims.

"What then shall you do?" Marian demanded. "What else but rise up and rebel like other slaves? What else but demand your rights as individuals? As partners in marriage, not worshipers at the feet of gods? Do not be afraid of losing the cloaks that hide your slavery when, by standing forth like Spartacus, you can make your needs known, and gain your rights."

Marian sat down to perfunctory applause. She had no reason to expect wholesale approval from a group, many of whom were walking case histories of the very thing she had been describing. Before the chairman could make the usual routine words of appreciation, however, a slender young woman stood up at the back of the room.

"My husband is a resident at Cedars of Lebanon Hospital, Dr. Crowder," she said. "I would like to ask you a question, if I may."

"Of course."

"In the specific case of medical marriages, why are you knocking something you haven't tried?"

"I did try it," said Marian. "Longer ago that I am going to admit publicly, I was married to a young doctor. Just like you appear to be doing, I worked to supplement what was then a very meager income and, for a while, kidded myself into believing, as many of you have done, that I was deliriously happy. Then came the day of reckoning. Two years out of medical school, while I was teaching embryology to support us during his residency, my husband had a chance to join a large clinic, whose head also had a daughter noted for her acquisitions where young doctors were concerned. The result was that I wound up out in the cold with a divorce."

"Did the desire to get ahead of him make you the success you are?" asked the questioner.

"Partly," Marian admitted. "But don't get the idea that I'm against all medical marriages. What I do say is that a woman who marries a doctor must work doubly hard to preserve her own identity and not become the sort of slave I've been talking about. Because if you don't stand up for your rights as an individual, you're going to wind up with the short end of the stick and a good chance of succumbing to the very symptoms I've just described to you."

ii

All things considered, she'd handled the luncheon speech very well, Marian told herself, as she walked through the passage connecting the Hotel Centralia and the hospital-medical school complex joining it to the Clinic Center. Reporters from all the newspapers covering the convention, plus the wire services and TV stations, had attended the press conference that followed. Several times she had been queried as to the purported sensation her speech to the convention OB-GYN section would cause tomorrow and each time she had managed to parry the question without giving any real information, yet preserve the suspense.

After the long noonday session, followed by the press conference, Marian would have preferred resting in her room and making some additional notes for the talk she was giving to another women's group that evening. But a paper dealing with inherited defects and their control through application of some new and dramatic work in the field of genetics was scheduled for three o'clock, so she had decided to attend that session before returning to the hotel to rest.

As she came up out of the underground passage beneath Auditorium Avenue to the exhibit floor of the convention, she saw Cary Poston moving along the corridor ahead and called to him to wait. When she caught up to him, she saw that his face was troubled.

"Anything wrong?" she asked.

"A lot. Where are you headed?"

"The OB-GYN section. A paper I want to hear is scheduled for three o'clock."

"I'm going to the CMA office to meet Hal Stimson and drive him to the airport." He looked at his watch. "We've got a half hour. Mind giving me some advice?"

"Not at all."

"Let's go up to the second floor lounge. We can talk there."

"The TV stations have offered a spot on the six o'clock broadcast for the Association to answer Spurgess' charges," said Cary, when they were seated in a comfortable corner of the lounge.

"Wouldn't that be a bit callous, coming right after his death?"

"That's my feeling. I think it would be more appropriate for Edward Danton to give a full-dress refutation of most of Spurgess' charges when he made his acceptance speech on Thursday morn—"

"Is Dr. Danton that confident of being elected?"

"Nobody doubts that he will be. The most we ever really hoped to do was force a change in Association policies, particularly a more enlightened approach to the question of how best to supply medical care for everybody. But after the diatribe Spurgess delivered this morning, the membership is angry enough to vote for the most conservative man who's nominated."

"Meaning Danton?"

"Who else? Doubtless much of what Spurgess said won't hold water, but like you say, it strikes me as being a little callous to call a man a liar publicly only a few hours after he's dead, no matter what he said about you."

"A lot of what Senator Spurgess said it true," she reminded him. "If organized medicine hadn't sat on its hands for the past twenty or thirty years where social reform was concerned, its back wouldn't be against the wall the way it is now."

"I know," Cary agreed. "Personally I'd like to see the CMA concentrate on remedying some of the deficiencies and the shortsighted policies Spurgess emphasized, but right now the consensus among the Establishment is to use the negative approach."

"Such as?"

"Spurgess charged that the medical profession has always opposed health insurance, which isn't true. The AMA merely insisted that insurance plans should not deprive a patient of the right to choose his own doctor. I suspect one reason why Spurgess attacked us today is because the government's own study shows that the AMA's Medicredit plan for total health care would run about a hundred and nine billion dollars a year by 1974, which is five billion or so less than the cost with the bill Spurgess introduced for full government control. Medicredit relies largely on voluntary private health insurance while Spurgess' plan makes the federal government responsible for everything."

"I remember reading that in one of the medical news magazines," said Marian. "But what struck me most was

171

the fact that the country will be spending close to a hundred billion a year on medical care by then anyway, even without a national plan."

"It's largely a matter of efficiency," Cary admitted. "The same issue of *The New York Times* Spurgess mentioned this morning quotes one clinic director saying the public now gets about fifty cents' worth of health care for each dollar spent, when, if the money were spent efficiently, they'd get eighty cents' worth. What it comes down to is that with the right kind of organization, the public could have complete care and still preserve the independence of doctors, patients and hospitals, with only a little more out of pocket spending than is happening now."

"I'm on the Admissions Committee at Hopkins," said Marian, "so I know personally that what he said about the medical profession fighting against expanding medical school facilities isn't true. Neither are his charges that blacks are denied admission."

"Most of his speech was just a political ploy designed to make headlines and gain votes," said Cary. "Actually there were eighty-six medical schools in 1961 and one hundred and three ten years later, with more opening up every year."

"You've got plenty of ammunition to refute most of his charges," Marian agreed. "But it's still too soon to attack a dead man."

"There's another factor," said Cary soberly. "Spurgess may have been murdered."

"But that's fantastic!"

"Exactly what I said at first. But one of our residents from India, Dr. Singh, was in charge of the aid station here in the Auditorium this morning. He comes from Nepal where aconite is often used in assassination and he's convinced that it caused Spurgess' death.

"I don't even remember much about aconite, except that it's a powerful heart drug and isn't used any more," Marian admitted, "How could such a thing happen?"

Cary gave her a quick summary of the events of the morning, culminating in the autopsy and Singh's insistence that the Senator had died of aconite poisoning, even though it had not been possible to demonstrate the drug in his body.

"The whole thing is utterly unbelievable," said Marian when he finished the account.

"Ordinarily I would respect any diagnosis Singh made but this time I had to go along with Kendall Thomas and Andy Huxtable—until I thought of getting the cups we drank from."

"That must have been like looking for a needle in a haystack?"

"Fortunately I remembered the location of the waste container we both tossed our cups into. A dozen were in the container and we took all of them to Kendall Thomas' laboratory. Aconite is highly soluble in alcohol—that's how the tincture that was a standard preparation in pharmacology years ago is made. We washed all the cups carefully with alcohol and then tested the solution."

"And found aconite?"

"The test was equivocal so now we have to assume that Spurgess was poisoned until we have positive proof that he wasn't."

"But how can you do that?"

"Kendall Thomas, our pharmacologist, is using a vacuum to evaporate off the alcohol that was used to wash out the cups because boiling might destroy the drug. If any residue remains after evaporation, he will dissolve it in a little alcohol and test again. It may be as late as midnight before we get a final report, though. Evaporation in a vacuum is a slow process."

"Will you let me know what you find as soon as the test is finished?"

"If that's what you want, but it may be late."

"I still want to know."

"Mind telling me why?"

"I don't know the answer to that myself, but something about this whole thing bothers me. Maybe it's just feminine intuition, but I want to know just the same."

"I'll call," he promised. "Or better still, I'll bring you the message myself, if you wish."

"Please do," she said. "I should be back from the sorority dinner I'm addressing tonight by ten-thirty or so."

iii

At the Central City Airport, Cary Poston and Hal Stimson stood with Agent Harvey Lawson of the Central City FBI, watching Senator Frank Spurgess' body in a plain shipping casket being loaded into the baggage compartment of a Boeing 737.

"I get the shakes when I think that just this morning we were in Washington and less than twelve hours later Frank is dead," said Stimson.

"It's like a bad dream," Cary agreed.

"Doesn't working in such close contact with death get to you sometimes, Cary?"

"In my field, we can usually see it coming—except with sudden heart attacks, of course."

"Are you convinced that the Senator died from heart involvement, Dr. Poston?" the FBI agent asked.

"Heart failure was what killed him—or rather heart arrest. The question is, what caused it?"

"I get the impression that you're leaning toward Dr. Singh's diagnosis, Cary," said Stimson. "Is that true?"

"Reluctantly, yes."

"Which means that some doctor at the convention is the murderer," said Lawson.

"Not necessarily," said Cary. "Senator Spurgess shot from the hip a lot and doctors weren't his only targets."

"Plenty of drug people are at the convention, too," said Stimson. "We were going after them next week and some of the stuff we've already dug up could put a few of the worst offenders behind bars."

"When you start making accusations, Hal, don't forget to give doctors credit for trying to help their patients even though they may prescribe a useless drug occasionally. We're not all charlatans, even if your former employer did try his best to smear us all with the same tar brush. Most doctors are dedicated men who have spent a considerable part of their lives preparing themselves for a very exacting job and as such they're just as worthy of their hire as any other profession. On the whole they don't make any more money, in proportion to what they've spent getting ready for their jobs than lawyers like you."

"What are you going to do if the solution Dr. Thomas is evaporating turns out to be loaded with that Nepalese drug—what was the name again?"

"Bikh?"

"Yes."

"The matter will be out of my hands, then," said Cary. "The Medical Examiner is required to report his findings concerning the cause of death and once that's done, it will be up to Lieutenant Klinger and Mr. Lawson here."

"Lieutenant Klinger and I are already acting upon the assumption that Senator Spurgess was poisoned," said the FBI man quietly. "And that the poison was really intended for you, Dr. Poston."

Cary gave him a startled look. "Whatever gave you that idea?"

"When you examine everything that happened this morning, you can hardly arrive at any other conclusion, Doctor."

"I certainly don't see it," said Hal Stimson.

"Nor I," said Cary. "Why would anybody want to kill me?"

"We haven't been able to answer that question yet," the FBI man admitted. "But it could be a paranoid former patient."

"That's as fantastic as thinking the poison was intended for Cary," Hal Stimson protested.

"No it isn't, Hal," said Cary soberly. "Someone whose wife or close relative died from heart disease could conceivably hold me responsible; it's a chance every doctor takes. In fact, a fraternity brother of mine was shot last year in his office by a former patient. My friend was a plastic surgeon and the murderer claimed he could have made him sexually adequate and didn't."

"This whole thing is beginning to sound more and more like a bad dream," Hal Stimson admitted. "Would you mind telling me how you and Lieutenant Klinger reached the conclusion that the poison wasn't really intended for Senator Spurgess, Mr. Lawson?"

"In the first place," said the FBI agent, "if aconite was really used as the death agent, the murderer must have made elaborate preparations beforehand in order to have such a powerful preparation of the drug available when he needed it. And in the second place, he would have had to know in advance both that Senator Spurgess would drink the beer and the route he would follow when he left the Auditorium."

"Actually the route was changed just before Spurgess went into the theater," said Cary. "When he saw how many people were going to be pouring out of that theater right after Spurgess finished speaking, the captain of the Civic Center security force decided that the Senator should leave by the rear loading ramp."

"The murderer would have had no way of knowing either the route Senator Spurgess and Dr. Poston were going to follow or that they would stop for a cup of beer," said Lawson. "So the only logical explanation is that he was following Dr. Poston, watching for an opportunity to poison him."

"And with plenty of opportunities," said Cary. "The chairman of the Arrangements Committee has to be on the run all the time and I often grab a bite and a drink wherever I find them."

"But how did the poison get into Frank Spurgess' cup— if it was intended for you, Cary?" Hal Stimson asked.

Harvey Lawson answered. "With a crowd jamming the exhibit floor, the murderer could easily have been jostled, as he was dropping the aconite into Dr. Poston's cup, causing him to miss."

"You're overlooking one other possibility," said Hal Stimson. "If the murderer is a doctor or someone connected with the pharmaceutical industry, he might have seen the opportunity to get rid of Senator Spurgess and taken it."

"That could have happened," Lawson conceded.

On the tarmac outside the boarding lounge, the coffin had been lifted into the baggage compartment of the airplane and the agent at the desk announced that the flight was now ready for departure.

"Thanks for your help." Hal Stimson shook hands with Cary and the FBI agent. "I'm sorry things turned out the way they did but I imagine a few of your members may be happy about the whole thing, Cary."

"Senator Spurgess would never have believed it, Hal, but most doctors would rather see even a critic alive than not," said Cary. "Every time we lose a patient, we've also lost a battle."

"Will you call me as soon as Dr. Huxtable makes a final diagnosis as to the cause of death?"

"Immediately," Cary promised. "Do you want the announcement to come from your office in Washington?"

"I think it had better, if Mr. Lawson doesn't object."

"We'd like to hold off announcing any diagnosis except heart stoppage for a few days, Mr. Stimson," said Lawson. "If the Senator was really killed accidentally while the murderer was trying to get Dr. Poston, he may become bold and try again."

"I guess you know what that makes you, Cary," said Hal.

"Yeah. A sitting duck."

CHAPTER XIV

The weather had changed to a fine drizzle when Carlota reported for work in the Polo Lounge at four. Shortly after five, George, the head bartender, called her to the phone.

"Sis?"

"Yes, Raul,"

"I'm h-home s-safe." He always stuttered a little when he was excited.

"What do you mean?"

"The doctors at the Induction Center turned me down."

"But how? Why?" Carlota was so relieved that she could hardly talk intelligibly.

"When I went in for the examination I could feel my heart pounding like it was going to jump right out of my throat. I guess my blood pressure was up, too; the guy taking it said he couldn't even get it on the machine."

"Tell me everything that happened," she urged.

"First they asked me whether we ever had any insanity in the family and I told them about Uncle Pancho Montez down in Mexico."

"What about Uncle Pancho?"

"You know—how he shot up a whole town."

"Uncle Pancho was drunk, Raul. He always shot up places when he was drunk."

"I figured what they didn't know wouldn't hurt 'em— or me. Then I told them about Aunt Elena."

"What about her?"

"After Uncle Rafael died, she shut herself up in the house and never came out again."

"And they turned you down on that?"

"I guess my blood pressure had something to do with it, too—that and the way my heart was skipping. They had me lie down a couple of hours and gave me a white tablet, but it didn't make any difference."

"You know it always skips when you're excited."

"What do you think I was today? Here I am stark naked with people punching me and sticking needles in me from all sides."

"Are you sure they really turned you down?"

"I got a paper to prove it. The major that gave it to me said go on back to school and forget about the draft. They can't do anything to me any more."

"Thank God!" said Carlota. "I've been praying to the Holy Mother all day that they wouldn't take you."

178

"She came through, Sis. I gotta run now. Don't expect me home 'til late. I'll be celebrating."

"Raul, be careful."

The phone clicked in Carlota's ear and she put it back upon its cradle. Then in sheer reaction to the sudden release of the tension she'd been under since yesterday, she began to laugh uncontrollably.

"You all right, Carlota?" the bartender asked.

"My brother phoned to say he was turned down by the draft. I guess I'm having hysterics."

"That really is something to celebrate. Why don't you take a break?"

"I do need time to get hold of myself, George. Besides, I've got to do something."

"Take a half hour. If anybody asks for you I'll tell 'em you weren't feeling well and went to get an aspirin."

Carlota was glad she hadn't given Raul the hundred dollars yet; in his excitement over having been turned down by the draft he might have spent it celebrating with his girl. But, now that she didn't need the money after all, it had to be returned to Dr. Paul Rice at once.

At this time of the afternoon he would probably still be at the medical meeting, she decided, so she could probably open the door of his room, drop the bills on the top of the dresser and get away without being seen.

Getting into Paul Rice's room posed no particular problem for her, familiar as she was with the housekeeping function in the great hotel. The maids on each floor had to have passkeys in order to make up the rooms but that work was finished before they went off duty at three o'clock. The keys wouldn't be needed again until the night maid went around turning down the beds, so they were left hanging on a hook in the floor utility room.

Getting the light poplin raincoat she'd worn to work from her locker in the basement, Carlota slipped it on to hide the distinctive uniform of the Polo Lounge waitresses and minimize the chance of recognition on the way to Paul Rice's room. Taking the service elevator, she quickly rose to the twelfth floor.

Only a moment was required to lift a master key from the hook in the utility room. Luck was still with her, and she reached Room 1276, which was near the elevator, without detection. There she knocked on the door, and when there was no answer, unlocked it quickly and slipped inside.

Leaving the two fifty-dollar bills on the chest of drawers, where she'd taken them from Paul Rice's wallet last night, or more correctly that same morning, Carlota had her hand on the doorknob, preparing to leave, when she heard the elevator door open in the corridor outside and quickly drew back.

Waiting for the sound of footsteps to pass the door, Carlota suddenly went rigid, when a key was inserted into the lock of 1276. With nowhere to hide, she could only stand, startled into a momentary paralysis, while the door opened and Paul Rice stepped inside.

Although obviously startled, he recovered before she did and turned to remove the key and close the door behind him. When he faced her again, he did not move away from the door.

"A little late, aren't you Miss—?"

"Montez. Carlota Montez." She found her tongue. "I—I came to bring back the hundred dollars you gave me last night."

Her words obviously surprised him.

"The two fifties are on the chest of drawers," Carlota added. "You can see for yourself."

"Did I give you the hundred?"

"I took it when I left," said Carlota. "You were asleep."

His eyes flicked to the dresser and the bills lying there, then back to her.

"Did I—?" He stopped and rubbed his eyes in a momentary gesture of uncertainty.

"Don't you remember anything?" she asked.

"Not after I came to the room and went to bed. Apparently I fell asleep."

"I tried to wake you, but I couldn't—so I left."

"I'm a very heavy sleeper," he admitted. "Please sit down, Miss Montez. It seems that we need to discuss something."

Glancing at her watch, Carlota saw that she still had twenty minutes of the half hour George had suggested—but she wasn't going to tell him that.

"I'm on duty," she said. "I only came to bring the money back."

"You're obviously a waitress in the Polo Lounge. I remember that, but not much more."

"You asked me to come to your room after midnight."

"Was a price mentioned?"

"A hundred dollars."

"At least I exercised a certain amount of discernment." His smile was wry. "But I'm afraid it wasn't very gallant of me to fall asleep. You're very pretty, Miss Montez. What surprises me is—"

"I'm not what you think," Carlota said quickly.

"No?"

"Mornings I'm a senior in college here, working for a degree in biochemistry. I only work nighttime in the Polo Lounge to pay my tuition."

"And supplement your income on the side? Or should I say on your back?"

Carlota winced. "I guess I deserved that—under the circumstances. But you're not exactly blameless, Dr. Rice."

"I suppose not," he addmitted. "Considering that I propositioned you in the first place."

"I'm not blaming you, after all, the skirts they make us wear are rather provocative. But you had another visitor last night as I was leaving, Doctor."

Paul Rice looked startled.

"It was Mrs. Danton," Carlota added pointedly.

"Did she stay after you left?"

"I guess finding me here surprised her—and made her mad, too. She apparently figured I was competition. Anyway she stalked out of here in a huff—and I followed, after taking the hundred that I needed pretty badly."

"I guess I owe you an apology, Miss Montez. Under the circumstances neither of us has a right to impugn the other's motives."

"What you do is your own business, Dr. Rice. I won't blame you if you turn me in to the hotel management."

"I haven't had much experience with call girls, Miss Montez. But I doubt very much that many of them go to the lengths you've gone to return payment, just because a service wasn't rendered."

It was Carlota's turn to smile. "I guess I'm not very good at being a call girl. But then this was my first—and last—time."

"Would you mind telling me why you made the bargain with me in the first place?"

"My brother had his physical for the draft today and he was going to Canada, if they took him. The hundred was for him."

"Yet you brought it back."

"Raul called me just now in the Polo Lounge to tell me he didn't pass the physical. I came right up to put the money back." Then her shoulders drooped. "I have to get back downstairs, Doctor. Mr. Kimball is the restaurant manager; you can call him and report me."

"I seem to have been something less than a gentleman, first in propositioning you downstairs and second in being so ungallant as to fall asleep before you got here. Please accept my apology—and this." He picked up the two fifties and held them out for her to take, but she made no move to do so.

"I don't want it, Dr. Rice," she said quickly. "And I am very grateful for your—your understanding."

He opened the door and glanced down the hall.

"The coast is clear," he reported. "You'd better run before someone comes up."

Carlota had to pass close to him as he stood back to let her out. And an impulse she couldn't have identified made her suddenly raise herself on tiptoes and kiss him on the cheek, before running for the service elevator.

ii

Alice had been almost ready to leave for the airport to meet Ted Jones, president of the Vibrassage Company, when a bellman brought a telegram from Jones saying he'd been delayed in Kansas City and wouldn't reach Central City for twenty-four and possibly forty-eight hours. In a way Jones's decision not to arrive that evening was a relief, for now she wouldn't have to face the unpleasant task of telling him her failing to remember the warning from the factory that the short-wave diathermy recently added to the regular Vibrassage line could stop a cardiac pacemaker had almost cost a potential customer his life. She would have to tell him sometime, however, so a delay of one or even two days wouldn't have been much of a help.

Alice was fortifying herself with a drink of the excellent Bourbon Ted Kraus had left in the room last night and morosely facing the decision to go down to the coffee shop for dinner alone, when the telephone rang.

"Miss Perrault?" a man's voice said.

"Yes."

"You may not remember me. This is Dr. Jethro Forbes —the one that started Dr. Downs's pacemaker this morning."

"I tried to call you earlier and thank you, Dr. Forbes," said Alice. "But you've become such a celebrity, your phone's been busy the past hour. They showed you on the six o'clock local TV news and also on Walter Cronkite."

"I know. It's all pretty embarrassing."

"You certainly deserve the recognition, Dr. Forbes. Not many people save somebody's life with a camera photographing a close-up view all the time."

"Watching myself on TV, I could almost believe the whole thing was staged."

"Believe me, it wasn't," said Alice fervently. "I still get the trembles when I think what mght have happened if you hadn't been in the next chair."

"I know its rather late," said Jethro, "but I was wondering whether you could have dinner with me this evening? Nothing formal; there's a Japanese Steak House here in Central City I like to go to when I come to the CMA conventions. If you don't have other plans, it might be sort of interesting."

"I'd love to have dinner with you, Dr. Forbes," said Alice. "My boss was supposed to be here but he wired that he couldn't make it."

"What time would suit you?" Jethro asked.

"About half an hour. I'll meet you in the lobby."

"Half an hour, then."

It was bound to be a dull evening, Alice thought as she began to dress, but she did owe the man an obligation. Momentarily, she considered pouring another drink before going down, in case the hayseed turned out to be a teetotaler, but decided against it.

It wouldn't hurt her to behave like a lady for one evening, she thought wryly. Especially when she was pretty sure Jethro Forbes wasn't the kind to expect the sort of ending she usually wound up in. Besides, after the day she'd had, going to bed before midnight would be a welcome change.

Jethro Forbes was waiting near the elevator when Alice came down. She thought he looked younger, but then things had happened so fast during the morning's episode of near disaster that he hadn't seemed much different then from the procession of men who shuffled in and out of the Vibrassage chairs, looking a little sheepish when the vibrations began to set their skins tingling.

Tonight there was a look of confidence, a strength of character in the almost Lincolnesque cragginess of Jethro's face that she hadn't noticed before, but which she liked immediately.

"Hope I didn't keep you waiting long," she said.

"I enjoy watching people's faces in hotel lobbies and trying to figure out what goes on behind them," he said as they were waiting for the doorman to get them a taxi.

"You aren't a psychiatrist by any chance?"

He laughed. "A general practitioner doesn't have time

184

for all that mumbo jumbo the psychiatrists use. He has to make his diagnosis in a hurry and hope he's right."

The taxicab came and he helped her in with an old-world sort of courtesy she hadn't experienced in a long time.

"The Japanese Steak House at Boulevard and Fifth," he told the driver.

"A doctor named Klein across from your booth and down the aisle a bit is a psychiatrist," said Jethro. "Not many people visit exhibits on mental disease—I guess they're afraid they'll recognize some of their own symptoms—so Klein and I have had a lot of time to talk."

"I know Dr. Klein but I don't particularly like him," said Alice. "He understands women too well."

Jethro laughed, a fell-bodied laugh like a man enjoying himself. "A GP has to do that, too, you know. At least three fourths of his patients are women."

"But you don't go around looking for the dirty linen in somebody's subsconscious."

"Most of the time we're too busy taking care of that sort of thing in people's conscious lives. I practiced in a small town in Kansas and I'll bet I could tell you more dirt on more people per capita there than any psychiatrist could dream of."

"You said practiced. Surely you aren't old enough to retire."

"Or rich enough, either. You might not think it to look at me, Miss Perrault, but I'm getting ready to embark on the greatest adventure of my life."

Before he could elaborate, the taxi drew up to a stop before what looked like a lovely Japanese garden, lit with the soft glow of recessed floodlights. Jethro handed her out as if she were a great lady descending from her coach.

"I discovered this place two conventions ago," he said as they followed a graveled path through the garden to the entrance of the restaurant. "It's so pretty it makes me forget about wanting to go to Japan when I was younger."

"I've always wanted to go there, too. But Mr. Jones, the

president of Vibrassage, is afraid to take the chairs to Japan. He says the Japanese will copy our machines and export them back to the U.S. cheaper than we can sell them."

"Usually I come here alone," he admitted. "But tonight I thought it would be nice to have somebody to enjoy it with, somebody nice like you."

If you only knew, Alice thought, and suddenly wanted to cry. Instead she took his arm and held on to it tightly as they crossed a delicate arching bridge leading to the pavilion in the center of the garden that housed the restaurant itself.

"I think that's the nicest thing anybody ever said to me," she said a little huskily. "Thank you, Jethro."

"This may all seem to be a little quaint to you, especially after the fancy hotels where conventions are usually held," he said. "But at least it's different."

"I know it's going to be lovely. Just seeing that garden makes the trip out here worthwhile."

"Let's have a drink first," he said, as a girl in a bright-colored kimono met them in the small lobby. "The lounge is on the other side of the dining room."

The interior of the cocktail lounge was as lovely as the surroundings outside had been—and Japanese down to tiny *bonsai* trees growing in pots there.

"I'm a Bourbon and water lover," said Jethro, when they'd found a table in the lounge and another of the kimono-clad waitresses appeared. "What would you like?"

"You just named it."

"Sarah—that's my wife—doesn't like me to drink in the house," he confessed while they were sipping an excellent Bourbon. "She's an officer in the W.C.T.U. at church and says the smell of whiskey nauseates her." He laughed again. "Won't even let it in the house, so I have to sneak mine into my workshop in the garage."

"You spoke of a great adventure just now," she reminded him. "I'm dying to hear about it."

"Later," he told her, "when I'm sure you won't laugh."

"I promise," she assured him.

"I guess having ideals sounds sort of silly nowadays, when young doctors are in such a hurry to get rich. You wouldn't think it to look at me, but I've always been sort of a romantic. When I was in medical school, everybody was reading things like De Kruif's *Microbe Hunters*."

"I remember that one. And *Not As a Stranger*—but I guess that came later."

"*Arrowsmith* and *An American Doctor's Odyssey* were two more of my favorites," he confessed. "I even used to dream of going to out-of-the way places where I could hunt down the causes of disease and destroy them the way other men did. You know, the kind of adventures Richard Halliburton wrote about."

"What happened?"

"A lot of things, most of them pretty dull." He studied his empty glass reflectively, then suddenly realized that hers was empty too. "You can tell I'm only a countryman —didn't even notice you had finished your drink. Would you like another?"

"If you would."

"One's usually my limit," he confessed. "Any more and I can't hide my breath from Sarah."

"Tonight you don't have to hide anything," she reminded him.

"In that case—" He signaled the waitress for two more drinks.

"You see what being a celebrity has done for you," Alice told him. "Already you're emancipated from the W.C.T.U."

iii

It was almost seven o'clock when Paul Rice entered the Polo Lounge and took a stool at the bar. Business was booming, the after-seven exodus to the excellent restaurants a convention-minded metropolis like Central City afforded had not yet begun.

"Good evening, Dr. Rice," said the bartender. "What can I serve you?"

"Gin and tonic," said Paul.

While he waited, he glanced around the room but didn't see Carlota anywhere.

"Don't you have a waitress named Montez?" he asked.

"We *did* have one—until an hour ago."

"What happened?"

"A guest complained to the management. Claimed she saw Carlota in another guest's room last night after midnight—a man naturally."

"Didn't Miss Montez defend herself?" Paul had a sinking feeling in the pit of his stomach.

"Why are you so interested, Doctor?"

"It appears that I was responsible," Paul admitted. "I had several drinks in here last night."

"I remember."

"I operated on a relative of Miss Montez's some time ago. She told me earlier today that she was worried about me after I left the lounge and went up to my room, when she got off duty, to see if I was all right. I was asleep, but someone must have seen her go in—or come out."

"If you'll pardon me for saying so, Doctor, that story is just screwy enough to be true," said George. "I know Carlota and I don't think she'd be in your room for any other reason. The way I heard it, though, a lady friend of yours must have come to visit you about the same time and caught Carlota in your room. When she saw Carlota working here tonight, she turned the girl in to the restaurant manager."

"When was that?"

"Hardly an hour ago."

Paul hesitated, then asked the question to which he was almost certain he already knew the answer. "Mind telling me who turned Miss Montez in?"

"It was Dr. Danton's wife. A party she was with came in about six and ordered drinks in that big booth over there in the corner. It's assigned to Carlota, and when Mrs. Danton saw her, I thought she was going to throw a fit. That was when she went to the manager and got the girl canned."

It was just the sort of thing a passionate and jealous woman like Aletha would do, Paul knew. And since he was responsible, he had to do what he could to protect the lovely girl who had risked her job to return the hundred dollars.

"Do you happen to know where Miss Montez lives, George?"

"I might." The bartender wiped a glass deliberately and put it down. "Why do you want to know, Doctor?"

"First, I'm going to try to convince the manager to take her back. Then I'm going to see her and apologize."

"In that case, it's 1410 Olivera Street."

The hotel restaurant manager was quite familiar with Paul Rice's medical reputation, as well as his being on the Arrangements Committee for the convention.

"You want me to employ Miss Montez again, is that it, Doctor?"

"Yes."

"Obviously I would accept your explanation without question—if the lady who made the complaint wasn't who she is."

"Why should that make any difference?"

"The Central Medical Association meets here annually, Dr. Rice, and next year Dr. Danton will probably be president. Under the circumstances, I can hardly afford to make an enemy of his wife by re-employing a cocktail waitress against whom she has just made a complaint, can I?"

"I suppose not."

"Nevertheless, Miss Montez is an excellent waitress. She's finishing college this year and I'd like to help her. Would it do if I let her come back to work Saturday, after the convention is over?"

"If that's all you can do, yes. But I feel badly because Miss Montez was discharged on my account."

"You have my word that she will be back on the payroll Saturday, Doctor," said the manager. "I'll have my secretary call the first thing in the morning and tell her."

"I'll tell her myself," said Paul and left the office, but

not without the conviction that the restaurant manager suspected there was a great deal more to the affair than he had admitted. Crossing the boulevard to the hospital parking lot, he got his car and headed south toward the Mexican section of Central City.

CHAPTER XV

With Daylight Saving Time, it was still not quite dark when Paul stopped his car in front of 1410 Olivera Street. The house wasn't large but both it and the garden surrounding it were well kept. Azaleas were blooming beside the walk that led from a gate in the white picket fence along the street side to the house. In front of the house were two beds of bright-colored pansies and at one end of the porch an old-fashioned wooden swing hung from its chains.

When he rang the doorbell, a tall woman with the profile of a Spanish aristocrat came to the door. The resemblance to Carlota was so marked that he didn't doubt she was the girl's mother.

"I would like to see Miss Carlota Montez, if she's home," he said.

"You're Dr. Rice, aren't you? The one who operated on Serafina?"

"Yes."

"Carlota got home a little while ago, Doctor. I'll tell her you are here."

It was nearly twenty minutes before the girl appeared. She had changed from the Polo Lounge uniform to a pale green spring dress and wore sandals now instead of boots. They made her a little shorter but even more lovely than she had been in the distinctive uniform of the cocktail waitress.

"I hope you don't mind my coming here," said Paul.

"But I thought you would like to know your job will be waiting for you again on Saturday."

The look of relief on her face was an ample reward for the drive to Olivera Street. "How did you manage it?" she asked.

"George told me what happened and this was the least I could do after you lost your job because of me. When I explained to Mr. Kimball that you felt responsible for me because of Serafina and came up to my room to see about me after you got off last night, because I appeared to have had too much to drink, he took my word."

Carlota smiled. "You're a remarkably persuasive man, Dr. Rice. I'm glad now that you didn't wake up last night."

"Have you had dinner yet?"

"No. I just got home."

"I hope my powers of persuasion are strong enough to convince you to have dinner with me."

She laughed. "If they weren't, my appetite would be. The news you brought me has made me very hungry."

"Where shall we go?"

"Some cousins of mine own a small restaurant on the river bank. We can go there."

"I noticed on your file in the hotel that you spell your first name with only one 't,' " he said as he started the car.

"I was named for Maximilian's Empress," she explained. "Grandmother always claimed Great-grandfather was a duke or something in the Emperor's court, but people usually like to think their ancestors were considerably more important than they really were. My sociology professor says it's a way of building self-esteem."

"Are you majoring in sociology?"

"I'm only taking it as a minor, my major is biochemistry. When I finish college next spring, I hope to get a grant to go on for a master's—and maybe a Doctorate. I've been offered a research position in Dr. Neighbors' laboratory at the medical school."

"His work on hormonal chemistry promises to be very important in medicine."

She nodded. "I'm doing my senior thesis in that field,

and plan to keep on with it, while I work in Dr. Neighbors' lab to pay my tuition in graduate school."

"Girls as lovely as you are don't always have that much ambition."

"When you're a Chicano, you learn early that if you're going to get anywhere in the world, you've got to lift yourself by your bootstraps, Dr. Rice."

"Please call me Paul."

She smiled. "All right. I hope you like Mexican food."

"Even the pepper, I've got a cast-iron stomach."

"I thought ulcers were an occupational disease with surgeons."

"Only successful ones. I'm a teacher, which puts me in another class."

"How does it feel to hold the life of a human being in your hands?"

"It's an awesome responsibility. But then you don't assume it until you're certain of your capability."

"I should think it would still put you under considerable tension."

"The tension helps keep you on your toes and makes you do a better job."

"And keeps you from being used, I suppose."

"People are suing doctors a lot," Paul admitted. "And after the way Senator Spurgess raked us over the coals this morning I suppose there'll be even more."

"From what the afternoon papers quoted him as saying about doctors' incomes, it would seem that all doctors are rich."

"Early in your career you have to decide whether you're going to make money out of medicine, or keep it the kind of calling it was with the old family doctors fifty years ago," he said.

"Are any of those left?"

"More than you'd think. Both my grandfather and my father were that kind of doctor, so I guess it was inevitable that I should go into teaching. Besides, you have a freedom in a university medical school setup that you wouldn't have in a practice—and a chance to do research."

"I'm looking forward to doing more of that when I get to graduate school."

"My partner, Jerry Warren, and I think it's the most important side of our work. I imagine you remember Katie Winters, the singer. She's Jerry's wife now."

"I still have several of her records. Imagine giving up a great career as a singer because you love a man and want to bear his children." Her voice was soft and, when he turned his head to look at her, the warmth in her eyes and her face stirred him.

"I guess that's the highest calling a woman can seek," she said.

Paul laughed. "I see you're not a believer in Fem Lib."

"We have a lot of them on campus and some of them make me sick, sleeping around and bragging about it. My grandmother worked as a peon in Mexico and wasn't ashamed of it. And my mother made Cuban sandwiches in a bakery—"

"The kind that are a yard long and split down the middle? I love 'em."

"You're not going to get away with feeding me on them tonight," she said, laughing. "Turn at the other end of the bridge here."

They were crossing the river that wound like a friendly serpent through one of the main sections of Central City.

"The restaurant is under the next bridge," she added. "A road along the bank leads to it."

"This is beautiful," said Paul as he parked on the riverbank in the shadow of the bridge. "Imagine being isolated from everything and still right in the middle of the city."

"That's why it's a favorite lunching place for businessmen in the Mexican community," Carlota told him as they walked through the garden, where lush flowers of every description and color were growing. "Nights, it's usually taken over by tourists, but business is slow on Mondays."

Carlota was welcomed warmly by the Flores family who ran the restaurant, a warmth that included Paul when she introduced him.

"Our poor establishment is honored by the presence of so important a surgeon, Señor Doctor," said the proprietor formally, shaking hands.

"Right now I'm a very hungry surgeon," said Paul. "And also a humble one in the presence of such a beautiful place."

"It is also our home, but we love it so much, we decided to share it with others," said Señor Flores. "Leave the dinner to us, you will not be sorry."

They were ushered ceremoniously to a table directly on the riverbank. In midstream, a young boy and girl were busy paddling a boat upstream, but most of the traffic on the river was lazy, drifting down with the current.

"How do they get back?" Paul asked.

"A friend upstream, near the main bridge, rents the boats to those who just like to drift, mainly young people in love," Carlota explained. "A mile or so downstream, they leave the boats and come ashore. His son meets them once an hour with a minibus."

"What about the boats?"

"In the morning, he comes down with an outboard and tows them all back, before many people are on the river."

"We'll have to take the trip someday—"

"In the motorboat?"

"No. The slow way—with the lovers."

When he reached across the table to cover her hand with his own, she didn't move it and he saw a delicate flush heighten the faint olive tint of her lovely skin.

From the kitchen, Señor Flores appeared, carrying a steaming tureen. Beaming with pride, he served the traditional Spanish bean soup. It was fragrant and savory and for a while they were busy with it and the crusty fresh bread. Finally, Carlota put down her spoon.

"I'll have to starve the rest of the week to even get into my Polo Lounge uniform Saturday. Will all the convention activities really be over by then?"

"The election is scheduled for Thursday noon and the convention ends afterward, except for a meeting of the Council and the newly elected officers that afternoon."

"The papers say you're running for president of the Association. Is Thursday when you'll be elected?"

Paul laughed. "I'm only what you might call a stalking horse, put into the race to gain concessions from those anxious to really win."

"What concessions?"

"Things like a firm stand on making adequate care available for everybody, something a lot of younger doctors have been fighting for—and not getting anywhere much."

"Why wouldn't they elect you when you're so capable? And so dedicated?"

"Medical politics are no different from the regular kind," he explained. "It isn't so much what you stand for as who you can talk into supporting you that really counts. A lot of us are unhappy with the system that has let the cost of medical care skyrocket the way it has, mostly because of inefficiency in hospital operation and in doctor's offices. But even more important, we think there has to be a set of controls on the activities of doctors."

"What do you mean?"

"If I'd wanted to be a plumber, I would have had to serve a long apprenticeship in my trade. Even then, the county or city government would send inspectors around periodically to check my work and if I didn't measure up, my license could be suspended."

"Don't you have boards to do that for doctors, too?"

"To a degree, particularly if you want to practice in a city where there's a hospital approved by the American Hospital Association, the AMA or the American College of Surgeons. I spent six years after graduation from medical school, getting certified in my specialty as a vascular surgeon, but a doctor who plans to practice in a small town that has a hospital rarely has to take more than a year's internship."

"Can he do anything with only that much experience?" she asked incredulously.

"Some states don't even require an internship, all doctors have to do is pass the examination of the State Board of Medical Examiners and after that they can do pretty much anything in the way of surgery they want to do, as long as they don't break a criminal law by performing an illegal abortion or something like that."

"But that's not fair to conscientious doctors like yourself who really train themselves in a specialty."

"No," he agreed. "Actually most small towns would be better off without a hospital because their doctors would have to send really sick people to a major medical center like a university medical school. It becomes a matter of civic pride to have a hospital, though, and besides, the average town doesn't have much of a chance of attracting doctors to practice there any more unless they do. So the citizens get together and raise some funds to build one."

"You mean there's no control at all over who operates?"

"Practically none. I wasn't allowed to operate alone until I was an assistant resident with three years of good training behind me. And even then one of the attending staff or the Chief Resident worked right with me while I was really learning my trade. In most small-town hospitals, though, the local doctors can do anything they've got the temerity to tackle. And believe me a lot of them aren't afraid of the devil himself—until they get into trouble and the patient has to be sent to a center like ours."

"That's terrible," she said. "What's the answer?"

The second course of their dinner and a bottle of red wine came just then, so discussion had to be deferred for a while.

"You were asking what the answer to quality medical care is," Paul said when he laid down knife and fork at last. "One of the main things is peer review."

"You mean by a jury of one's peers?"

"Exactly. A board of experienced doctors to ride herd on those who don't bother to keep themselves up to date. Or who operate on conditions they really aren't qualified to tackle. Most important of all, the peer review board must have the authority to lower the boom where it's needed."

"Why would a really competent doctor object to that?"

"Most of us are individualists, considering the responsibilities we have in our work we have to be. And most of us would resent a government agency or even a committee from the medical society—looking over our shoulders. But I've been talking your arm off with medical shop talk," he apologized. "And after you went to all the trouble to order a perfect dinner."

"All I did was to tell Cousin Manuel you're something special. He did the rest."

"And nobly."

"As for your shop talk, I think it's fascinating."

"I still haven't discovered a thing about you—except how lovely you are."

"Things won't be so lovely for me if I don't get back to my books," said Carlota.

"I'll take you home on one condition."

She gave him a quick, searching look. "What is it?"

"That you go to the convention banquet and dinner dance with me Wednesday evening."

"To ease your conscience because I was fired?"

"You're hired again, remember? I'm asking you because I'd like to know you better."

"In that case the answer's yes."

"It's a real stuffed-shirt occasion."

"It will be a treat to see the upper crust at play," she said with a smile, then sobered. "But Mrs. Danton may not like it."

"To hell with Mrs. Danton." For the first time since the convention had begun, Paul felt really emancipated. "The cocktail party starts at six-thirty but we won't need to be there before seven; you already know I'm not much when it comes to drinking. Shall I pick you up at home a little after six?"

"That will be fine."

"We'll have a table with Jerry and Katie Warren and some other younger members of the medical school faculty. You'll like them, I know."

At 1410 Olivera Street, the radio was blaring and a

group of boys and girls were dancing in the living room. When Paul opened the door and let Carlota out of the car, she moved quickly against him in the darkness and kissed him.

"That's for giving me such a lovely evening," she said. "And for getting my job back."

"It's hard to believe we met less than twenty-four hours ago, but then it hasn't exactly been an ordinary acquaintance."

"Hardly." Carlota laughed. "You could almost say you made a fallen woman of me—without even waking up."

ii

Shortly before ten that evening Cary Poston received a call from Dr. Kendall Thomas.

"Can you come over to my laboratory, Cary?" The pharmacologist's tone was sober and Cary didn't ask any questions.

In Thomas' private laboratory, he found, besides the pharmacologist, Lieutenant Klinger, Mr. Lawson and Dr. Huxtable, the Medical Examiner. A glance at the rack of test tubes on the laboratory table told the story for each contained the reddish crystalline precipitate characteristic of a positive reaction for aconite.

"Dr. Singh was right, Cary," said Dr. Thomas. "We finished evaporating the alcoholic solution from the cups in that waste container a few minutes ago. It still had enough pseudaconitine in it to kill an average man."

"So Senator Spurgess was murdered?"

"No doubt about it now," said Dr. Huxtable. "I'll have to give the official cause of death as poisoning by aconite —at the hands of a person or persons unknown."

Cary took a deep breath. "So where do we go from here?"

Lieutenant Klinger answered: "I've asked Dr. Huxtable to defer announcing the cause of death until tomorrow noon at the earliest, Doctor. Mr. Lawson tells me you agree with his belief that the poison was probably intended for you."

"I can't refute Mr. Lawson's logic, Lieutenant. But I still can't figure out why I would be the target."

"If you ask me, the idea of someone stalking you is pretty farfetched, Cary," said Dr. Thomas.

"If the murderer had been planning from the start to assassinate Senator Spurgess, he would have used some weapon other than poison, Dr. Thomas," said Klinger.

"Why? It's almost as lethal as a bullet."

"He would have had no way of knowing the Senator would drink anything while he was in the building. Or even which route the Spurgess party would take when they left."

"The route was changed at the last minute too, because of the crowded condition on the exhibit floor," Cary Poston added.

"The murderer could still have followed when you and the others left the theater, Cary," said Kendall Thomas. "And it would have been a simple matter to drop poison into Spurgess' cup."

"We have to deal with probabilities, not possibilities, Dr. Thomas," said the FBI agent. "Granted that the murderer did drop the poison into the Senator's drink, the fact remains that he had no way of knowing Senator Spurgess would even stop to drink on the way out, so he couldn't have planned it that way. The only logical answer is that he must have followed Dr. Poston, in fact, had probably been following him for some time, looking for the opportunity he needed. When he saw Dr. Poston and Senator Spurgess drinking beer, he managed to jostle them and drop the lethal dose into one of the cups."

"At one time or another, practically everybody at the convention drinks at least one beer at the Central Pharmaceutical exhibit," said Cary. "All the murderer had to do was wait nearby until I got thirsty. And the worst part is I don't have the least idea who could possibly hate me enough to try to kill me."

"What about the beer?" Dr. Huxtable asked.

"I checked the taps as soon as the post-mortem was over," said Lieutenant Klinger. "They were clear and people had been drinking before and after Dr. Poston got the two cups. Which means that the poison had to be given *after* Dr. Poston left the Central Pharmaceutical Company booth. Both cups were drawn from the same tap, near the middle of the keg."

"You still haven't told me what you want me to do," Cary reminded the lieutenant.

"We have two choices, Doctor," said Klinger. "We can make the announcement to the press and admit that a killer is on the loose—"

"But that would stampede the convention."

"And probably insure that we would never know who the killer actually is," Klinger agreed.

"I guess I don't have to ask the other alternative," Cary admitted. "But it's not very comfortable being bait for a trap, with a good chance of winding up dead, whether you catch my killer or not."

"We'll take every possible precaution to protect you, of course, Doctor," said Klinger. "What we need more than anything else right now is an effective antidote that will be quickly available, in case the murderer tries again and we aren't able to keep him from actually poisoning you!"

"Atropine in large doses rather effectively combats the effects of aconite," said the pharmacologist. "I can have two hypodermics of atropine, say one and two-tenths milligrams each, put up in a sterile packet so Dr. Poston can give himself an injection of atropine as soon as he realizes that he has taken aconite."

"Could you recognize the symptoms of poisoning in time to take the antidote, Dr. Poston?" Lieutenant Klinger asked.

"I'd better," said Cary grimly. "The first symptom is a sharp tingling in the mucous membranes of the throat and upper esophagus. Now that I know what to expect, I should be able to treat myself in time."

"Let's hope so," said Klinger briskly. "Suppose we adjourn then and meet in the Medical Examiner's office tomorrow morning about nine o'clock. Maybe by that time some of us will have figured out how to catch the murderer."

iii

After the conference in Dr. Kendall Thomas' laboratory was over, Cary stopped by the hospital Emergency Room to get the packet containing two syringes of atropine solution, with sterile needles ready for injection. When he telephoned Marian at the hotel, she answered at once.

"How was the banquet?" he asked.

"Like hundreds of others I've been to: Chicken and ham Mornay, tough broccoli, cold rolls, a parfait and too much coffee."

"You sound really sorry for yourself. How about letting me come over and cheer you up?"

"I don't think so, Cary. I need time to think, without the distraction of having a man in bed with me."

"Was I a distraction last night?"

"Last night was entertainment, after all this *is* a convention. I've been working so hard lately I'd almost forgotten how pleasant making love with you can be but I need a little time now to weigh the advantages against the disadvantages."

"I'll be glad to list the advantages for you."

"I can see those for myself. What I've got to do now is dig up some disadvantages before I go off the deep end. Right in the middle of my speech tonight, I suddenly asked myself what I wanted to be liberated from and I couldn't think of a thing. That's what you've done to me since I got off the plane yesterday afternoon."

"I thought you were enjoying it."

"I am—very much. But I keep asking myself whether this isn't something we can both enjoy and look back upon when we're old, the way you reminisce about something pleasant that happened long ago."

"I've got a cabin down in the Big Bend country that's a wonderful place for continuing a romantic episode. We can be there before dark Thursday, after the convention is over."

"I don't know, Cary. I was hurt badly once and I don't want to be hurt again. You're everything any woman could want in a lover—"

"Or a husband?"

"Yes."

"They can be the same, you know."

"Can be, yes. But we both know they almost never are. Good night, Cary. I'll see you tomorrow morning, after my paper to the OB-GYN section."

iv

It was after ten when Jethro and Alice came out of the Japanese Steak House into the garden around it. They were pleasantly satiated with delicious food and the sort of comfortable talk that comes easily when neither tries to impress the other.

"It's so lovely here I hate to leave," said Alice. "Let's walk awhile in the garden outside before we go back to the hotel."

The night was warm with the promise of summer. The garden was lovely with its graveled walks, banks of flowers, delicately arched bridges over a narrow, meandering brook, and the tiny, almost grotesque trees the Japanese like to grow, sometimes to an age of many hundreds of years.

It was almost eleven when Jethro asked the parking attendant at the front of the restaurant to call them a taxi and they were driven back to the hotel. Both were reluctant to bring the evening to a close, but when they looked in the door of the Falstaff Room, as the Regency House cocktail lounge was called, they saw that it was jammed and noisy.

"It would be a shame to end the lovely evening we've had in a noisy place like that," said Alice. "I have some Bourbon in my room, we could have a good-night drink there."

"Are you sure that wouldn't be putting you out?"

"After what you've given me?" She was actually beautiful when she laughed, the hardness of the years and the men she'd known erased for the moment. "That's the least I can do."

The Bourbon was old and mellow, the place, although only another hotel room, comfortable. Alice slipped off her shoes and put her feet on the coffee table. When Jethro did the same they laughed at the hole in his sock. Sarah was getting to be a worse housekeeper every day, but he didn't want to be reminded of her tonight, so he hid that foot with the other one.

"I'm still curious about this great adventure of yours," said Alice. "Or am I prying?"

"Of course not. It's just that the idea of a forty-five-year-old man pulling up stakes and starting out again in a strange place seems sort of ridiculous to most people."

"If that's what you really want, Jethro, it's not ridiculous at all. But wouldn't it mean giving up your practice?"

"I've given up everything already, except a little income I have from stocks, plus enough money for my plane fare to Guatemala and some side expenses."

"But how can you be sure you'll be happy there?"

"A classmate from medical school named Trevor Hart runs a hospital in the highlands. It's only a shoestring operation but he's happy there and wants me to come with him."

"How does your wife feel about this?"

"She doesn't know it—and won't."

"You're leaving her?"

"I'm making a clean break. Sarah doesn't even know where I am right now."

"Is that fair?"

"She hasn't worried much about me for ten years or so. We were married when she became pregnant while we were going together. The baby was stillborn, and she hasn't wanted any other."

"What a shame," said Alice. "Are you going to get a divorce?"

"No."

"Wouldn't it be fairer to her?"

"Not really. When a man divorces his wife in a small town like Revere, it sort of casts an aspersion on her. But if he just up and leaves for no apparent cause, the people always suspect another woman is involved and he becomes the villain. Then everybody sympathizes with his wife."

"You've spent the better part of twenty-odd years building up a reputation there," she protested. "Surely everybody knows you're a good man, Jethro. Why would they suddenly think the worst of you."

Jethro studied the rich color of the whiskey in his glass for a moment before he answered.

"I guess human nature is pretty much the same wherever you find it," he said. "We like to think our gods have feet of clay, and when our belief is proved right, we're a little pleased and smug about it. That's what will happen in Revere when I drop out of sight—not that I'm a god there but a lot of people do think something of me. Sarah will be a martyr and I think she'll enjoy the role. I've arranged things so she'll be financially well fixed with an annuity she can't squander. She never did know anything much about money."

"And you, Jethro? What about you?"

"I'll be free to do the things I want to do." His face crinkled into a smile, like a piece of soft old parchment crushed in one's hand, so weatherbeaten was it from the years of Kansas sun. "It's a little too late to become another Richard Halliburton, but I'll have a little money coming in. And if Guatemala doesn't work out, freighter travel is always cheap. Anyway I won't have to always be in a hurry, like I was in Revere."

"It sounds like heaven," she said wistfully. "I had two years nursing and was going into the Navy when I graduated—quite a while ago. But a man I thought loved me came along and disrupted that scheme. Then I went to work for Vibrassage and I've been convention hopping ever since."

Jethro drained his glass and put it down. "You must be tired. I guess I'd better go and let you get some sleep."

Alice looked at him, the craggy face, the brown eyes that revealed the warm soul of the man back of them, the lean almost ungainly body in the brown tweed suit she was sure had come off a rack at the Emporium Department Store in Revere—or its thousand-times-repeated equivalent over the country.

She looked at the gentle hands whose strength was evident in the long fingers, the prominent knuckles which she knew could be quite as gentle helping a woman out of a taxicab as they undoubtedly were ushering a baby into the the world. And the decision which had been forming ever since he'd taken her arm to guide her across the delicately arching bridge into the garden of the Japanese Steak House suddenly crystallized.

"You don't have to go unless you want to, Jethro," she said softly. "You must have been lonely for a long, long time."

v

As he was walking from the hospital parking lot toward the hotel entrance, Paul Rice noticed a light burning in the Laboratory of Experimental Surgery and detoured to enter the building. He found Otto, the old technician, working at a glassblower's bench, where he often made special pieces of apparatus for other laboratories in the hospital, a skill he'd brought with him from Austria many years ago.

"You're out late, Dr. Rice," said Otto.

"And I'm beginning to think you never sleep," said Paul with a smile. "No matter when I look in, you're always at work. What are you making this time?"

Reaching up, Otto removed the jeweler's magnifier he was wearing and shut off the flame of the burner he'd been using for the delicate task of blowing glass to form new apparatus.

"A special retort for some hormone assays Dr. Poston is doing," he said. "Dr. Warren came by earlier. I think he came back for a meeting of the Young Turks Steering Committee."

"Dr. Warren takes this business of medical politics pretty seriously, but there's a lot of talk without much action, as far as the rest of the group is concerned. You know how young doctors are, Otto."

"Most young doctors," Otto corected him. "In their youth they can see clearly what is wrong and even try to do something about it with storefront clinics and such. But when they graduate and take on responsibilities that squeeze their pocketbooks, their viewpoint begins to change. It's the same with any profession."

"You've watched medicine develop for a long time, Otto. Where do you think it's going?"

"It's over half a century since I first learned to use a microtome in the old Allgemeine Krankenhaus in Vienna, Dr. Rice. Some doctors were still arguing then about whether germs caused disease."

"And now we know a lot of human ills have nothing to do with germs. Is that progress?"

"More people are being saved to grow old. You could call that progress, but not very many grow much older than their fathers did even now."

"At least the problems are different."

"Not the problems, Dr. Rice—just the way of handling them. In the old days a young doctor learned what was called the art of medicine through apprenticing himself to an older physician. Nowadays that same art is needed to treat old people who have lost the desire to live, except that they call it geriatrics."

"You still have the *joie de vivre*, Otto. How do you keep it?"

The old man moved over to a cage and stood looking down at the dog he and Jerry Warren had operated upon late Sunday night.

"I will tell you a secret, Doctor," he said. "My patients have only me. I feed them, I groom them, and sometimes when I know they are in pain, I slip something into their food. They have only one master and no worries about tomorrow, so they're happy with me and I'm happy with them."

"It would be a lot simpler if human patients reacted the way canine ones do."

"And maybe a lot better for medicine. Most doctors are good men—like yourself. They have a genuine desire to relieve suffering and restore health. But lately, so many other things must be considered."

"Like malpractice insurance," said Paul wryly. "I paid mine last week and the premium was twenty-five per cent more, for the third successive time."

"Yet you've never been sued, or the university because of you."

"True."

"Always many must pay for the mistakes of the few, especially with so many people anxious to profit from what they think are mistakes. My patients don't sue me, they love me too much for that. In the end most human patients are grateful to their doctors, too, especially if they are dedicated men like you. I think you will not have to worry about malpractice any more than I worry about troubles from my patients here."

"How about this fellow? Anything new?"

Through the wire of the cage Paul scratched the ears of the Great Dane Jerry and Otto had operated on yesterday. The dog had been sleeping quietly but opened his eyes and wagged his tail.

"Only what we knew this morning," said Otto, handing Paul a clipboard on which was a sheet of graph paper.

Lines joined two sets of readings to form two graphs on the same sheet, so they could easily be compared. One set of readings had been taken directly from a cannula in the lower end of the carotid artery, where it came off the aorta just above the heart. The other set was from the arterial system at the base of the brain.

As had already been apparent that morning, a marked difference existed between the pressure of the blood flowing through the artificial connection between the main arterial system of the body and the beginning of the brain's private, so to speak, circulation. In the latter, the pressure drop between heart and brain was easily detectible, while through the connection with the superficial circulation, blood was shunted directly to the brain at approximately the same pressure as that with which it left the heart itself.

"There doesn't seem to be any doubt that it's possible to deliver blood to the brain under considerably greater pressure than when it takes the normal route by way of the carotid arteries, which are usually made less elastic by sclerosis in such patients anyway," said Paul.

"I'm sure of it," said Otto. "This is a brilliant idea of yours, Dr. Rice."

"Not mine, Dr. Danton's. I only wish I had thought of it first."

"You can use it on me when my old brain begins to run out of steam because my arteries have been hardened by too much beer and knockwurst," Otto assured him.

"I still wonder how many people we may kill with this operation by bringing on a stroke from the increased pressure," Paul demurred.

"If you can make even half the old people who come to you think more clearly and perhaps remember some of the good things about life they had forgotten, who is the loser?"

"The ones who die from brain artery rupture because the pressure is too high," said Paul.

"In my time pneumonia was called the 'Old Man's Friend,' Dr. Rice. It carried him off before he could become a mere vegetable, because the arteries in his brain had turned to pipestems. But penicillin stopped that—"

"Are you saying blood-vessel surgeons should become the executioners of elderly people?"

"Not executioners, Doctor—friends. If a man's failing brain cannot be revived, then he's better off dead and you will be doing him a favor by trying to send more blood to it whether the operation succeeds or fails."

"Why should I have to make that decision?" Paul protested. "You'd have me substituting for God."

"Every doctor has to substitute for God sometime. I only hope that if that time ever comes with me, Dr. Rice, a conscientious man like you will be there to make the decisions."

vi

Neither Jethro nor Alice had seen Caleb Downs when they looked into the Falstaff Room at the Regency House. He'd been sitting at the far end of the long curving bar, nursing his second double scotch and silently cursing the bad luck that had let Cary Poston slip from his grasp earlier that day.

"The double-crossing bitch," he muttered when he saw Alice and Jethro together. "I'll make her pay for that."

The man on the next stool turned to look at him "Did you say something partner?" he asked in a broad Texas accent.

"Just saw a gal I tried to pick up this morning go by with another fellow. She told me her boss would be in town tonight, but the guy she's with isn't her boss."

"Cheer up!" said the Texan. "There's always plenty around during a convention—a lot of it free, too."

"I guess you're right." Caleb pushed a bill across the polished wooden surface to the bartender to pay for his drinks. "But I sort of had my eye on this one."

"I'm a gynecologist," said the Texan with a shrug. "From my point of view, they all look the same."

vii

In their tower suite at the Hotel Centralia, Aletha and H. Edward Danton were undressing for bed. Aletha was still smoothing on night cream when Danton finished putting on his pajamas. When she saw his reflection in the dressing table mirror as he was shaking a Nembutal capsule out of a bottle from his shaving kit, she turned on the bench to face him.

"Aren't you taking a lot of those lately?" she asked.

"Tomorrow's a big day." He swallowed the barbiturate. "Got to be sure of a good night's sleep."

209

"The final caucus is tomorrow afternoon, isn't it?"

"Four o'clock, but I have to introduce Marian Crowder in the morning. And then I want to hear the paper Paul and Jerry are giving on their artificial heart."

"Did what I learned from Paul help you?"

H. Edward Danton moved over to kiss the still satin-smooth skin of her shoulder. "You're indispensable, darling. Thanks to you, I know what to expect—and what to do."

"Go easy on Paul, dear. You were young once—and ambitious."

"A little raking over won't hurt him," Danton assured her. "And it could help me a lot in the election Thursday."

"You're not going to stay so involved in politics after the election that you'll put off going to Houston again, are you?"

"Scout's honor," he promised. "I've got an appointment next week."

"I wish I could hear Marian Crowder's talk," said Aletha. "But the chairman of the Auxiliary's Historical Exhibit Committee came down with a virus and I've got to cover the exhibit for her all day tomorrow."

"The newspapers and TV will give her paper a big play. You can read about it tomorrow."

"Want to tell me now what you're going to do about Paul's paper?" she asked casually.

"You can read about that, too. On the front page."

CHAPTER XVI

Caleb Downs's anger at seeing Alice Perrault and Jethro Forbes together the night before hadn't been enough to disturb the purely logical operation of his mind. The more he thought about it, the more convinced he became that he should cover his tracks more than they had been covered. And what better way than by using the police themselves as an alibi?

Before going downstairs for breakfast Tuesday morning, he telephoned police headquarters and asked for Lieutenant Klinger.

"The lieutenant has gone to the University Hospital," he was told.

"Do you have any idea where I might reach him there?"

"He was going to the office of the Medical Examiner for a conference at nine o'clock."

Caleb hung up the telephone. As he started to leave for breakfast, he saw lying on the carpet in front of the door a copy of the morning paper provided to guests of Regency House by the management. Picking it up, he went back inside and sat down to read it.

The paper carried a lengthy account of Senator Spurgess' speech before the CMA Convention and his sudden death shortly afterward from what was given only as "heart arrest." Caleb read the newspaper story word for word, but could find nothing in it, or elsewhere in the morning edition, to indicate that anyone considered the Senator's death as possibly having come from anything except natural causes. And yet, if Lieutenant Klinger was having a conference with the Medical Examiner so early in the morning, it could mean that someone besides Dr. Singh was suspicious. All of which made it even more vital that Caleb throw the police lieutenant off the scent.

Telephoning the hospital, he asked for the office of the Medical Examiner and shortly was speaking to Klinger himself.

"This is Caleb Downs, president of Central Pharmaceutical Company," he said. "You may remember talking with me yesterday in the Auditorium Restaurant."

"Oh yes, Mr. Downs. What can I do for you?"

"There's a rumor going around the hotels that some rare drug caused the death of Senator Spurgess. I've been subpoenaed to testify next week before his committee, along with a lot of other pharmaceutical manufacturers, and I don't want a rumor getting started that he got it at my booth."

"As a matter of fact, Mr. Downs, the Senator was given some beer from your booth by Dr. Poston just before he died."

"Then I'm glad I called you, Lieutenant. Could you inspect our setup first thing this morning?"

"Certainly, Mr. Downs. Do you have any reason to suspect anything was wrong at the booth yesterday?"

"Oh no. But with so many people at the convention and the Senator about to launch an attack upon drug manufacturers before he died, all kinds of rumors can spread. I just want to be ahead of them with a clean bill of health."

"I can understand how such a rumor could hurt your business," said Klinger. "I'll be coming over to the Convention Hall about ten. Will that be all right?"

"Ten would be fine, Lieutenant," said Downs. "I'd like to get it over with before the first break comes at ten-thirty. The crowd is always thirsty by then."

"Ten sharp then. I'll pretend to be from the Health Department making a routine check, so your salesmen won't get suspicious."

"Fine. I'll be expecting you."

Caleb was smiling as he hung up the phone. Calling Klinger had been a smart move, he assured himself. Not only would the police be disarmed now but during the inspection he intended to learn just how much the lieutenant really knew about the death of Senator Frank Spurgess.

As Caleb Downs came out of his hotel room, he recognized the tall, somewhat stooped, form of Jethro Forbes ahead of him. Jethro, too, was moving toward the elevators and Caleb caught up with him as he was pressing the "Down" button.

"Good morning, Dr. Forbes." Caleb was feeling jovial after his talk with the police officer. "I didn't get to thank you properly for saving my life yesterday."

"We were both lucky," said Jethro. "If I hadn't listened

to a tape on demand pacemakers a couple of weeks ago, while I was making a house call, and if Mr. Kraus hadn't shown me that ophthalmic magnet yesterday morning, things might have turned out differently."

"And if we didn't have rooms on the same floor, I wouldn't have the opportunity to buy your breakfast as a small token of gratitude to you for my being alive," said Caleb. "Will you join me?"

"I'd be happy to," said Jethro. "I must confess that I had two beers at your booth during the day," he added as the elevator was descending to the lobby floor.

"Feel free to have as many as you like all during the convention," said Caleb cordially. "That's what it's there for."

The hostess ushered them to a table in the busy downstairs dining room.

"I'm a stockholder in your company, Mr. Downs," said Jethro while they were eating. "Bought a thousand shares, when you first went public."

"You've got a valuable nest egg, then. I hope you kept it."

"Every share. What with splits and stock dividends, I now have close to twenty thousand shares."

"That makes you almost as much an owner of the company as I am," Caleb assured him. Then he added casually, "Staying through Thursday?"

"Friday. I have some business to attend to. How about you?"

"I'd like nothing better than to stick around and play golf. My doctor says I'm not getting the exercise an ex-coronary patient ought to take, but I'll have to get back to the factory Thursday afternoon. A number of us in the pharmaceutical manufacturing business had been subpoenaed to testify before the Senate Medical Subcommittee prior to Senator Spurgess' death yesterday. I don't know what will happen now but I think I'd better be ready, in case someone else takes over."

"Somebody will, I imagine," said Jethro. "Doctors and

drug people are good targets for ambitious politicians and the liberal element in the Democratic Party doesn't overlook many chances to attack us both."

"I guess we can expect that sort of thing as long as they're in control of Congress." Caleb took a cigar case from his pocket and offered Jethro one of the expensive slender Panatellas it contained, but he refused.

"I never had time for smoking," he said. "Which makes me lucky, I suppose."

"Damn near dying with a coronary at my age taught me to enjoy life while I can." Caleb lit the cigar and drew on it with obvious relish. "By the way, I saw you and Miss Perrault from the Vibrassage booth come into the hotel about eleven last night. She's quite a saleswoman. Wish I could get her to work for me."

"Her employer was supposed to arrive yesterday afternoon but telegraphed her around six that he'd be delayed a day of two," said Jethro. "She didn't have any plans and I'm here alone, so we had dinner together at the Japanese Steak House. She's very nice."

"And quite a looker, too. You certainly know how to pick women, Dr. Forbes."

ii

The group who gathered in Dr. Huxtable's office shortly after nine included a new face, that of the County Prosecutor, Mr. Anthony Sparks. Once again Cary repeated the story of the events just before and after the death of Senator Frank Spurgess, stopping every few moments to answer questions posed by the prosecutor and the police officers. But when he finished, they were no nearer a clue to the identity of the killer than they had been at the beginning.

"It looks like we're up against a blank wall," the County Prosecutor admitted at last. "The best we can do is list it as murder, by person or persons unknown."

"People will jump at once to the conclusion that Spurgess was killed by a doctor," Cary objected.

"With over two thousand physicians here for the convention, and most of them disliking the deceased, that would seem to be the logical conclusion," said Mr. Sparks.

"I can't help being convinced that the answer to this whole puzzle is right under my fingers somewhere," said Klinger as he looked at his watch. "I have an appointment on the convention floor at ten."

At the door, Lieutenant Klinger turned back. "Don't be surprised if you see someone watching you pretty closely, Dr. Poston. He's there for your protection."

The conference broke up, without having made any progress toward identifying the murderer. Outside the office of the Medical Examiner, Dr. Singh fell into step beside Lieutenant Klinger.

"I'm going to the Civic Center aid station," he said. "Mind if I accompany you, Lieutenant?"

"Not at all."

"I have a confession to make," Singh admitted when they were out of the Medical Examiner's office.

"So?"

"I am afraid I accidentally revealed the cause of the Senator's death yesterday."

"Not to the press?" Klinger asked quickly.

"No. To Mr. Downs, the man whose heart stopped yesterday morning."

Remembering the telephone call from Downs that morning, Klinger was suddenly alert.

"How did it happen, Doctor?" he asked.

"Mr. Downs spent nearly an hour lying down in the aid station, after Dr. Forbes started his heart beating again. I suggested that he be admitted to the hospital, but he refused."

"Did he say why? From what I saw and heard on TV, he had a pretty close shave with that pacemaker."

"He insisted that he felt all right and appeared to be in good condition. The pacemaker was working perfectly, too, so I didn't insist, after he signed a release. But while we were talking in the aid station, I happened to mention

215

my suspicion that Senator Spurgess had been killed with bikh."

"Was he familiar with the drug?"

"He didn't seem to be, but he was very much interested in it. I knew he was a drug manufacturer, though, so I thought nothing of it."

"Did you tell him anything else?" Klinger asked.

Singh shook his head. "I realized that I might have made a mistake in mentioning bikh and asked him not to say anything about it. He promised that he wouldn't, but since bikh has been proved to be the real agent, I thought I ought to tell you about the incident."

"You did right, Doctor," said Klinger. "I'll be talking to Mr. Downs this morning. Don't worry about it any more."

"Thank you, Lieutenant." Singh stopped before the door of the aid station. "I feel a lot better already."

Briefly Klinger considered facing Caleb Downs with the fact that he'd known for some twenty hours about the possibility of aconite poisoning, but had only mentioned a rumor allegedly going through the hotels when he called that morning. On second thought, however, he gave up the idea. If Downs was involved in the Spurgess murder, he had certainly covered his tracks well so far, and it made more sense to give him his head, so to speak, hoping he would make a mistake that would also brand him as a murderer.

iii

"Looks like you've got a clean bill of health here, Mr. Downs," Klinger said when he finished the inspection. He had carefully examined the kegs of beer brought in earlier that morning to assuage the thirst of more than two thousand doctors and exhibitors, as well as the apparatus for dispensing it.

"I appreciate your coming so early," said Caleb. "How about a beer before you go?"

"I rarely drink anything with alcohol in it because of my stomach, but I *am* thirsty."

Caleb drew two foaming cups of beer from the tap and handed one to Klinger, keeping the other for himself.

"I pay premium prices for this stuff because doctors are used to drinking only the best," he said. "But before handing over the beer, we see that each doctor gets free samples of my products and literature, so in spite of the cost, this is one of the cheapest forms of advertising I could invest in."

"How much do you know about drugs, Mr. Downs—besides selling them?" Klinger hoped the other man didn't notice that he was holding his cup gingerly so as not to blot the prints made by Caleb Downs's fingers on the waxy surface.

"I have a degree in biochemistry and I've also done some pharmaceutical research while developing my products. Why do you ask. Lieutenant?"

"I'm interested in that rumor you heard. Was the name of the poison mentioned?"

"Yes. Aconite."

"Know anything about it?"

Something in Klinger's voice rang a warning bell in Caleb's mind.

"Only that it's one of the old drugs—not used any more that I know of," he said casually. "Come to think of it, though, Dr. Singh did mention aconite to me yesterday, when I was lying down in the aid station. He says it's still a favorite poisoning agent in Nepal—where he came from. The whole thing sounds almost like a paperback who-done-it, doesn't it?"

"You could say that, yes."

"Got any leads on a possible killer?"

Klinger shook his head. "So far the murderer has managed to cover his tracks completely. But if my theory is right that he was trying to kill someone else, and accidentally poisoned Senator Spurgess, he'll have to strike again to get the real intended victim. Ever since Dr. Thomas identified aconite in the cup Senator Spurgess threw away, we've had the Civic Center under close police surveillance.

If the murderer tries to kill again, we've got a good chance to nail him."

"Are you letting the newspapers know the real cause of death?"

"Not yet," said Klinger. "In fact, I wouldn't have spoken of it to you, if Dr. Singh hadn't told me just now that he'd mentioned the possibility of aconite poisoning to you yesterday."

"You can rely on my discretion, Lieutenant," Caleb said quickly. "And for any help I can give."

"You can help most by not mentioning this conversation or the one with Dr. Singh, Mr. Downs. As long as the murderer doesn't know we're pretty sure what killed Senator Spurgess, he'll feel free to move. And the freer he feels, the more likely we are to catch him."

Klinger moved out into the aisle, still carrying his cup, which was almost half full.

"I've got to run, thanks for the beer. You've been very cooperative, Mr. Downs, and I appreciate it."

Caleb's laugh was unforced for he was quite certain now that he had lulled any suspicions Lieutenant Klinger might have had about him. "It isn't very comforting to know a killer is on the loose in a big medical convention, Lieutenant, but the only person who'd want to get rid of me would be a competitor."

He'd handled the whole thing rather well, Caleb told himself, as he watched Klinger turn into a side aisle and disappear from view. Telling about his conversation yesterday with Dr. Singh had been pure inspiration, extricating him from what could have been a very sticky situation, considering that Klinger had already known of it.

Caleb might not have been quite so elated, however, if he had seen Lieutenant Klinger empty the cup into a waste container and then wrap it carefully in a handkerchief to preserve the fingerprints that were on it.

iv

The paper by Paul Rice and Jerry Warren on their work in developing the so-called artificial heart was scheduled to be read before the Thoracic and Vascular Surgery section of the convention at ten o'clock Tuesday morning. Paul was to deliver the paper itself, while Jerry supervised the showing of the film that was an integral part of the presentation.

The last person Paul expected to see enter the room just as the paper was announced was H. Edward Danton.

The subject "Temporary Support to the Badly Damaged Heart by Means of Closed Chest Transarterial Bypass" was not even an arresting title. But word had gone out that it was a particularly effective form of the so-called artificial heart over which he and Danton had quarrelled while he was at the Danton Clinic, so the room was filled with doctors, many of them from the Danton camp.

Looking back afterward on what happened that morning, Paul knew he should have been forewarned by Danton's presence. It simply never occurred to him, however, that he was being set up for the kill.

"The heart is a remarkably effective pump," Paul began. "And all the more so because a sharp pressure differential exists between its two halves. The right half, which sends blood through the lungs for oxygenation and removal of carbon dioxide waste, operates at roughly one fifth the pressure that must be delivered by the left ventricle in order to drive blood through the extremities and the rest of the body. It is not surprising, then, that the left heart far more often requires help of various kinds from both cardiologists and surgeons than does the right.

"For about five years, my associate, Dr. Jerry Warren, and I have been studying the possibility of assisting the left side of the heart, particularly after it has been damaged by blocking of the coronary arteries that bring blood to it. Our first endeavors were directed toward devising a mechanical pump which could be implanted in the chest to take the place of the human heart, either temporarily or permanently. Here is a series of slides showing some of our early attempts."

As Jerry flashed a slide upon the screen, he also dimmed the lights by means of a rheostat, leaving only the small light over the lectern where Paul was reading.

"The difficulties inherent in devising and implanting such a pump are considerable," Paul continued. "As these slides show, our first pumping devices were rather crude, accounting no doubt for their failure even under experimental conditions. During the past two years, therefore, Dr. Warren and I have centered our work on aiding the left heart—splinting it temporarily while it recovers from the severe shock of a coronary attack and allowing it to heal itself.

"The technique we use seems to offer great promise with the added advantage that no major surgical interference, such as opening the chest and inserting of the many types of left ventricular assistance devices now being studied in several clinics, is involved. I am sure all of you are aware that avoiding the shock of a major procedure in a patient already at or near *extremis* is extremely important.

"In our technique, a small incision is first made in the armpit and the brachial artery is exposed."

Once again Jerry began to flash a series of colored slides upon the screen, illustrating each point Paul was making. The audience was quiet for most of them, being intimately concerned with these same problems, were intent upon the presentation.

"A polyurethane glass-reinforced cannula is then passed into the artery and through it a catheter is directed along the arterial system toward the heart, until it is inside the ascending aorta," Paul continued. "After checking position by X ray, the catheter is then pushed through the aortic valve into the left ventricle itself, where it takes blood directly from the left heart, thus reducing the load on that vital portion of the body's central pump.

"Meanwhile, a second cannula is placed in the femoral artery of the upper thigh, very much as is done in preparing a patient for cardiopulmonary bypass with the heart-lung machine. A simple roller pump is next placed between the catheter that takes blood from the left ventricle and the one which delivers it into the arterial system through the femoral."

Leaning down from the platform, Paul handed the nearest doctor on the front row of spectators a model of the pump he had described.

"The advantages of transarterial bypass are several," he continued, as the pump was being passed from hand to hand. "By taking blood directly from a left heart damaged by coronary thrombosis and pumping it back into the arterial system through the cannula in the femoral artery, most of the load on a weakened left ventricle is relieved, giving it a chance to recover strength and function. Equally important is the fact that this method can be used on a patient who is almost moribund from ventricular fibrillation due to a severe coronary attack, without subjecting him to an open operation to insert one of the conventional types of so-called artificial hearts.

"It is to be hoped that with the use of this relatively simple type of pump in a large number of severe cases of coronary thrombosis, or simple heart failure, a considerable improvement can be made in the prognosis and more patients carried successfully through the period of ventricular arrhythmia which often forms such a serious hazard. The rest of my presentation will consist of a film demonstrating the technique of left ventricular bypass in several patients, after which I will speak briefly on our progress in developing an implantable pump which can, with considerable reason, be called an artificial heart."

At the back of the room, Jerry Warren switched on a motion picture projector and dimmed the lights again. When the film was finished Paul moved back to the podium, as the lights went up.

"In all, we have now used the method you have just seen in twenty cases of severe and apparently irreversible cardiac shock with fibrillation," he said. "In at least half of these, the method was apparently successful in reversing the deterioration in heart function by splinting the left ventricle until it was able to function for itself once again. Admittedly, this is only a stopgap procedure, since it requires that the patient be in the hospital and under intensive cardiac care, a very costly situation. But it does appear to be lifesaving in a substantial percentage of patients with otherwise fatal coronary thrombosis.

"In our experimental work," Paul continued, "Dr. Warren and I have sought to build a better device. We had tried many, but the one we are now using, with considerable success in both dogs and calves, involves the implantation of a balloon-type compressing unit inside the first portion of the aorta just above the heart itself.

"Actually the balloons we use are in two sections, which can be inflated in sequence, the first portion nearest the heart and the aortic valve, the second within the arch of the aorta beyond it."

From a table beside the podium, Paul held up a board to which one of the balloons he was describing had been attached, with a small, battery-driven air pump.

"If you will watch closely," he said as he pressed a switch to start the pump, "you will see that the first inflation in each pumping cycle acts to block any blackflow of blood into the ventricle, following which the second portion of the balloon inflates to fill the aorta for a distance of perhaps eight inches, becoming in essence a true artificial heart operating inside the aorta. Both parts of the balloon are inflated with air by means of tubes brought out through the chest wall and attached to the small, but extremely efficient, air pump you see in actual operation here upon the board. The pump is driven by long life batteries and contact electrodes attached to the ventricle itself which control its pumping cycle, enabling it to follow the intrinsic rhythm of the heart itself, thus keeping the artificial heart and the real one from acting at cross purposes."

Looking down at the audience as the lights went up, Paul recognized at least a half dozen of the most famous names in this, the most dramatic branch of surgery—including the dean of them all, Dr. H. Edward Danton, whose somewhat florid face was quite impassive.

"I give credit freely to Dr. Warren and our technical assistant, Mr. Otto Heinrich, for their skill in constructing both the balloons and the pump," Paul continued. "The problem of clotting on the surface of the balloons has been largely removed, as with most artificial blood vessels now widely used, by the growth of cells from the normal intimal lining of the aorta across its surface. We have implanted two of these pumps, one in a dog and the other in a calf, and they have been functioning successfully for a little more than three months."

When Paul took his seat, the section chairman called upon several men engaged in heart and blood-vessel surgery, to whom Paul had sent copies of the paper in advance, to discuss it.

As usual the discussion added little except to afford the discussers an opportunity to publicize some of their own work and get their names attached at the end of the article, when it was published in the highly prestigious *Journal of the Central Medical Association*. The chairman was about to call upon Paul for a final summation when Danton stood up.

"Mr. Chairman," he said in his raspy voice. "May I have the privilege of the floor to discuss this paper?"

"Certainly, Dr. Danton," said the chairman. "Please come to the platform."

Danton's pace was unhurried and, when he faced the audience, he did not begin his remarks by congratulating Paul on his presentation, as the other discussers had done.

"As one with considerable experience in heart surgery and research over the years," Danton began, "I feel it necessary to warn you against using seemingly simple procedures, such as you have just heard described during this presentation, in severe heart disease. The procedure described is, of course, not new; it has been used by several clinics over the country, including my own, and is therefor not a cure-all."

Seeing Jerry Warren suddenly stiffen, where he was standing beside the motion picture projector, Paul shook his head in a warning gesture. Danton's purpose was quite apparent, to cut Paul to pieces publicly on a professional question and humiliate him before his fellow experts in this most rapidly growing field of surgery. But however much he might resent Danton's tactics, he had no wish to engage in a public altercation with his former chief.

"The danger of these seemingly simple temporary measures," Danton continued, "is that they may create a false sense of security in both surgeon and cardiologist, making them less likely to realize when the condition is no longer yielding to what had best be described as a palliative measure and that a different and more forthright attack is needed."

Danton paused, as if reluctant to say more, then added: "I had not intended to speak of it at this time, because our research is not yet complete. In our clinic we have now made considerable progress toward developing a device which can effectively take over the function of a diseased heart for an indefinite period of time. Moreover, it is so small that it can be implanted in the chest and leave the patient free to live a practically normal life. In good time, after our device has had a sufficiently long clinical trial, we shall make a full report on it to this section of our Association."

Danton sat down to considerable applause and the chairman looked inquiringly at Paul, who rose to speak.

"Dr. Danton's experience is far greater than mine, of course." Paul was carefully controlling his own anger. "And I am sure no one is happier than I am to know that he has finally solved the problem on which we have all been working, that of developing a long-term substitute for the severely diseased heart.

"If you will look at your programs, you will see that my own paper is titled merely 'Temporary Support to the Badly Damaged Heart by Means of Closed Chest Trans-arterial Bypass,' which is all we try to do with this procedure. In our hands, it has done just that very effectively in a number of cases and we felt that those working in this field should know about it."

v

Between the end of one paper and the beginning of the next, there was always considerable traffic in and out of the meeting rooms, as the conventioneers chose presentations being given in other areas where they had a particular interest.

When he saw Danton leave the room with Elton Brooks at his elbow, Paul rose with Jerry beside him, and left also. He wasn't surprised to see Danton move toward the press area off the second floor lobby of the Civic Center where reporters gathered immediately after the presentations to interview those giving papers and cull material for their stories from the authors themselves.

A TV camera had been set up in one corner of the lobby with a reporter ready to interview those selected by the CMA hierarchy for presentation on the air, and it was to this that Danton headed directly. Only a few news-papermen remained to question Paul about his paper, but the press release issued to them had carried a description of his work, plus a diagram of the artificial heart. Danton, however, was still the lion and never more so than after so dramatically announcing his successful development of the artificial heart.

"The scene-stealing bastard," said Jerry bitterly. "He just made that announcement to stave off the publicity you would have gotten!"

"He's put us behind the eight ball all right," Paul agreed.

"If you ask me, they're no nearer making an artificial

225

heart than we are," said Jerry. "There's Elton Brooks, let's put the screws on him."

Brooks had been left behind by Danton, always a solo performer. He tried to escape back into the meeting room when he saw Paul and Jerry bearing down upon him, but Jerry managed to head him off before he could reach the door.

"Let's have a beer together for old times, Elton," said Paul. "A booth downstairs is dispensing it free."

"Well, I—"

"Your boss is busy with publicity," said Jerry. "And you can bet your scalpel he's not going to let you in on it."

The other surgeon shrugged, and fell into step between Jerry and Paul.

"This wasn't my idea," he said. "When Jerry told me about this pump of yours yesterday—"

"Did you mention it to Danton?" Jerry asked quickly.

"Yes—but I didn't think he would—"

"Nobody, but nobody, is going to get ahead of H. Edward Danton," said Jerry, as they paused before the Central Pharmaceutical booth, where a line was waiting for paper cups to be filled with cold draft beer. "What I can't understand is that when I talked to you yesterday you didn't even mention this wonderful new artificial heart being developed down there at the Danton Clinic, Elton."

Brooks looked even more uncomfortable. "Well, you see it's been under wraps—until today."

"Are you sure anything's under those wraps?" Paul asked bluntly. "Except the one Jerry and I had worked on before I left the clinic?"

"Come clean, Elton," Jerry Warren urged. "We know the chief can be a chronic liar when he wants to boost his own stock. And nothing is going to boost it more just before this election than to have the newspapers come out with word that he's developed an artificial heart. Have you really got anything better than our transarterial bypass?"

Brooks shrugged. "We don't have anything as good—

but don't quote me on it. Danton's pushing everybody so hard to develop an artificial heart that can be implanted in the chest and run under its own power, the staff is about ready to rebel."

"If he's no nearer than that to a workable heart, why would he cut the ground from under us by making people believe our work is no good?" Jerry demanded.

Elton Brooks looked embarrassed. "Don't be too hard on Danton, Jerry. After all he taught the three of us most of what we know about cardiovascular surgery."

"We don't deny that," said Paul. "All we ask is why the vendetta against us?"

"It's not really against you. The presidency of both the CMA and the AMA mean an awful lot to Dr. Danton."

"He's been moving steadily upward in medical politics for ten years at least," said Paul. "Why the sudden spurt?"

"The chief's not as young as he used to be, for one thing."

"He looks pretty healthy to me," said Jerry, then added pointedly, "are you telling us something's wrong with him?"

"Why do you ask that?" Elton Brooks countered, but Paul noted that he did not look at Jerry when he spoke.

"For one thing that change of hands during the infarct operation."

Elton Brooks looked startled. "What are you talking about?"

"You know damned well what I'm talking about," said Jerry. "Danton would never have let you finish that job, if he'd been able to do it himself."

"You're imagining things."

"I'm not so dumb that I can't tell the difference between a size eight and a size seven surgical glove, Elton," said Jerry. "If you're the kind of friend you used to be, you'll tell us what this is all about."

Elton Brooks flushed, but held his temper. "There's no use trying to pry something out of me, Jerry," he said. "Even if there's anything to tell, I'm not going to do it."

"If Danton's disabled, how's he going to function as president of either the Central or the AMA? Both those jobs require a lot of traveling and speechmaking."

"I didn't say he was disabled. And don't you go telling it around that I did."

"Or you might get the ax like we did?"

"They've got something exciting in the way of a new teaching center at Phoenix. I've been invited to join them."

"And the price of a recommendation by Dr. Danton is your silence about whatever trouble he's having?" Paul asked.

Elton Brooks shrugged. "If you fellows are through with your inquisition, there's a paper I want to hear in the Internal Medicine Section."

"Who's going to be Number Two at the Danton Clinic when you leave?" Paul asked as Brooks got up to leave.

"We have a couple of bright young men coming along."

"Far enough to take over in the middle of removing a cardiac infarct?"

"Almost. And I wouldn't be leaving anyway until next fall."

"Of all the ungrateful bastards," Jerry exclaimed when the other surgeon was out of earshot. "He was green as hell, when he first came to the clinic, and you and I showed him the ropes."

"Don't be too hard on Elton," Paul admonished his partner. "He's obviously had to swear not to reveal anything about this disability of Danton's. Besides, he's right about all three of us owing a lot to the chief. You and I could never have learned as much about cardiovascular surgery anywhere else as we did while we were with Danton."

"Are you saying we should lay off him?"

"Maybe a little."

"Like how?"

"By not voicing our suspicion that something's wrong, when we don't know what it is. Besides, when he isn't on a crusade, like he is now with medical politics, Danton can

228

be a pretty decent man. Don't forget the time Katie had the automobile accident while she was pregnant and crushed one of her renal arteries. If Danton hadn't been able to make her another one out of Dacron, she'd have lost a kidney and probably little Jerry."

"I guess we do owe him a lot," Jerry admitted. "But I wish to hell he'd stop picking on us."

Paul chuckled. "You should feel complimented. Believe me, Danton wouldn't bother to cut anybody down, if he didn't think they were standing pretty tall in the first place."

The answer seemed to satisfy Jerry, and he left the theater floor for the exhibit area and their booth. But remembering Aletha's visit to his room yesterday afternoon and her implied promise of intimacy before the convention ended, Paul was convinced now that luring him back to the Danton Clinic had been her idea all along.

For H. Edward Danton would hardly have gone to the trouble of cutting him down to size publicly, if he'd had any idea of trying to get him to return to the clinic.

CHAPTER XVII

Fifteen minutes before Marian Crowder was scheduled to begin her guest lecture to the OB-GYN section of the CMA Convention, the room was jammed. With a large crowd in the hall outside clamoring to get in, the Convention Arrangements Committee hurriedly moved the location to the much larger Civic Center Theater which was not scheduled to be used for another hour, when the Second General Session of the convention would meet there.

Marian's talk to the Auxiliary leaders, plus the television and newspaper publicity the author of *Sexual Slavery* had enjoyed since the book was published, would have been enough to fill the smaller hall. But the announced change in the topic of her address to "Life *Without* Father"—shrewdly deferred to the last minute by Marian herself—promised to be even more sensational. As eleven o'clock approached on Tuesday morning, the other scientific sections meeting at the same period found only a few people in attendance.

Sitting on the platform from which she was to speak, Marian was the picture of reserved loveliness, the rare scientist who combined beauty with brains.

Promptly at eleven, Dr. H. Edward Danton himself, quite conscious of the advantage that would accrue to his political campaign by introducing what could hardly be termed less than the lioness of the convention, rose and tapped with a pencil against the microphone.

"We welcome to the Seventy-fifth Annual Convention of the Central Medical Association, oldest in the country, one of the brightest female luminaries in the field of medical science—as well as one of the most beautiful."

Danton was interrupted by a round of applause and waited for it to subside.

"I feel sure," he continued, that if Carrie Nation had been half as lovely and accomplished as our next speaker, we'd all still be drinking moonshine. Graduating from Johns Hopkins at the tender age of twenty-two and first in her class, she embarked upon a program of research designed to prove that, speaking literally, the female is more deadly than the male. Speaking *figuratively* only, however, I need not tell you that she can hold her own with any of today's film stars."

A roar of laughter greeted this rather heavy-handed example of medical humor.

"Since Dr. Marian Crowder has long since made a name in her own right in the field of embryology, I won't take up your time with a list of her scientific accomplishments," Danton continued. "More recently she has earned a high place as a best-selling author with the publication of her first book—which I confess to not yet having had time to read—*Sexual Slavery*. But whether or not you have read the book, I am sure the masculine portion of the audience will join me in paraphrasing the famous words of Patrick Henry: 'If this be slavery, make the most of it.'

"Fellow members of the CMA and guests, I give you Dr. Marian Crowder who will speak on 'Life *Without*—' " Here Danton's eyebrows rose in a mock expression of amazement that brought laughter once again from the audience—" 'Father?' "

As Marian moved to the platform, her eyes searched the crowd. No matter how many times she spoke, this moment when she looked down upon the faces staring up at her never failed to generate a panicky fear that she would find herself with nothing to say. But when she saw Cary Poston standing at the back of the room beside the projector and his hand rose with thumb and forefinger touching to form a circle, confidence came flooding back.

Placing her manuscript upon the lectern, she switched on the small light that cast a circle of brilliance upon its top sheet.

"Fellow members and guests," she said, "I am honored indeed that Dr. Danton was able to take time from politicking to introduce me."

A gust of laughter from the crowd interrupted her for a few moments.

"My study of the professional program tells me that I am the only woman physician scheduled to speak at this convention, which gives you some idea of the odds against women in medicine. To give you another example of the odds in this world against my sex, let me also remind you that each month, the average woman releases one female germ cell, the ovum, from a follicle in the ovary. But once a week—or more often depending upon use and circumstance—the male of the species releases something like three million spermatozoa.

"Think about these odds again, please—three million to one. Then tell me how could it be that, prior to the coming of that great female emancipator, the Pill, every woman with either a marriage license, the courage of her convictions—or both—wasn't pregnant all the time?

"Don't tell me woman hasn't been discriminated against when, until now, she must wait upon the whim of a man to reproduce her own kind. But be assured, my friends, that the facts of life have changed. Human reproduction has now been achieved without the presence of even so much as one of those three million sperm. And with a chemical stimulant, I have repeatedly fertilized human ova in my laboratory and carried them well past the morula stage of embryo development."

From a shelf beneath the lectern, she took a model of a morula. About the size of an orange, it had a pebbly appearance, like a raspberry.

"The morula this model demonstrates is a rapidly dividing mass of cells, soon to be differentiated into the homunculus called man," she said. "From this point, I assure you, it will be just a short step to achieving implantation of these embryos into the uteri of women who cannot otherwise bear children, where they can grow as a normal pregnancy.

"Creating an artificial womb, where babies can be carried to birth, so to speak, outside the body, is a little further away—but only a little. *Life* without father is already a reality. *Birth* without father is the next goal in our experiment."

There was no laughter now, and not even much disbelief in the sea of faces staring at her from the packed rows of the theater.

"For those of you not familiar with the phenomenon— or the word—parthenogenesis means fertilization of a female germ cell without the presence of a male cell. Anyone who grows roses knows, I am sure, that aphids, a form of plant lice, reproduce themselves in summer without the benefit of the male. Which, when you think of it, is not really surprising since aphids reproduce so rapidly that there would be no time for romantic dallying! Male aphids appear only in the autumn and, typical to the male, fertilize only one female cell for each individual aphid. These fertilized ova then restart the annual multiplication once more in spring, after which the male cells are no longer needed. Other insects, notably wasps and a few others of that group, have done away entirely with males and seem to be prospering, as your gardens will attest."

From the elevated stage where she was speaking, Marian saw a tall man enter the room and tap Cary Poston on the shoulder. To her surprise, Cary rose and left the theater and she couldn't help being a little miffed at his leaving while she was in the midst of her paper.

"The now classic experiments in parthenogenesis were first done nearly a hundred years ago using the eggs of sea urchins," Marian continued. "These were found to be casily fertilizable by the addition of magnesium chloride and other chemicals to the water in which they were placed and by 1952, no less than three hundred and seventy-one ways of reproducing sea urchins asexually had been reported. But eggs, too, can be fertilized by a number of agents, both chemical and mechanical, some of them merely by pricking the egg membrane with a very sharp needle.

"From the sea urchin, it was but a short step to the rabbit and here cold proved to be an effective fertilizing agent. I am sure the male rabbit, considering the well-known fertility of the species, must have been shocked to learn that he could be replaced by an ice cube."

Laughter was perfunctory, which didn't surprise Marian for she'd noticed much the same reaction in smaller, largely male groups, when she had reported on her work at some of the monthly hospital staff meetings.

"Being the most advanced form of life from an evolutionary standpoint, as well as the most complicated anatomically and physiologically, man could be expected to be the last animal to be reproduced parthenogenetically," she continued. "To the surprise of many workers, including myself, it has been discovered, however, that the human ovum sometimes begins a spontaneous parthenogenetic development as an embryo before leaving the ovary for its journey down the tube into the uterus— without fertilization by a male cell having occurred.

"Speaking purely from a statistical point of view, it would appear, that such a 'virgin birth' can be expected to occur once in roughly every 1.6 million pregnancies, although a British medical journal, the *Lancet,* estimated the incidence of spontaneous human parthenogenesis at about once in every three billion births. Studies recently made in England have apparently yielded a case, too, where it appears to be established without question that human pregnancy and birth of a living child did occur without the presence of male spermatozoa—a true case of life without father."

The audience was tense now and Marian could see that the look in many eyes was actually hostile to the startling revelations she was making.

"Whatever your religious convictions—and I certainly have no intention of getting involved in that aspect of controversy—it appears that, given a world population of nearly four billion people, an actual 'virgin birth' can occur at least once every five years. All of which means that a number of people living today are fatherless— though certainly not bastards—without knowing it. The major difficulty in this line of reasoning, of course, is that while practically all of us have actual proof, through the witness of a doctor, midwife or an occasional policeman, who officiated at our birth, that we are a child of our mother, the question of who the father is can be based, as some wag has said, only on circumstantial evidence."

The joke, in spite of its age, brought a laugh from the audience, breaking the tension engendered by her startling revelations.

"In our own laboratory," Marian continued, "we have repeatedly produced human ova by hormone injection and placed them in a special medium. After bringing about fertilization by either chemical or mechanical means, we have grown the resultant embryo in an atmosphere rich in oxygen, using a hyperbaric pressure chamber, and then implanted a healthy embryo into the uterus of women who might not otherwise have given birth. Several of these have gone on to complete development and the birth of girl babies since the absence of the sex-determining chromosome present in normal fertilization by male cells prevents the production of males."

Marian paused as a sudden buzz of low-voiced conversation told her the full significance of the last observation had penetrated the consciousness of even the most resistant members of the audience. When the buzz died away, she leaned forward and started to deliver the *coup de grâce*.

"As a fellow physician," she said, "I feel I should warn you that the women of this world are now fast approaching the point where we can destroy the male on a number of counts. Not only do we outnumber you, we also live longer. And now that a means of reproduction without your presence, however pleasant that may be, is available, we don't need you—except perhaps for recreation.

"It has taken ten years of research to reach this state of affairs, but I remind you that the twenty-five million years preceding it had not accomplished anything at all on this point, except perhaps a few isolated cases of conception without male participation.

"Give me another ten years and with the experience I and my co-workers have gained, I guarantee that the so-called artificial womb will become a reality. Then ova can be carried to full development and the infant allowed to be born, merely by severing the connection to an artificial placenta by which it has been nourished and its waste products removed.

"When that day comes, gentlemen, you will be in grave danger of becoming extinct and the world will be ours—unless we choose, of course, to allow the presence of a certain number of males in the world for various purposes. Sexual activity, a considerably different thing from reproduction, can then be separated entirely from it and women will be freed from the burden of a daily dose of a drug which does not always redound to their welfare, plus the increased danger of thromboembolic disease alleged to be a hazard in those who take the Pill.

"Many people far more versed in philosophical consideration than I have considered the question of the ideal male-female relationship which will then result, with its sharing of mutual understanding between the sexes and the highly desirable human-to-human relationship which will then have a chance to exist. Aldous Huxley in *Brave New World* saw glimmerings of the possibilities in such a situation, but we have tended to consider it a thing of the considerably distant future. Actually, however, we have the means of its accomplishment almost within our grasp at the present moment.

"With selective reproduction possible under rigidly controlled conditions through parthenogenesis, the creation of 'Men Like Gods' would not appear to be far from an accomplishable fact. People will then be untroubled by Original Sin because no sin will exist in the most intimate personal communion possible between the inhabitants of the earth, whatever their sex. And with passion completely eradicated from this true master race, a perfect world will once again exist, as it did before Adam and Eve, lured by the serpent, felt the need to cover themselves with fig leaves."

The stunned audience was silent for a moment after Marian finished her address, then gave her a perfunctory round of applause. She had expected this, since the audience was composed largely of men who, as she very well knew, clung stubbornly to the position of dominance that mere maleness gave them.

Finally, H. Edward Danton rose.

"Thank you, Dr. Crowder, for a glimpse into the female-designed world of the future," he said with a note of smugness in his voice. "I, for one, can only say that if this perfect world, where no passion exists, should come into being at any time in the near future, I can be thankful that what I like to call my 'salad days' are behind me. And I can assure you that a world in which not only are individuals indistinguishable from each other, but presumably also the sexes, will be considerably less attractive than the one in which we now exist, in spite of its admitted imperfections."

A solid round of applause greeted Danton's words and the session broke immediately.

ii

A group of reporters was waiting in the second floor lobby when Marian came out of the meeting hall. In the forefront was a slender young woman, her nearsighted eyes aglow behind the steel rims of her granny glasses.

"You certainly put them in their places, Dr. Crowder," she said. "Some of us managed to get into the projection booth behind the balcony where we could hear and use small tape recorders."

"Was that exactly cricket?" Marian was tired and not a little cross at Edward Danton and the audience, but particularly miffed at Cary Poston for leaving almost before she had started.

"It's hard enough for women to get ahead of men in this business," said the woman reporter. "We have to take advantages where we can find them. I'm off to write my story."

As she disappeared, a TV camera manipulated by a young man with a classic beard zoomed in on Marian for a close-up reminding her that she was perspiring and that her hair was probably mussed. But it was too late to remedy that.

"Did you really tell them men aren't needed in reproduction any more, Doctor—only in sex?" The young man with the microphone shoved it at her.

"Words to that effect."

"Just how far have your personal experiments gone, Doctor?" he asked a bit smugly—which did nothing to quell Marian's temper.

"We have been able to produce babies without fathers."

"Hell, that's been happening ever since Adam and Eve,"

said a craggy-faced reporter "Tell us something new, Doctor."

"Why don't you read the CMA publicity sheets then?" Marian snapped.

"Do you really think women will ever be able to get along without men?" another reporter asked.

"I get along without them very well," she answered.

"What a pity," said the questioner, who sounded genuine. "All that beauty wasted on a world run by a gaggle of females."

"I didn't say there would be no males," Marian insisted. "Merely that they would be bred selectively."

"For brains, Doctor—or body?" It was the smug reporter and his implications didn't help Marian's temper.

"Both," she said shortly. "And always a certain number as beasts of burden. Now if you'll excuse me, I'm going to lunch."

"Alone, I imagine, Doctor," the TV reporter said. "After this morning, I'll bet any real man would be afraid to get near you. It's a scientific fact, isn't it, that the black widow eats her mate after she's through with him?"

Marian curbed the impulse to throw the microphone she had been holding at him and left for the Ladies Room. Closing the door behind her with a vicious slam, she refurbished her complexion, which was not as much disturbed, she was glad to see, as she had feared. Then having applied fresh lipstick, she left the lobby and moved down an escalator to the ground floor and the restaurant where she had promised to meet Cary for lunch.

Cary was late, which didn't improve Marian's temper.

"Dr. Poston's table, please," she told the hostess.

"Certainly, Dr. Crowder." The woman was tall, glossy haired, and well girdled.

"I read your book," she added as she escorted Marian to the back of the room.

By now Marian had learned to sense opinions from the tone and manner of the speaker when they were voiced. This one, she decided, was adverse.

"What didn't you like about it?" she asked, taking the bull by the horns.

"Well, I didn't say—"

"You just expressed an opinion by showing me to a table so near the kitchen that I'd be dodging trays throughout lunch."

The woman looked startled. "Would you rather—?"

"I certainly would," said Marian crisply. "Dr. Poston happens to be chairman of the Committee on Arrangements for the Central Medical Association and no law says it has to keep on meeting in Central City."

The woman looked stunned. "We're rather crowded but I just noticed a table in the corner, away from the noise. Please follow me, Doctor."

"This is much nicer," Marian agreed when she was seated. "And nothing says you have to like my book."

"As a matter of fact, the only part I disliked was the first chapter. You know where you describe—"

"The Marquis de Sade is pretty explicit. I only used that portion to show just how subservient the woman usually is in the sex relationship."

"You can say that again." The hostess was thawing rapidly. "But I'll say one thing; once you finished that first chapter, you were bound to go on with the book. Can I order anything for you from the bar while you're waiting for Dr. Poston?"

"A bloody mary, please. I just finished addressing an audience of men."

"And told them off properly, I hear."

Marian looked at her watch; it had been less than twenty minutes since she'd finished her speech.

"How in the world did you know that?" she asked.

"The young man, who handles the slide projector for the convention, came down to lunch before you did and was telling the waitresses about it. There've been plenty of times when I could have wished for a world without men."

By the time Marian's drink arrived, Cary appeared, looking composed and cool as usual. Which only made

Marian the more conscious that she was irritated and mussed.

"Bring me one of those and then we'll order," he told the waitress, and turned to Marian. "You weren't kidding, were you, when you promised the girls of the Auxiliary to drop a bomb?"

"How would you know?" she demanded tartly. "You left before I got started."

"I was outside with a television reporter," he said. "The loudspeakers were on in the lounge and I could hear what you were saying."

"But you still didn't want anyone to know you were listening?"

"I'm sorry if I hurt your feelings, darling. I gave my paper early this morning and the TV people weren't here then. They wanted an interview covering the subject, and the reporter for the afternoon edition wanted one, too. Both of them had a noon deadline to meet."

"What earthshaking revelation did you make? They barely interviewed me."

"I mentioned it to you coming in from the airport. We were having so many pregnancies among the students that we started a program of postcoital contraception. Nothing new, of course; they've been doing it at a number of colleges but we've accumulated a couple of thousand cases. If the girl reports to the student health service within three days after exposure we can pretty well guarantee that she won't have a baby. What we do is give her a package containing ten tablets of diethylstilbestrol, twenty-five milligrams each, with instructions to take two daily for five days."

"How many pregnancies did you say you would expect in such a group?"

"The statistical expectancy would be about eighty in the two thousand cases we reported, more if coitus occurred more than once. But not a single pregnancy resulted."

"How about side effects?"

"Over half had no symptoms worth mentioning and none of the others were serious, usually mild stomach upsets and the like. The press didn't realize just what the paper was about when I gave it this morning until somebody tipped them off. But someone labeled it the 'Morning-after Pill' and now they're having a ball. Which reminds me—"

"I can take care of myself," said Marian shortly. "I'm not exactly a college girl, you know."

"I certainly do know," he said. "And speaking of the bomb you dropped—"

Marian stiffened, for the inflection was there even though faint. "I take it you didn't approve," she said frostily.

"As a scientific presentation? Or as a blockbuster?"

"Both."

"It was certainly a blockbuster, but I'm sure you'd be the first to admit that it wasn't exactly the scientific paper one would expect from the greatest living embryologist."

"What would you have said?" Marian's tone was icier than the bloody mary she had just finished.

"I've read your early reports so I know your work is very thorough, as I expected it to be. You have the scientific data to back up everything you said this morning about your work, except that a lot of it is probably considerably further in the future than you intimated."

"Are you calling me a liar?" Marian demanded.

"Of course not. But Marian Crowder is a great medical scientist who can't afford to slant her work to create publicity. Besides you're also the woman I love. Or haven't I told you before?"

"Certain channels of communication have been opened."

"That's a new way of saying it, but—"

"The crust of H. Edward Danton," Marian spluttered. "Trying to humiliate me before that crowd of—of males."

"Danton was crude, but he got more applause than you did, darling. Let's face it: No man likes to hear a woman tell him he's extinct, when it comes to reproduction, where a lot of us are inclined to be a bit sensitive. After all, a couple of glands that can produce three million spermatozoa in one shot can't be all bad."

"Now you're making fun of me."

"Just trying to restore your sense of balance and humor," he assured her. "Right now you're feeling sorry for yourself because Danton got the last word. But the Dantons of this world usually do, that's why so many of them rise to positions of leadership without much ability, though I'll have to admit H. Edward is an exception there. What would you like for lunch?"

"I'm not sure I want anything else." Marian picked up her glass and drained the final drop of the drink.

"In that case," said Cary with a grin, "why don't we each have another one of these and go over to your hotel?"

"So you can prove your vaunted prowess in reproduction?"

"That's the general—or rather the purely physical—idea."

"If that's all you have to say, I might as well go to my room—alone." Marian pushed back her chair and got to her feet. "You can buy lunch for the hostess, she's already read my book so she knows what would be expected of her."

She was gone before he could protest, back straight, head high and very lovely, as she threaded her way between the tables. As she disappeared through the doorway, Alex Klein, who was being escorted to a table for one by the hostess, stopped beside Cary.

"Eating alone?" he asked.

"I was going to have lunch with Marian."

"I just saw her leaving in what looked like a huff. Have you been stood up?"

"If a pride of lions had been nearby, I'd have been thrown to them," Cary admitted wryly. "When will I ever learn that when it comes to themselves women have no sense of humor?"

"If you ever do, you'll be halfway at least to becoming a psychiatrist," said Alex. "Mind if I join you? Or would you rather lick your wounds in solitude?"

242

"Sit down," said Cary. "I guess I need a shoulder to cry on."

"This one's round, so the tears run off easily." Klein lowered his not inconsiderable bulk into the chair across from Cary and signaled the waitress, pointing to Cary's empty glass and holding up two fingers.

"I thought you two had a thing going," he said.

"So did I. We had a brief affair in medical school, nothing really permanent—"

"Making love in the back seat of an automobile never was a very satisfactory way of encouraging a grand passion."

"Then she went off the deep end for this curly-haired wolf of a resident. By the time that broke up, I was married."

"And happily," Alex Klein reminded him. "I know because neither you nor Mary ever used my couch—which is more than I can say for half the medical school faculty and their wives."

Their drinks came and they ordered lunch: salad and a small steak for Cary, beef Stroganoff for the psychiatrist.

"I know I'm courting death from cholesterol build-up," said Klein, when he saw Cary's eyebrows lift at the lunch he had ordered. "But I know myself well enough by now to be sure the frustration of not being able to eat what I like would cause a damn sight more stress inside my psychophysical mechanism than the damage a few calories and cholesterol can ever do. When you come down to it, it's the strain of modern living that really kills us."

Cary smiled. "I never would have expected you to be a stress victim, Alex. You're the happiest man I know."

"Only because my wife's a loving and passionate woman. The way to live without temptation in a world where there's a plethora of women, my friend—about a five-to-one ratio around here when you include nurses, technicians, aides and an occasional nubile member of the Hospital Volunteer Corps, whose husband is out traveling so she can live comfortably when she's a widow—is to stay well drained. But getting back to your girl friend—"

"Ex-girl friend."

"Don't you believe it; I read her book. What these women liberationists are crying to be liberated from is the kind of man most of them wind up with. And you, my friend, are about as attractive a male as any I know."

When Cary looked startled, Alex Klein grinned impishly, like a fat cherub who has discovered a way to raise a little hell in heaven.

"Not that you attract me—except as a friend," he said. "Though considering how much enjoyment my homosexual patients seem to get out of each other, I'm beginning to think the heterosexual relationship is somewhat overrated. One of them told me his current inamorata had the prettiest behind in the world. He pointed the guy out to me one day, too, and damned if he wasn't right."

Cary found himself laughing in spite of his worry over the tiff with Marian. "I'm always wondering how much of the stuff you come up with is true," he admitted.

"What difference does it make?" Alex Klein attacked his beef Stroganoff with enthusiasm and relish. "A novelist friend of mine says any story worth telling is worth telling well. Mind disclosing what set the beautiful Dr. Crowder off?"

"I just happened to be in the line of fire. She was already angry."

"Over the way her paper was received?"

"Yes."

"Didn't she know a male audience will never accept the idea of a possible world populated only by women and a few kept studs?"

"I think she took the natural masculine resistance to the idea of a world without males as a rejection of her role as a scientist," said Cary. "And I added insult to injury by telling her she had let her emotions run away with her scientific acumen."

"Is she really getting anywhere with this parthenogenesis thing?"

"Judging from her preliminary report, she's ahead of anybody else in the world at the moment. If she sticks to the genetic side of embryology, trying to prevent things like muscular dystrophy, hemophilia—the whole line of disease with hereditary factors—she'll probably wind up with a Nobel prize in a year or two."

"Meanwhile she's making a killing on the book-club and lecture circuit." Alex put his fork down on his empty plate and wiped his mouth with a napkin. "It's the old question: Shall I do what really needs to be done for that bunch of cruds called my fellow man? Or shall I look out for Number One?"

"What's your choice?"

"Same as yours. We choose to teach full time at twenty-five thousand a year when we could easily be grossing seventy-five in private practice. I'm not really complaining though. For me, being on a medical faculty combines the best of two worlds."

"I guess you're right." Cary had eaten half of his salad and only toyed with his steak. "But Marian could have both, plus the kind of fulfillment successful marriage can bring—the kind I had."

"Cheer up." Alex signaled the waitress to bring the dessert cart. "If your lady love is as smart as I think she is, all will go well. And if she isn't, there are always plenty of opportunities around for a handsome widower. Let's talk politics for a change. How many votes do you think Paul Rice can pull after that clobbering Danton gave him this morning over the artificial heart—that is, if Paul lets himself be nominated?"

"Is there any doubt that he will?"

"I, for one, am beginning to worry a little—"

"He couldn't possibly feel any loyalty to Danton, could he?"

"Loyalty, hell!" said Alex. "I have a friend inside the Danton Clinic who swears the old man had no grounds to fire Paul and Jerry, except that they were on the verge of a breakthrough with this artificial heart business, probably something along the lines Paul spoke about in his paper. But H. Edward isn't going to let anybody take credit for work at the clinic except himself, whether he had anything to do with the actual work or not, so he booted the boys out."

"Then why would Paul back down when it comes to making even a token opposition to Danton for president-elect?"

"H. Edward not only has a monstrous ego, he's also got a secret weapon where young men are concerned—Aletha."

Cary whistled softly. "I never thought of that."

"You mean she's never made a pass at a handsome guy like you?"

"Come to think of it there have been—shall we say opportunities?"

"And you never took advantage of them, I suppose." Klein shook his head resignedly. "What a dope! I hear she's quite a performer in the sack."

"Are you saying she might buy Paul off that way?"

"All I go by are the facts, man. Item one: He was nuts about her two years ago. Item two: Hotel gossip is that she went to his room Sunday night after midnight. What's your opinion?"

Cary whistled softly. "No wonder Paul's been looking a bit troubled the past two days. I take it that you think she's got to him already."

"Or vice versa; we should know at the Young Turks caucus this afternoon." Alex stood up. "Got to get back to the exhibit floor. I'm trying to convince myself I can afford one of those Vibrassage chairs."

"They aren't that expensive, are they?"

"It's me I'm worrying about, not the chair. Jed Porter keeps one in his bedroom. He says making love in one of them damn near drives him and Helen up the wall. See you at the caucus."

CHAPTER XVIII

Paul Rice was in the audio-visual center of the Auditorium, working with the technician showing the closed-circuit films to put a projection machine that had blown a tube back in operation, when Jerry Warren reached him by way of the pocket pager.

"Where are you, Jerry?" he asked.

"In the second floor lounge, buttonholing doctors between the scientific papers and rounding up votes for this afternoon. Is anything badly wrong with the projector?"

"Nothing the technician and I can't fix. They called me when they couldn't find you."

"I've been busy all afternoon bending people's arms before the caucus and left my pager in the lab. Have you seen the afternoon paper?"

"No."

"Better get one before they're all sold out. You and Danton are all over the front page—along with Dr. Poston's Morning-after Pill. That's naturally more important than heart surgery."

"I'm surprised we even made the news, after the shellacking Danton gave us."

"I guess from what Elton Brooks *didn't* tell us, Danton's got more problems than we have."

"He can't really hurt us," Paul agreed. "Our paper will be published in the CMA *Journal* anyway. We do have to get to work on one thing as soon as the convention is over, though."

"The external temporal operation?"

"That, too, but mainly the left ventricular bypass. I've been holding off before until we had more results on the balloon pump. But after this morning we need to go right ahead and apply for an exhibit booth and a place on the program at the clinical meeting of the AMA this coming winter."

"Maybe we can make it," said Jerry. "Danton won't be in the AMA hierarchy by then, they won't even elect him a vice-president until after he serves his year as president of the CMA."

"We've built a better mousetrap, Jerry; the way Danton attacked us proves that," said Paul. "All we have to do now is let the surgical world beat a path to our door."

"I wish I was as optimistic as you are," said Jerry. "Be sure to get a newspaper as soon as you can. It would help our campaign, too, if you would say a few words, after you're voted the nominee by the caucus this afternoon—enough at least to give the lie to Danton. Gotta run, good-by."

"Jerry, I—" Paul tried to keep Jerry on the line but knew he'd failed, when the telephone clicked in his ear and the dial tone came on. After hanging up the receiver, he looked at it thoroughly for a few moments, then picked it up again and dialed an outside number.

"Katie," he said when Jerry's wife answered the ring in their apartment a few blocks away.

"Paul!" she cried. "Have you seen the paper?"

"Jerry just called to tell me. He's running around collecting votes."

"I should think he would be," she said indignantly. "Has Dr. Danton really got a working artificial heart that's better than yours and Jerry's?"

"Elton Brooks says he doesn't have any, but we don't want to get Elton into trouble by quoting him in the press. He's trying to get a job in the new center at Phoenix."

"Dr. Brooks is a nice guy," said Katie. "I never could understand how he has stayed with Dr. Danton as long as he has."

"I called to ask you to do me a favor, Katie."

"Anything short of being untrue to my husband. Come to think of it I might even be talked into that, if you're in the neighborhood."

"All right, you sexy dame." Paul laughed. "This is about a girl."

"Have you got one at last, Paul? I was beginning to think you might be one of *them.*"

"Seriously, Katie, I'm taking a girl named Carlota Montez to the convention dinner dance Wednesday night. Can you get a table together on such short notice, say three or four couples?"

"Sure. There are always plenty of us downtrodden minority group members around. What's she like?"

"A senior at Central U, majoring in biochemistry."

"Not the hen medic type?"

Paul laughed. "No. Her great-great-grandfather was a count or something at the court of Emperor Maximilian in Mexico City. In real life she's a waitress in the Polo Lounge."

"That means she's a knockout," said Katie. "I'm not sure we plain girls ought to let her in the club."

"You're about as plain as Nefertiti," he assured her. "Take down Carlota's telephone number and give her a call. She's got a lot of your records."

"What shall I tell her?"

"What to wear and things like that. You know, woman stuff."

"How about letting her know she's stirred the interest of the most eligible bachelor-doctor in Central City?"

"Make the best case you can for me, I sort of like the girl. See you tomorrow night."

While the technician finished fixing the projector, Paul stepped outside the convention hall to where a rack of newspapers stood near the curb at the loading zone. The story he was looking for wasn't hard to find, for a headline, SURGEONS QUARREL OVER ARTIFICIAL HEART, was spread across the front page, with a story beneath it and pictures of both Paul and Danton.

Glancing over the three-column spread, Paul saw that the writer had given his and Jerry's project more play than Jerry had implied, which didn't surprise him, since it was a Central City newspaper. The reporting was reasonably exact, too, and the sketch of their pump had turned out rather well.

"The press gave you quite a spread, Dr. Rice." The tall, slightly stooped man standing just inside the entrance to the Auditorium seemed familiar, and when Paul read the name on his badge he knew why.

"Almost as much as you got yesterday, Dr. Forbes," he said. "And with less reason."

"If you'd lost as many coronary cases as I have from shock in the first few hours, you wouldn't say that," Jethro Forbes told him. "I just hope when I get mine, it will be while both of us are in Central City. Did you get to the president's luncheon?"

Paul shook his head. "I was going but a projector broke down. I'm chairman of that section of the Arrangements Committee, so I had to stop and see that it was fixed. Did anything new come up?"

"Nothing we didn't know already. The Secretary for Health in HEW told us Medicare will bankrupt the nation, if better ways aren't worked out to cut costs. But he didn't tell us how to do that, except through HMOs."

Paul was familiar with the term: Health Maintenance Organizations were the new government ploy to solve some of the thorny problems of providing medical care. Essentially the idea was centered around groups of doctors, usually working through a big hospital. The theory was that one HMO to an area would provide complete medical care, with the whole thing being paid for through a universal system of health insurance. Those who could would pay monthly premiums covering regular medical care and also various portions of catastrophic costs, depending upon which of the proposed plans was adopted. Those who couldn't would be covered by a Medicare-like setup.

"Do you think an HMO can really save on costs?" Paul asked as he and Jethro were walking through the exhibit area, on the way to the ramps leading upward to the meeting halls.

"The government certainly thinks so," said Jethro. "According to the secretary, judging from the experience of such clinics as the Kaiser-Permanente ones and a number of others, a well-organized group can cut hospital days by nearly twenty-five per cent and admissions almost as much. That means lowering the costs in the hospital sector that account for roughly forty per cent of medical-care expense today."

When Paul looked startled and instinctively turned his head to study the speciality designation on Jethro's badge, the older doctor chuckled.

"It's GP, Dr. Rice—and that's what I am."

"But—"

"You shouldn't be surprised that I'm interested in the socio-economic side of medicine. Those of us in general practice are involved in all the problems that beset medicine in general, perhaps even more than most doctors because we're right at the root of the whole question, the sick individual. I got interested in the subject nearly twenty years ago when I was in medical school. Read a book called *That None Should Die,* published, I believe, about 1941. The author, a doctor, had a plan of medical care all worked out at a time when group practice was still a dirty word to most doctors and health insurance even worse."

"What was the plan?"

"It involved organizing medical facilities and personnel throughout the country into districts with hospitals and a professional group or groups providing each area with complete medical care, much like the government is proposing that the HMOs do today. The lower income groups would have their costs paid by the government, pretty much like so-called charity hospitals do now. The middle income section was to be covered with nationwide group insurance, collected like a tax and paid out by an autonomous commission to keep it out of politics. The upper income groups could buy their own health insurance wherever they wished."

"Sounds complete enough."

"It's the nearest to a perfect system I've ever seen, even

though it was devised a good thirty years or more ago."
Jethro chuckled again. "Which goes to show you that a
prophet is without honor in his own land and there's nothing new under the sun." He glanced at his watch. "I've
got to run. There's a paper starting a few minutes from
now on malaria in the communicable disease section and
I don't want to miss it."

Paul was halfway through the passageway beneath Auditorium Avenue, on the way to the Hotel Centralia to
see if there were any messages for him, when it occurred
to him to wonder why a general practitioner from Revere,
Kansas—the town typed on Jethro's Forbes's convention
badge beneath his name—would need to study malaria.

ii

Cary Poston was making a note on the chart of the last
patient he was scheduled to see in his office that afternoon, when the telephone rang. It was Marian.

"Can I talk to you somewhere, Cary?" she asked.

"Sure. Is anything wrong?"

"Nothing except that I made a fool of myself at lunch
today."

"You were tired and upset over Edward Danton. Are
you dressed?"

"Yes."

"How about a drink in the Polo Lounge?"

"I'd rather make it coffee in the hotel coffee shop.
We're supposed to have cocktails with Edward and Aletha
Danton at seven."

"Good Lord! I'd forgotten that. Want me to call it off?"

"No. We'll discuss it when I see you. Ten minutes?"

"Fine."

He was there in nine minutes, followed by the detective
who'd been his shadow since the conference in the Medical Examiner's office the night before. When Marian
stepped out of the elevator, he was waiting.

The coffee shop was almost empty, although the Polo

Lounge was already doing a thriving business even before five o'clock.

"I owe you an apology for blowing up the way I did at lunch," said Marian when they were seated. "It must have been embarrassing for you."

"Don't even think about it. After all, you were under a strain."

"Things did sort of pile up on me," she admitted. "I was planning to drop a blockbuster with my paper but I'm afraid the whole thing fizzled. You got more publicity with that Morning-after Pill."

"Your turn will come," he told her. "You finished your presentation too late to make the afternoon editions."

"To be completely honest, it doesn't make much difference any more."

"Your work is valuable—and definitive. It's bound to be recognized as such by people who really count in the fields of embryology and genetics."

"I'm even less confident of that now than I was a few days ago," she admitted.

"Surely not because Edward Danton saw a chance to cop the limelight by putting you down?"

"No. I can hold my own in that kind of a dogfight when I need to. I guess deep down, it's you that's disturbing me."

"Why?"

"You don't fit the pattern."

He chuckled. "Give me another ten years. I've been working so hard to sweep you off your feet, because we don't have as much time as we might have."

"I've spent most of my life proving I can be independent of men and hold my own in any field," said Marian. "Then you turn me into a simpering schoolgirl overnight. I ought to hate you for it, but I can't—damn it."

"That's the best news I've heard since I met you at the airport Sunday."

"I guess I was really running away from my own weakness today when I stood you up in the restaurant," she

253

admitted. "Let's change the subject. What have you been doing?"

"Trying not to look like a man who's being followed."

"Why?" she asked in a tone of quick concern.

"We're trying to keep it under wraps, so as not to stampede the convention," said Cary. "The tests show that Senator Spurgess was poisoned—with aconite."

"Oh, Cary! That's terrible! Does anyone have an idea why?"

"A lot of people here at the convention hated him."

"Doctors don't go around killing politicians just because they don't like what men like Spurgess say."

"Everybody at the conference we had this morning was convinced that the poisoner is after me."

"No, Cary!" Marian caught her breath in a gasp of protest—and fear. "Who would hate you enough to want to kill you?"

"The only person I could think of would be one of your rejected suitors." He laughed. "Do you know of anybody who would be jealous enough of me to want to kill me?"

"Of course not. I was practically a hermit until you swept me off my feet at the airport, and put me right up on Cloud Nine."

"Stay there until I can persuade you to marry me."

"Seriously, Cary. Who could possibly want to kill you?"

"None of us has the least idea, but both Andy Huxtable and Lieutenant Klinger are so certain of their theory, they insisted that I take precautions."

"What precautions could you take?"

"The police are taking them for me," he explained. "See the man there at the end of the counter—the broad-shouldered one?"

"Yes."

"He's half of a team that's watching me day and night."

"But what good could they do?"

"Spurgess collapsed after drinking beer. Apparently someone managed to drop a lethal dose of aconite in his cup and the police believe it was intended for me."

"Where did the beer come from?"

"The Central Pharmaceutical exhibit."

"Why don't the police look there?"

"Lieutenant Klinger did. Hundreds of people drank from the same keg yesterday morning, including both Spurgess and myself. The cups were in stacks and it would be impossible to know which cup would be given to me, so Lieutenant Klinger is certain the Central Pharmaceutical exhibit wasn't the source of the poison."

"Doesn't that mean it will be even harder for you to protect yourself?"

"Impossible would seem to be the word," he admitted soberly.

"So what can you do?"

"Atropine appears to be the only answer. Aconite acts first on the cardiac inhibitory center of the brain, so the first symptom is slowing of the pulse by way of the vagus nerve. In the kind of dosage this murderer has been using, it quickly reaches the heart through the digestive tract and the circulation. By acting directly on both the cardiac muscle and the nervous system of the heart itself, it causes paralysis very quickly and death a few minutes later."

"But if you were in coma, you wouldn't be able to give yourself an injection of atropine."

"Strangely enough, the cerebrum itself isn't affected by aconite until the very last moments before death. The major action is on the lower brain centers in the region of the medulla oblongata, which means that the victim is conscious right up to the moment of death and might have time to take an antidote."

"Is there one—besides atropine?"

"Not really. Of course anything that induces vomiting would help remove the drug from the stomach. But according to Dr. Singh, one of our residents from Nepal, the poison that killed Spurgess is so potent that death occurs before you could possibly wash out the stomach of a victim. Only atropine given rapidly in large doses, and preferably intravenously, would have a chance of being effective."

From his coat pocket Cary took the small, cloth-wrapped package prepared for him last night in the hospital Emergency Room.

"Two sterile syringes are in here, each loaded with one point two milligrams of atropine," he told Marian. "My pulse is always a little fast whenever I'm with you. If it ever starts slowing down, give me one of those ampules hypodermically as fast as you can."

"This isn't anything to joke about, Cary."

"Nobody's joking, darling. I only wish I were. It's not very pleasant being the bait that we hope will lure a murderer into trying again, so we can trap him."

"How long did you say it would take us to fly down to that cottage of yours in the Big Bend?" she asked suddenly.

"A couple of hours."

"Let's go, Cary."

"Of course—the moment the convention is over on Thursday—"

"I mean now. This afternoon."

He put his hand over hers on the table and found it damp and trembling. "Running away wouldn't accomplish anything, Marian. We both know that."

"I only know I don't want to become a widow, before I've even decided to become a wife." She was near to crying. "If you really love me the way you say you do—"

"You don't mean that, darling."

"Then promise me one thing."

"Anything—except running away."

"Bring your toothbrush when you come to pick me up for cocktails with the Dantons at seven. And stay with me until the police capture the murderer."

"Best offer I've had in two days." Cary smiled and lifted her hand to kiss it. "I'll see you at seven and give the policeman who's guarding me the night off."

iii

A dozen doctors filled the suite in the Hotel Centralia which Dr. H. Edward Danton had rented as his headquarters for the political campaign to make him president-elect of the CMA. By the time Danton himself arrived about four-thirty for the final pre-election caucus, the level of whiskey in the bottles on the table in the corner, along with various necessities for making drinks, had been lowered considerably.

All the men there were over forty, most of them past fifty. Well dressed and obviously successful, they made up the hierarchy which had controlled the operation of the Central Medical Association for close to a decade.

"Pour me some scotch and water, John, I'm bushed," Danton told Dr. John Towers. The current president-elect, Towers, would take office at the Third General Session just before noon on Thursday to serve a year in the highest office of the CMA.

As Towers moved to the table where the bottles stood, Alex Klein spoke from the back of the room. A member of the Association's governing Council, he'd been invited to the caucus, even though known to be a supporter of Paul Rice's candidacy for president-elect.

"The way I hear it, a lot of young men among the membership are pretty hot over the way you attacked Paul Rice and Jerry Warren this morning on a purely scientific question, Danton," said Klein. "What's the matter? Running scared?"

"Of course not." Danton took the glass Dr. Towers handed him. "I taught Paul everything he knows about heart surgery and now I'm giving him a crash course in medical politics. One day he'll realize I'm doing him a favor."

"You still didn't gain any votes this morning, Edward," said Dr. Towers bluntly. "And you didn't help CMA either. The days when a few of us could run the Association pretty much the way we wanted to run it are over, just like they're over for all of medicine."

"Maybe I was a little rough on Paul." Danton put down his glass. "If it will make the rest of you happy I'll apologize, and even appoint him chairman of an important committee when I'm president."

"The Association certainly needs some new blood," a doctor said from the back of the room. "We all made a helluva mess by failing to anticipate the country's need for medical care—from the AMA right down to the county medical societies. Now we're practically certain to have something we don't want rammed down our throats by the federal government."

"We won't get anywhere by turning this caucus into a gripe session against government medicine," said Danton. "A strong sentiment is building up in the country against any more federal participation in people's lives. All we need to do is give it time to fulfill its role."

"But can we hold off the radical element in the profession that long?" said Towers: "Especially after Spurgess delivered that diatribe yesterday."

"In my acceptance speech on Thursday, I'm going to refute Spurgess' charges one by one," Danton promised. "Then I'll go on to show how this plan would cost eight per cent of the GNP in a few years or, roughly, five times as much as the Vietnam war cost in its most expensive year. We'll get full coverage from press, radio and TV, so we ought to be able to scare hell out of a lot of people who have been conned into believing the U.S. doesn't really have the best medical-care set up in the world."

Danton drained his glass and handed it to Dr. Towers for a refill. "Now let's get down to the business of the caucus. All of you are on the Council so you ought to know how sentiment is running. We'll start with the Central City District. What do you say, Klein?"

"The younger faculty members are highly organized," said Alex. "If it came to a showdown, they could outvote the conservatives and I'm inclined to go along with them."

"What do you suggest?"

"Nominate Paul Rice for a lower echelon post, at the very least a member of the Council."

"That's out," said Danton flatly.

"Are you sure this isn't a purely personal vendetta you're waging against Paul because he and Jerry have forged far ahead in the race for an artificial heart?"

258

Danton ignored the question, but as the surgeon turned to Dr. John Towers, Alex Klein saw that a tortuous artery visible beneath the skin at his left temple was throbbing dangerously.

"All right, John," said Danton. "What about your district?"

"The rank and file among the membership are supporting you just like they've always supported whoever the Nominating Committee has put up in the past," said Towers. "But among the medical school faculties, the younger men are clamoring for more of a say in the organization."

"I've promised to give Paul Rice a committee post a year from now," said Danton. "If you appoint someone his age to a high spot this year it will appease the liberal element and give us time to work something out."

"I'm already working on that," said Towers.

"Good," said Danton. "Let's hear from the rest of you."

One by one the Council, representing leading members of the medical profession in the entire central part of the United States, responded. And everywhere the sentiment was much the same. Physicians in private practice, particularly those who operated their own offices as individuals —as opposed to groups—were generally too busy making money to bother much with medical politics and could be counted upon to deliver a routine vote for the organization candidates. But with the younger element, who were more likely to become faculty members of medical schools or work with larger groups. the story was different. Knowing no time when a considerable portion of medical-care costs had not been covered by some form of insurance, often government sponsored through Medicare and Medicaid, they recognized that the old "fee for service" principle was long since dead and must be replaced by something that would really work.

When the reports were finished, most of the men there were sober. However well they'd been able to dominate medical politics throughout the central states in the past, hardly any of them failed to realize that control was rapidly slipping from their hands. And almost none, except Alex Klein, could be really happy about the prospect, since most members of the Council had ambitions one day to occupy the position for which Danton was the announced candidate.

"I'd say we have them licked," Danton summed up the results of the caucus somewhat more optimistically than many of the others would have done. "The thing now is to get out the vote among the segment of the profession we can depend upon. That means each of you has got to work like hell between now and Thursday."

"We'll have to spend a lot of money for liquor," said a doctor from Texas with the leathery countenance of one who spent a great deal of time in the sun. "A few slugs of free Bourbon will get votes a damned sight faster than all the oratory and logic you can muster."

"Spend it them, I'll foot the bill." Danton looked at his watch. "Bring as many votes as you can with you to the General Session Thursday. I want to see a real turnout."

He rose to his feet but swayed suddenly and might have fallen if Dr. John Towers, who was standing nearby, hadn't caught his arm. For an instant, it almost seemed as if Danton had lost touch with his surroundings. He quickly recovered, however, and shaking off Towers' hand, started to leave the room. But when Alex Klein saw that Danton's right foot dragged ever so slightly and the fingers of his right hand tended to curl, the psychiatrist's eyes narrowed.

Before Klein could say anything, however, Danton had left the room. And by the time the psychiatrist reached the door, from which he could see Danton moving down the hall with Dr. Towers, the slight drag of the right foot and cramping in the fingers of the right hand seemed to have disappeared.

Nevertheless, Klein went to the hotel telephone and rang the central operator at University Hospital across the street. When she answered, he asked to be connected with the paging operator, whose task it was to communicate with doctors carrying the small electronic pagers required of all staff personnel wherever they went.

"Where are you, Paul?" Klein asked when Paul Rice's voice sounded in the receiver.

"At the Auditorium. The audio-visual technician has been having some trouble with one of the films to be shown on closed-circuit TV."

"I want to talk to you about something," said Klein. "Don't leave before I get there."

CHAPTER XIX

Paul was watching a film on a small monitor when Alex Klein came into the room.

"Keep on with whatever you're doing," said the psychiatrist. "We've got an hour before the Young Turk caucus starts."

"Seen Jerry lately?" Paul asked.

"Not since lunch. I thought he'd be with you."

"Jerry's taking my candidacy seriously. Apparently he's out corralling votes."

"Wouldn't you expect him to? After all, he worships you."

"I wish I deserved it more."

"You'll do—'til something better comes along. I just came from the Danton pre-election caucus."

"Is it ethical for you to be here, when I'm supposed to be a candidate?"

"I told Danton flat out I'd rather vote for you than him."

"Still I wish Jerry hadn't talked me into letting my name be entered. Now everybody's saying it's only a grudge fight between Danton and myself because he kicked us out of the clinic and attacked us this morning."

"Isn't it?"

"Not really. Nobody could deny that Danton deserves to be president more than anybody else in the CMA."

"I have to agree," said Alex. "But I still don't like the son of a bitch."

"Jerry feels the same way; with him this is a grudge fight."

"And with good reason."

"Maybe so, but I'm more concerned that Danton's election may generally be considered a victory for the reactionary faction in the CMA and the medical profession as a whole. That could slow down what progress we're beginning to achieve toward making the kind of medical care we give in university centers available to all."

"I'm sure Jerry would like nothing better than to give your old chief a swift kick," said Klein. "But from what I saw just now at the caucus, I'm not so sure Danton hasn't already done that to himself—without even being a contortionist."

"What are you talking about, Alex?"

The psychiatrist described the brief attack Danton appeared to have had at the end of the caucus and his remarkably quick recovery.

"What do you make of it?" Paul asked.

"From where I sat, it looked like transient cerebral ischemia."

"Vascular surgeons move faster and call it TCI," said Paul. "When General Eisenhower had one, it was thought to be a slight stroke from spasm of one of the smaller arteries of the brain. Nowadays we know it can have a number of causes, all of them bad. Did Danton appear to be okay just before it happened?"

"He was his usual repulsive self," said Klein. "I'm afraid I riled him a little, though—by saying I'd rather vote for you. That might have brought on the TCI."

"Anger can do it, if the basic cause is already there. Did he appear to lose consciousness?"

"No. But he did sway against John Towers. Could have been a little vertigo, I suppose."

"You said his right foot was dragging, didn't you?"

"Not for long. By the time I got to the door, where I could watch him walking down the hall, he seemed to have recovered." Alex frowned. "You don't seem surprised. What do you know that I don't, Paul?"

"Have you seen Danton's film on excision of a cardiac infarct? It's being shown nights on closed-circuit TV."

"I don't look at surgical films," said Klein. "It's all I can do to keep up on progress in my own field."

"In the middle of the film another surgeon took over. Jerry and I recognized the difference in the size of the surgeon's hands."

"Do you think Danton had a TCI attack in the middle of the operation?"

"Probably. We've learned from other sources that he has practically stopped doing major cardiac surgery."

Alex Klein gave Paul a quick look. "If Danton's afraid to operate because a TCI might catch him in the middle of an important procedure, he's pretty vulnerable. All you have to do is reveal——"

"No, Alex."

"Why not? He certainly hasn't done you any favors lately."

"I'm not going to make a political advantage out of another surgeon's physical weakness." Paul switched off the monitor he had been watching and got to his feet. "Where would you expect Elton Brooks to be about now?"

"In the Polo Lounge—or the Auditorium cocktail lounge. It's that time of day."

"Let's go."

As Alex Klein had suggested, Elton Brooks was in the Auditorium cocktail lounge, nursing a double scotch.

"I was about to have you paged, Paul," he said before Paul could speak.

"That's a coincidence. I'm looking for you."

"It's no coincidence," said Brooks soberly. "I suppose Alex told you about Dr. Danton's TCI attack, as the caucus was breaking up just now. I was in the corridor outside the caucus room and saw it."

"This isn't the first one either, is it?" Paul asked and the other young heart surgeon shook his head.

"I was waiting for the chief to warn him that I was going to tell you why we had to change surgeons in the middle of the infarct operation and came in here to fortify my conscience a little."

"You didn't have to tell me so you didn't break your word," said Paul quickly. "I knew the answer as soon as Alex told me about the attack. How long has this been going on?"

"About three months. But they're getting more frequent."

"No wonder he's been pushing hell for leather to get that vote over with Thursday," said Paul. "Imagine having everything you've worked for almost within your grasp and then seeing your chances fade because part of your brain sometimes doesn't function properly."

"I tried to tell you this morning that Danton isn't entirely to blame for the way he's been going after you, Paul. But I couldn't quite manage it without revealing the whole thing. Danton's fighting to win the election—"

"And I just happen to be in the way," said Paul. "Fortunately I can remedy that."

"How?" Alex Klein asked.

"By stopping Jerry from nominating me."

Alex Klein looked at his watch. "The Young Turk caucus is being held in Parlor C at the Hotel Centralia. It's probably already started so you'd better get Jerry on the pager and head him off."

Paul picked up the telephone and dialed the hospital paging operator. "Would you call Dr. Jerry Warren for me?" he asked.

"I've been trying to get Dr. Warren for someone else for more than ten minutes, Dr. Rice. He doesn't answer."

"Thank you." Paul hung up the phone and started for the door. "I just remembered Jerry telling me earlier that he wasn't carrying the pager, Alex. We'll have to catch him before the caucus."

ii

"I wonder where Paul is." Jerry Warren was standing with Cary Poston at the door of Parlor C, watching a stream of doctors, most of them from the younger section of the membership, pour into the meeting room. "He was helping fix a projector when I talked to him awhile ago but he ought to be through over there by now."

"We're getting a good turnout," Cary observed. "Maybe that's a good sign."

"And a lot of women doctors. They're always more socially conscious than men."

"Paul's being young and handsome should influence that vote, too," said Cary. "Pete Sanders tells me there are roughly a hundred and fifty women registered so far, out of nearly two thousand total."

"Seven per cent is roughly the national average of women doctors."

Cary turned into the doorway and glanced toward the dais at the far end of the room, where a podium and a microphone had been placed on a small platform.

"Looks like they're about ready to call the Young Turks Committee to order," he said.

"I'm supposed to be up front," said Jerry. "Try to corral Paul when he comes in, Dr. Poston, and ride herd on him until I can get him nominated. He's been pretty skittish since yesterday about going through with it. I left my pager in the lab this afternoon so he couldn't get me."

"Some achieve greatness, others have it thrust upon them," said Cary.

"This time the reason is Aletha Danton," said Jerry. "Paul had quite a crush on her our last year at the clinic and the grapevine says she's been making a play for him, since she and Danton got to Central City."

"A lot of men I know would like to have her making a play for them," said Cary.

"Paul can have her. Just so long as he doesn't let her talk him out of running against H. Edward."

265

"I'll hang on to him when he gets here," Cary promised. "But if you think there's a possibility of his refusing to be nominated, you'd better get up front where he can't get to you so easily."

On the podium, the heavily bearded temporary chairman of the Young Turks Committee—self-elected, Cary suspected—was pounding with his gavel to bring the meeting to order. Spotting Jethro Forbes in the back row of seats near the aisle, Cary took a seat beside him, where he could see the doorway, if Paul Rice came in.

A permanent chairman was quickly elected. Naturally it was the one already in the chair, an assistant professor of family practice in a Texas medical school.

"Gentlemen," said the chairman, when the buzz of conversation had subsided after considerable gavel banging, "let me have your attention, please."

A conference on procedure seemed to be going on between the new presiding officer on the dais and several other doctors, including Jerry Warren, who was standing behind it. Meanwhile, the buzz of conversation filled the room.

"First we need to elect a secretary," the chairman announced finally. "Do I hear a nomination?"

Another man with a beard was duly nominated and quickly elected.

"The way this thing's going, it will soon look like a Shaker Convention," Cary said in disgust as, notebook already in hand, the secretary moved up to the dais and took a seat beside the chairman.

Jethro chuckled. "It's strange that when people decide to rebel against one kind of rule, they always wind up using the same tactics as those they're rebelling against."

"I guess you're right," said Cary. "If those guys up there are put into office, they'll be further to the right in six months than the hierarchy we already have."

"Is your man any better?" Jethro asked.

"We hope so. At least if Paul Rice gets elected, you won't feel like you're being manipulated either by guys with beards like those up there or smooth ones like Danton."

"I took a patient to Danton years ago," said Jethro. "He certainly rules the roost down there."

"Danton's the usual megalomaniac, the kind that rides roughshod over everybody else and finally winds up with all the marbles."

"A lot of good they do them though," said Jethro. "Even in a small town like Revere, you can't help seeing that the people who are always pushing to get ahead usually wind up in the soup together. Once they reach the point where they can't go any higher, the main driving force in their lives sort of peters out on them. The next thing you know they've been clobbered by a coronary or a stroke."

On the platform the chairman was pounding vigorously with his gavel once again.

"Will those of you in the back stop talking, please," he said severely. "The medical profession stands at the crossroads—"

"Oh, my God! Not another standing-at-the-crossroads speech," said Cary.

"The Central Medical Association has been run by a handful of willful men," the chairman continued. "And we have all followed them like sheep."

"Hear, hear!" said a pudgy man with a British accent.

"What right does he have to applaud?" said Cary, *sotto voce*. "He left England in the first place to escape National Health Insurance and that's what they're trying to ram down our throats again."

"Now we're being asked to vote a man into the highest office of the CMA who is further to the right than his predecessors have ever been," the chairman continued: "I ask you, is this the way to act, when young doctors are clamoring everywhere for more social consciousness in our profession?"

Cries of "No!" "Never!" and "Down with the Establishment!" sounded here and there. The chairman pounded on the gavel, but not too heavily, until they subsided.

"I want you to hear from a leader among the young men who will shortly be taking your place and mine," he said. "The president of Students for Modernizing Medicine, Mr. Johnathan Peters, a senior at Central University Medical School."

Johnathan Peters had long hair, a droopy mustache and a small pointed beard.

"That guy was flunking his second year, until he hit on the sociology kick and got himself elected president of the student body," said Cary. "Then the faculty was afraid to fire him for fear of stirring up a riot."

"I thought that only happened to school boards in small towns," said Jethro with a chuckle. "Mind if I ask how you voted?"

"I'm a maverick, so I voted to can the guy."

"Do you feel any better for having taken a stand?"

"We mavericks always feel good when we've got our backs up about something, but then, so do the rest of the paranoiacs." Cary had spoken the last word without really thinking about it, but the significance of the word "paranoiac" struck him now like a body blow. Instinctively, he turned to look at the back of the room and felt a sudden surge of relief at the sight of the solid-looking man in the blue serge suit who was his guardian on the daytime shift.

"Ladies and gentlemen, fellow members of the medical profession, I will take only a few moments of your time." The words rolled off Johnathan Peters' tongue in an obviously well-rehearsed speech. "The medical students of America are determined that our profession shall not continue down the old paths."

"We're being bombarded with clichés today," said Cary.

"Next to the treatment of illness—and sometimes before it—we have a grave responsibility for the welfare of the souls of men," said the speaker. "To cure the body we must no longer be concerned only with what happens after bacteria strike or the degenerative process has already begun. We must look at the entire picture, the whole aspect of man as a social animal."

There was a spatter of applause and the speaker waited patiently for it to subside.

"Which means that we must cure not only a patient's physical ills but his emotional and social ills as well, because the three cannot be separated. It means making certain that every family has a living income, adequate medical care, and most important of all, the right to live in a normal environment that will let their children grow up to be well-rounded human beings."

Jethro Forbes chuckled. "What he's describing is a fat bastard who refuses to work but enthusiastically fertilizes every ovum he can get to. When young Dr. Peters gets out into practice and starts paying taxes to achieve this Utopia he's yapping about, you'll find him singing a different tune."

"That, gentlemen, must be our goal," the speaker's voice took on an even more portentous note. "And since it is, we must use every means to reach our objective through the voice of the most influential medical society short of the AMA. We must put forth a candidate for president-elect who possesses conviction and the determination to defeat the hierarchy represented by H. Edward Danton."

The applause this time was heavy, to Cary's surprise. When he looked at Jethro he saw that the older doctor was applauding, too, although the crooked smile was back on his face again.

"If you don't believe what he said, why the applause?" Cary asked.

"For one thing it will get him off the platform," said Jethro. "For another, some things need to be applauded: Motherhood, the flag, the President, the church. Hell, man, this country would fall on its face without them."

The chairman was holding up his hand for attention, but it was a while before the applause subsided.

"Thank you, Johnathan," he said when the room was quiet again. "I know you're going to be a leader in our profession—"

"If he ever passes the National Board," said Cary Poston to Jethro.

"Now we come to our most important task," the chairman announced. "The selection of a rump candidate who will be nominated from the floor to oppose Dr. H. Edward Danton in the election on Thursday morning. I recognize Dr. Jerry Warren."

iii

"And, so, ladies and gentlemen—" On the platform, Jerry was winding up the brief nominating speech when Paul entered the room with Alex Klein—"I wish to place in nomination for sponsorship by this group the name of a man whom most of you know by reputation as the coming young cardiac surgeon of the country."

"How does it feel to be eulogized without having to be in a coffin?" said Alex, when the applause momentarily interrupted Jerry's speech.

"I don't like it." Paul had moved farther into the room and was standing at the end of the aisle where Cary and Jethro were sitting.

"One of the coming young men of medicine in America," Jerry continued, "Dr. Paul Rice, professor of cardiovascular surgery in the Central University Medical School."

The round of applause that followed was punctuated suddenly by Paul's voice: "Mr. Chairman!"

He had spoken loudly and everybody on the platform looked startled, most of all Jerry Warren.

"Dr. Rice, isn't it?" said the chairman. "The light isn't very good back there."

"Paul Rice, Mr. Chairman," Paul's voice was clear, as was his determination. "I wish to withdraw my nomination."

"That is your privilege, Dr. Rice." The chairman stroked his beard. "But this is most un—"

Paul had been casting about in his mind for a logical public explanation to support his announcement. He found it now in the gesture the chairman had just made.

"My reason for refusing the honor done me by my colleague, Dr. Warren, and which would have been done

270

by all of you, had you seen fit to elect me, is simply this: I have not been active in this movement before, due to the demands of organizing a service and getting a research program under way here at Central University Medical School. Therefore, it would not be fitting for me to accept this honor, when there are those in this room, particularly one on the platform, who deserve it so much more than I. It is an honor, therefore, Mr. Chairman, to place your name in nomination."

He sat down amid cries of "Move the nominations be closed" and "Question! Question!"

The chairman was quickly elected, to his evident pleasure, and people began to filter from the room bound for the bars of the various hotels.

"I must say you surprised me, Dr. Rice," said Jethro Forbes as the three of them were leaving the meeting room. "Though I was hoping you would do just what you did."

"Mind telling me why?"

"Medical society elections are always rigged," said Jethro. "The candidates are chosen by nominating committees in the medical equivalent of smoke-filled rooms, not on any meeting floor. I'm sure you would have gotten more votes than any other rump candidate I can think of, but you would have been clobbered just the same. And it doesn't do a future candidate any good to have the record of a loss in his dossier."

Jethro's eyes twinkled. "Besides, whoever labeled the last-minute entry a rump candidate knew what he was talking about. They're always at the ass-end of the line and out in the cold."

"You'd better run, Paul," said Cary. "I see Jerry heading this way with murder in his eye."

Paul didn't quite make it, for Jerry caught up with him just before he reached the door and followed him outside.

"What the hell was the idea of making me look like a damned fool just now?" he demanded angrily.

"I didn't intend it that way, Jerry. It's just that at the last minute I couldn't go through with it."

"What happened? That's what I want to know."

"I don't even know myself, Jerry. I've been in doubt ever since we discovered that Danton seemed to be in trouble physically. Maybe it was too much like kicking a guy when he's down."

iv

H. Edward Danton was taking an afternoon nap in his suite, when Aletha stormed in, a folded afternoon newspaper under her arm. Tossing it in his direction without speaking, she went to the tray of bottles and glasses on the chest, poured a double shot of Bourbon and drank it neat, before turning to face him.

"Of all the damn fool stunts!" she snapped. "You were planning all along to knife Paul in the back when he gave his paper, weren't you?"

"Of course. That's politics."

"Did you know he withdrew his nomination by the Young Turks Committee?"

Danton looked up quickly. "When did you hear that?"

"Just now. I've been working all afternoon in the medical history exhibit of the Auxiliary and Cary Poston told me about it, when I ran into him in the hotel lobby downstairs. Do you have any idea why Paul withdrew?"

"Because he knew he'd be clobbered in the election. What else?"

"He did it because he's too decent to take advantage of you by publicizing those attacks of yours. John Towers was with you right after the caucus yesterday. He told me he thought you were going to collapse."

"It was nothing—"

"Just like the others were nothing? Especially the one that made you turn over the heart operation to Elton Brooks in the middle of the film?"

"It wasn't that bad."

"Can you be sure how bad the next one will be?"

"Of course not."

"Or that Elton can always handle something you start?

272

He's not the surgeon Paul Rice is, you know. If a patient dies because you aren't able to complete an operation, the clinic will be wide open to a suit for damages."

Danton shrugged. "I've taken care of Paul Rice, that was the important thing."

"And destroyed all the progress I've made toward getting Paul in the mood to come back to the clinic, if this trouble you're having gets worse."

"Or if I die suddenly with a stroke?" Danton's eyes narrowed. "That's what you're really working for, isn't it?"

"And what's wrong with making certain the work you've done will go on?" she demanded angrily. "Especially when you're doing everything you can to make that impossible by driving away the one surgeon who could step in and take your place."

"In my clinic? Or in my bed? Which would it be, Aletha?"

She didn't back down. "What's wrong with both? We've worked hard to build something that can be a monument to both of us. We've never balked at anything that had to be done and I don't plan to throw it all away, just to build your ego."

Moving to the dressing table, she sprayed perfume upon her neck and shoulders with an atomizer and turned to the door.

"Where are you going?" he asked.

"To make up to Paul for what you did today. And don't ask me how."

v

Paul had just come into his hotel room, after the caucus in Parlor C, when there was a knock on the door. He half expected it to be Jerry, still indignant over his withdrawal. To his surprise it was Aletha Danton.

"Aren't you going to invite me in, darling?" she said.

"Of course. Excuse me please, I'm a little upset."

She brushed against him as she came into the room and he would have had to be a monk not to be conscious of the perfume she was wearing and the strong allure of her body as it touched his.

"Was Jerry very much disturbed because you withdrew your name?" she asked.

"How did you know that so soon?"

"Cary Poston told me in the lobby. I came to tell you how much I appreciate what you did for *me.*"

She was standing so close that he could easily have taken her in his arms and he moved away lest his resolve weaken in the face of what her coming this afternoon, and the warm intimacy of her tone, implied.

"How much trouble is Dr. Danton having, Aletha?" he asked.

"What do you mean?" There was a wary note in her voice.

"Didn't Elton Brooks tell you Jerry and I noticed the change of surgeons during the film on cardiac infarct excision?"

"No."

"But you did know about the TCI attack Dr. Danton had this afternoon at the end of his caucus?"

"John Towers told me about that," she admitted. "Edward has had a few of them. But what difference does that make to you?"

"Stop playing games, Aletha. We both know you didn't come here Sunday night after midnight just to say hello. And my chances of winning the election couldn't have been important enough for you to give—or maybe I should say, sell—yourself to me so I wouldn't go on with it."

Ignoring her angry gasp of protest he added, "So there's only one other answer. You intended to tie me so closely to yourself that I'd be willing to take Dr. Danton's place, if he's no longer able to operate."

"You scum!" The tautness in her voice told him her temper was near the eruption point, but he didn't realize quite how near in time to duck. Her right hand, driven with all the force of a body kept lithe with tennis and golf, struck him on the right cheek with a force that threw him off balance and dropped him momentarily to his knees.

A sudden sticking pain in his cheek told him the large diamond ring she wore had found something distinctly softer than itself and for an instant he thought she was going to strike him again. Then she whirled and was through the door and into the hall before he could get back to his feet.

Closing the door behind her, he went to the bathroom mirror and bathed the tiny deep cut the diamond had made before covering it with a Band-Aid. His cheek still hurt but it was amazing how free he felt, with the weight that had been heavy upon his mind ever since he'd learned that Aletha Danton was in Central City now lifted.

CHAPTER XX

Alice Perrault and Jethro Forbes had finished dinner, this time at a fake Polynesian restaurant called the Luau. But if the surroundings were fake, compared to the nighttime loveliness of the Japanese garden at the Steak House where they had eaten the night before, the food was savory and authentic—even to the suckling pig roasted in a pit with fruits and vegetables surrounding it, and the orange-flavored liqueur they were enjoying now in fragile brandy snifters.

"I'm going to love the tropics," said Jethro.

"How can you be so sure?" she asked.

"Did you ever spend a winter in Revere, Kansas?"

"It couldn't be much worse than West Virginia. I left there as soon as I finished high school to study nursing." Her tone became bitter for the first time that evening. "When you've knocked around as much as I have, one part of the country is pretty much like another—except for the distance between the convention hall and the hotel."

"A pharmaceutical house in Kansas City organizes several medical tours every year," said Jethro. "They arrange to have enough clinical papers read wherever you go to make the whole thing a legitimate tax deduction, so it's pretty attractive to doctors who want to take a vacation. I read about the Mayan ruins in Guatemala years ago, and when I got some literature on a medical tour there, I decided to go."

"Ever since I read a book about those stone statues with the big heads, I've wanted to visit Easter Island," Alice said wistfully. "But I guess I'll never get to go."

Jethro Forbes reached across the small table and covered her hand with his own. "A travel agency in New York organizes trips to Easter. Would you let me take you there?"

Alice caught her breath, and suddenly had to fight back the tears, for she knew him well enough by now to realize that the offer was genuine.

"Your wife wouldn't like that," she managed to say.

"I told you I'm not going back to Revere—or to her."

"Then you certainly don't want to become involved with a blonde who runs a commercial booth at conventions."

"I want to become involved with you," he said simply. "What or where you've been up to now doesn't matter at all."

"Tell me more about Guatemala." Alice deliberately changed the subject.

"It won't be wholly a bed of roses," he admitted. "There are always some drawbacks—like stepping into an ant hill in the darkness."

Alice smiled. "I sat down on one when I was on a picnic in Florida. Talk about hot pants! I invented them then and there."

"The country's everything you've read about in the *National Geographic,* but I wanted something more primitive," said Jethro. "While the others were hunting for a couple of days, I went to Tikal and Antigua—"

"Antigua's an island, isn't it?"

"There's an island with that name but it's also the name of a city in Guatemala, one of the oldest in the Western Hemisphere. In Spanish days it was the foremost center south of Mexico, but now it's just a sleepy town that's so beautiful it takes your breath away."

"And that's where you're going."

"Not far away. Trevor Hart and I were in medical school together. He got fed up with life here in the States where he was a successful surgeon—you know the kind who's busy fighting for positions on hospital staffs, climbing the social ladder, the whole business. So after his wife died, he pulled up stakes and started this hospital in a village not far from Antigua. I spent two days there while the rest of the doctors on the tour were hunting and fell in love with the place. Trevor invited me to come back and head up the medical section of the hospital."

"How can you be sure your wife wouldn't like it there?"

"Sarah in Guatemala?" Jethro's laugh was warm and natural, as was everything about him. "Revere and television are her whole world. You could even narrow that down to our home, the Methodist Church that's only a block away, and the W.C.T.U. Do you have any idea what it's like to spend the greater part of your life in a squirrel cage like that?"

Alice nodded. "Mine isn't much larger. The Vibrassage booth in convention halls of a hundred cities, a nearby hotel, the bar and men on the make to get you liquored up so you'll go to bed with them. The inside of a 727, a DC-9 or what-have-you, and the long walk from a debarking ramp to the baggage claim area. We're all living in squirrel cages, darling; only the bars they're made of are so thick we'll never saw our way out."

"I've already started sawing mine," said Jethro. "When I got to the airport Sunday, I went straight to the Braniff counter and bought a ticket to Guatemala City. From there I can hire a taxi for ten dollars that will take me up into the hills where I want to go."

"You certainly know what you want."

"And who I want to be with me," he said. "Say the word and I'll go to the phone booth outside the restaurant and reserve another seat. Mine's one way but I'll even make yours a round trip, if that will make you any more comfortable."

"You really have burned your bridges, haven't you?"

"I bought Sarah an annuity that will take care of her for life. The house is hers and she can sell the practice to the next M.D. who's willing to shut himself up in that squirrel cage. But I'll be free."

Alice looked away and it was a long moment before she spoke again.

"Suppose I only stayed a few weeks and then decided to come back?"

"I told you I'd make that second ticket a round trip—and give you the return half."

"You're a pretty swell guy, Jethro Forbes." Alice's voice was suddenly husky. "Why couldn't I have met you when I was a nursing student? Before I let a guy I didn't even love knock me up, because I wanted people to believe I was more sophisticated than a small-town girl from West Virginia could possibly be?"

"Neither one of us might have been ready then," he said. "But I am now—and I think you are, too."

"You saved my job for me the other day. I do owe—"

"You didn't owe me anything to start with and last night more than repaid whatever you might have thought you owed. We'll be starting even—"

Alice laughed shakily. "In this light you can pass for a Lochinvar. But I'm still a hell of an example of a blushing maiden fair."

"The offer still holds."

She put her hand on his in a pleading gesture. "Will you give me a rain check just for a few days, Jethro?"

"Of course."

"We'd better go, then. I think they want to close up and we're the last customers."

Toward morning he was awakened by the dampness of her tears against the bare skin of his chest. And when he put his arm about her, he felt her shoulders shaking spasmodically in soundless sobbing.

"I guess I'm not much of a lover," he said wryly.

"Please, Jethro, it's not that."

"Then what?"

"I'm just sad because I didn't meet someone like you a long time ago."

"We can still have a full life together, Alice. The hospital in Guatemala desperately needs nursing help and you've had two years. It shouldn't take you long to get the hang of things again."

"I'm not worrying about that, darling. It's just that you deserve something better than a woman who's been knocked around for years by so many men she can't even count them any more."

"Then it's because I wasn't able to bring you to a climax?"

"That hasn't happened in a long time either—not since I was a schoolgirl at home. You deserve more than half a woman, darling. When I lost my baby, infection destroyed all possibility of my ever having another child."

Jethro laughed and drew her closer. "I guess it's a bit late for either of us to become parents. Now go back to sleep and we'll talk about it tomorrow night."

She went to sleep almost immediately but it was Jethro who lay awake now. He'd come to Central City fairly bubbling with excitement over the step he was going to take on Friday, when the convention was finished and he boarded an airplane for Mexico City and then on to Guatemala. But now the prospect had lost much of its allure.

At another time, in another place, he might have been able to see the wry humor in the situation: a man running away from the humdrum of life with the woman who was his wife, only to fall in love like a schoolboy with another instead. But there was no humor in it now, only heartbreak.

For he could no longer be sure that the work he'd looked forward to so much as an anodyne for those years of loneliness while Sara sat transfixed before the television screen, wouldn't lose most of its attraction for him, unless the woman sleeping in his arms was there, too.

ii

The sound of the vacuum cleaner in the next suite awakened Marian about eight-thirty Wednesday morning; Cary had left shortly after six. She lay there for a while half awake and half asleep, reveling in the knowledge that she need not get up unless she chose. Then, remembering a paper she wanted to hear that morning, left the bed and began to dress.

It was a little after nine when she took the elevator down to the lobby floor and the main hotel restaurant. The receptionist gave her a table by the window overlooking an inner court and garden.

iii

Caleb Downs hadn't slept well. Twice during the night he had been awakened by the dull ache in his left shoulder and arm that he'd learned from experience was a warning of an impending attack of angina pectoris. Which, in turn, was a sharp reminder that the circulation to his highly vulnerable heart muscle was being buffeted by the emotional strain of the past several days.

The pain was quickly relieved when he placed one of the small tablets of nitroglycerine he always carried with him beneath his tongue; taken that way the drug worked even more rapidly than if given by hypodermic injection. But he knew the threat of an impending coronary represented by the arm pain still existed, unless the frustration that caused it was removed.

He'd switched on the TV when he got out of bed and

was shaving, when the news headlines of the eight o'clock broadcast reached his ears. Moving quickly back into the bedroom, he stood watching the newscaster for the local station.

"As yet unconfirmed reports from doctors attending the Central Medical Association Convention at the Civic Center Auditorium suggests that the death of Senator Spurgess on Monday, shortly after he had delivered a scathing attack upon the assembled doctors, was more than the heart attack announced by local medical authorities," said the newscaster. "Reliable sources at the convention report that Senator Spurgess was almost certainly killed by a powerful oriental poison, probably dropped into a drink he was carrying, as he passed through the crowded exhibit floor of the convention on the way to a luncheon in his honor sponsored by local Democratic Party leaders.

"If these reports are true, this is by far the most sensational event to occur during a convention characterized by an internal political power struggle between conservative and liberal forces among the membership, as well as controversy over an artificial heart developed by Dr. Paul Rice and Dr. Jerry Warren of the Central University Medical School faculty.

"At this hour neither the police nor the office of Dr. Andrew Huxtable, County Medical Examiner, will confirm or deny the rumor, but an official statement concerning the cause of Senator Spurgess' death is expected this morning. We will of course interrupt all programs to bring you any further developments in this dramatic murder, if indeed such is the case."

Moving back to the bathroom, Caleb finished shaving, and dressed. In a way he felt relieved that the truth of Monday morning's events had finally become known, although it meant that he had to move quickly now, or not at all. He hadn't gotten where he was by giving up, however, and determined to get on with what had to be done, he stopped in the coffee shop for coffee and a sweet roll, then took a taxi to the Hotel Centralia.

Picking up a house phone in the lobby, Caleb rang Marian Crowder's suite. A maid answered and told him Marian was probably in the dining room at breakfast. This was considerably better luck than he had hoped for and, moving across the lobby to the entrance to the main restaurant, he looked in and saw Marian at a table near a glass window overlooking an inner court around which the hotel was built.

She was beginning her breakfast, so he was sure of time to put into effect the plan that had taken form in his mind with the news that Marian was in the dining room.

iv

Leaving the hotel, Caleb crossed the street to a public telephone booth at the corner. Closing the glass door behind him, he looked up the hotel number and dialed it.

"This is Dr. Sanderson of the Convention Arrangements Committee," he told the operator who answered. "I called Dr. Marian Crowder's room but she didn't answer, so she may be in one of the restaurants. I don't want to interupt her breakfast, but would you call her in the restaurant at ten minutes to ten and tell her the paper she wanted to hear in the Embryology Section will be given at ten o'clock?"

"Certainly, Doctor." The operator was obviously eager to please a member of the powerful Arrangements Committee. "I'll call her at ten minutes before the hour."

Leaving the telephone booth, Caleb crossed the street again and entered the hotel gift shop. He'd already noted that because of Marian's presence at the convention a stack of copies of *Sexual Slavery* had been placed just inside the door. Now he bought one, paid for it in cash and went into the restaurant with it under his arm. Crossing the room, he stopped before Marian's table.

"I'm Caleb Downs, president of Central Pharmaceutical, Dr. Crowder," he said. "I'm also a great admirer of yours. Would you mind autographing your book for me?"

Marian smiled. She was feeling too happy this morning to resent anyone's intrusion upon her privacy.

"Would you care for some coffee?" she asked as she handed the autographed copy of *Sexual Slavery* back to him."

"That's kind of you." Caleb sat down in the chair across from her.

"Your face somehow seems familiar, Mr. Downs. Haven't we met somewhere else before?"

"Not unless you've had some of the free beer at our booth across the street at the convention."

"I don't drink beer so I haven't visited your booth as yet," she said.

"Just coffee for me," Caleb told the waitress who came to the table when he sat down. He turned back to Marian. "The main reason why I'm sure we've never met before, Doctor, is that no man could fail to remember meeting anyone as attractive as you."

By now Marian was accustomed to men on the make, rarely did one of them employ a maneuver with which she was unfamiliar. And yet, she couldn't repress the odd conviction that Caleb Downs was something more than what he pretended to be.

"Most men don't agree with my book," she said.

"I don't either," he said as the waitress put a fresh Thermos pitcher of coffee on the table. "No woman has to be a sexual slave, Doctor. She can enjoy sex as much as a man, and still be free—if she wants it that way."

"What about household chores, Mr. Downs? And children?"

"Modern-day technology has done away with housework. And the Pill with children."

"You seem to have strong convictions."

"A woman can have just as strong ones. I'd be willing to bet you do."

"I'm a scientist, Mr. Downs," Marian spoke with some severity. She was already regretting having invited him to have coffee with her but didn't want to offend him when he'd paid seven ninety-five for her book.

Detecting the signs of restlessnes on Marian's part, Caleb glanced at the clock over the door. The time was exactly ten minutes to ten and he was silently cursing the hotel telephone operator, who had promised to give Marian the message he'd phoned in from the booth across the street, when a waitress approached the table.

"There's a call for you, Dr. Crowder," she said. "You can take it at the cashier's desk."

"Will you excuse me, Mr. Downs?" Marian moved away without waiting for an answer.

A quick glance around the restaurant told Caleb nobody appeared to be watching him. And when he saw a salesman from one of the other pharmaceutical houses exhibiting at the convention having breakfast at a nearby table, he suddenly saw a way to give himself an alibi.

Rising from his chair he managed to drop one of the tiny effervescent tablets of bikhaconite into each coffee cup before moving over to shake hands with the salesman. When he saw Marian returning to her table he quickly moved back and poured fresh coffee from the Thermos pitcher left by the waitress into each cup before Marian was close enough to notice the slight bubbles of effervescence as the bikh he'd dropped into the cups was dissolved.

"A strange thing just happened," she said as he helped her with her chair. "A Dr. Sanderson left a message with the hotel operator to remind me of a paper he said I wanted to hear at the convention. But I don't know anything about it, or anyone with that name."

"It must have been for somebody else and the operator made a mistake; they're always doing that to me."

Caleb lifted the cup to his lips, but was careful to drink only a small amount, although he kept it to his lips until Marian drank and put down her cup.

"I asked the operator if she couldn't be mistaken," Marian added. "But she said Dr. Sanderson told her to call me at ten of ten."

"Sounds weird." Caleb pushed his chair back from the table. He'd been careful to drink only a small amount of the poisoned coffee but, even so, knew he couldn't afford to waste any time in giving himself the antidote he always carried.

"I've inflicted myself on you long enough, Doctor," he said. "Everybody has a right to enjoy a second cup of coffee and the morning paper in peace. Good-by."

"Good-by, Mr. Downs," Marian said absentmindedly, still worried about that strange message.

As he left the restaurant, Caleb saw her lift the half-filled cup to her lips and drink again. Hurrying across the lobby he took the 'Down" escalator to the lower level and, pushing open the door to the Men's Room, plunged into a toilet enclosure. With trembling fingers he injected the atropine he'd taken the precaution to carry against the possibility of accidental self-poisoning and leaned against the wall until he felt it begin to take effect.

Picking up her bag and newspaper, Marian had meanwhile left the table and was halfway from the restaurant to the bank of elevators, when she became conscious of the tingling sensation in her mouth and throat. Suddenly remembering what Cary had told her about the symptoms of aconite poisoning, she hurried into an empty elevator and punched the button for her floor.

By the time the elevator door opened at her floor the tingling was so severe that she could no longer doubt its source. Breathing was becoming difficult, too, for a heavy weight seemed to be pressing upon her chest. Even her eyes no longer focused properly and she had trouble inserting the key into her door. When it finally opened, she staggered across the room and dialed the hotel operator.

"Call Dr. Cary Poston at the hospital," she gasped. "Tell him I've been poisoned."

But even as she tried to put the telephone back on its cradle, Marian felt herself falling into blackness and knew no more.

Meanwhile, Caleb Downs was halfway across the mall to the University Hospital and the neon sign that spelled EMERGENCY.

"Call a doctor, I've been poisoned with aconite," he

shouted, as he staggered past the clerk at the desk to collapse into a chair in what he was sure was a perfect imitation of a man dying from the Nepalese assassination drug.

CHAPTER XXI

Paul Rice was scheduled to cover his and Jerry Warren's exhibit Wednesday morning and heard the TV news broadcast shortly after eight that morning in his room while he was shaving. By nine, Dr. Huxtable and Lieutenant Klinger had issued a statement to the press, confirming the fact that Senator Spurgess had been killed by a powerful poison, administered by an unknown person. No public announcement had as yet been made of the attempt, hardly an hour before, on the lives of Caleb Downs and Marian Crowder, but the hotels and the Civic Center were already abuzz with it.

Since the convention was winding down toward its close some thirty-six hours later, there were no lines at the registration desk just inside the entrance. Queues were already beginning to form at the airlines' ticket booth to one side of the lobby, however, although the young women who had staffed the booth since the convention opened had not yet arrived. The flow of doctors through the gates to the exhibit floor and the meeting rooms upstairs was noticeably less, too, than on previous mornings by this time.

"Looks like the exodus has already begun," Paul said to the guard who admitted him to the exhibit floor.

"Can't say I blame 'em, Doctor," said the guard. "It gives me the shivers to think that a murderer has been going in and out of the convention for the past three days, probably right through this gate, without anybody even knowing who he is."

At the booth, Paul flicked on the switch that illuminated the panels of the exhibit and tested the projector at the back which allowed a short moving picture of a coronary bypass operation to be shown, merely by depressing the switch. Everything was working smoothly, so he moved along one of the radiating aisles that crisscrossed the exhibit floor to where he could see Alex Klein opening his own exhibit.

"Jerry here?" Klein asked.

"It was my turn to open up this morning," said Paul. "I haven't seen Jerry since he chewed me out yesterday afternoon following the caucus."

"He was pretty upset, but he'll come around."

"I hope so. My date and I are supposed to be at the same table with Jerry and Katie and some others tonight."

"The way people are leaving, there'll be plenty of empty tables," said Alex. "John has called an emergency meeting of the Council for ten-thirty this morning. I guess Danton is getting worried about anybody being here to vote tomorrow."

"Do the police have any leads on the murderer?"

"Not that I know of. Maybe I can find out something when the Council meets. If I do, I'll let you know."

When Paul got back to the booth, he saw Jerry Warren standing before it, a troubled look on his normally happy countenance.

"Morning, Jerry," said Paul.

"Morning. I—"

"I—" Both had spoken simultaneously and both stopped, leaving the conversation hanging in the air. Jerry was the first to speak again.

"What hit you?" he asked.

"Just a mishap," said Paul. "I owe you an apology for yesterday afternoon."

"I'm the one who should apologize," said Jerry. "I was so busy resenting being caught with egg on my face, I didn't even consider that you had the right to make your own decision."

"I really did try to reach you and tell you I couldn't

let myself be nominated, Jerry. But the paging operator couldn't raise you."

"I guess it was sort of a comedy of errors," Jerry admitted. "I was afraid you might decide against the nomination, so I deliberately made it hard for you to reach me before I nominated you. And after I was caught, I got mad at you when I should have been mad at myself."

"Did you know Danton had a TCI at the end of his caucus yesterday afternoon?"

"No. Are you sure?"

"Alex Klein saw it. And Elton Brooks's conscience made him confirm it."

"That would explain the change of surgeons in the middle of the infarct film," said Jerry.

"And also the shunt operation using the external maxillary artery."

"Danton's in a bind all right. He can't very well start any really delicate surgery, when he doesn't know whether one of those little strokes will leave him with a paralyzed hand, or even drop him in his tracks."

"There's another thing—and it confirms what we suspect," said Paul. "After I withdrew from the race yesterday afternoon, Aletha came to my room. I guess she saw herself as Lady Bountiful, come to reward a loyal subject. Anyway she practically told me Danton is incapacitated and the clinic could be mine, if his condition gets any worse."

"Congrat—"

"I turned her down, Jerry—once and for all. She took it as a personal affront." Paul put his hand up to the Band-Aid on his cheek. "Put her mark on me, too, with that big diamond she wears on her right hand."

"You didn't have to do that because I shot off my face—"

"You had nothing to do with it, Jerry. I don't mind telling you I've felt better ever since."

"I still don't entirely understand why."

"A lot of things were involved, things I've been blind to since leaving Danton because I couldn't see beyond

Aletha. Anyway it's done and I'm damned glad it is." He held out his hand. "Are we back in double harness again?"

Jerry shook hands. "I better call Katie. She gave me hell last night for having the gall to insinuate that your love life--if any--would influence your decision where medicine is concerned. And, by the way, Katie talked to your new girl friend on the telephone. She was very much impressed with her."

"So am I," said Paul. "I guess that was another reason why Aletha looked a little old for the first time yesterday afternoon."

ii

Jethro Forbes winked when Alice Perrault looked up from the order blank she was filling in for a portly and prosperous looking doctor.

"We'll have a chair ready for you in a few minutes, Dr. Forbes," she said formally.

"Looks like your business is holding up well in spite of this poison scare, Miss Perrault," said the plump doctor, as he signed the order blank and started making out a check.

"You know what the saying is about building a better mousetrap, Dr. Pancoast." Alice gave him her warmest smile as she leaned over to stamp the words VIBRASSAGE CORPORATION in the middle of the check.

"You've been very kind, Miss Perrault," said Dr. Pancoast. "Perhaps you'd have a drink with me after the convention closes this afternoon."

"I'm so sorry, Dr. Pancoast." Alice sounded really sincere. "My boss will be in town this afternoon and we've got to go over sales reports this evening."

"Another time, then?"

"I hope so. It's very nice of you to offer it." Alice's tone was throaty and intimate, as she tore off a copy of the sales agreement and handed it to him. "Here's your copy.

289

You can start depreciating your chair on your income tax right away. It's eligible for investment credit, too."

As the portly doctor left the booth Alice turned to Jethro. "Just take off your jacket and lie down, Dr. Forbes. We'll have you relaxed in no time.

"You look good enough to eat this morning," Jethro told her as he took off his coat and hung it up. "Let me put you under my magic spell and day after tomorrow you'll wake up with a toucan staring at you from a bush outside the window."

"I woke up this morning with *you* staring at me," she said in a low voice. "What's the difference?"

"A toucan is a light-colored bird with a huge beak—something like a parrot. You'll love them."

Alice flipped the switch and the couch began to vibrate, sending a pleasurable warmth through Jethro's body, reminiscent of that he'd experienced last night with her in his arms.

"How's that?" she asked.

"I like the saleswoman better. Where shall we go tonight?"

"The way I feel now, I'm going to bed." Then her voice softened. "I really believe you're starved for love."

"And still only half fed."

"Did you hear about the close shave Mr. Downs had this morning?" she asked.

"Not the details. I came to the convention hall early to hear a symposium on tropical diseases."

"Mr. Downs was having breakfast in the dining room at the Centralia with Dr. Crowder. Someone apparently managed to poison them both with the same drug that was used on Senator Spurgess. Downs suspected what happened and made a bee line for the hospital Emergency Room. They gave him atropine and he didn't even have to be admitted."

"Downs must be more of a charmer than he appears to be," said Jethro. "I thought Dr. Cary Poston had the inside track with Dr. Crowder."

Alice glanced toward the Central Pharmaceutical

booth where a line had just begun to form. "Downs has something—animal magnetism, I suppose. A woman can sense that sort of a thing in a man, even if she's afraid of him."

"Why would you be afraid of Downs?" Jethro asked.

Alice shivered a little, although the room wasn't cold. "I guess because he could still make me lose my job. And cause trouble for Vibrassage, too."

"He'd have a hard time finding you in Guatemala," Jethro assured her. "Stop worrying about Downs and think about how nice it's going to be down there—with our own private toucan looking in the window."

"Oh Jethro, I really want to. But I can't make a change like that overnight."

"It's the way I'm doing it. Say the word and I'll reserve another seat on the plane."

"Let me have tonight to think and I'll give you my answer early Thursday morning."

"At breakfast?"

"At breakfast, I promise."

"Say eight-thirty, in the Regency House coffee shop?"

"Right. Now run on, please. I see a customer who looks like he's ready to buy a chair."

iii

A grim-looking group of doctors gathered in the temporary office of the Central Medical Association at ten-thirty. Since he would take office as president at tomorrow's General Session, Dr. John Towers presided over the informal meeting of the Council governing body of the Association between conventions.

"Do you have any idea how many members have left already, Pete?" Towers asked the executive secretary.

"I just finished making a check by telephone with the hotels," said Sanders. "They say checkouts have been unusually heavy this morning for the third day of the convention. With the banquet coming up tonight, this would ordinarily be one of the busiest days."

"The airlines report every available seat filled through Saturday," said H. Edward Danton glumly. "Aletha checked with them just before I left the hotel."

"I think a few will be left to vote tomorrow, Edward," said Dr. Hanson dryly. "Let's hope someone doesn't decide to poison you before then."

"Where's Cary Poston?" Dr. Towers asked the room in general.

"He's been with Marian Crowder since she was admitted to the hospital," said Alex Klein. "I hear it's still touch and go with her."

"What about that fellow Downs?"

"He apparently didn't get much of the poison. I saw him at the exhibit just before I came up here."

"What gets me about this business is the lack of a pattern," said Danton. "I called Andy Huxtable as soon as I heard the news broadcast this morning. He says they think the murderer tried to kill Cary originally and got Senator Spurgess by mistake. But with Marian Crowder and this fellow Downs both getting poisoned this morning, that theory seems to have gone out the window."

"Maybe he hates doctors," said Towers. "How about that, Alex?"

"There are plenty of psychotics running loose with the potentialities this person seems to have," said Klein. "The trouble is most people are a little paranoid, so you can't tell who's really dangerous, until something pops—like now."

"So what can we do?" Danton asked.

"Nothing," said Dr. Towers. "Except hope some of us will be here tomorrow."

"What about calling off the rest of the convention?" Dr. Hanson asked.

"That's out of the question," said Danton brusquely. "The rest of you can leave, if you want to, but I'm not letting some nut run me off before I've finished here."

"Anybody vote for ending the convention?" Towers asked.

When nobody spoke up, the meeting ended with nothing accomplished, for the good reason that no one could figure out what to do.

CHAPTER XXII

Jethro and Alice Perrault had a late lunch in the Auditorium cafeteria.

"I'm so sure you're going with me that I bought another ticket for Guatemala City this morning," he told her. "They had two cancellations; we can leave Friday afternoon at three."

She looked at him and thought how wonderful these past three days had been because of the gentle man whose work-gnarled hands touched hers on the table cover. With the certain knowledge that he would cherish and care for her as long as she lived, she asked herself for the tenth time at least why she still hesitated, trying to evade facing the answer she already knew: that she could never know real happiness, as long as the purely animal drive of passion which was like a cancer within her sought a fulfillment her unconscious mind refused to permit. And knowing it was there, she also knew she could never subject Jethro to the shock of her going to some other man, driven by the insatiable demands of her body for the release no man had been able to give her since that day so long ago when she'd been raped by Henry Perrault.

"Jethro—I—"

"Don't say it," he begged. "The ticket's a round trip, like I told you, so you won't be burning any bridges. You can even call it a vacation; just give me a chance to show you what we'll have down there and I know you'll love it the way I do."

"It's not that—"

"I'm sure it troubles you that I'm too old to ever be

the lover you're entitled to have." He smiled wryly. "I was a little out of practice before last Monday night, but I'm learning. You have to admit that."

"You're perfect, Jethro. No woman could want more in a man."

"Then what is it?"

"I feel an obligation to my boss."

"You can call him."

"I won't have to. He's finally going to stop by this afternoon. I had a wire from him this morning."

"That means I won't see you tonight?"

"I don't have to sleep with Ted Jones to keep my job, Jethro. He always takes the ten o'clock plane out of Central City and I'll have to go with him to the airport. But I can meet you, say about eleven, in the Falstaff Room at the hotel. All we'll miss is dinner."

"And you'll tell him about us?"

She nodded. "It's only fair to him. Now I'd better get back to the booth. I spoke to one of the airlines' girls in the Ladies Lounge. She says doctors are leaving Central City in droves, since the news broke about the poisonings. With the convention ending tomorrow after the election, this afternoon is our last chance to improve the record for Vibrassage sales."

She stood up and picked up her handbag but, as she was turning away from the table, reached out suddenly and put her hand on Jethro's arm, gripping it so tightly that he felt the pressure of her nails through the sleeve of his coat.

"What is it?" Jethro was counting out coins for the tip.

"Caleb Downs is sitting over there by the window. The way he looks at me makes me afraid."

"The way practically every man looks at you makes *me* afraid, afraid I'm dreaming," said Jethro. "If Downs had you and I didn't, I guess I'd be looking and wishing, too. He had a close shave this morning, maybe he just feels lousy."

It wasn't as simple as that, Alice knew. No matter

how she tried to resist it, something about Downs had a strange effect on her. Part of what she felt could be fear because of what had happened on Monday, she knew, and what could still happen if he chose to make trouble because of it. But more than that was the strange fascination Downs stirred within her, somewhat, she imagined, like the fascination felt by a cobra's victim as it watched the swaying head in the brief moment before death struck. And that fascination, she knew, was purely sexual.

"Don't forget. At eleven in the Falstaff Room." Jethro reminded her as they parted outside the restaurant.

"I'll be there. And if you should change your mind about Guatemala before then, I'll understand."

She walked away before he could ask her the meaning of that strange last sentence. But as he moved toward the main entrance of the now almost deserted Auditorium, Jethro's brow was creased by a frown of puzzlement.

CHAPTER XXIII

Caleb Downs waited until Jethro and Alice left the restaurant, then paid his check and followed. Emerging from the door he almost collided with Cary Poston, who was moving along the corridor in the same direction.

"I've been wanting to talk to you, Mr. Downs," said Cary. "Mind if I walk back to the exhibit floor with you?"

"Not at all." Caleb had intended to follow Alice Perrault and start making his final play, but reluctantly put the idea aside for the moment, knowing it would be bad policy to antagonize the other man.

"I haven't seen you since you were almost poisoned this morning in the Centralia restaurant," said Cary. "Are you all right now?"

"A little dry from the atropine they gave me in the Emergency Room but otherwise okay."

"Do you mind answering a few questions about what happened?"

"Not at all," said Caleb. "I went over the whole thing with the police in the Emergency Room but I'll be happy to give you a rundown on it, too."

"I hope to marry Dr. Crowder," said Cary. "So I'm naturally interested in protecting her until the murderer can be caught."

"I've got something of a vested interest in catching him myself," said Caleb. "If the doctor in the Emergency Room hadn't given me atropine first and asked questions afterward, I wouldn't be here."

"Dr. Crowder had a very close call too. After injecting the atropine, I had to give her CPR in the hotel room to keep her circulation going until the drug could be carried to the vital centers of the brain where aconite exerts its main effect."

"She was lucky you happened to have atropine with you."

"It didn't just happen. Lieutenant Klinger thinks I'm one of the targets of whoever's on this murder spree. He insisted that I carry it."

"Who would want to kill you, Dr. Poston?"

"Neither the police nor I have the answer to that," Cary admitted. "I was hoping you might remember noticing someone near Dr. Crowder's table who might have been acting oddly."

"I was at the table while she went to the phone, except for a moment or two, when I spoke to a friend from another pharmaceutical house."

"And you don't remember anything unusual?"

"Sorry, not a thing." Caleb Downs forced a casual note into his voice. "I hope you're guarding Dr. Crowder.

"Lieutenant Klinger has given both of us police protection. I'm sure he'd do the same for you—"

Caleb laughed. "I was raised a Presbyterian and we

figure that what is to be will be, Doctor. If a policeman was looking over my shoulder all the time, it would make me so nervous that anybody who wanted to kill me could do it easily."

"I don't particularly like it myself," Cary admitted.

"How is Dr. Crowder?"

"Fine, thank you. Of course she'll feel the effects of the atropine for five or six hours yet. I'm keeping her in the hospital where we can guard her closely."

"Well, I enjoyed talking to you, Doctor," said Downs. "Stop by the exhibit and have a beer before we close up shop. I'll draw it personally, so you'll be sure it's okay."

"I might do that," said Cary. "Thanks for letting me take up your time."

The dumb bastard, Caleb thought contemptuously, as he watched the tall figure of the cardiologist disappear along another corridor. If things go right, he just set himself up for death.

ii

In order to be close to the convention, Lieutenant Klinger had practically taken up residence, since Senator Spurgess' death, in the office of the Medical Examiner. Cary found him there immediately after his talk with Caleb Downs, and gave him a replay of their conversation.

"I'm afraid I didn't learn anything," he admitted.

"Downs is a cool one, whether he's the murderer or not," said Klinger.

"Do you really think he could be?"

"The more I see of him, the more I believe it," said Klinger. "But it's still only a hunch."

"Any report on the fingerprints you took off the beer cup?"

"We got a preliminary report by teletype this afternoon. Downs was fingerprinted when he was arrested on a traffic violation in Kansas City several years ago, but that's all anybody seems to have on him. No background or anything."

"Isn't that unusual?"

"Not if he's the solid citizen he seems to be. Apparently he turned up about ten years ago in this Arkansas town where his factory is located and started manufacturing pharmaceuticals. His business prospered from the start and now he's at least a millionaire, but nobody seems to know anything else about him. Oh yes, he did have what was called a 'nervous breakdown' last year. Spent about a month in a private hospital for nervous troubles outside Kansas City."

"Was the diagnosis 'nervous breakdown'?"

"No, paranoid psychosis. The psychiatrist who runs the place tried to have him legally committed to a state hospital, but he talked the judge out of it."

"Paranoids quite frequently do," said Cary. "Their symptoms so often appear to be merely exaggerations of normal personality traits that it's hard to make the diagnosis stick legally."

"We run up against it all the time, too," said Klinger. "That's why so many potential murderers are running loose."

"And you found out nothing else?"

"As far as the records we've been able to discover go, Downs could have been born the day before he appeared in this Arkansas town and started to build his factory. One thing I wish you hadn't done, though, Doctor."

"What's that?"

"Told him you're going to marry Dr. Crowder. If he really wants to kill her for some reason she doesn't even remember, you may have put yourself back in the position of Possible Victim Number One."

iii

Marian Crowder came back to consciousness in a bright and cheery hospital room—with no memory of how she had come to be there. The fact that she was alive was reassuring and she let herself drift back into the Nirvana of sleep that surrounded her like a soft cocoon.

When she awakened again, Cary Poston was standing by the bed, feeling her pulse.

"For a while I thought you'd decided to withdraw from the world," he told her.

"How long was I out?"

"Nearly six hours. I was in the tunnel when the pager got me, so I reached your room just after you passed out. As soon as I felt how slow your pulse was, I gave you a jolt of atropine—"

"It must have been a big one. My mouth still feels like parchment, and my chest is so sore I can hardly breathe."

"Blame me for that. Your heart stopped before the atropine could take effect and I had to give you cardiopulmonary resuscitation to keep blood flowing to your brain until the atropine could neutralize the aconite."

"Drink some of this." He gave her some ice water. "It will wet your whistle and make talking easier."

"I love you," she said, when he took the glass away. "Or hadn't I told you?"

"Not in so many words, but there have been certain favorable indications."

Suddenly remembering the events just before she lost consciousness, she sat straight up in bed.

"Did they catch Caleb Downs?" she asked.

"He got to the Emergency Room in time. The resident on duty said he showed only mild effects."

"What are you talking about, Cary?"

"Downs was poisoned at the same time you were. Fortunately for him, he recognized the symptoms and made it to the hospital Emergency Room. The resident there gave him atropine. He didn't even have to stay in the hospital."

"But Downs gave the stuff to me—in coffee."

"It was in the coffee all right. The restaurant crew was very busy this morning and the dishes hadn't been washed before Lieutenant Klinger got to them. We found bikh in both cups."

"But that's impossible."

"I'm afraid not. Suppose you tell me exactly what happened before you lost consciousness. Maybe it will give us a clue as to just how you got the drug."

"I had almost finished eating when Caleb Downs came into the restaurant," she said. "He'd bought a copy of *Sexual Slavery* and wanted me to autograph it for him. Ordinarily I don't consort with men I don't know, but I guess you've mellowed me since I've been here. I invited him to join me, then the telephone call came."

"For him?"

"No. The hotel operator called the restaurant and asked for me, so I went to the cashier's desk to take the call. The operator said a Dr. Sanderson had left word for me to be called at ten minutes to ten. He told her I'd asked him to remind me of a paper I wanted to hear at the convention at ten o'clock."

"Who is Sanderson?"

"That's the strange part. I don't know anyone by that name and I hadn't asked anyone to call me. Wait a minute, though! He said he was from your committee, Cary —Arrangements."

"There's no Dr. Sanderson on the committee. Or on the faculty, either, for that matter." Cary's face was grave now. "Whoever had you called to the phone wanted to get you away from your table long enough to put the poison in your coffee."

"But Caleb Downs was at the table."

"Not all the time."

"How can you be so sure?"

"He remembers leaving the table while you were telephoning and speaking to a salesman for another pharmaceutical house, who was having breakfast in the restaurant."

"He could be lying."

"The other man confirms the story."

"Then how could it have happened?"

"That's what Lieutenant Klinger is trying to find out. He'll be up later and talk to you, I wouldn't let him until I was sure you were all right. Feel up to it now?"

"Any time. Do you suppose whoever the murderer is could be after both of us?"

"Lieutenant Klinger asked me the same question. But until last Sunday, I hadn't seen you since we were in medical school."

"That must be it! The only thing you and I have in common is that we were in the same class in medical school."

"Except that we were in love then and we're in love now."

"The second case just happened, but anybody clever enough to work out such a scheme must have been working on it for quite a while. That means our being in love now couldn't be the reason the murderer wants to get rid of us—if he does. It would have to be something else, Cary, something that goes a long way back."

"But what?"

"I don't have the least idea," said Marian. "Besides, how could anyone who wanted to murder us both know we'd be here for this particular convention?"

"The programs were printed a whole month before the convention started," he reminded her. "Anybody who looked at one of them would know we'd both be here."

"Sitting ducks!"

"Maybe he's just a paranoiac who hates doctors, like some people are claiming."

"Does that answer satisfy you?"

"No. But neither does anything else I've thought of. And why did he also try to poison Downs this morning?"

"That could have been an accident like Senator Spurgess' death was. If the murderer came to the table, while I was at the telephone and Mr. Downs was talking to the other pharmaceutical salesman, he would have no way to be sure which cup was mine, so he had to poison both."

"There just might be something to that theory," said

301

Cary. "Lieutenant Klinger did notice that no lipstick marks were on either cup."

"That's what getting rich from *Sexual Slavery* did for me," said Marian. "I use an indelible lipstick that's very expensive but has the advantage of not coming off easily. The murderer had already killed once, when he got Senator Spurgess instead of you, so killing two more instead of one wouldn't bother him."

Cary looked at his watch. "I have one more patient to see this afternoon. Don't drink anything you don't see opened right before your eyes. I'll be back to check out your dinner tray."

"I'm not going to let you be a taster for me—and risk your life."

"The Queen's Taster—I'd like that," he said, kissing her again. "Better get some rest. I'll be back later to watch your dinner tray being prepared."

"Thanks for being in that tunnel this morning," she said. "If you'd had to travel all the way from the hospital to the hotel, I guess I wouldn't be here now.

iv

In the office of Dr. Andrew Huxtable, Lieutenant Klinger relaxed by the desk with a long slender cigar, the kind taken up by many heavy smokers after cigarettes were indicted as a major cause of lung cancer.

"Think there's anything to this business about smoking and lung cancer, Doctor?" the lieutenant asked.

"Stay around here long enough to see some of the lungs I cut into and you'll be convinced," Huxtable told him. "Between emphysema and early malignant changes, they'll scare the hell out of you."

"The early reports scared the hell out of me a long time ago," said Klinger. "These cigars are a darned sight more expensive than the cigarettes I used to smoke, though. Sometimes I wonder if the tobacco industry isn't really putting something over on me."

"I'll give you a concrete example," said Huxtable.

"When the statistics about cigarette smoking and cancer first came out in England, people paid very little attention to them just like over here. But doctors do watch mortality statistics and a lot of English medics cut out cigarettes or switched to other ways of smoking. The first figures on a study of lung cancer in English doctors came out the other day. They show something like a third less deaths from it than before, while the incidence in the general population didn't change much. Does that convince you?"

"I guess I'm stuck with an expensive habit." Lieutenant Klinger sighed. "Since you're so bugs on logic, Doctor, did it ever strike you that there's a startling relationship between that fellow Downs and those deaths from poisoning we've been investigating?"

"Can't say that it has," Huxtable admitted. "Of course I stay pretty well isolated down in this stinking basement. What's your evidence?"

"Item one—Senator Spurgess' death occurred right after the victim drank a cup of beer from Downs's exhibit."

"But you checked the exhibit and found nothing."

"True."

"And, besides, probably a thousand doctors at least have drunk beer from that exhibit and lived. It's always one of the most popular places at the big conventions."

"Somebody still has to be handing out those fatal doses of what Dr. Singh called bikh, Doctor. And where could it be done more easily than at the beer exhibit?"

"Nowhere, I guess."

"Item two," said Klinger. "Downs was having breakfast, or at least coffee, with Dr. Crowder this morning."

"She's a damned attractive woman. I wouldn't mind having breakfast with her myself."

"That's reason enough. But with one death, plus two other attempts already, all occurring while the same man is in close proximity, I naturally get suspicious."

"Your theory might hold up, Lieutenant—except for one thing."

"I know—Downs getting a dose of the drug himself. You're pretty sure he did get it, by the way?"

"No question about that; specimens of saliva from both him and Dr. Crowder were positive for aconite. Whoever put the poison in her coffee put it in Downs's, too. Fortunately she's a physician and recognized the symptoms in time for Cary Poston to give her atropine and combat the drug."

"Downs recognized them, too," said Klinger. "Doesn't that strike you as coming in a little handy, to say the least?"

"You're forgetting one thing, Lieutenant. Downs is a trained pharmacologist in his own right, which brings us back to your starting point and gets us nowhere."

"Maybe yes, maybe no," said Klinger. "I learned long ago in police work not to go afield for suspects, when I have a prime one right under my nose."

"Downs again?"

"In person. Now let me pose you a hypothetical question."

"I thought you were working up to something in your usual evasive fashion," said the Medical Examiner. "What is it?"

"Could an expert in pharmaceutics, or whatever you call it, deliberately take less than a lethal dose of aconite himself, but still enough to produce symptoms? Especially if he went directly to an Emergency Room, and told the doctor there he should be given atropine because he suspected he'd been poisoned with aconite?"

"You've got a lot of 'ifs' in there," Huxtable objected.

"But could it happen?"

"I suppose so. The trouble is that preparations of aconite are extracts of alkaloids—we call them tinctures because the solvent is usually alcohol. No two of them have exactly the same potency."

"I've been reading up on aconite myself," the lieutenant admitted. "With ordinary extracts of the various forms of monkshood or related plants, a fairly large dose is required to produce a lethal effect. Right?"

"The British Pharmacopoeia says no more than five drops of the alcoholic tincture should be given therapeutically at a time. Which probably means that a lethal dose would be several times that much, since there's always a considerable leeway for error in giving drugs. It's hard to see how the poisoner has been getting a lethal dose to his victims without being detected. Or at least why the poison in the beer or coffee they drink isn't discovered because of the taste."

"Suppose he's isolated a far more potent, and therefore more virulent, form of the drug," said Klinger. "Say something extracted from the root of *aconitum ferox*— you remember Dr. Singh spoke of this being used in Nepal for assassinations. And suppose he's been able to crystallize—or whatever it is chemists do—this compound to where he has a rapidly soluble preparation. Wouldn't it be possible then to give an exceedingly small dose that might not be detected, perhaps by dropping it into a cup of coffee?"

"Possibly. But I've never heard of such a preparation."

"Probably because aconite is hardly ever used any more in medicine."

"Maybe. But with such a concentrated dose, it would be difficult for Downs to have taken any of it, if that's what you're hinting at now, without getting a dangerous amount himself."

Suppose he was willing to take that risk in order to destroy Dr. Crowder?"

"Why would he hate her that much, when you tell me she doesn't remember ever seeing him before?"

"I haven't figured out the answer to that yet," Klinger admitted.

"Are you going to arrest him?"

"Not just yet. We don't have enough evidence to go on and what little we do have is strictly circumstantial."

"Meanwhile?"

"Dr. Crowder should be safe in the hospital. I just talked to Dr. Poston about her and he will see that special precautions are taken about her food."

"Are you sure that's enough protection?"

"Those precautions are just routine," Klinger assured the Medical Examiner. "Between the FBI and the Central City Police Department, the Civic Center is fairly swarming with officers, some in uniform but most of them not. Dr. Poston has been warned not to let down his guard, either, and I've got a man watching everything Downs does."

"You do seem to be doing your job," Huxtable conceded.

"I learned one interesting thing," said Klinger. "Dr. Poston and Dr. Crowder were in the same class in medical school. I've wired Johns Hopkins for a class picture and maybe one of them will recognize a classmate or a fellow student who would want to kill them both."

"Anything else I can help you with?" Huxtable asked. "I'm supposed to take my wife to the convention dinner dance this evening."

"Nothing I can think of just now. I'll be glad when this damned convention is over."

"Cheer up," said the Medical Examiner. "The national organization of morticians will be in town next week. That ought to be a gay old time."

CHAPTER XXIV

It was still daylight when Paul Rice stopped his car before the Montez home in the Mexican quarter of Central City. The president's cocktail party that always preceded the dinner dance of the CMA Convention, began at six-thirty in the Grand Ballroom of the Hotel Centralia. Paul had arranged for them to meet Jerry and Katie Warren and some other couples from the younger faculty members in the lobby of the ballroom at seven, when the festivities would be starting to shift into high gear.

Supposed to be a strictly social affair, the reception and dinner, with the dance to follow, was also the last opportunity for active politicking on a large scale before tomorrow's final General Session with its crucial election. At the dinner dance, the outgoing president and his wife made their last social bow before a new team with Dr. John Towers as president took the helm of the Association.

Carlota had chosen to accentuate, rather than play down, her Mexican heritage. Her dress was white, the skirt long, and the low-cut bodice left her shoulders bare, setting off perfectly the slight olive tint of skin. Her almost raven-black hair was piled high and held in place by a jeweled comb. For a wrap, she carried a lacy mantilla.

"Did I tell you how beautiful you are?" Paul asked as he opened the door of the car for her.

"At least I'm a little more covered up than I am in the Polo Lounge." Carlota laughed, but he could tell she was pleased. "Mr. Kimball called to say I can come back to work Saturday afternoon, as soon as the convention is over."

"It's all but over now. Since the news broke this morning about the way Senator Spurgess was poisoned and the afternoon papers carried a story on the attempted murder of Dr. Crowder and Mr. Downs, people have been leaving in droves. There'll be plenty of empty tables at the dinner tonight. In fact, the police may well outnumber the guests."

"At least that story about the murder pushed you off the front pages," she said. "Or didn't you want it that way?"

"It suited me fine. Jerry and I got a lot of publicity for our new heart pump—"

"Even though Dr. Danton said it isn't any good?"

"The element of controversy only made the story more newsworthy."

"Did you know in advance that he was going to denounce you to the newspapers?"

"I should have expected it. He made the same statements when he discussed my paper in the meeting room right after I presented it."

"Is he really on the verge of some major discovery?"

Paul shrugged. "Everybody at the Danton Clinic is working on an artificial heart but that's nothing new. Jerry and I were doing that before we left there. We still haven't quite ironed out the bugs in ours but on balance I'd say we're well ahead of any work being done at the Danton Clinic."

"Did he give the newspaper interview before or after you withdrew from the race for president-elect?"

"Before."

"And you still didn't run against him?"

"Actually it's too bad that this question of who has a working heart pump and who doesn't ever got blown up into an issue between Dr. Danton and myself. When I saw after my paper yesterday that it was becoming something of a *cause célèbre,* I thought it was time to stop it."

"I still don't exactly understand why," she said.

"What Jerry and I are trying to develop is a pump that can substitute for the left side of a heart badly damaged from coronary disease and keep the patient alive through the period of initial shock, so we can operate later and give his heart a new blood supply."

"That certainly makes sense."

"Making progress in developing a workable temporary pump is much more important to us than who gets the credit for an artificial heart. But in the eyes of the public, anybody who can claim to have an artificial heart that really works will be a medical hero, like Dr. Barnard was with the first transplant. Dr. Danton is much more publicity conscious than I am, so it seemed better not to make an issue of it by going on with the election."

"Plus the fact that he would have clobbered you anyway?"

Paul smiled. "Who have you been talking to?"

"Not talking—listening. A cocktail waitress who keeps her eyes and ears open can learn a lot about the internal politics of organizations that hold conventions in Central City."

"And particularly if she's got the kind of a brain that makes her spend the other half of her time going to college and getting an education."

"I was determined to graduate from college as far back as I can remember," said Carlota. "Even when I was a little girl, I refused to speak Spanish most of the time like the other Mexican children."

"What got you interested in biochemistry?"

"I suppose because it's the nearest thing to medicine I found in the curriculum at Central U. By juggling college classes, I can work in the five or six hours I spend working in the Polo Lounge, particularly over weekends when business is best anyway, but I'd never be able to pay my tuition in medical school that way. Once I really got into biochemistry, I decided I'd rather work in a hospital research laboratory anyway. Fortunately, I can combine that job with working on a master's degree."

"Compared to you, I was born with a silver spoon in my mouth," said Paul. "My father was a hard-working GP back in Missouri, but he made a good living. I didn't have to work my way through like Jerry Warren and a lot of other doctors I know did."

"When Katie Warren talked to me yesterday afternoon, she said her husband was pretty upset about your withdrawing from the race."

"He was—for a while. But Jerry understands my reasoning now. Dr. Danton is ill and it didn't seem fair to take advantage of that."

"I suppose it all makes sense to an idealist," she conceded. "But I doubt that many doctors would look at it the same way."

"Admittedly, medicine is far more of a business and less of a calling than it was in my father's day," said Paul. "But Jerry and I look at it the same way Dad did and I suspect a lot of others do, too. Dr. Forbes, the one who made the headlines on Monday when he started a stopped pacemaker and saved a man's life, is a general practitioner in a small town. Jerry was talking to him a few hours before he made the headlines and he says you couldn't find a more typical cracker-barrel philosopher if you tried—or a better doctor. And certainly people like Dr. Cary Poston, the cardiologist who works with us quite a bit, could easily make twice as much in practice as he does teaching in the medical school."

"I imagine you could, too," she said.

"I was offered three times my salary by a large private clinic in California, before I took the job here at Central City. But in California I would have had practically no time for research, which is the most important part of my work."

He changed the subject as they swung into the busy traffic of the downtown expressway. "I think you're going to like the people at our table tonight. I trust that you don't have any prejudice against black skins."

"Prejudice! Don't forget that I'm a member of a minority group, too."

"The great-granddaughter of a duke in Emperor Maximilian's court?"

Carlota laughed. "You've been taking Mother's stories too literally."

"She looks enough like nobility for them to be true, and so do you. And you *are* named for an empress."

"Poor Carlota and Maximilian, sold down the river by people they trusted. I think I'll like being a biochemist far more than I would being a countess or a duchess back then. At least I know I'm not going to lose my head." She chuckled suddenly. "Though from the look on Mrs. Danton's face just before she went to Mr. Kimball to get me fired, I think she would have loved sending me to the guillotine."

ii

Jack Reeves whistled softly when he opened the door of Paul Rice's car and saw Carlota.

"Hello, Jack," she said, smiling. "Cinderella has come to the ball."

"Hasn't she ever!" said Jack. "Good evening, Dr. Rice. Saw you yesterday on the twelve o'clock news."

Paul laughed. "The wounds don't show, but they're still there, Jack. Will you take care of the car for me, please?"

"Of course." Jack Reeves blew his whistle for a parking lot attendant. "Better be careful, Cinderella." His eyes twinkled as he helped Carlota from the car. "I think the Wicked Witch is inside."

"Sounds like the hotel grapevine is as efficient as the hospital one," said Paul as they came into the lobby.

"You haven't seen anything to the way the wires will hum when Jack starts passing word around that I came with you," said Carlota, as they moved toward the elevators leading to the ballroom on the roof overlooking the city. "The next time he calls for a porter to take a set of bags up to the lobby for an arriving guest, he'll alert the switchboard and phones will start ringing from the boiler room to the rooftop lounge."

"It will be all over the hospital, too, before morning," said Paul. "I'll be the most envied single doctor on the staff."

The lobby of the ballroom where the elevator disgorged passengers was crowded and noisy. Paul gave their tickets to the attendant at the door and took Carlota's arm, guiding her toward the ballroom itself, where people were milling about like Grand Central Station at five o'clock in the afternoon.

Spying Jerry Warren and the two other couples standing a little outside the stream of people going into the ballroom, Paul guided Carlota through the crowd toward them. Jerry and Katie Warren in particular made a striking pair. Both were a light-golden brown in color and Katie sparkled with the personality that had made her a hit in show business.

"Katie and Jerry Warren, Carlota Montez," Paul introduced her.

"How lovely you are!" Katie exclaimed. "I didn't think

Paul ever got far enough from the laboratory and the operating room to make a catch like you. I can't even get Jerry away from the TV once he gets home."

"I'm bugs on doctor programs, Miss Montez," said Jerry. "Get some of my best research ideas there."

Paul introduced Carlota to the others. Jacob Stein, a saturnine-looking Jew and a brilliant conversationalist, was a resident in surgery. His wife, Dorothy, was dark and intense. The other couple were from India, their name was Vanda. The man—a resident in pathology—was short, his skin darker than either Jerry or Katie Warren's, while his wife was a tiny fragile-looking girl in a lovely silver-colored sari.

"My name is Jahnsi, Miss Montez." Dr. Vanda's white teeth flashed in his dark face. "Most people call me John. My child bride here is Sirsa, mother of four."

"Four!" Carlota exclaimed. "Oh, I'm sorry, I didn't mean—"

"Everybody's surprised," the tiny Sirsa assured her. "But we love our children."

"Of course you do," said Carlota. "Mexican families tend to be large, too."

"Shall we go through the receiving line?" said Paul. "It's to the left of the door there."

Carlota gave a quick glance at the line of distinguished-looking people waiting to greet the guests. When she didn't see Aletha Danton, she drew a deep breath of relief.

The reception-line greetings were perfunctory and, after a few moments in the line, they were free to find their table, which was toward the back of the huge room.

"You mean Danton the Great didn't invite you to sit with his group, Paul?" Dorothy Stein's black eyebrows rose dramatically.

"Fat chance of that."

"Do you work in the hospital, Miss Montez?" Dorothy Stein asked, when they were seated and had begun to tackle the inevitable fruit cup with which all convention banquets begin.

Carlota wasn't sure she liked Dorothy Stein and decided to get things out in the open from the start.

"Daytime I'm a senior at Central U," she explained. "Six nights a week I moonlight in the Polo Lounge after classes as a cocktail waitress."

"Guess that will hold you, Dorothy." Jacob Stein chuckled. "Incidentally, Carlota, I found her clerking in a five-and-ten."

"Just a little old oppressed minority group, aren't we, friends?" said Katie Warren. "We could start a demonstration except that it would embarrass Paul."

"I love your records," Carlota told Katie. "I have several of them."

"The word is 'loved,' " said Katie with her gamin smile. "I never was real sure I had a career waiting as a singer. Then this gorgeous hunk of Afro-American came along and I've been pregnant practically ever since, so I guess I'll never know."

"How many children do you have?"

"Three so far. The Pill and God willing, only one more —but late, to keep us company after the others leave for college. I've seen too many medical marriages flounder, once the children were educated."

"Tell me, Miss Montez," said Dorothy Stein, "when you're working in the Polo Lounge, do you ever—?"

"What she means is do the men give you a feel, à la *Butterfield 8?*" said Jacob Stein. "The next time I go into the Polo Lounge the answer will definitely be 'yes.' May I say, Miss Montez, that rarely have I ever encountered a more feelable member of the opposite sex—present company excepted, of course."

"You crud!" Dorothy Stein didn't appear to be the least bit offended. "If you weren't such a demon in bed, I'd have ditched you long ago."

"We sometimes have our moments, Mrs. Stein," said Carlota.

"Call me Dorothy, please. My somewhat acerbic manner actually covers the heart of gold of a typical Jewish mama. And by the way, how did you happen to meet our adored Paul here?"

"In the Polo Lounge," said Carlota, "when he propositioned me."

"Well, well," said Katie Warren. "When did you take up philandering, darling?"

"Maybe you'll appreciate me more from now on, Katie."

Paul, Carlota saw, wasn't even embarrassed by the badinage of his friends. She was seeing a side of him she hadn't known before and found herself liking him even more.

"I hope you accepted the proposition, Carlota," said Dorothy Stein. "I've been dying to seduce him ever since he came to Central City."

"Now I know what you do, when I'm on emergency duty for thirty-six hours straight," said Stein. "Take care, woman! I'll sneak home some evening and surprise you with your lover."

"Don't pay any attention to us, Carlota," said Katie Warren. "We're all really very uptight characters, like John and Sirsa here. We women know we'll be spending the rest of our lives driving kids and grandchildren to and from nursery school, kindergarten, music, speech, ballet and Boy Scouts—God, what a dismal prospect—while we wait for husbands who never come home from their work."

"You have one consolation, Katie," said John Vanda. "At least you'll all be rich."

"What shall it avail a woman if she gains the whole world and loses her husband to a nurse fifteen years younger than she is, who's smart enough to know how nylon clings to a well-turned behind? By the way, what philosopher said that?"

"One named Katie Warren, who knows she's speaking guff, I suspect," said Paul.

"You can talk, slave driver," said Katie darkly. "Just wait 'til somebody nails you down and you start joining your big chromosomes to her little ones."

"The way I heard it, the females are stronger than the males when it comes to chromosomes." Carlota was enjoying the good-natured banter hugely. "I took a course in genetics last year and it seemed to me that a lot of adverse inherited factors are transmitted by the male."

"That's what Dr. Crowder was holding forth about in her lecture on 'Life Without Father' yesterday," said Paul.

"Isn't she the author of *Sexual Slavery?*" Carlota asked.

"The same," said Jerry. "She and Dr. Poston have the hottest thing going, since Cleopatra rolled herself up in that rug to snare Julius Caesar. Have you read the book?"

"What woman hasn't?" said Dorothy Stein.

"If you ask me, it's the men who are slaves," said Jacob Stein. "I come home from a hard day's work on service and what do I get? A list of things that need to be done in the apartment and people we ought to visit."

"And who do you think has been slaving all day in the library reference department?" Dorothy demanded indignantly. "All you want when you come home is sex and food."

"In that order?" Katie's eyebrows lifted. "Jake certainly must find something at the hospital that Jerry doesn't."

"Please," said Sirsa. "You're embarrassing Carlota and prejudicing her against marriage, when we've all been trying for years to get Paul snared by somebody we could approve of. Besides, in India a woman who loves her husband is happy to bear him children."

"Hear! Hear!" said Katie Warren. "Three cheers for motherhood."

"Mexican families are very close, too," said Carlota. "I guess it's because we usually live together in the same part of town."

"You disappoint me, Carlota," said Jacob Stein. "I always imagined myself snaring a sultry señorita and dancing around the kitchen, until I got caught by this female dynamo here. Do any of you know what it is to be married to an ambitious Jewish mother? She can't wait for the time when I get my certification behind me and go out into the world to prey on unsuspecting women with slightly enlarged uteri."

"Is it like this all the time when they're together?" Carlota asked Paul in mock seriousness.

"Wait 'til they've had a few more drinks," he warned her. "They're absolutely unbearable then."

iii

The music for the dance that followed the annual banquet of the CMA began with a waltz while the tables were being cleared.

"Let's dance, Paul," said Carlota. "I love waltzes."

The floor was not yet crowded, so they had room to dance.

"I love your friends," she said. "But don't they know anything except medical shop talk?"

"You just put your finger on one of the main reasons for the high rate of medical divorces. Enjoying yourself otherwise?"

"I'm having a wonderful time. Oh! Oh!" She moved closer to him. "Don't look now but we're being raked with a broadside."

He swung her around and came face to face with Aletha Danton, who was dancing with Elton Brooks. She was hardly three feet away, and obeying a sudden perverse impulse, Paul moved quickly toward the other two and broke in, drawing Carlota with him before she had time to protest.

"Mrs. Danton, Dr. Brooks. May I present Miss Carlota Montez?" he said.

Carlota nodded courteously, as did Elton Brooks, but Aletha looked as if Paul had struck her in the face.

"Miss Montez and I have already met," she said icily.

"Then you'll be interested to know that Carlota is a great-granddaughter of a member of Emperor Maximilian's court in Mexico City and a student at Central University."

"I enjoyed our dance, Mrs. Danton." Elton Brooks was obviously anxious to change partners. "May I have this dance, Miss Montez?"

As Brooks and Carlota moved away, Paul put his arm around Aletha's rigid waist. "This seems to be our dance, Aletha," he said.

"You son-of-a-bitch," she said between clenched teeth. "What the hell do you think you're doing?"

"Giving you a little taste of what your husband did to me yesterday."

"Introducing me to a prostitute—?"

"Better watch your language. Carlota realized I'd had too much to drink in the Polo Lounge Sunday night and came up to my room to check up on me when she went off duty."

"Do you think anybody would believe that?" she demanded furiously.

"As many as would believe you came there for the same reason."

Dancing nearby with a somewhat apprehensive Elton Brooks, Carlota sensed the tension. Slipping out of her partner's embrace, while still holding him by the hand, she moved quickly to Paul's side.

"Come, Paul," she said loud enough for those at Danton's table and the surrounding area to hear distinctly. "You know I don't like you dancing with older women."

CHAPTER XXV

In Marian Crowder's hospital room, Cary Poston kissed her good night. "Do you have to go?" she asked.

"Afraid so. The hospital authorities don't approve of in-room debauchery. But you're safe, that's the most important thing."

"If you hadn't arrived with the atropine, I'd be dead."

"That gives me a lien on you."

"Let me out of here and I'll pay up tonight."

"You're not going to get out that easy, my sweet. I'll settle for nothing less than complete foreclosure."

"I'm close to that, too. When can I leave the hospital?"

"When we've caught whoever tried to kill you this morning."

"But that might be never."

"I've got a strange feeling that things are moving rapidly to a climax," Cary's voice was sober. "The convention ends tomorrow, so the murderer must be getting desperate to try to kill you and Caleb Downs in an open place like the hotel restaurant. With only one more day before CMA members will nearly all be going in different directions, he almost has to make another play in the next twenty-four hours."

"I'm scared, Cary."

"So am I. He's failed once with both of us, so he has to try again soon, if he's to get us before the convention is over."

"Maybe he'll just give up."

"The worst thing we could do now would be to assume that," said Cary. "Paranoiacs don't admit failure, as a rule. That's what makes them so dangerous."

ii

Things still weren't going right, Caleb Downs was forced to admit as he sat in the Falstaff Room about ten-thirty Wednesday evening. The room was only half filled, most of the doctors still in Central City being at the Centralia where the convention dinner dance was in progress.

Being a pragmatist, Caleb couldn't deny that he had failed so far on nearly all counts, but the admission didn't make the truth any less galling. Cary Poston and Marian Crowder were still alive, and with both under police protection, it simply didn't make sense to risk losing everything in a final attempt to destroy them. Especially since he had one accomplishment at least of which to be proud —the elimination of Senator Frank Spurgess as a threat to the pharmaceutical manufacturing industry.

Earlier that evening, Caleb had tried to get in touch with Alice Perrault. But her room didn't answer and he judged that she was out with that hayseed doctor who had become famous, merely by waving a magnet over his, Caleb's, chest. Certain that there'd been a definite invitation in the blonde's eyes more than once since Monday, and convinced that the possibilities she offered weren't something a man could easily walk away from, Caleb had hung around the Falstaff Room all evening, hoping the two of them would show up and he'd be able to take her away from Jethro Forbes.

The frustration of having spent four days with nothing accomplished hadn't been good for Caleb's heart, either. Twice that afternoon he'd experienced a dull ache in his left arm and shoulder portending an attack of angina pectoris. Each time he'd been able to relieve the pain by placing a tiny nitroglycerine tablet under his tongue, but the relief had been only temporary. And, as he sat nursing his third drink, he could feel the familiar warning starting in his left arm.

Then his pulse took a sudden leap when he saw Alice enter the lounge. She was alone and looked around, obviously seeking someone—Jethro Forbes, he supposed. Not finding him, she crossed to the bar and took a stool. But before she could give her order to the barman, Caleb moved to the stool beside her.

iii

As Alice had told Jethro, Ted Jones, the president of Vibrassage, usually took the ten o'clock plane out of Central City for Chicago, when he visited the CMA conventions. Tonight, however, Jones had been going on to Kansas City, where the traveling Vibrassage unit was scheduled to set up Sunday afternoon for business at the State Medical Association meeting starting there on Monday.

When Jones's plane departed at nine-thirty, Alice took a cab back to the hotel. She called Jethro's room and not finding him in, went down to the bar of the Falstaff Room for a drink while she waited to meet him at eleven, as she had promised.

She knew Jethro would expect a final answer in the morning about going with him to Guatemala so it wasn't fair to hold him in suspense any longer. And yet she still wasn't sure she could trust herself to be what he would have every right to expect, if she went with him.

She hadn't told Ted Jones about the possibility of her going for the same reason that she didn't know the answer herself. And that, she realized, wasn't being fair to Jones either. He paid her a good salary, never argued about her expense account, and made no demands upon her, except to sell as many Vibrassage units as she could. And there, she was proud to say, she had never let him down. All of which contributed to her emotional turmoil when she took a stool at the bar and ordered a drink. Nor was she really surprised when Caleb Downs took the stool beside her for that sort of thing happened to her frequently in hotels.

"Drinking alone?" he asked.

She nodded but didn't answer. Something about the bearded man in the expensively tailored suit still both attracted and repelled her, in spite of the lulling effect of alcohol.

The attraction she knew from long experience was purely sexual and that troubled her even more, for it posed a grave threat to her relationship with Jethro, if she dared to take a chance at keeping the quiet happiness she'd experienced these past few days with him.

As Caleb put his own drink on the bar in front of him, he touched her arm. It was a casual gesture but the sudden quickening of her pulse and the heady sense of expectation, even desire, she experienced, warned her that the compulsion which kept driving her into the arms of men, seeking a release she never obtained, was quite as strong and as impossible to control as ever—and that the denouement of their meeting in the bar would be just as it always was, the lulling sensation of the small vibrator upon her aching lower body and the dubious solace of a red capsule.

"Where's the boy friend?" Caleb asked.

"If you mean Dr. Forbes, I don't know."

"Looks like he stood you up."

"My boss flew in from Chicago and we spent the afternoon going over sales results."

"Which aren't as good as they could be. I've noticed it in my business, too, even before the convention, and I know the reason."

"Why?" she asked.

"Doctors are notorious suckers, when it comes to investments. Every boiler shop took sales operation has a list of high flying speculators in the medical profession. I think a lot of them thought everything was coming up roses, when the market hot up after the 1970 recession. But when it started down again they got clipped, so they're not buying any gadgets like those chairs of yours."

"My boss said much the same thing tonight."

"Smart man." Her presence and the certainty that the convention wouldn't be a total loss was beginning to warm Caleb's soul. "Can I buy you another drink?"

"No thanks," said Alice. "I'm going up to bed in a few minutes."

"Alone?" Caleb Downs's bushy eyebrows rose. "What a shame."

It was the pitch, but Alice hadn't doubted he would be making it soon after he sat down on the stool beside her at the bar, even though half the other stools were already vacant. She felt a sudden urge of anger at herself for responding, like a schoolgirl eager to be kissed, but that didn't diminish the reality of the response.

"I like my privacy," she said a little shortly.

"And your job?" His voice had changed and the bantering note was gone.

"Of course."

"Be a shame if you should lose it."

"I sell more Vibrassage units than any salesman in the company," Alice said indignantly. "Why would Mr. Jones fire me?"

"Maybe because someone brought a damage suit against

321

you and the company for, say, a million dollars. It's worth that, you know, to have your heart stopped by a machine that's not being properly operated."

The same cold fear settled around Alice's heart that had been there on Monday morning after the accident happened. When nothing had arisen since then to make her think Caleb Downs would make trouble, the fear had almost left her. Now she was faced with a naked threat, one she didn't doubt for a second that he would carry through.

"The machine was properly operated." She hoped he wouldn't notice that she had started trembling. "What happened to you was just an accident."

"You could get some argument on that in court. Reports of demand pacemakers being stopped by various short-wave machines, even as ordinary as the kind of microwave ovens restaurants use to heat up hamburgers and wieners, have been appearing in medical literature for several years now. An operator who was on the ball would have asked me whether I had a pacemaker before she turned on that diathermy machine."

"If you knew it, why didn't you—?"

"How should I know what kind of waves you were going to start shooting into my body?" he asked blandly.

Alice knew she was licked. If the case ever came to a trial and he started giving that sort of testimony to a jury, the company could easily be taken for that million he'd mentioned. And he had only to tell Ted Jones what had happened and threaten to sue for her to be out on her ear.

Her hand was shaking as she picked up the glass and drained the contents in a single gulp.

"Wh—what do you want?" she asked almost in a whisper, although she was sure now that the answer was.

"Just your company for a little while," he told her. "I've got a bottle in my room upstairs, we could finish this conversation a lot more comfortably up there. Besides, you don't want this sort of thing being discussed openly where people might hear and get the wrong idea, do you?"

Alice felt a surge of relief at the knowledge that his

threat of a suit had been just a ploy to make her go to bed with him, something she would have done anyway in the natural course of events before the evening was over, if Jethro Forbes didn't come along soon—and maybe if he did.

"If *that's* what you're after," she said, "let's go."

She slid off the stool and started for the door. If Jethro had gotten her note, he might turn up at any moment and it was very important now that they get away before he did.

Caleb was fumbling for money—she let him pay for her drinks and his—but reached her at the door to the lobby and took her arm, drawing her closely against him.

"You're playing it smart the way I figured you would, baby," he said. "You and me are going to celebrate to-night."

"Celebrate what?" She turned to look at him as they pushed on through and so didn't see Jethro come in through the street entrance to the bar and stop short, as if he had been slapped in the face. When the door closed behind them, he moved to the bar with the dragging steps of an old man and ordered a double Bourbon.

iv

The Warrens and the Steins had to leave the dance before eleven to take their baby-sitters home, so Paul and Carlota left at the same time. He drove her home and parked in front of the small house on Olivera Street, all of whose inhabitants appeared to be asleep, along with those in the neighborhood.

"Do you suppose we could sit for a while in your porch swing?" Paul asked. "We had one at home when I was growing up but I haven't been in one since."

"Certainly," she said. "I often sit there for a few minutes and have a Coke after I get home from the Polo Lounge. Would you like something to drink?"

"I've enjoyed this evening so much, all I want is to sit and talk."

"You're very serious about your work, aren't you?" she asked as they opened the front gate, which creaked a little on its hinges, and started up the walk.

"Too serious, I guess. It's only when I'm with someone like you that I realize how much I've missed by keeping my nose to the grindstone."

"Jerry Warren was telling me about your work while we were dancing. He says you left the Danton Clinic because of him."

"It was more like both of us being kicked out together."

It was pleasant to sit in the darkness of the vine-surrounded porch with the old wooden swing moving gently, a fitting ending to an evening he had enjoyed immensely. Mainly, he knew, because of the lovely girl beside him who fitted so naturally into the curve of his arm.

"Jerry said you didn't have to go to bat for him and make an issue of his being fired, just because he happened to say something about the work you both were doing at a medical meeting," she said.

"But it was *our* work."

"For which Dr. Danton wanted to take the credit?"

"In a way I guess Danton had a right to be angry, too. He wouldn't have gotten where he is if he hadn't sometimes ridden roughshod over people who weren't quite so convinced of their own purpose as he is of his. He taught me everything I know about my specialty, too, so even when he slugs me the way he did yesterday morning, I can't really hold a grudge against him very long. After all, a lot of people with heart trouble are alive today who wouldn't be, if he hadn't driven ahead—"

"And damn the torpedoes?"

"Yes. Jerry and I were only invited to take part in that particular symposium because we were working in the Danton Clinic, so we could have been considered to be speaking for it."

"It still wasn't fair for him to fire you."

"Actually, he did us a favor. I might have hung around the clinic awhile longer."

"Under Danton's shadow?"

Paul chuckled. "You don't work there otherwise."

"I like Katie and Jerry very much," she said.

"Katie's a doll, and Jerry's one of the most brilliant research surgeons I've ever known," said Paul. "We work together so smoothly in the operating room and the laboratory that an outsider can hardly tell who's the surgeon and who's the assistant."

"Would you go back to the Danton Clinic without Jerry?"

"Of course not. Where did you ever get that idea?"

"The others were talking while you were dancing with Sirsa. They said Dr. Danton may never be able to operate again and his wife wants you to come back and take over. That was why she came to your room the night she found me there, wasn't it?"

"And all along I thought it was my manly charm. You've just taken me down a peg."

"Oh, you've got the manly charm all right," Carlota assured him. "I recognized it the first time I saw you, that night in the Polo Lounge. I needed that hundred pretty badly, but I wouldn't have taken it from just any man who asked me."

"That's being pretty frank." Paul felt his pulse beat a little faster.

"That little episode with Mrs. Danton this evening had something to do with me, too, didn't it?" she asked.

"I got angry when she called you a—" He stopped.

"A prostitute?"

"Yes."

"I am—technically."

"You certainly aren't," he said indignantly. "Nothing happened."

"If you hadn't been out cold it would have—and all because you were angry at yourself for wanting her."

"You must have been studying psychology." Paul managed to laugh although he was feeling pretty uncomfortable. "The Freudian branch."

"It's still true, isn't it?"

"I suppose so, since we're letting our hair down."

"I think you took me to the banquet tonight as an act of defiance to show her you're not a puppet to be manipulated, when she wants to pull the strings."

"You're wrong there," he said. "I've told you already that you're a very attractive girl."

Her eyes twinkled. "And you nearly got me into bed once—"

"That had nothing to do with it, either."

She kissed him quickly on the lips, a warm light kiss.

"I believe you," she said. "And I also think it's time we said good night."

"Can I see you again soon?"

"Does that mean you're going to stay in Central City?"

"I don't think I ever really seriously considered leaving. I have just about everything I could wish here—now."

"For that," she told him, "You can kiss *me* good night."

v

Jethro Forbes had been disturbed by Alice's words when he'd left her after lunch that afternoon. He'd sat through a paper on toxemia of pregnancy in the OB-GYN section without really hearing what was being said. Since Alice was tied up for dinner with her boss, he'd eaten a soggy fish sandwich before going to a movie that turned out to be largely a parade of naked womanhood, revealed during a flimsy story that seemed to have no purpose except justifying the exposure.

"Skin-flick," a fellow sitting near him had called the picture but Jethro didn't see even one in the large cast that could compare with Alice.

Something was troubling her, he'd sensed that almost from the beginning. And what disturbed him most was his utter inability to help her exorcise her own particular demon.

Not expecting to see her at the Falstaff Room until eleven, he'd walked back to the hotel the long way, arriving just in time to see her leave the bar, quite willingly it seemed, with Caleb Downs. From the half darkness of the bar he'd watched them take the elevator, obviously bound for one or the other's room.

About a half-hour later Jethro was weaving a little as he opened the door of his room. He knew he had no real claim on Alice Perrault. She hadn't made him any promises and he'd recognized from the skill with which she made love that she'd had plenty of experience there. So if she'd decided to choose another man for tonight, he had no real right to be resentful—none of which made the pain he felt any less.

Moving across the room, he switched on the TV set but the news was just going off and all he heard was a fragment about a tornado striking somewhere. Which didn't excite him, since Revere was located in the center of the Midwest tornado belt and he'd been through his share of them in the past fifteen years.

Pulling off his clothes, he dropped them across a chair and climbed into bed. It was the first time he had slept alone since Sunday night and he turned his face to the wall, so he couldn't see the empty side of the bed.

CHAPTER XXVI

Watching from the bed where she lay beneath the sheet, as Caleb Downs came out of the bathroom, Alice felt a sudden panic grip her. It was a panic she hadn't experienced since she was sixteen and she knew its source at once. Caleb had left the ceiling light on in spite of her protests, and seen now in a light almost as bright as the sunlight shining through the window of another bedroom so long ago, he was almost the image of Henry Perrault.

The broad shoulders were matted with dark hair, tufts of which also stood out over his shoulder blades. His hips were narrow and he moved with the same deliberate intention her father had used that terrible afternoon. Caleb had sprayed himself with cologne in the bathroom, too, and when the reek of it reached her nostrils, as he moved toward the bed, she could have sworn it was the same scent her father always used.

Feeling her heart start to pound and her muscles tense as the memory of that other afternoon so long ago came flooding back, Alice fought against the surge of desire threatening to seize her—and knew in a moment fraught with sheer horror and guilt that she was powerless to resist.

Could there really be any truth in what the pudgy psychiatrist had told her? She asked herself desperately. Was the unwillingness to admit to herself that her body had responded that afternoon, in spite of the prohibitions of her fundamentalist upbringing, really the mental block that had kept her from experiencing that same response since? The real reason she had embroiled herself with a succession of men? Seeking always to convince the other Alice that despite the deep-seated prohibition of her unconscious mind against incest, her body hadn't really responded even while her mind was paralyzed with horror and guilt at what her father's embrace had meant.

Caleb Downs gave her no time to contemplate or dredge up old memories. Seizing the top hem of the sheet she had pulled up across her breasts for protection against the glare of the ceiling light, he jerked it down, leaving her completely exposed.

"Man! Oh, man!" he gloated. "You're something special! Something real special, baby, just like I knew you'd be."

Frantically Alice reached for the sheet but he jerked it from her hand and off the bed.

"I won't need that pacemaker tonight," he chortled. "You've got my old ticker in high gear."

"Maybe you shouldn't—" Alice's words ended in a cry of pain and protest as Caleb seized her in a bearlike embrace, crushing her breasts against the matted hair upon his chest.

"Too late for that now." His mouth on hers shut away any further words, even her cry as his body was joined roughly to hers. The cry was not so much of pain, however, as it was a protest against the answering clamor within her own body aroused by the similarity between the situation now and that afternoon long ago—a similarity assailing all the structure of defense she had built up against the horror of her own demanding response.

In panic now as control of her own sensation was stripped away, to be replaced by an overpowering urge to respond, Alice reached up and seized Caleb Downs by the shoulders, desperately fighting to push him away long enough to detach herself from his body. But when her fingers closed around the tufts of coarse hair sprouting from his shoulder blades, the memory of almost identical tufts upon her father's body suddenly loosed a roaring tornado inside her, driving out all thought, all reason, everything except the clamor of her senses.

No longer under the control of the will, her body writhed in an instinctual response until the purely animal force of desire generated in her by Caleb Downs's rough lovemaking matched and exceeded his own, sweeping them both upon a surging tide of emotion toward the inevitable peak which each so desperately sought to achieve.

Then suddenly his weight was a crushing burden upon her, driving him deep within her loins and triggering in her own body the final spasm of climatic response. No longer did she fight against the tide but let herself be swept on its crest to a height of ecstasy far beyond what she'd felt that afternoon in her father's embrace.

Momentarily, Alice was sure she'd blacked out under the surging force of that tornado of emotion. Fighting for room to breathe beneath the weight of Caleb Downs's body, she pushed against his shoulder and was startled when he rolled clear of her body and lay, gasping for breath, on his back.

Only when she saw him stagger from the bed and fumble frantically in the pocket of his jacket, where it had fallen to the floor when he'd undressed hurriedly, did Alice realize that he was in the grip of something more than simply the aftermath of explosive sexual relief. For his breathing was labored, as his lungs sought to pull in enough air to supply the needs of his body for oxygen, and his face twisted in pain.

"What's wrong?" she cried.

Caleb didn't answer. His frantic probing in the pockets of his jacket had yielded a small brown bottle, and with trembling fingers he emptied a few small tablets on the bedside table. Seizing one, he placed it under his tongue, before he collapsed upon the bed.

He would have crushed Alice with his own weight as he fell, if she hadn't scrambled out of the way. Swinging her legs off the bed, she stood beside it, looking down with horror at the stricken man.

"My heart!" he gasped. "Another nitroglycerine tablet!"

Then, as she watched, he tried desperately to push himself up with his hands upon the mattress, apparently trying to spit out the tablet he had just placed beneath his tongue. But his strength failed and he fell back.

"Get atrop—" His tongue suddenly seemed to be without control and only a babble of sounds that had no meaning came from his mouth.

Terrified, Alice realized that she was nude and reached down to pick up her slip, where he had knocked over the chair on which she had placed her clothing. As she pulled it over her head with frantic haste, the stertorous sound of his breathing filled the room, its rate growing perceptibly slower while the seconds passed.

Searching frantically for some way to get help without involving herself, Alice suddenly remembered that Jethro Forbes's room was on the same floor. She knew she had no right to ask Jethro for any favors, after she had stood him up and gone to bed with Caleb Downs. But Jethro was a dedicated doctor and she could at least appeal to him in that capacity.

Picking up the telephone beside the bed, she dialed 7 and then 1030, the number of Jethro's room, knowing the inside call would not register with the operator of the hotel switchboard.

"I'm in Caleb Downs's room," she said when he answered. "I think he's had another heart attack."

"I'll be right there."

The telephone clicked in Alice's ear as Jethro hung up and, turning to Caleb Downs again, she saw that he was unconscious. In addition to the slowing of his respirations, their depth was also perceptibly less than it had been a few moments before.

She knew there wasn't any point in trying to fool Jethro about what had happened: The mussed bed, the half-filled whiskey bottle, the empty glasses, and most of all Caleb's naked body with the skin already beginning to turn blue from oxygen lack, all spoke for themselves. Alice had only time to pull her dress on over her head, when there was a light tap on the door. She went to let Jethro in, sobbing with relief at the sight of his homely, comforting face.

"Take your clothes and go to my room, the door's ajar," he told her. "Get into bed."

"B—but—"

"You weren't in this room at all tonight, understand? You've been with me ever since you left the bar downstairs."

"But how did you—?"

"I came in just as you and Downs were leaving." He was reaching for Caleb Downs's wrist as he spoke. "Did you give him anything."

"He took a tablet—nitroglycerine, I think he said—under his tongue. The bottle was in his jacket pocket."

"Be sure you take everything that's yours with you. You haven't been here at all, understand?"

She nodded. "Thank you, Jethro."

"The corridor outside was empty just now. You ought to make it this time of night without anybody seeing you."

As she moved to the door, Alice saw Jethro place his ear on the unconscious man's chest. She heard him give a muffled exclamation of surprise before she closed it behind her, but didn't stop to see what had occasioned it.

ii

Jethro didn't even hear the door close behind Alice. With his ear against Caleb Downs's chest, he heard the slowing of the heart, the sound of the beats growing ever fainter and farther apart, like a metronome running down, until he could hear no more.

Cardiac compression, he knew, could be dangerous with a pacemaker inside Downs's chest and the metal spring electrodes, by which its impulses were transmitted to the organ itself, penetrating the heart muscle. But no other course was open, even though Jethro's clinical sense told him it, too, would be fruitless.

As he exterted rhythmic pressure upon the breastbone of the dying man, pushing it back gainst the spine and compressing the heart to drive blood out of it and into the circulation, Jethro's gaze centered upon a strange scar on Caleb Downs's chest just above the surgical incision that had told him on Monday a pacemaker had probably been placed inside his chest.

The scar's whiteness made it stand out sharply against the cyanotic bluish hue of the surrounding skin. The pattern, a triangle within a circle, was familiar, too, for Jethro bore the same scar upon his own chest, burned there many years ago during the initiation into Alpha Kappa medical fraternity. He even recognized the school, for in one point of the triangular part of the scar, the Greek letter Iota, identifying the Johns Hopkins chapter, could be seen.

There had been no time for Jethro to call for help; the strenuous effort of CPR—cardiopulmonary resuscitation—left time for nothing else. But when some ten minutes of rhythmic pressure upon Downs's chest alternating with mouth-to-mouth breathing brought no evidence of a heartbeat, he finally stopped, sure now that death had come to the other man.

The bottle of tablets, one of which Caleb Downs had placed under his tongue, had spilled over the bedside table in the stricken man's frantic haste to relieve the stabbing pain of angina. Several of the small tablets it contained lay beside the mouth of the bottle but the bottle itself bore no label.

When Jethro examined the tablets more closely, he was struck immediately by the fact that they seemed a little larger than the ordinary dose of one hundred and fiftieth of a grain of nitroglycerine, used almost universally as a temporary method of relieving the stabbing pains of angina pectoris.

Moistening the end of his index finger with water from the bathroom faucet, he touched one of the tablets, then touched the tip of his tongue.

The sharp tingling sensation on his tongue told him the identity of the drug Downs had taken by mistake, when the effort of sexual union had been too much for an already overtaxed heart. It also sent him hurrying to the bathroom to rinse out his mouth again and again. Returning to the bedside table, Jethro picked up the telephone and dialed the hotel operator.

"This is Dr. Jethro Forbes," he told her. "I have an emergency here with one of the guests. Please give me the paging operator at University Hospital."

The voice of the paging operator sounded almost immediately in Jethro's ear.

"Can you locate Dr. Cary Poston for me?" he asked. "This is Dr. Jethro Forbes. I need him at once in Room 1030 at the Regency House."

"Dr. Poston is staying in the hospital," said the operator. "I'll ring him, Doctor Forbes."

"Please tell him to come here immediately."

The stinging sensation in Jethro's mouth had stopped now. And when he felt his own pulse, the beat was a little faster than normal, about what he would expect it to be with the realization that he had absorbed even a small dose of the lethal drug which had already killed one man and sent Marian Crowder to the hospital. By which he judged that he had not absorbed enough of the powerful preparation of aconite to be in danger himself.

While he waited for Cary Poston to reach the hotel, Jethro carefully searched the room to make certain no evidence of Alice's having been there that evening remained. In the dead man's right-hand coat pocket, he found the vial Downs had undoubtedly intended to get.

It was a small familiar bottle labeled "Nitroglycerine, 1/150 gr." with the directions "Place under tongue for chest pain."

iii

"What's wrong, Jethro?" Cary Poston asked when the other doctor opened the door of Room 1030, roughly fifteen minutes after Jethro's call.

"Downs is dead," said Jethro.

Cary moved quickly to the bed and lifted the dead man's wrist for a moment before dropping it and turning back to Jethro.

"What happened here?"

"I got a call maybe twenty minutes ago. My room is on the same floor as this."

"Why would Downs call you?"

"I met him in the corridor one morning and we had breakfast together so he must have thought of me and dialed my room directly."

"Was he dead when you got here?"

"Almost. I gave him CPR but his pulse just slowed down and stopped—a typical aconite effect."

"How could anyone give aconite to him?"

"They didn't have to." Jethro picked up a small white tablet that was lying on the bedside table with several others. "He seems to have made the mistake of taking his own medicine."

"Are you saying Downs is—was the murderer?"

"That's what everything adds up to. The way I figure it he must have had an attack of angina and tried to take a nitroglycerine tablet but got the wrong drug. These were in his coat pocket."

Picking up the small bottle labeled "Nitroglycerine,

1/150 gr.," Jethro handed it to Cary. "The tablets are right much alike and the bottles, too—except that the nitroglycerine is labeled."

"Then he must have taken bikh by mistake?"

"I don't see any other explanation."

"But why would—?"

"Take a look at this." Jethro pointed to the dead man's chest just below the left collar bone. Against the bluish tint of oxygen lack, the white scar with the triangle and tiny Greek letter inscribed, stood out sharply.

"Look familiar?" Jethro asked.

"Our fraternity brand!" Cary examined the scar more closely. "Is the small letter Iota?"

"Looks like it to me. Iota's the signature Greek letter of your chapter of Alpha Kappa, isn't it?"

"Yes."

"Downs looks like he's about your age, so you both may have been in the same chapter at Hopkins at roughly the same time. Does anything about him look familiar?"

Cary shook his head. "Marian has always claimed she'd known him somewhere. She told me she mentioned it to Downs, too, but he denied it."

Jethro pointed to a small scar in the lower part of the dead man's neck. "What do you make of that?"

"Obviously he's had a tracheotomy, probably when he had the heart attack that left him in need of a pacemaker." Cary rubbed his chin thoughtfully. "That would account for a change in voice, he always sounded a bit hoarse. And the beard would hide his features."

"He certainly had a built-in disguise."

"That's it!" Cary cried. "There was a fellow in our chapter named Eric Sands who was about Downs's size. But he failed at the end of the first year, got kicked out for cheating. He was sort of a genius, too—in pharmacology."

"Go on," said Jethro. "The whole thing is beginning to fall into place like a whodunit."

"When Sands was kicked out, he accused Marian and

me of turning him in for cheating. Raised quite a stink about it, in fact."

"Did you?"

"No." Cary shook his head unbelievingly. "It's fantastic, isn't it? Do you suppose he's planned all these years to kill us?"

"Looks like it," said Jethro. "Senator Spurgess must have gotten the poison in a cup of beer intended for you."

"Imagine letting something like that warp your mind to the point where you'd be willing to murder two people years later."

"My guess is that he'd been planning it for a long time," said Jethro. "A skilled pharmacologist would be able to select a sophisticated drug like bikhaconite and Sands was a genius in the field. I bought some stock in his company about five years ago. It's now worth around a hundred times what I paid for it."

"Better sell it first thing in the morning," Cary told him. "When this gets out, the bottom will probably fall out of Central Pharmaceutical. Well, I'd better call Lieutenant Klinger and tell him we've wrapped up his case for him."

iv

Alice was asleep in the bed, curled up like a child, when Jethro returned to his room. Careful not to make any noise, he undressed and switched off the shower stall light before slipping into the bed beside her.

Her body was warm when it touched his in the darkness and, though still asleep, she moved closer to him. But when his arm instinctively went around her, he felt her body suddenly grow rigid and heard the start of a scream in her throat.

"It's Jethro," he said quickly. "Everything's all right."

After a brief moment, while the remembered panic she had experienced earlier, seized her once again, Alice relaxed and moved closer to him, holding him tightly as if afraid he would leave her. For a long time they lay there, until her body began to relax.

336

"Is—is it over?" she asked.

"Downs is dead—from a heart attack."

"He was going to sue Vibrassage—and me, Jethro. I had to do what he wanted me to."

"It's all right, darling."

"Then you don't hate me because I—"

"Downs was the one who's been poisoning people. He would have killed you, too, if you hadn't let him have his way."

She shivered and clung to him again.

"Nobody knows you were in Downs's room tonight," he told her. "If the police ask questions, you've been here with me ever since you left the bar downstairs, just like you're going to be with me always."

"I'd like that," she said, and moved deeper into his embrace. "Make love to me, darling, so I'll know the past hour was nothing but a bad dream."

In Jethro's arms Alice discovered that in the terrible moment when she had cried out in one final agony of guilt against the response of her own body the specter which had haunted her since she was sixteen had been dissipated at last, even as the dying body of the man who had called himself Caleb Downs had threatened to crush her beneath its weight.

v

Dr. Andrew Huxtable came into the autopsy room carrying a paper cup of coffee in his hand.

"A helluva fine pair of friends you turned out to be, rousting me out of bed when I'd just fallen asleep after dancing with a lot of faculty wives--middle-aged ones mostly," he said. "Don't you know we have refrigerators to keep stiffs on ice until a decent hour of the morning?"

"Sorry, Doc," said Lieutenant Klinger. "We need an analysis of this guy's stomach contents and saliva before there's a chemical change."

"Also a report on these." From his pocket Cary took a small envelope in which he had placed the tiny tablets he'd found scattered on Caleb Downs's bedside table. "We think they're what's been killing pople around here, including Sands."

"Handle those things carefully will you, Cary?" said Huxtable. "We'll have to get Kendall Thomas to check them."

Going to the phone, he looked up a number in the directory hanging from it and dialed.

"Kendall's got a short fuse," Huxtable confided while the phone was ringing. "Here, you talk to him, Cary. If I don't have Downs's stomach out before Kendall gets here he'll be madder'n hell at me for fouling him up."

As Huxtable picked up a razor-sharp autopsy knife from the tray beside the long table, the voice of Dr. Kendall Thomas sounded sleepily in Cary's ear.

"That you, Kendall?" Cary asked.

"Of course it's me, Cary. Who the hell do you think I've got sleeping in my bed? Some hen medic bucking for an 'A' in pharmacology?"

"We need you in Andy Huxtable's department, Kendall. The murderer seems to have taken some of his own drug by mouth, thinking it was nitroglycerine."

"Who is it?"

"Caleb Downs, head of Central Pharmaceutical."

"My God! I had a beer at that booth late this afternoon."

"You're safe. As potent as this stuff appears to be, you'd have been dead long ago if Downs wanted you that way."

"I'll be right over," said Thomas. "Tell Andy to be sure to save me the stomach contents."

"He's taking the stomach out now, intact. We'll keep it for you."

When Cary went back to the autopsy table, Huxtable had half completed the examination.

"Nothing in this guy except the bikh, if that's what killed him, Cary," he said. "Plus an old coronary scar and a pacemaker. Kendall coming over?"

"As soon as he can get dressed. Said for you to be sure and save the stomach contents."

"What the hell kind of a Medical Examiner does he think I am? Anything else you want, Klinger?"

Huxtable's knife was moving with slashing rapidity as he spoke, removing pieces of the innermost tissues of the body for later examination by chemical and microscopic tests. At the head of the table, a technician was already at work with a bone saw, removing the top of the cranium so the brain could be lifted out in one piece, after the stem extending down into the spinal column was cut.

"Let's go into the office," said Klinger to Cary Poston. "I've seen hundreds of these things, but when they start to use the bone saw, it always gets to me."

In the office, Klinger closed the door so the noise didn't intrude.

"What I want to be sure of here is the sequence of events, Dr. Poston," he said. "If Downs was after you and Dr. Crowder all the time, I can understand his getting Senator Spurgess accidentally. But would he risk the gas chamber just to destroy Dr. Crowder?"

"A paranoiac would," said Cary.

"Why did he call Dr. Forbes instead of the hotel physician?"

"Forbes was close by, a few doors down the hall. He'd saved Downs's life on Monday, so Downs naturally thought of him."

"Would Downs have had time to dial the operator?"

"He didn't have to. Just dailing 7 and then 1030 would ring Dr. Forbes's room."

"I'll accept that," said Klinger. "Now answer me this since you're a heart specialist. Why would Downs—or Sands—need nitroglycerine tablets with a pacemaker already in his heart?"

"Pacemakers only control the rate of the heart," Cary explained. "If Downs had a severe coronary once, which is why most pacemakers are put in, his heart circulation could be so decreased by hardening of the arteries that he'd be liable to attacks of angina."

"Even when he was asleep?"

"Angina patients are often wakened by the pain; sometimes they can even remember having a bad dream that brought on the attack. My guess, though, is that Downs—or Sands—was frustrated at not being able to get to Dr. Crowder or me. That in itself would be enough to cause tension, and tension can bring on angina in anyone whose arteries are already in trouble."

"Would he have the pills?"

"Most cardiacs of this type keep nitroglycerine with them all the time. It relieves the pain of angina quicker than anything else."

"Then it was logical for him to try to take a nitroglycerine tablet?"

"Absolutely. I'll even go you one further. Nitroglycerine is usually placed under the tongue because it dissolves almost as quickly there as if given intravenously. Downs had to have a form of aconite that would act with about the same rapidity as nitroglycerine in order to kill as quickly as it's been doing. If you would care to put one of these little tablets under your tongue as a test, Lieutenant—"

"I'll take your word for it," Klinger assured him. "Go on."

"Downs undoubtedly woke up with a severe anginal pain. One of the accompaniments is a profound fear of death so he must have been in a real panic while he was fumbling for nitroglycerine in his jacket and put the pseudaconite tablet under his tongue instead by mistake. That stuff causes a severe burning, or tingling, of the mucous membranes when it's absorbed, so he knew right away what had happened. That's when he rang Dr. Forbes. We found a syringe with atropine that Downs—or Sands- carried with him as a precaution but the drug hit him so fast he didn't get to use it. He knew Dr. Forbes could, though, since he's a doctor. The trouble was, by the time Forbes got to the room, Downs was practically dead from the poison."

"That's the part I'm not sure of," Klinger interrupted.

"In the cases of both Senator Spurgess and Dr. Crowder, five or even ten minutes elapsed while the drug was being absorbed. Why didn't Downs have time to give himself a shot of atropine?"

"I've already explained that," said Cary. "A nitroglycerine tablet under the tongue acts in seconds. The pseudaconite tablet Sands put under his tongue by mistake seems to have been equally rapid."

Any further discussion was put off by the arrival of Dr. Kendall Thomas carrying a rack of test tubes and two bottles of reagent, one clear and the other a deep purple color.

"I stopped by my laboratory and brought down the chemicals for a preliminary test," he said.

"Here's your saliva specimen, Kendall." The Medical Examiner gave the pharmacologist a test tube containing a small amount of an opalescent fluid.

Dividing the contents of the test tube into several portions, Dr. Thomas added acetic acid to one and then the purple potassium permanganate solution. Immediately a heavy reddish precipitate clouded the tube.

"You can be sure that precipitate will be crystalline when I filter it out," he said. "There's your cause of death, Lieutenant."

"Thanks, Kendall," said Cary. "You can go on back to bed now."

"I've never seen a form of aconite as deadly as this one appears to be," said the pharmacologist. "If the lieutenant will let me have one of those tablets, I'm going to analyze it and find out what the exact chemical structure is."

"Be my guest." Klinger gingerly handed over the envelope with the several tablets in it as if he were glad to get rid of it. "Just save a couple for evidence, in case it turns out that anybody else is involved in this caper."

"I don't see how Downs could have afforded to work any way except alone," said Cary as he and Lieutenant Klinger crossed the hospital lobby. "He couldn't trust anybody else with the knowledge of what he was about."

"It's a good thing he wasn't down on the whole medical profession the way I once thought the murderer might be," said Klinger. "All he would have had to do was drop a few of those tablets into one of his beer kegs and he could have killed half the doctors at the convention."

"And implicated himself."

"Not if he were smart enough to take a small dose the way he did with Dr. Crowder. Well, I'm off to bed. At least I can get a few hours of sleep, now that the Convention Murder Case is solved. Can I drop you somewhere, Dr. Poston?"

"My apartment is only a couple of blocks away and the walk will do me good," said Cary. "There's no need for you to bother."

"I'll just follow you in the car until you're safely home," said Klinger. "It would be a shame for you to come through all this unscathed and then have somebody mug you between here and your apartment."

CHAPTER XXVII

It was barely six o'clock Thursday morning when the telephone beside Paul Rice's bed in the Hotel Centralia rang sharply.

"Paul." It was Cary Poston's voice. "We've got trouble."

"Another poisoning?"

"Not this time, thank God. Edward Danton has had a stroke."

"When?"

"About thirty minutes ago. He always gets up early. This morning he went to the bathroom and woke Aletha up when he fell off the seat, unconscious."

"What a tough break! The election's today."

"Danton's got more to worry about than elections. His right side is paralyzed and he can't speak."

"Is he still in the hotel?"

"No. I had him brought over to Medical Private. When can you see him?"

"Are you still there?" Cary asked when Paul didn't answer immediately.

"How does Aletha feel about it? We had words last night."

"Danton is my responsibility now and you're the best surgeon this side of Houston for treating a cerebral embolus. Room 510, Medical Private."

"I'll be there in fifteen minutes," said Paul.

"Shall I alert an OR?"

"Not at the moment, but you can call Jerry for me. We may have to do an arteriogram."

"Will do," said Cary and hung up.

When Paul walked into one of the plush VIP suites on the Private Medical ward of University Hospital, he saw Aletha Danton walking back and forth in the adjoining sitting room. Cary Poston stood at one side of Edward Danton's bed; at the other was Dr. Cedric Moriarity, a full professor in the Department of Neurology.

"Morning, Paul," said the neurologist. "This is a classic case of internal carotid embolism. Came on while straining."

H. Edward Danton was in an Intensive Care hospital bed. His eyes were open and his left hand was moving upon the covers in a constant twitching, but there was no movement of the right. Nor did he show any recognition of Paul's presence.

A block between the will and the muscles that must carry out the commands of that will, caused by the cessation of blood flow through a major artery to one side of the brain, aphasia and paralysis of that severity were indicative of a severe insult to the brain, ordinarily referred to as a stroke.

With a stethoscope Paul listened over Danton's neck directly opposite the spot where the great artery carrying blood to one side of the head divided into the internal carotid branch, forming an important source of supply for one side of the brain, and the external channel that brought blood to many of the important facial structures outside the skull.

The bruit he expected to hear was easily audible on the left side, a steady whooshing sound in cadence with the beating of the heart. The bruit itself was diagnostic of an obstruction inside the artery interfering with the flow of blood and causing the sound, just as scarring of a heart valve from rheumatic fever caused a murmur that could be heard by listening over the heart itself.

When Paul moved the bell of the stethoscope upward, the sound became less noticeable and abruptly disappeared just under Danton's ear. On the opposite side of the neck, it was not audible at all.

"The bruit is quite characteristic," said Paul.

"So are the neurological signs," said Dr. Moriarty.

"What about the rest of the physical findings?"

"Blood pressure's not too high—one fifty over ninety," said Cary. "There's no cardiac enlargement and only moderate hardening of the arteries in the eye grounds."

Study of the inside of the eye, where the arteries supplying the sensitive retina and other structures of the eyeball spread out in a treelike pattern that was easily seen with an ophthalmoscope by looking directly through the pupil, was extremely important in determining the extent of hardening of the blood vessels generally over the body.

"Do you think he understands anything we say?" Paul asked Dr. Moriarty.

"He may. But communication is gone due to the aphasia."

"I just talked to Houston." Aletha spoke from the back of the room; Paul hadn't realized she had come in from the adjoining sitting room. "Dr. DeBakey's in Europe. Won't be back for a week."

"Do you agree that immediate surgery is indicated. Paul?" Dr. Moriarty asked.

"What would you do?" Aletha asked quickly before Paul could answer.

"A clot has broken loose, probably from an ulcerated area inside one of the brain arteries where the wall has hardened," said Paul. "Usually it's close to where the main carotid divides to form the most important section of the brain's blood supply. We need to operate immediately and remove the clot."

"He told me yesterday they'd found a hardening in the X rays at the clinic a couple of weeks ago," said Aletha. "What do you call it? An arteriogram?"

"Yes."

"He was going to see Dr. DeBakey as soon as we got back and have the area removed."

"It's too bad he didn't go to Houston when the plaque was first diagnosed," said Paul.

"Edward was determined to win the election first," said Aletha bitterly and Paul knew what she was thinking— that if the Young Turk movement to run him for president-elect hadn't gained momentum and required so much effort on Danton's part to combat it, the stroke might not have happened.

"Edward's been carrying a potential explosion around inside his skull as long as that arteriosclerotic plaque has been there, Aletha," said Cary pointedly. "If anyone's to blame for this, it's Edward himself. The most important thing now is to get the embolus, and its cause, if possible, out of the artery before his brain is damaged permanently."

"Do you want me to operate?" Paul asked Aletha. "Or would you rather have someone else?"

"How long can you wait?"

Dr. Moriarity answered the question. "Every hour increases the danger that the clot will enlarge and block off more and more important arteries, Mrs. Danton. I'd say your husband should be operated on as soon as Dr. Rice can get ready."

"I'll need your permission," Paul told Aletha.

He was not surprised to see her still hesitate, considering how angry she had been with him the evening before.

"You said he could understand, didn't you, Dr. Moriarity?" she asked finally.

"He may still be able to," said the neurologist. "But I

can't guarantee how long he will go on understanding— or that the clot will not enlarge and begin to shut down the blood flow to vital centers. It usually does, once the blood begins to back up behind the embolus."

"I can't take the responsibility myself without trying to ask him," said Aletha.

"You've known Dr. Danton longer than I have, Cary," said Moriarity. "Why don't you try to get through to him?"

Cary Poston moved closer to the bed and stood looking down at Edward Danton.

"I'm sure you know as well as we do what has happened, Edward," he said. "An embolus in the internal carotid on the left side has caused a stroke. We all feel that Paul should operate at once to remove it and clean out the artery if he can."

"Will that cure him of these attacks?" Aletha asked.

"Operation is successful in ninety to ninety-five per cent of the cases where a carotid plaque is diagnosed," said Paul. "Once it's removed, blood can flow through the artery unimpeded, if the patient continues to take drugs to prevent clotting while the inside of the artery heals."

"If you're willing for Paul to operate, Edward, please try to communicate with us," said Cary.

For several minutes they watched the inert figure upon the bed anxiously, his eyes, the left arm in which movement still remained, even the left leg which he could also move.

"The aphasia is too deep," Cary said finally, when there was no response that any of them could discern. "You'll have to make the decision, Aletha."

"Go ahead and operate then." Her voice had a flat, almost metallic tone.

"I'll have an operating room made ready while I talk to Ed Balentine, the roentgenologist at the Danton Clinic," said Paul. "If he can tell us enough about the location of this plaque, we may be able to go ahead without having to do a second set of arteriograms. I don't want to put any more pressure behind that clot than I have to."

ii

It was seven o'clock and already light outside the hotel window when the phone in Jethro Forbes's room rang. He picked it up and spoke softly, so as not to awaken Alice. After the explosive climax of their lovemaking, when he came back from Caleb Downs's room, she'd dropped into a deep sleep in his arms.

"Jethro?" He recognized the voice even from hundreds of miles away. It was Wiley Blackston, the mayor of Revere.

"Yes, Wiley."

"Thank God I found you! Sarah thought you had gone to a medical meeting in Chicago but I remembered that the news broadcast about the way you started that fellow's heart came from Central City. The operator had to call four hotels before we found you."

"What's wrong, Wiley?"

"Wrong! Didn't you see the TV news?"

"Not last night. I was doing something else."

"Making out with some broad, I hope." His old breakfast companion chuckled. "I hope you've had enough. How soon can you get a flight home?"

"The convention isn't over yet."

"It's over for you," said Wiley. "A tornado came through here about nine o'clock last night and flattened Revere. We've turned the Baptist Church into an emergency hospital but water pipes are all torn up and the Health Department people say we could have an epidemic any time. The residents of Revere have to be immunized against typhoid right away but there's nobody available except Joe Painter and you know what that means."

A poor doctor at best, Painter was in his seventies, Jethro knew. And the chances of getting a young doctor to come to Revere, with or without the emergency, were practically nil.

"We need you here, Jethro," said Wiley Blackston. "Need you bad."

"Is Sarah——?"

"The tornado missed your house. I don't think Sarah even stopped looking at the TV."

"No." Jethro hardly recognized the voice as his own. "She wouldn't."

"Got any idea when you can get a flight out of there?"

Jethro looked at Alice, and saw that she was awake, watching him.

"You still there, Jethro?" Wiley Blackston's voice was anxious.

"I'll have to check the airlines and call you back."

"Another tornado warning just came over the radio, so the people are panicky. If I can tell them you'll be here before nightfall, it will help a lot."

"I'll call you back as soon as I can check the airline schedules, Wiley," Jethro promised and hung up the phone.

Alice sat up, pulling the sheet around her. "What's happened?" she asked.

"That was Wiley Blackston, the mayor of Revere. A tornado nearly destroyed the town last night."

"I heard about it on the radio coming back from the airport, but I didn't recognize the name of the town. Is your wife——"

"Didn't turn a hair, Wiley said, but the rest of the town's in a mess. He wants me to come home right away."

"Aren't there any other doctors?"

"Only one—and he's not much help."

"You're going, aren't you?"

He nodded. "I have to. People—some I brought into the world myself—need me."

"What about Guatemala?"

He took a deep breath. "I guess that was just a dream. Dr. Klein said yesterday that there comes a time in everybody's life when duty won't let you change directions any longer. He called it the point of no return. I've been trying to tell myself I hadn't passed it, but I suppose I have."

"And me?"

Jethro smiled. "You'll be all right—now that you've laid your particular ghost."

She leaned over to kiss him and both of them knew it was a gesture of farewell.

"Something like you should happen to every woman once in her lifetime, at least, Jethro," she said softly. "I'm glad it happened to me, but I guess I knew all along I didn't deserve you enough to keep you for my own."

"Guatemala isn't going to disappear," he said. "Neither are we or the CMA. If you see me in one of those Vibrassage chairs next spring, don't be surprised."

iii

Word that important surgery was about to be performed on Dr. H. Edward Danton spread quickly through the hospital. By the time Paul finished talking to the Danton Clinic radiologist by long-distance telephone, breakfast tables in the coffee shops of the hotels, where the greater part of the doctors attending the convention was staying, had also started to buzz with the dramatic news.

By the time Paul started scrubbing, the observation gallery of the main operating theater was packed, with hundreds clamoring to get in. After a quick conference between Cary Poston and other members of the Arrangements Committee, the closed-circuit TV system, by which surgical operations could be piped to monitor screens placed in strategic locations throughout the Civic Center, as well as in hotel rooms, had been activated.

Crowds quickly gathered around the monitors, leaving the meeting rooms, where the final scientific papers of the convention were being presented, almost deserted.

Jerry Warren was in the scrub room when Paul came in, busy scrubbing his hands and arms with green soap. Both he and Paul, as well as those already busy in the adjoining operating room, wore green operating pajamas, caps, masks and cloth boots over their shoes to keep down airborne infections.

"Who would have thought, when Danton was lambasting you day before yesterday, that you'd have his life in your hands this morning?" said Jerry. "From the way people were talking in the elevator, you're well on the way to being the hero of the hour."

"And the bastard at a family reunion, if I don't extract that embolus," said Paul wryly. *"Sic transit* something or other."

"If you succeed, every female in the neighborhood will be ready to climb into the sack with you—including, I am pained to admit, my wife."

"I'll start there first," Paul assured him. "I've had my eye on that chick of yours for some time."

"If our next child has blue eyes, I'll know where to start shooting," said Jerry. "The *droit de seigneur* business went out with the end of the Civil War."

"We can always revive it."

"If this operation turns out like it should," said Jerry, "it could reinstate you as the Great White Hope to succeed Danton, in his clinic as well as in his marital bed— where you've already been, if you know how to take opportunity by the forelock."

"That's the damnedest simile I ever heard." Such preoperative banter, often grisly, served to relax tension and put the operating team at ease before important surgery.

"Actually you can blame Carlota," Paul added.

"Now there's a chick you ought to dig. Of all the females who have tried to put their hooks into you so far, I'd grade her Number One. No wonder Aletha's jealous."

"That's all over." Paul gave Jerry a quick account of Aletha's visit to his room after the caucus and the way Carlota had told her off on the dance floor.

"It may be over for you and I hope it is. But don't forget that 'Hell hath no fury like a woman scorned.' And you can't scorn a woman much more than by refusing to go to bed with her when she's got a case of hot pants over you." Jerry shook his head. "For my money, turning down that was above and beyond practically everything. By the way, when are you going to see Carlota again?"

"Tonight, if she'll let me. She goes back to work in the Polo Lounge Saturday night, after the convention is over."

"Don't let her get away from you." Jerry dropped the brush he was using into the sink and immersed his hands and arms in a basin of antiseptic solution. "What's your plan of operation for our former employer?"

"I just finished talking to Ed Balentine. Aletha said she thought an arteriogram was done a few weeks ago and Ed confirmed that Danton's got an ulcerated plaque right near the bifurcation of the common carotid. It's been spilling small emboli into his brain arteries for at least a month, causing those TCI attacks. Ed and the others down there begged him to go to DeBakey in Houston instead of coming to Central City for the convention, but Danton's had his sights set on the presidency of CMA for years and wouldn't give in."

"He's just bullheaded enough to take the risk," Jerry agreed.

"We'll use the conventional approach through the left side of the neck over the carotid bifurcation," said Paul. "Unless I'm mistaken that clot has already filled most of the large branches of the internal carotid, so we may have some trouble getting it out."

"Thank God, the brain's got a fine collateral circulation. Once we shut off the carotid itself, the backflow from the other side should help flush out the smaller arteries."

"I'm counting on that," said Paul. "Plus the heparin we'll inject into both carotids to help dissolve any little clots we can't get to."

Jerry stepped to the door leading to the main operating theater and looked up at the glass-fronted gallery where visitors, usually medical students and house staff, could watch with no danger of bringing contaminants into the operating room itself.

"Joe's starting the anesthetic," he said. "I notice you're not using hypothermia."

"Would you?"

"Under the circumstances, no. I'd say Danton's brain has had enough of an insult for one day."

Hypothermia, lowering the body temperature by means of ice, lessened the need of sensitive cells for oxygen. A protective measure used by some blood-vessel surgeons in operations upon the circulatory system leading to the brain—as well as its more frequent use in open-heart surgery where a heart-lung pump was practically standard operating procedure—it was particularly valuable, when the circulation on one side was already damaged by artery hardening or by a free-floating clot called an embolus like the one that had felled H. Edward Danton.

Neither Dr. Moriarity's examination, confirmed by Paul himself, nor the X-ray studies reported over the telephone to Paul by the Danton Clinic radiologist indicated any failure of the right side of the brain's arterial tree, however. So under the circumstances it seemed best not to add the cellular damage always done by cold to that already inflicted upon the brain cells of the left side by interference with their blood supply.

After soaking his hands and forearms in an antiseptic solution, Paul lifted them and, holding the fingers upright so the excess dripped off his elbows and did not contaminate his scrubbed hands and arms, walked through into the operating room. A nurse in sterile garb handed him a sterile towel. Drying his hands and arms, again moving from the fingers toward the elbow for the same reason, he dropped the towel and extended his hands while she held up an open gown for him to thrust his arms into the sleeves.

Behind him, a nurse wearing a cap and mask but not scrubbed—a "dirty nurse" in operating room parlance—quickly tied the strings of his gown. While Paul powdered his hands, the one who was scrubbed—naturally the "sterile" or "scrub nurse"—lifted a rubber glove with her own gloved fingers inside the cuff, where they would not touch his bare skin. Holding the glove so he could thrust his hand deep into it, she repeated the maneuver with the left hand.

In teaching hospitals, the surgeon was usually in direct voice communication with watchers in the gallery, while a closed-circuit TV camera inside the main operating room light transmitted a more detailed picture of the surgical field to monitor screens on each side of the gallery.

The dirty nurse followed Paul as he moved toward the operating table, which had been wheeled into the center of the room. Now she plugged the cord running from a throat microphone he had tied on before beginning to scrub into the operating room P.A. system through a jack in the floor.

H. Edward Danton lay with his head turned slightly to the right, extending the tissues of the neck and causing the muscle that traversed that side diagonally, in anatomic parlance the sternocleidomastoid, to stand out. His neck and the lower part of the head had been freshly shaven in an area extending well up behind the ear.

"Ready for draping?" Paul asked the anesthetist, who sat at the end of the table, holding the mask that was strapped over Danton's mouth and nose.

"Whenever you are. I'm carrying him as light as possible. Let me know when you want the blood pressure to rise."

"As soon as we get the common carotid clamped," said Paul. "We'll give the word."

The network of arteries in the brain, many connected across the midline to form what was called the collateral circulation, was quite plentiful. By raising the blood pressure in the general circulation with vasopressor -blood-pressure elevating- drugs, blood would flow across from the unblocked arterial tree into the small branches on the blocked side, tending to push the obstructing clot in a reverse direction and thereby assist in removing the damaging embolus.

Jerry extended his hand and the scrub nurse popped into his glove the handle of a long forcep holding a folded square of gauze in its jaws. Dipping the gauze into the basin of antiseptic she held out for him with the other hand, he began to paint Danton's neck with the yellow-tinged fluid, putting on two liberal coats.

"This patient suffered what appears to be a massive

embolism of the internal carotid artery less than two hours ago, causing hemiplegia and complete aphasia." While he waited for Jerry to complete the application of the antiseptic to the skin, Paul addressed the crowd that filled the gallery. "Twenty, perhaps as little as ten, years ago, we would have called this simply an apoplectic stroke and written him off as a permanent paralytic. Fortunately, we know now that many cases of what we call stroke are really emboli, clots floating in the bloodstream until they obstruct an artery branch.

"The use of artificial heart valves has increased the occurrence of what we call embolic phenomena in the brain, but the larger number of these strokes are still caused by an area of hardening and often ulceration in the carotid artery system, with clot formation at the point of ulceration, where the inner layer of the artery—the intima—often undergoes degeneration."

Jerry had moved to the other side of the table while Paul was speaking. The two of them now drapped Danton's body with sterile towels and larger sheets, leaving bare only a rectangle on the left side of the neck extending from the lower part of the skull down to the collarbone.

"I don't have to tell a medical audience that our concept of what the word 'stroke' means has undergone drastic changes in a few short years," Paul continued. "Perhaps we should reserve the word 'stroke' itself for the classic type of hemorrhage into the brain from rapture of an artery, causing the familiar picture of paralysis, coma and, not infrequently, death. Or, if the patient lives, loss of function in a leg, an arm or both, frequently leaving them invalids and unable to care for themselves.

"I wish I had an X-ray study of the carotid artery system—an arteriogram—to show you in this case, but they were done about a month ago at the Danton Clinic, when the patient had his first attack of transient cerebral ischemia, TCI for short. This brief and often largely overlooked failure of function in a small area of the brain is frequently due to interruption of its blood supply by an embolus or by blocking of a vessel itself with a thrombus or fixed clot.

"Had endarterectomy—removal of the ulcerated lining of the artery—been done a month ago, when the condition was first discovered, the patient could have been spared the shock to his brain which has occurred because of the embolus. Unless our diagnosis is all wrong, however, no blood vessel has actually ruptured here, so if we are able to remove both the embolus and the plaque which caused it, Dr. Danton should be almost as good as new. Unfortunately, however, we must now carry out two operations—embolectomy and endarterectomy—where a month ago, we would have been able to control the condition with only the latter."

CHAPTER XXVIII

In the temporary office of the Central Medical Association, a group of doctors from the Association Council had begun to gather as soon as H. Edward Danton was taken to the operating room. At the moment, the monitor screen in one corner of the room showed only the main operating theater at University Hospital with the hurried, but obviously orderly, preparations for major surgery.

"We've got some decisions to make, gentlemen, and not much time," said Dr. John Towers. "The final General Session is scheduled for eleven o'clock."

"What can we do?" said Dr. Jack Hanson. "We don't even know whether Danton will come through this—or what condition he'll be in, if he does come through."

"If you ask me, this gets us off the hook," said Dr. Heath. "We can put up a compromise candidate the younger men won't object to and stop this revolution that's been brewing the past year or so before it goes any further and starts tearing the Association apart."

"With one of the medical-care bills that's up before Congress certain to be passed next year, this is no time to be quarreling among ourselves," Dr. Hanson agreed. "We need to make a common front with the AMA and work out some sort of a national compromise doctors all over the country can live with."

"Danton's got a big following among the older and more conservative members," Dr. Towers warned. "If they think we're using his illness to give them the runaround and elect a more liberal slate, there's liable to be a rebellion on the right even stronger and more violent than the Young Turk movement on the left. The last thing any major medical organization wants at a time like this is wider polarization of the membership than we've already got."

"Why don't we nominate Cary Poston as what you might call the organization candidate, then?" Dr. Heath suggested. "Everybody likes him and he'd make a perfect dark horse."

"I'm sure Cary wouldn't take it." Alex Klein had come into the room in time to hear Heath's suggestion.

"Why not?" Dr. Heath asked.

"For one thing, he doesn't like medical politics. For another, I happen to know he's slated to be named provost in charge of the entire medical side of the University in another year, when the present provost retires. Cary was acting dean two years ago when Dr. Chancellor, the present provost, was seriously ill for six months. He was the one who brought Paul and Jerry Warren to Central."

"That removes him from consideration," Dr. Towers said. "We've always had a tradition in the CMA that only a practicing doctor should be president."

"Besides, that would mean jumping Cary over the three vice-presidents we already have," Dr. Hanson reminded the others. "They certainly wouldn't like that."

On the monitor screen the inert form of Dr. H. Edward Danton was now being wheeled into the operating room.

"There but for the grace of God could go you or me, Jack," said Towers. "We've both got enough years and probably enough cerebral arteriosclerosis to be candidates for a stroke some day."

356

"Not me," said Hanson. "I jog three miles a day and haven't eaten bacon in a year."

"I guess I should have realized something was wrong with Danton the other day, when he had that little spell after the caucus," Dr. Towers admitted. "But this concept of strokes caused by small cerebral emboli is so new that I didn't think of it."

"What could you have done?" Alex Klein asked.

"Nothing," Towers admitted. "Edward knew exactly what was happening to him all the time, yet he insisted on going through with the election."

"This isn't getting our problem solved," Dr. Heath reminded them. "Do you have another idea?"

There was a momentary silence, then Alex Klein spoke.

"I can think of one way to handle the situation," he said.

"Let us have it then, Alex," said Hanson. "There isn't much time."

"I've watched Paul do a number of these endarterectomies," said the psychiatrist. "It rarely takes more than an hour, so we should know by ten o'clock, at the latest, whether Danton is going to come through it."

"We can't wait until then to plan what we're going to do," Dr. Heath objected. "Unless we have the slate of candidates filled when the General Session starts, there'll be all sorts of nominations from the floor and the election could end in bedlam."

"My idea is to go ahead and nominate Danton the way you intended to do, Tom," said Alex Klein. "If it turns out that Danton isn't around next spring to become president, or isn't able to fill the office, John here can keep it a second year."

"I don't see where that accomplishes anything," Heath objected.

"Give me time, Tom; you young fellows are too damned impatient. In addition to nominating Danton for president-elect, we also nominate Paul Rice for third vice-president. That means putting him at the bottom of the ladder instead of the second rung from the top, but the group who were pulling for him, until he withdrew the other day, will take this as a concession from what they call the Establishment. In other words, they'll jump at the chance to get their man elected a vice-president instead of making the token race for president-elect, which everybody knew they couldn't win anyway."

"There's merit to the idea," Dr. Hanson conceded. "But why will the liberal element think that's so much of a victory?"

"All vice-presidents are on the Executive Committee and the Council that rules the Association between conventions," Alex reminded the others. "That means Paul will be privy to the innermost decisions of the Association. Even more important, he'll be recognized as spokesman for the younger doctors and can fight any change in policy he thinks isn't forward-looking enough, besides pushing through changes that we all agree need to be made anyway."

"I'll buy that idea, Alex," said Dr. Hanson.

"So will I," said Towers. "How about you, Tom?"

"It sounds involved enough to be good politics," the younger doctor admitted. "But can you be sure Paul will accept?"

"I'll undertake to convince him, if he needs convincing, which I don't think he will," said Alex Klein. "I was with Paul the other afternoon, just before he withdrew from the race for president-elect. I know most of his reasons for withdrawing then and none of them would apply to the nomination for vice-president. I think he'd feel that he was letting down the people who've been supporting him, if he doesn't take that job when it's offered to him."

"Then it's settled?" asked Dr. Towers.

Nobody objected.

"We'll go into the election with a full slate." Towers glanced at the monitor. "Looks like the operation is beginning so what say we adjourn to the lounge? They've got a large screen out there."

"I've seen enough endarterectomies to know Paul will do a good job," said Alex. "I'm going out and corral the leaders among the Young Turks and convince them they're getting a better deal than if they voted for their own slate."

ii

When Paul held out his hand, the nurse handling sutures and instruments slapped a scalpel into it smartly. Picking up a gauze square, he pressed upon the skin of Danton's neck to make it tense while across the table from him Jerry did the same.

The knife flashed down in a slicing cut, following the border of the muscle that stood out there, and laying the tissues open down to the edge of the muscle itself. For the next few minutes there was no sound except the clicking of hemostatic forceps as their jaws closed off the mouths of small blood vessels in the skin incision. Larger ones were tied off with very fine catgut, Jerry's hands moving swiftly as he placed the knots while Paul held up the forceps.

"I don't have to remind a medical audience," Paul said while Jerry was tying off the cut vessels, "that a left-sided brain lesion causes paralysis on the opposite side, as it does here."

When the wound was reasonably dry, they redraped the skin edges to prevent further contact with them, since it was impossible completely to destroy all the bacteria normally found upon the skin. Swiftly Paul freed the skin edges so they could be pulled back to give exposure of the deeper tissues. Then placing a U-shaped instrument with rakelike jaws at the end and a ratchet in the middle, he separated the skin edges mechanically with the retractor, holding the incision open to allow free access to the deeper tissues.

Moving slowly and carefully, Paul began to free the tissues in the depths of the wound. As he worked, a white tube began to appear in the lower portion of the incision toward the collarbone. Roughly the size of a little finger, it pulsated strongly with each heartbeat.

"I think you can see the pulsation of the common carotid artery at the lower angle of the wound on your small screens," he told the onlookers after a few moments of dissection. "The fact that it does pulsate would tend to indicate that the clot does not extend down that far. All of which is in keeping with the fact that the Danton Clinic roentgenologist localized the offending plaque just above the beginning of the internal carotid artery with an arteriogram several weeks ago."

With a small curved forcep he next freed the artery and, slipping the forceps beneath it, caught the end of a piece of cloth tape Jerry placed between the paws. Pulling the tape through, he clamped it so the artery could be quickly controlled in case of severe hemorrhage.

"The common cartoid is now under control," he announced. "The next step is to free the internal carotid above the point of division into the internal and the external branches. You will notice as we expose the internal carotid artery—" He was working as he talked—"that there is almost no pulsation here, indicating that it is blocked by the embolus we seek to remove."

Four hands moved almost as one, so in tune were Paul and Jerry with each other's minds from long practice. When a second tape had secured the internal carotid, where it began to branch out like a tree several inches above the lower tape, Paul carefully sponged the area clean. Then he moved his hands away so the crowd in the gallery could easily see the course of the artery in the depths of the wound, either by direct vision or on the monitor screens.

"As you know, pressure directly over the carotid body—" Here he indicated a small lump of tissue lying just over the area where the larger artery divided to form the two smaller ones—"can cause collapse or even sudden death, so we will be careful not to disturb it." He looked up to the gallery. "It's hard to believe pressure over such a tiny area could kill a man, but skilled assassins have known for centuries how to use it to render people instantly unconscious."

"Shut off the common carotid, please," said Paul and Jerry Warren expertly applied a forcep closing off the flow.

"You can add the vasopressor to the drip," Paul told the anesthetist.

Moments later the pressure line rose sharply on the monitor screen by which vital life functions such as arterial and venous pressure, blood oxygen, electrocardiogram and respirations were being constantly recorded visually.

Picking up a delicately pointed blade, Paul slit the artery open over the area just below the bifurcation and extending upward along the course of the inner branch. Only a small amount of blood oozed from the cut, mute evidence of the block above it, and even those in the gallery could now see the surface of the dark red clot that had felled H. Edward Danton as surely as a bludgeon. It almost filled the inside of the internal carotid and extended up past the point where the artery disappeared inside the skull on the way to supply the brain with blood. The lower end of the clot ended about half an inch above where Jerry had clamped the larger vessel.

"If the arteries on the right side were not open and functioning well, it might be dangerous to clamp the common carotid for more than a few moments, since a good portion of the blood supply to this half of the brain would be shut off," Paul explained to the watchers in the gallery and on TV. "Fortunately, there are widespread connections between the arteries of both sides. And since the X-ray studies of this patient previously made at the Danton Clinic show the cerebral circulation on the opposite side to be intact, the brain can be adequately supplied long enough for us to complete our work."

Picking up a forcep with delicate teeth at the end of its jaws, Paul gingerly seized the lower end of the clot and began to pull gently downward, seeking to dislodge it base first, as one might extract the woody part of a tree from inside its bark by removing the larger parts first and then the smaller branches in descending order.

At first the clot moved only slightly and Paul gingerly exerted a slightly greater pull upon it. With its branches growing steadily smaller like those of a tree, there was grave danger of breaking off smaller ones deep inside the brain, where they would still obstruct blood flow and damage brain function.

"A little more vasopressor effect, Jack?" he asked the anesthetist, who nodded and thrust the needle of a syringe containing the blood pressure-elevating drug through the wall of the intravenous tubing, injecting the contents.

Immediately the moving line marking the blood pressure curve on the monitor screen where vital functions were being closely watched rose sharply. And with the increased back pressure from the normal arterial tree on the right side, by way of small cross-communicating arteries of the collateral circulation, the clot began to move of its own accord, telling Paul it was safe to exert more pull.

From then on it was smooth sailing, as the branching clot was extracted intact through the opening Paul had made in the internal carotid, first the trunklike lower portion, then the smaller branches above.

"We're being helped here by back pressure from the communicating arteries," Paul explained. "In other words, blood is pouring in above this clot, helping to push it out. Fortunately, the embolus doesn't seem to have been attached to any part of the brain's arterial tree. And with the current from below no longer jamming it into the base of the internal carotid, extraction is not proving particularly difficult."

Across the table from him, Jerry Warren's eyelids crinkled above his mask. "Reminds me of pulling a rabbit out of one of the box traps I used to set on the farm in Alabama where I grew up—tail first by the hind feet."

As the smaller branches of the treelike embolus began to appear, blood started to flow from portions of the internal carotid which, until a few moments before, had been blocked, evidence in itself that removal of the embolus was approaching completion.

"Ready to clamp?" Paul spoke quietly, his eyes never leaving the dark clot which was now several inches long, with a large number of smaller branches making their appearance as it was extracted.

Jerry's hand moved at the upper edge of the incision and the jaws of the forceps touched the outside of the artery.

"Now," Paul said, as the complete treelike structure of the embolus suddenly popped from the incision in the wall of the artery, followed by a spurt of blood.

The jaws of the forceps Jerry held were quickly shut and the flow of blood ceased. Lifting the embolus on a piece of gauze and holding it up for the audience to see, Paul straightened out the branches so its treelike character was apparent.

"Embolectomy is complete," he said as he put the gauze down on the nurse's table. "Be sure and save that. We don't often get them that large or that complete."

When Jerry Warren gently sponged away the blood which had filled the incision area, the cause of all the trouble was immediately apparent. A raised, rough-surfaced plaque occupied nearly the first inch of the inner lining of the internal carotid artery, beyond the point where it formed a major branch of the larger common vessel below. At the center of the yellowish plaque, the ulceration from which Paul had detached the base of the embolus was plainly visible.

"This is a classical demonstration," he told the audience. "The plaque should be easy to remove."

"Aren't you going to use the temporary shunt?" Jerry Warren asked.

Paul nodded. "Upstream first. We'll have less pressure that way."

The nurse handed him a small tube and, slipping one end into the carotid just above the plaque, he pushed it upward toward the brain. When Jerry momentarily removed the clamp which had prevented a backflow of blood, Paul slid the tube up past where the clamp had been placed and by tightening the strip of tape around the vessel with the shunt tube inside it, Jerry was able to create a blood-tight joint.

Holding the other end of the tube, Paul loosened the clamp that closed it, allowing the tube to fill with blood by backflow from above. Next he slipped the lower end into the carotid artery and, pushing it downward toward the heart, left it in place after Jerry tightened the tape around it once again to make a tight joint.

"We're using what is called an internal shunt so blood can flow through to the brain," Paul explained. "As you can see, the shunt is simply a small tube, purposely left with a loop in the middle, so it can be pulled to one side, allowing access to the damaged area while still supplying the left side of the brain with blood."

The shunt, with its small loop, was already pulsating as blood was forced through it with each heartbeat to the no longer threatened left side of the brain. Drawing the loop carefully aside, Paul now exposed the ulcerated plaque in the artery wall and gently dissected it free, until it could be peeled off the inner lining, then dropped it upon another square of gauze.

"We will enlarge the size of the artery in this area by adding a knitted Dacron patch graft," he told the audience. "Actually this may not be necessary, however, since we have removed the area of hardening and ulceration that caused the embolus. But we want to be sure there's plenty of room for the normal circulation to be re-established and that our sutures enclosing the arterial wall will not narrow it.

"Of course the patient will be given drugs to discourage clotting of the blood, so the area where the inner lining of the artery has been removed will have a chance to heal over and be smooth once again," he added. "In our experience, dealing with several hundred cases, Dr. Danton should suffer no ill effects from this surgery. Unless there are other plaques which we have not yet been able to see, he should be able to live a normal life."

After the delicate job of extracting the embolus and removing the ulcerated plaque, sewing the Dacron patch into place where the artery had been opened, removing the shunt tube just before the last sutures were tightened, required little more than a skilled piece of hemstitching. Not much more than an hour had passed when Paul stepped back from the table and nodded to Jerry to apply the dressing to the skin incision.

The gallery was already nearly empty, most of the visitors having left after what had easily been the most dramatic event of the whole convention.

"I was too busy to ask how he was during the operation," Paul said to the anesthetist as he pulled off his gown and gloves.

"I kept his pressure up with the vasopressor drip just to be sure his brain cells wouldn't suffer from any sudden change when you removed the embolus," said the anesthesiologist. "As far as I could tell, it didn't bother him at all."

iii

Cary Poston came into the Doctors' Lounge outside the operating room suite, while Paul was changing from operating clothes to regular garb.

"The whole convention saw that operation on closed-circuit TV, Paul," said the internist. "You're the man of the hour."

"Right now I'm a hollow man of the hour," Paul said as Jerry Warren came in. "This sort of work shouldn't be done on an empty stomach."

"A lot of news and TV people are waiting to talk to you," said Cary. "I put them in the small lecture room at the end of the hall."

"Can't I just escape down the back stairs?"

"Not a chance," said Cary. "John Towers is in the CMA office at the Auditorium right now, wording a motion to make Edward Danton president-elect by acclamation, when the General Session convenes a couple of hours from now at eleven-thirty."

"That figures," said Jerry, somewhat bitterly. "Everybody will feel sorry for Danton, so he'll be a shoo-in. And tomorrow they will have forgotten Paul."

"Not quite," said Cary. "The success of the Young Turk campaign to run Paul against Danton for president-elect really shook up the Old Guard, even though Paul finally withdrew from the race. Alex Klein was called to an emergency meeting of the Council this morning."

"I'm glad something has finally shaken up the Old Guard," said Jerry. "Membership in all the big medical associations has been falling because the younger men haven't been joining for the same reason they don't go to church any more. They're tired of being treated to old sermons on professional responsibility dredged up to hide the fact that the Old Guard have been sitting on their collective asses for years and not doing anything about social reform."

"While they kept raising dues to support a lobby against government participation in the whole field of medical care," said Paul. "So why should I help keep them in power, Cary?"

"You can't unseat the present hierarchy," said Cary. "And enough members will always rubber stamp anyone they nominate to elect him."

"When that happens," Jerry said dourly, "the younger men will start leaving the Association in droves."

"Alex has figured out a way to prevent that," said Cary. "But it requires your co-operation, Paul."

"Isn't it enough that I just saved the next president-elect from being a hemiplegic invalid the rest of his life?"

"Alex and I think this is the time to make a deal," said Cary. "On the principle that if you can't lick 'em, join 'em."

"Isn't that what we're fighting?" Paul asked.

"Sometimes you have to fight the enemy with his own weapons, so you can find out where he's weak," said Cary. "We'll go along with the election of Danton by acclamation, but only if John Towers agrees to have the nominating committee put you up for third vice-president, which automatically makes you a member of the Council."

"The whole thing still smacks of crookedness to me," said Paul.

"Politics." Cary corrected him.

"Is there a difference?"

"Most of the time, no—whether it's an alderman running for re-election to control his ward, or a doctor running for the presidency of his state medical society, so he can deliver the vote in the AMA council. But that's the way it's done—in both worlds."

"You've got to go along, Paul," Jerry urged. "With an important seat in the CMA hierarchy, you'll be in a position to fight for more representation by local societies and less control from the top by the old die-hards, plus a broader form of health insurance that neither the profession nor the government will control. And most important, peer review to make sure incompetent butchers no longer use the operating rooms of small-town hospitals to get rich by taking out every loose organ in sight."

"I'm still not sure," said Paul. "I'm a surgeon, not a politician."

"Right now you're a hero and this looks like the only way to keep the shysters in the medical profession from wrecking Blue Cross and Blue Shield. If they do that the government will step in and we'll all be up the creek."

"What I want most in life at the moment is two scrambled eggs, a hunk of ham, some toast and two cups of coffee," said Paul. "But if you and Alex think this is the thing to do, Cary, I'll go along."

"Stay hungry a half hour longer and I'll pay for steak and eggs," said Cary. "We need to cash in on this operation for all it's worth and you can start by talking to the press. The publicity will help, too, when we ask the regents for an increase next year in the budget for cardiovascular research here at Central."

Cary's last words were the clincher. Medical schools were constantly doing battle with the lay boards of regents that controlled them over the necessity for research. The steadily rising cost of medical care, particularly for those who couldn't pay, had sharply restricted research budgets, yet these same patients were vitally necessary to progress.

Paul and Jerry could have used twice the facilities available to them in the cardiovascular research unit at Central Medical School, so if the dramatic character of the operation he had just performed on one of the most famous doctors in the world would help gain support for their work, he couldn't very well refuse to cash in on it.

"All right," Paul said wearily. "Where are your newspapermen?"

iv

The small surgical auditorium was jammed when Paul came in, flanked by Jerry Warren. The table on the dais was festooned with microphones and three television cameras plus several powerful lights were beamed upon the two chairs at the table. One of the chairs was empty, obviously waiting for him. In the other, lovely, cool and seemingly not in the least disturbed, was Aletha Danton.

At the sight of her, Paul started to turn back, but Jerry's firm hand on his arm propelled him forward, so he had no choice except to move to the empty chair, or create a scene.

"Thank you for saving my husband, Dr. Rice." Aletha smiled warmly, her pique at him seemingly forgotten—at least for the cameras. "Dr. Poston just brought word that the operation is over and he's in good condition."

"Any one of a hundred surgeons in the country could have done what I did," said Paul. "In fact, Dr. Danton originated this particular operation."

"Weren't you trained by Dr. Danton, Dr. Rice?" a newsman in the front row asked.

"I did my residency at the Danton Clinic and stayed on for several years afterward as a staff member."

"Wouldn't you say it was particularly fitting for the disciple to save the life of the master?" the reporter asked.

Behind him Paul heard Jerry Warren snort and knew what his friend was thinking, that under any other circumstances Paul was the last person Danton would have selected to operate on him.

"You can say that if you wish," he conceded.

"Would you describe what you did at the operation, Doctor?" another reporter asked.

"A clot had formed in one of the most important arteries

368

of the brain, so Dr. Warren and I opened the artery and extracted the clot—the technical name for the operation is an embolectomy."

"Wasn't that a very delicate and dangerous procedure?"

"Dr. Warren made a very apt observation during the operation," said Paul. "He compared it to the way he pulled rabbits out of box traps back in Alabama, when he was a boy."

There was a snicker of laughter from the crowd and Aletha's face momentarily showed a look of annoyance.

"Dr. Rice has always been very modest about his professional achievements," she said. "I happen to know my husband considers him the most brilliant young surgeon he has ever trained."

"Your description of the operation doesn't sound very dramatic, Dr. Rice," said another newsman.

"Dramatic operations are very often failures," said Paul. "The well-trained surgeon operates only when he's sure of what he's dealing with and how he will cure it. In Dr. Danton's case, the clot came from a rough area—an ulcerated atheromatous plaque, if you wish a technical name—inside one of his brain arteries. Once we extracted the embolus, removing the source was relatively simple."

"I've seen films of my husband performing these operations," added Aletha, "and believe me they scare me to death. In my husband's grave condition, I wouldn't think of letting someone he didn't have the greatest confidence in operate. And I've already told you he had the greatest confidence in Dr. Rice's ability."

"What now, Dr. Rice?" a newsman asked.

"Dr. Warren and I are going out and order the biggest breakfast we can find."

"And Dr. Danton?"

"He should be awake soon. If you will excuse us, I'm sure Mrs. Danton will want to be with him." Turning to Aletha, he added: "Don't worry, I think your husband is going to be all right."

"How about you and Katie having dinner tonight with

Carlota and me, if Carlota doesn't have a class?" Paul asked Jerry as they were leaving the surgical auditorium.

"How about your taking her to some quiet romantic spot and convincing her Aletha Danton doesn't have the hooks on you?"

"Why would she think that?"

"When those TV films hit the boob tube at noon showing you and Aletha apparently all lovie-dovie after you've preserved the Great One for posterity, you're going to have to do some convincing—that is, if you want to hold on to our lovely Mex friend."

"That's one thing I do want."

"Then get busy and take her some place; I'll cover the service and even resist the impulse to put arsenic into Danton's I-V. But take your pager with you, in case he throws another embolus before we get his clotting time under control with heparin."

Jerry chuckled. "Danton could never carry the Southern vote, when he comes up for Presidency of the AMA a few year hence, if I had to go in alone and it ever became known that a black doctor operated on him."

v

Cary Poston came into Marian Crowder's room, while Paul was being questioned by the press. He found her sitting in a chair eating breakfast from a tray, fully dressed.

"What's this?" he said. "I haven't discharged you from the hospital."

"But you're going to, aren't you?"

"I'm not sure. You see I like having you around."

"I've been thinking of doing a little traveling."

"So? Where?"

"Somebody was telling me the Big Bend country is very nice this time of the year. I was thinking of going down there for a few days—if I can find anyone to take me."

"I think that could be arranged—after a little matter is attended to first at City Hall."

"I sort of took that for granted," she confessed.

"When did you decide?"

"This morning, when I heard the news about Eric Sands and realized how close I had come to causing your death."

"And yours, too. Don't forget that."

"I'm not forgetting it," she said soberly. "The whole thing made me realize that I've been given a second chance, not only at life but at having you. And I'm not going to let you escape again."

"I'll have the airport get the plane ready," he told her. "We can attend to that business at City Hall and still make the Big Bend by dark."

CHAPTER XXIX

For the final General Session of the CMA Convention, the main theater was barely half filled. The sole business was the election of officers and that proceeded with rubber-stamp efficiency.

H. Edward Danton was named president-elect by acclamation and Paul, third vice-president with equal alacrity.

"Dr. Klein," said Dr. John Towers when the election was finished, "since you placed Dr. Rice's name in nomination, will you escort him to the platform?"

"Let's go, Paul," said Alex. "Your first step toward one day becoming president of the AMA."

"In that case, I'll go the other way," said Paul as they started up the aisle toward the platform.

The applause began at the back of the room and was taken up by each row as they passed, until by the time they reached the platform, the entire audience was standing. Paul knew the applause was a tribute to the fact that, less than three hours before, he had saved the brain, and perhaps the life, of a man who had cut him to pieces just two days earlier before many of those seated in the theater, but who was nevertheless one of the greats in world medicine, more than it was to his own election but that in no way lessened the lift it gave him.

As he shook hands with Dr. Towers and started to take the empty chair on the platform, someone in the audience shouted, Speech!" and the cry was quickly taken up by others until it filled the hall.

"They want you, Dr. Rice," said Towers. "The floor is yours."

As Paul moved across the stage toward the podium, the shouts slowly died away.

"I have no prepared speech, for which I am sure you will be grateful," he said. "But I need no preparation to tell you I appreciate, more than any words I might prepare could possibly say, the trust you have placed in me by electing ne to be even the lowest man on the totem pole.

"Years ago, when I was still in high school, I read some words written by Robert Louis Stevenson that impressed me very much, so much, in fact that they may have been responsible for my becoming a doctor. Because they express better than I could ever say what I feel about our profession, I memorized them later and would like to share them with you:

> *"There are men and classes of men that stand above the common herd: the soldier, the sailor, and the shepherd not unfrequently; the artist rarely; rarelier still, the clergyman; the physician almost as a rule. . . . Generosity he has, such as is possible to those who practise an art, never to those who drive a trade; discretion, tested by a hundred secrets; tact, tried in a thousand embarrassments; and what are more important, Heraclean cheerfulness and courage.*

"I am sure most of you realize, as I do, that my being on the platform this morning, with the title of third vice-president of the Central Medical Association, is the result of a compromise. In this Association, as in medical schools

372

and among younger members of the medical profession everywhere, the forces of activism have been growing rapidly in the past several years. This does not mean that those of us who feel it is time for a change are trying to turn medical practice over to the federal government, as some of you believe. It does mean that more and more doctors are seeking to solve major problems in the delivery of health care which also concern a great number of people outside our profession.

"All of which boils down to the fact that medicine is still as much an art as it is a science, even in a day of machines that can almost take over the function of the human heart. Like prayer, which is a private relationship between a man and God, the cure of disease involves a private relationship between the patient and his doctor. Admittedly, with the rising cost of medical care, a third and purely economic influence has to come into the patient-physician relationship, making it less close than it was even twenty years ago. But what every doctor worth his salt wants is to be certain that, while this third economic force must necessarily *enter* into the patient-doctor relationship, it shall not come *between* them. For when that happens, the rapport necessary for a cure is broken.

"It has been estimated from reliable public-health studies that roughly sixty diseases could be eradicated within a few years, if as little as ten per cent of the money spent on the Vietnam war had been devoted to a concentrated battle against disease. Syphilis and gonorrhea are now major scourges, particularly among the young, yet it is generally conceded that $100 million properly spent in a well-organized program could eradicate syphilis as effectively as smallpox has been eradicated through vaccination.

"Recently a cry has gone up for more medical schools and they are certainly needed. Yet a ten per cent drop in war expenditures would influence the health of the American people far more than building ten more medical schools.

"Many of you, I suspect," Paul continued, "voted for

me this morning as the lesser of two evils, knowing there are those among the younger registrants at this convention who would turn our lucrative profession upside down. It will remain to be seen whether the profession as a whole, and the health of the people we serve, might not in the final determination have been better off if you had chosen one of them instead of me.

"I am by nature a research scientist and much prefer the laboratory and the operating room to politicking. But I am also pragmatic enough to know that practical politics are absolutely vital to the preservation of medicine as a profession. I therefore accept the office to which you have elected me, humbly and with appreciation, but also with the warning that, although I may be *in* what is called the Establishment, I am not *of* it.

"As a physician, I am responsible to society in a very particular way, being one half of a partnership in which the consumer of health care has as many rights as the provider. When the time comes that I no longer represent the consumer as much as I do the provider in helping to establish the policies of this organization, I will resign, but not before I have done everything in my power to guard the rights of both."

Paul sat down while the applause ebbed about him.

"Thank you, Dr. Rice," said Dr. Towers, when it had subsided. "I can assure you that the greater part of what you call the Establishment share your feeling about the trust the members of this Association have placed in us by electing us to office. The Third and last General Session of the Seventy-fifth Convention of the Central Medical Association stands adjourned. The Seventy-sixth Convention will meet here in Central City starting on Monday, May 4, of next year. The Council will convene this afternoon at two o'clock in the temporary offices of the Association on the second floor of this building to wind up convention affairs. Thank you and goodby."

"That was a masterly speech." Cary Poston had waited until Paul came down from the platform, after receiving the congratulations of many who had heard it. "I saw the